T0065441

Locusts Are Here Again

Locusts Are Here Again

BY

Bright A. Okoro

malthouse 〰P

Malthouse Press Limited

Lagos, Benin, Ibadan, Jos,Port-Harcourt, Zaria

© Bright A. Okoro 2021

First Published 2021

ISBN: 978-978-58298-3-9

Published in Nigeria by

Malthouse Press Limited
43 Onitana Street, Off Stadium Hotel Road,
Off Western Avenue, Lagos Mainland
E-mail: malthouselagos@gmail.com
Facebook:@malthouselagos
Twitter:@malthouselagos
Istagram:@malthouselagos
Tel: 0802 600 3203

Distributors:

African Books Collective Ltd, Oxford, UK
Email: orders@africanbookscollective.com
Website: http://www.africanbookscollective.com

Dedication

Dedicated to God Almighty for giving me the inspiration to write

CHAPTER ONE

'Papa has come! Papa has come…!' chorused the children repeatedly as they ran to their father who was just returning from a trip to Safa, for a warm embrace. The competitive race was always very intense among the children because the first two among them, to get to their father would take his portfolio and the polythene bag which were highly coveted by them. The polythene bag was expected to contain some biscuits, bread and candies which Chief Akpovire's children considered a luxury. Other children in the community hardly tasted such township delicacies. The children became more excited as they met and danced around their father who too became more affectionate, all broad smiles, as it gave him great delight to see his children feeling very elated with importance, in welcoming him back home and expecting their township goodies. As the children were handed their bread, biscuits and candies, they jumped up and down repeatedly with great excitement. Other children in the immediate neighbourhood who were with Chief Akpovire's children then were lucky to share in the luxury, as Chief Akpovire saw himself as the father of all in the community.

Chief Akpovire often travelled to Safa, the predominant town with some relative peculiarities of Europe in the locality. It had one of the major seaports in the country which had attracted many sailors and foreign nationals from Europe and the Middle East, particularly Britons, Italians and Lebanese, who came with their merchandise. One of such imported wares in Safa was the sea slang which had come to dominate the fashion of English spoken in the town. The influence of these whites who were essentially tourists in attitude had been great in the town.

Safa was substantially a colonial creation. It started as a trading post, where many European traders bought timbers and natural rubber to Europe and brought in manufactured European goods. Very soon, the trading post started developing into a major commercial centre in the coastal region of the country. As the town developed, several manufacturing companies in Europe began to open their depots in Safa to showcase their products. United African Company, UAC, was prominent among them. Later, few local firms started emerging too. Over time, Safa became a relatively sophisticated town with prodigious European presence. This happened alongside colonial administration.

When the country came under full British colonial administration, following the historic *Berlin Conference*[1] Safa was made a municipality in recognition of its cosmopolitan composition. Even with the British colonial municipal administration, the influence of sailors and merchandise remained dominant in the town. There were several recreational centres like hotels, night-clubs and cinemas. And the local inhabitants were remarkably influenced by Western lifestyle in various ways. The boys wore jeans, jackets and sometimes hats in the fashion of the Italian sailors or after the actors they watched in cowboy films in cinema centres. Some of the local girls were dating white men and had begun to lighten their skins and hair with creams to impress and be more acceptable to their white lovers. They were making all efforts to look like white ladies, to wits: becoming grotesque caricatures of their preferred look. A handful of them had also started smoking cigarettes in imitation of the lights of their lives. The local men with some Europe learning often wore coats or complete suits and glasses, sometimes with hats to look the Victorian gentleman; they also liked to speak in British Standard English to exhibit their claim to 'high civilization' and high social status in the society. Most of these men had attended at least the 'Standard School,' which was the basic education and the only formal education available then, in the early stage of British colonial administration of the country. These men were next to the whites in the various administrative offices and business centres of the town. To boost their social status, they had the highly prized coveted 'locomotive' of the time – superb white bicycle which they rode to their various places of work. Their wives also liked to look modern, doing nothing else other than house-keeping - just making the home comfortable. Those who were barely literate among such women sometimes engaged in reading small story books and newspapers when the children had gone to school, as the tradition of the people only assigned domestic duties except subsistence farming to the women then. These literate ones saw themselves as ladies of European type, so they had housemaids from their villages who took care of their children and chores in their homes.

There was the exclusive business class. They were not the petty traders in the open markets or the hawkers who hauled their wares from place to place. They were exclusive entrepreneurs who dealt in timber or natural rubber.

---

[1] A conference in Berlin where European powers decided how Africa should be partitioned among themselves in their colonial quests in 1884.

2

Most of them were the middlemen between the white merchants and the local producers. They would go to the hinterland to buy natural rubber which they sold to the white merchants in large quantities after they had been processed into rubber sheets and smoke-dried in large ovens, which in turn the white merchants shipped overseas. Over time, some of the more enterprising ones started competing with the whites by buying in bulk from other middlemen and direct producers and were shipping directly overseas themselves. They had an advantage over their white counterparts as they had direct contact to the source. When they became more prosperous, they started giving out money and lorries to other local middlemen who would account for them in the produce they would turn in subsequently. This swiftly encouraged many local buyers at the grassroots and wealth was created and circulated in the hinterland.

The tactics eventually forced some white men out of the rubber and timber businesses as they could not adjust themselves to this kind of keen competition which they were not used to. Some of them soon abandoned the business altogether. But they never left the town rather they turned to other businesses that were still the preserve of the whites in Safa.

Timber business was most dominant in Safa, evidence of which was seen in the existence of a very large and well organised timber processing factory in Safa – the only one in the whole country which had become the largest employer of labour in the town – its entire management were exclusively Europeans.

Safa happened to be on the fringe of the forest belt in the region, which harboured abundance of timber trees. At first, this singular factory in Safa was the major buyer of timber in the entire sub-region. It processed timber into refined planks and shipped them overseas for sale, besides few other British traders. Some of the local businessmen, who sold to this large European factory and other British traders, took a cue from their fellow local rubber merchants. After sometime they began to acquire sawmills to process their timber into planks and started buying from other smaller local businessmen and began to ship their processed products directly overseas for sale. This raised the tempo of the competition in the trade. There were other minor export merchandise in Safa like palm kernel and palm oil.

All these business activities heightened the enterprising spirit of the town, which gave expression to other entrepreneurial activities. Very soon, plastic and shoe-making industries started emerging. Later, a mineral water factory that was indigenously managed followed. The establishment of primary and secondary schools which were hitherto the preserve of Christian missionaries and British colonial administration became another vista of business opportunity among the local entrepreneurs. These individual initiatives in education were to cater for the growing interest in Western civilization in the town, relative to the strong western influence and the high volume of economic activities in Safa.

All these various socio-economic activities had a profound influence on the physical development of the town. First, was the white residential area which was nick-named 'European Quarter' – for, apart from the few Lebanese who operated the cinema centres and the major hotels in the town, all the other whites were Europeans especially Britons. All the whites in Safa irrespective of their nationalities were residing there: an area that had all the peculiarities of some settlements in Britain.

The residential area was carefully planned and built by the colonial administration in Safa. All the houses were clearly detached from one another with fences of well-kept flowers, most cases with barbed wires in addition. Within each compound were flowering plants and shrub. A well-kept lawn surrounded every house with one or two path-ways that were neatly cut out. The houses were usually two in each residence, the main house which was either a bungalow or a duplex, depending on the status of the real occupant; this was the master's house, the white man. Beside it but with some comfortable distance, to separate them apart, was a small house of three to four rooms. This small house was named 'the boys' quarter' by the master. This was where the master's servants, such as his steward, driver, gate-keeper/gardener who were blacks, stayed. Though, they might be men with wives and children, their families were not allowed to stay with them in his master's residence.

Into each residence was a drive leading directly from one of the main streets. All the streets were tarred. Along the streets of this all-white residential area were lines of tall shaded flowering trees which shielded the entire lanes and streets from the penetrating eye of the sun in such a manner that the entire white settlement was one large range of magnificent scenery of comfort – cool, flowery and serene with birds sometimes singing pleasant melodies upon the atmosphere. This was well complemented by the gentle breeze that blew from the river from time to time into the settlement; to caress and shuffle tenderly the flowering trees into some regular swaying dance to entertain its residents. For, the quarter was located in an area where the river that ran past the town had a meander. This made it possible for many of the whites in the 'European Quarter' to have direct access to the river, and those who were fortunate to have their houses along its bank, had mini-jetties constructed on their side of the bank, thereby having good luxurious outlets into the river where they kept their speed-boats, which they used for pleasure-sail at weekend.

The other part of the all-white residential area which faced the main town was where several colonial administrative buildings were located: the court, municipal office, the police station, the public hospital and the customs office and several others. Between the all-white residential settlement and the administrative buildings was a large field with a building. It was the social rendezvous of the white community, where they relaxed and had fun in the evening after their official engagements. The field was a golf-course while the building was their guest-house where they accommodated colonial guests from the central colonial administration at the country's capital or from the 'Colonial Office' in London. But on ordinary day, it just the convergent place for recreation among the white community in Safa, where they drank in a convivial atmosphere. Sometimes, some of them talked about wild and interesting stories about the local people to amuse themselves as they drank together in the guest-house.

They also received the latest news about Europe through the grapevine here, particularly the recent developments at the 'Colonial Office' in London which was of prime interest to them. The central colonial administration at the country's capital was another area of interest, as all the administrative policies and directives were all directly from there. Every one of them, apart from relaxation often came to this evening social rendezvous to hear some gossips about the two most powerful centres of administration whose decisions or indecisions affected them directly.

Parallel to the 'European Quarter' was the main town of Safa where the cream of the local society lived, especially the business class and the privileged literate local people who were next to the white man in the ladder of social ranking. Their houses were fashioned after the white man's, but with so much distortion. They made a caricature of the houses in the white settlement. Just as their white counterparts, they either built a storey or a bungalow. But rather than occupy it all alone with some domestic aides like the white man, they had part of it partitioned into rooms for letting. In most cases, they also imitated the white man by including a "boys' quarter", merely to increase the number of tenants in the compound. But the landlord with his family was quite distinguished in the house. He and his family occupied the only apartment in the house, a large living room with two or three bed-rooms, while the tenants had a single room or two rooms each, depending on their incomes. There was a corridor in the house in most cases, to demarcate the landlord's apartment from the tenants' occupancy. Latrines and bathrooms built at the back of the house were also separated. Those of the landlord and his household were always under lock and key and were tagged 'private only'.

The main roads in this side of the town enjoyed the privilege of being tarred. The area was the heart of Safa with all the liveliness and warmth of an urban sprawl. Restaurants and beer parlours were scattered within it for people to enjoy themselves. Also, the cinema centres and club-houses were located in the main town. A few of the notable landlords had come off materially like the whites – having the luxury of the white man's car. Some other ones had a lorry for commercial transport.

Immediately following the area where there was a cluster of administrative buildings, after the public square, was the commercial nerve centre of Safa. The main market was situated here, sprawling over the entire area, to include some big shops and warehouses, which were managed by whites as the representatives of some major trading firms in Europe. The port which was not more than a ship-yard where few ships berthed was a few metres away from the main market within the area. During the day, the commercial centre was the heartbeats of Safa, as many traders from different parts of the country would come there to buy wares while others came from the neighbouring villages to sell agricultural produce and foodstuffs. It was as a result of all these business activities with their importing and exporting extension that made some of the whites see Safa as the future Liverpool of the country that was worth investing in.

Behind the commercial centre in the extreme west of the town was a slum. The houses in the slum were so similar that a first time visitor would find it hard to differentiate them. The houses were shanties, built with planks or mud, sometimes plastered with cement. The shanties were crowded together, sprawling over a large stretch of land without roads and streets and was thickly populated. Endless streams of people like lines of ants were always on the many crooked paths, which did not particularly lead to any direction. There were children running and playing with wild excitement at a near-by open ground, the only space available in the slum, near their dump. These slum urchins understood every nook and cranny of their surroundings and they knew how to make themselves happy in it. Many of the children saw the open ground as their possession. They were mostly always there playing during the day, which showed how addicted they were to such plays and running. One other thing they liked doing too, was to go to the refuse heaps from the white settlement, to scavenge for something to take or sell to others in the slum at very cheap prices, and there were always willing buyers. The little amount of money they made from the scavenging was enough to make them happy, as they bought candies, plantain chips, beans cakes etc, which they shared among themselves and jumped around like little rats in the area.

All the modern amenities like tap water, electricity and tarred roads were completely absent in this part of the town. The inhabitants were people without regular incomes; mainly living on daily paid jobs as they could find. But they were happy somehow. They seemed to be happy among themselves and did not feel their indigent conditions as they lived a communal life. They shared each other's burdens and helped one another in their daily struggle of life. There were petty traders with their few articles in sheds in the slum, where most of the men often gathered together to play draughts while they drank *ogogoro** or palm wine and smoked cigarettes which they often bought on credit and laughed away their sorrows in their squalid congenial environment. The area was a squatter community. Many new comers into the town particularly those who had not been able to settle to any stable jobs saw the slum as a temporary place of abode. But oftentimes they got stuck in it and would become permanent residents of the area. That was how the slum was developed. The inhabitants were a salad of very irregular and low-income earners mainly labourers and other unskilled workers from different parts of the country and beyond. As a result, they creatively coded a Pidgin English which non-residents might find difficult to comprehend. This invention was to enable them relate to one another clearly to overcome the difficulty in understanding themselves without recourse to their various indigenous languages since they found it very difficult to use the English language well, as they were mainly illiterates and had little or no contact with either the whites or the educated local people in the town.

---

* Locally brewed strong colourless alcoholic liquor, mostly from palm trees

Chief Akpovire was one of the landlords in the prestigious main town of Safa. He had been a very successful businessman and accomplished community leader at Akpobaro, his birth place. At this time, it was customary for a successful man to have several wives, for wives and children and a large compound were the show room of wealth and Chief Akpovire had enough to show for his prosperity. He had one wife with four children at Safa and three wives with thirteen children at Akpobaro. The temptation to marry more was still there as the people of Akpobaro still beckoned to him for their daughters, whenever they had a singularly promising beauty in their families which they thought he deserved, as every family wanted to identify with his stupendous wealth and prestige, while having the prospect of making their lucky daughter have the singular luxury and privilege of living in Safa as *a* lady totally free from the laborious farm life of the village.

Chief Akpovire was the most distinguished man in the community of Akpobaro as he was the only man among them who owned a *white man building* in Safa. In the community too, he had the only magnificent edifice; a large bungalow built like the one in Safa with a modern latrine and two bathrooms. Before Chief Akpovire ventured into the flourishing timber business in Safa, he was a Councillor representing the newly created Omaurhie District at Western Ahwotu Divisional Headquarters. This was made possible following the 'Macpherson Constitution' which increased the elective offices tremendously and extended active politics to all the nooks and crannies of the country to allow full participation of the indigenous peoples in their own affairs, in response to the criticisms that trailed the previous colonial constitutional review in the country, as it was widely criticised for lack of local inputs. The nationalist politicians were not consulted before the review. The criticisms were so loud and popular in the country that a deputation was sent among the nationalist politicians to protest against the 'Richard Constitution' at the 'Colonial Office' in London. So when the next Governor General, Sir Macpherson was to review his predecessor's, he did what was right to ensure that his constitution did not suffer the same fate. He consulted extensively among the local peoples whose views formed the framework of the 'Macpherson Constitution,' which invariably became the engine of active politics in the country; as it afforded many people the opportunity to be part of the political process. Many new wards were created for Council elections and all other elections were to proceed from there through a chain of Electoral College which made the electoral process less expensive.

Chief Akpovire was one of the beneficiaries of the 'Macpherson Constitution'. Before then, he was a sales clerk in UAC, in Safa when he had struggled to complete his Standard Six. After some years, he became disenchanted with the job, as a result of his white boss' high-handedness towards his local workers. For, Chief Akpovire was a man, quite conscious of his proud ancestry, so he was not happy with the job. His disgust at working for a white man was further accentuated as he drew understanding daily from the fountain of ideas in *Nationalist* newspaper which spotlighted the brazen oppressions and injustices of the colonial administration, and the discriminatory and exploitative tendencies of the whites in the country. The writers of such articles and reports were usually prominent politicians in the nationalist struggle that attended higher education in Britain or the US, and were inspired by powerful political agitations of great American blacks of the past. These firebrand nationalists always couched their agitations in *Old Major's* style[2] – remove the common enemy and life would be pretty good.

Chief Akpovire had also been watching with envy the progress of his fellow compatriots in the timber and rubber businesses and how they had become prosperous. Most importantly, the respect their wealth had earned them even among the whites who saw them as business counterparts. He had been ruminating upon the idea of going into the booming timber or rubber business, considering all the possible risks.

While he was still thinking over such idea, the *Macpherson* Constitution threw open a new vista of opportunity and he quickly took advantage of it, and became a councillor in the Council in his area, representing the newly-created Omaurhie Ward. Chief Akpovire was rather fortunate with his election: his election was by consensus; without any agitation as the newly created Omaurhie Ward was too remote from party politics.

Three weeks after the *Macpherson* Constitution was signed into law, two white officials drove to Akpobaro and other neighbouring villages to announce to the elders to choose within two weeks an *educated person* among their people who would represent them at the Council. Unfortunately, the privileged few Standard Six certificate holders from the clan had all left the

---

[2]Old Major was the character whose speech stirred the revolt in *Animal Farm* by George Orwell. It stressed that once their common enemy – man - was removed, there would be abundant life for all the animals.

community, and were working either as teachers or clerks in the civil service or other establishments in urban centres. Being so disenchanted with his work, Chief Akpovire quickly made himself available when he received the information and saved the elders the difficulty of getting someone to represent them.

When Chief Akpovire came to the Council, he observed that he was the only independent candidate, and to his amazing delight, he found himself being wooed by the two dominant political parties in the region; he became an object of intense struggle between the two rival parties. But he was very careful. He took time to consider the options before him, and was wise enough to join the party in control of the region, although, the party did not enjoy the same popularity among his people. For his ethnic people preferred the 'National Party' which was the rival party. Chief Akpovire calculated that over time, the colonial administration would allow political parties to control government at the regional level, as the nationalist struggle was gaining more ground, and the most popular party was likely to take over. He thought once that happened, he would use his position to bring some development to his remote district that had never been touched by the least colonial development save the exploitation of timber in its vast natural forest.

To his pleasant surprise, his dream did not take time before it materialised. The next constitutional review granted self-government to two regions, leaving only one in the hand of a colonial administrator. Expectedly, his party captured the government of his region by majority votes. Immediately, his party started the implementation of its well-articulated programmes, one of which was 'free primary education,' which was extended to all the nooks and crannies of the entire region. The slogan 'knowledge is power' mounted by his party paid off handsomely – many people embraced the new programme. In Chief Akpovire's district, several villages now had primary schools which hitherto were non-existent. This brought about great learning among the children and teenagers in the area. With his influence in the party, two dispensaries were also sited in Omaurhie Ward. Also, Chief Akpovire was able to influence the award of some petty contracts at the Council to some Akpobaro's chiefs, such as the supply of benches to the primary schools in the area.

The only road in the district which was hitherto a journey into the wilderness was expanded and upgraded by the Council to a major feeder road to Safa. The Council employed some men to maintain the road throughout

10

the seasons. All these were no mean developments to the people of Omaurhie where he came from, and Chief Akpovire's image and personality soared like the eagle to the sky; he was so held with awe throughout the length and breadth of Omaurhie that his re-election was just a mere formality : nobody came forward to challenge his candidacy.

He became so popular and respected in the community that hardly was any major decision taken in his village, Akpobaro, without his approval. Any time he returned from Ugbevwe, the Council headquarters, the chiefs in his village would pay him visits in his newly built ultra-modern edifice, to relate to him all that had transpired in his absence and how they were handled. They would want to know his view on each of such matters, as they saw him as the foremost leader who knew far more than they were and could always give them the best idea. Some other persons in the area also considered it a mark of respect to pay him visits whenever he returned from the Council, considering his tremendous influence in government, especially the privileged few, working for Council. For instance, the headmaster and teachers in Akpobaro often paid him respect, as he always saw to their needs and interests at the Council. And for this singular enviable recognition and respect accorded him in the entire community, he was determined to do all he could for them.

Within the party, Chief Akpovire had also become very influential. Immediately the party formed the government at the regional level, they began to control the local councils in the region and so many people started flooding into the party in the province. But before this time, Chief Akpovire had become one of the leading party faithful in the province. As a result, he was always among the privileged few who represented the province at crucial meetings of the party at regional and central levels. This further raised his profile. He had met face-to-face with all the great nationalist politicians across the country at crucial national meetings, where several important issues affecting the country, vis-à-vis colonial rule were discussed. This had increased his political awareness that he had come to have a clear perception of the country's political aspirations, which were beginning to shape his political thoughts and vision.

CHAPTER TWO

After Chief Akpovire had completed the maximum two terms at the Council, he decided to live among his people where he thought he could be more helpful. He had planned to settle down to two things: for the four years he had been in politics he had seen great progress in the lives of his people. Many of those who began the 'new standard school' created by his party government in the area would soon begin to work as teachers, clerks, etc., on completion of their primary education. And some others who had business inclination might like to start retail trading. The most daring among them might venture into the exclusive timber or rubber business. Most importantly, some of such pupils would like to further their education. By this reckoning, Chief Akpovire saw the need to extend the educational frontier in the area. He decided to establish a 'modern secondary school'[3], which was like a junior college then, with the mind of setting up a full college later. He had a vision of using this educational space to farm for the community a formidable educated class who could bring great development to the area. He had no illusion about the future: he knew from all he had seen in the country, that the future belonged to those that attended school, and he would not want his people to be left behind. He had planned to leave the day-to-day running of his schools to the teachers while he engaged himself in the timber or rubber business which had been his earlier consideration.

When Chief Akpovire eventually settled down among his people in Akpobaro, their joy knew no bound. They never expected a man of such a high status to live among them. They had thought he would eventually go back to Safa after his two tenures. They were further thrilled when he built his 'modern secondary school' at the outskirts of Akpobaro, and it turned out more successful than Chief Akpovire had anticipated; every pupil wanted to be there after his or her primary education. The success of the 'modern secondary school' after seven years motivated Chief Akpovire to go ahead with the idea of establishing a College in the area. He had acquired a large expanse of land in the next village for it but lack of funds became his major

---

[3]Trade/technical school (Modern School, for short) meant for primary school leavers before or not proceeding to boarding schools for O'level studies. The latter were initially called College and then Secondary School in the old Western Nigeria as Teachers Colleges and other Colleges were created.

impediment. He went to all the banks in Safa to obtain loan. Unfortunately, no bank was willing to accept his 'modern secondary school' in a remote village as security. He realised he needed time to raise enough money for the college. Although, his timber business was doing well, he was committing much of its profit to the building of his personal house in Safa, for him to consolidate in his business. Besides his commitment to his business, he still made out time to attend to his community's affairs. He had initiated several ideas and regulations which had greatly enhanced the harmony and progress of Akpobaro. Whenever there was an intractable dispute between two individuals or villages it was usually brought to him to resolve. He had settled many marriage and land disputes that were very problematic and would have been taken to court in Safa, which saved the community's members a lot of time and money.

He had also become a channel of admission for the indigenes of Akpobaro into colleges at Safa, as the people did not know how to apply for admission for their children or were rather too timid to do so.

In appreciation of his immense contributions to the development of Akpobaro, he was given the highest chieftaincy title of 'the *Ohworode** of Akpobaro'. Individuals within the community sometimes offered him their choice produce as a form of homage. Many a hunter who had a prize game like wild pig would send him one limb and some other vital parts. A fisherman who caught many fish also sent him some. During harvest, gifts of yams would fill his barn. Parents who had exceptionally beautiful daughter would want the chief to marry her. As a result, he had married three more beautiful women to the only wife he had before he left Safa for politics. At Christmas, he usually received several expensive imported spirits and greeting cards from the community's natives working in urban centres. Government officials like the tax collectors who had an assignment in the community passed through him to accomplish their tasks without difficulty, as they knew that he had the people in his grip. The police superintendent in charge of the area had maintained a personal relationship with him on this account.

As Chief Akpovire relaxed with all dignity, in his specially made deck-chair in the frontage of his edifice, luxuriating in the cool refreshing evening breeze that day, having returned from yet another successful business trip in

---

* "Big Person"…important personality

Safa, he became absorbed in his own sense of accomplishments. His poise was that of a great man who had the entire world under his control.

The children had gone back to their play and other things they were doing before. His wives returned from their farms that evening. For, they engaged in skeletal farming. They were very happy to ride their bicycles into the presence of their amiable husband, who had been away for two weeks. With all smiles, they stood their luxurious bicycles, for they were the only women that rode bicycles to farm in the village, and hurried to greet their husband whom they fondly called 'Masa,' a corrupt form of Master.

'Is it long you came, Masa?' the most senior wife said in a most respectful voice, revealing a smile of great delight. By virtue of her position, she was expected to lead the other two in all the domestic conducts and activities in the family. She initiated every action for the rest two in matters affecting them as wives of Chief Akpovire; for seniority in marriage was accorded high recognition in this part of the country.

'Not quite long, how is the home?' returned Chief Akpovire.

'We're fine,' the three women answered almost together.

'There's a loaf of bread and a sardine on the dining table for you,' said Chief Akpovire.

'*Miguo*[4] Masa,' they curtseyed in greeting.

His three wives smiled into his bungalow and returned with the bread and the sardine to their own house opposite their husband's, where each of them with her children had two-room apartment, except the teenage male-children who stayed separately together in their own two- room apartment in the wives' abode.

That night after dinner, Chief Akpovire was relaxing in front of his house under the congenial bright moonlight. By his sides were his wives. The moon was in its full circle and its attraction was irresistible to the Akpobaro folk who knew nothing about electricity. The children usually entertained themselves with stories or riddles in the congenial moonlight. Sometimes, they indulged in play while the adults sat outside enjoying conversation and gossips amidst laughter. There were times also when the children sat in front of their parents to learn riddles and stories, which formed part of their upbringing. They related such stories and riddles again among themselves in their own

---

[4] Respectful greeting of an older person, literally meaning "I am kneeling" or "my knees are down".

gathering, and in this way, such stories and riddles were passed to the next generation and their upcoming children. Some of such stories sometimes included family or the community histories.

As Chief Akpovire sat there with his wives who were amusing him with interesting stories that transpired in the village while he was away, his children were busy playing nearby. At a time, the children became too noisy; Chief Akpovire felt he should rather bring them into his fold. He was just thinking of an interesting story to tell them, when his mind flashed back to the historic misfortune that occurred in Akpobaro many years ago when he was a boy. The unfortunate event was already buried in the distant memory of the community. He realized how evanescent events could be. Looking at the community now, it appeared such a calamity never occurred; not even a single sign of it remained to remind the community of the misfortune, as Akpobaro had recovered from it fully and had even improved far beyond that time. Since then, a lot of other events had occurred in quick succession, so much that the community had lost memory of many of them, too. *How kaleidoscopic human society can be?* he mused. But now he wanted to tell the story to his children to show that life could be so unpredictable.

'Many years ago, that is about forty years now,' he began after calling the children together in his front to hear the story.

'Hmm, forty years now?' exclaimed Otabunor, his first wife.

'Yes, that is a long time now. There occurred a great famine in our land.'

'Great famine!' reacted the children.

'What's famine papa?' said Onajome, the youngest child, with much agitation.

'Keep quiet! you always like to ask questions,' Iroro, his older sister silenced him.

'One day everybody woke up to find that locusts had covered the entire farmlands,' continued Chief Akpovire, without bothering about the interruption, knowing full well that by the end of the story, everything would be clear to Onajome who was just three years old. 'They were so numerous and plenty, covering everywhere, and it was almost harvest time when everyone was preparing to reap his sweat and labour of the year. The yields of that year were very promising as there was enough rainfall and sunshine. Encouraged by the good weather and the favourable prices of produce of the previous year, the people went to farm at cockcrow and returned when the mother hen with its chicks was just returning to roost. The people of

15

Akpobaro worked tirelessly throughout the season for a bumper harvest, only to wake up one day to find the most unexpected on their farmlands - it was unbelievable! The men gnashed their teeth helplessly in pain at the sight of the locusts on their farms. The women and mothers wailed uncontrollably. True to their nature, the locusts destroyed everything, not a single crop remained on the farmland. It seemed the world had come to an end. Not a few people died that year. Some could not stand the cry of their children starving and their miserable look - they jumped into wells. Some others hanged themselves in frustration while many others migrated to other places like pods dispersing their peas in cracking explosion in the dry season. There was acute hunger and suffering in Akpobaro. Many children died that year and the year that followed. So many young girls were given away in marriage in a hurry to men in other lands, like produce that were sold away by a far-away farmer when he realised suddenly that the market was about to end, in the belief that such girls could support their parents' families from their marriages. Nobody ever thought the community would ever recover from the unmitigated disaster. It was like an unending eclipse. The community bore this huge burden of sorrow for a very long time. It took rare strength of perseverance to survive the famine. But looking at Akpobaro now, will you believe that such unmentionable and unparalled misfortune ever occurred?'

The children shook their heads, trying vainly to capture the imagination of the disaster.

'You see how life changes,' Chief Akpovire concluded.

'Papa, did any of our family member die?' Efe, the oldest of the children said with some heaviness on his mind.

'One of the two of my father's brothers hanged himself and his wife took his children to where only God knows. Till today, we are still waiting to see them. Our family made all efforts to find them but there was no trace.'

'Masa, you never told me about this,' Otabunor his most senior wife said with accusing concern.

'It's not everything a man experienced that he likes to talk about, my dear. There are things, sometimes, too heavy for the mouth to say. You cannot understand because you're a woman. I must appreciate the fact that the woman is giving the man a great hand behind in the battle of daily living. But it is not everything she can comprehend like the one in the front who receives the blows of life directly,' answered Chief Akpovire calmly.

There was some awkward silence for sometime.

'Papa, will the locusts come again?' Onajome broke the silence in a whimper.

'Heaven forbid!' Ogevwe, the second wife of Chief Akpovire reacted swiftly. Overwhelmed with the solemnity of the story, they all went to sleep immediately as time had gone far into the night.

CHAPTER THREE

That night news went round Akpobaro that Chief Akpovire had returned from Safa. So the next morning, his fellow chiefs started trickling into his house for a visit.

The chief of the chiefs was always expecting such visits as it had become usual to receive many callers after staying away in Safa for sometime. The first to visit that morning was Mudiaga with three others. Mudiaga was very close to Chief Akpovire. He was his devoted companion. As he entered the expansive compound, he shouted, 'Where are my people?' This was his customary way of referring to the wives and children of Chief Akpovire in the compound, and the discordant voices of *miguo* started coming from the different doors and corners of the compound. Mudiaga and his company went specifically towards the kitchen house to meet the most senior wife whom they saw as they answered the greetings.

'*Avwebo,*[5] is *my person* in?' Mudiaga asked excitedly with all expectation as he turned his walking stick in the direction of Chief Akpovire's edifice.

'Yes, he is,' Otabunor answered after another greeting, and Mudiaga with his company moved in the direction of the bungalow.

When they got very close they hailed, '*Olorogun!*[6]

'*Ilorogun!,*' Chief Akpovire who had recognised their voices answered enthusiastically with a broad smile as he sat in his specially cushioned armchair – his personal preserve – the only one of such beautifully designed chairs in the community. And they quickened their steps into the house to exchange warm greetings with their adored.

After they had sat down, Chief Akpovire went into his bedroom and came back with one of his bottles of herbal *roots*. He peered at it. The drink inside was little.

'Ochuko, Ochuko!' he called and his second son ran down from the other side of the compound. 'Take the bottle at the right corner of the dining room and tell Umuko to fill it for me,' Chief Akpovire instructed Ochuko after giving him money.

---

[5] A favourite wife, usually in polygamous social setting.
[6] Traditional chiefs or notable persons among the Urhobo. *Ilorogun* for more than one.

Ochuko soon returned with the bottle now filled with *ogogoro,* the popular local gin.

'Turn the drink into the roots,' Chief Akpovire directed.

While his son, Ochuko, was doing that, he went to his cupboard and brought a kola-nut and a saucer. He put the kola-nut in the saucer by the drink at the centre of the table.

'My people, there is drink on the table. Kola-nut is by it, also.'

'*Olorogun!*' hailed the rest of them in appreciation.

The man next to the eldest by age then stood up.

'*Olorogun,* the drink and the kola-nut you offer us, we accept with gladness. Let's break the kola-nut and share the drink. This is what our eldest says. We thank you.'

The eldest man who was incidentally was Mudiaga broke the kola-nut according to its parts and there were five lobes.

'Ah, the kola-nut has shared itself,' he announced joyfully as they were five in the house and they all laughed. He prayed with the kola-nut first. First, to Chief Akpovire who offered it. Obire followed, being the one who accepted the offer on behalf of everyone that was present in the house and the rest two were given according to age before Mudiaga took the last lobe. He also prayed with the drink accordingly as he offered each person a shot. Lastly, he held a shot of the *ogogoro* and prayed with it to the spirits of their forebears and asked for blessings for the land, and for the general well-being of the community.

'But whoever curses the land not to be good for someone, I do not pray for that evil person!' he concluded and the rest persons in the house answered, '*Ise*'[7] in unison.

He poured some of the drink on the floor before downing the rest. After that first round, they started taking their turns one after another.

'The roots taste very good. Who prepared it for you?' Akpotu enthused.

'You're right, Akpotu. The quality of the roots is exceptionally good,' Oseme added as he gulped down his shot.

'Akpokonah prepared it for me when I was having some stomach ache and since then I notice that the root is good for the body system generally, apart from tasting well. If your stomach is rioting or making you go to the

---

[7]Amen. Variously spelt "Ise" and "Isie"

back of the house, frequently. Just take a shot of it and the whole storm in your belly will cease at once,' explained Chief Akpovire.

And they all nodded their heads in agreement with what Chief Akpovire had said.

Akpotu peered through the bottle closely and examined the roots if he could recognise them.

'They are not the ones that I know,' he shook his head disappointingly.

'It is foolish to think that you can know all roots in the bush. There are numerous herbs and roots in our bushes that we have not yet known their uses. Even Omojevwe that is so good at knowing the treatments of herbs and roots has not been able to identify many,' remarked Oseme.

'That's why each time I see those men that come here, plying the whole village on market days, with *oyibo* medicines which they say are better than our roots and herbs, I 'm not happy.' Mudiaga said. 'They sell to our people medicines they do not understand neither how they are made. But these herbs and roots around us are what we have been using and they work very well. If my daughter, Oke, contracts fever, I just go into the bush and get the herbs or roots for her. That's all. She bounces back to her full health between four and seven days of drinking and bathing with them. But that their own, you will have to pay money and yet they don't work well. They even say if you take them more than what you should, you'll get another sickness or even die. No, not for me!' he shrugged his shoulders in total rejection of modern medicines with some amusing effect.

And all of them burst into laughter including Chief Akpovire.

'That means we are at the mercy of the peddlers because we don't really know how those medicines are taken. We simply rely on what they tell us and our enemies can use them against us. They can tell us to take more than required and we shall just be dying without knowing where the deaths are coming from,' noted Oseme.

'That's true! Those peddlers could fall into the hands of our enemies to bring us ruin. We have to really be careful with them,' Mudiaga alerted.

'Councillor,' for that was what they called Chief Akpovire, as a mark of respect for him, 'you should know better, don't you think those medicine sellers should be banned from our community before they cause great havoc among our people?' asked he.

Chief Akpovire laughed.

'Mudiaga, if you go to Safa, you'll see that most of our people that live there no longer take these herbs and roots we are so proud of here. They only take the medicines of the white man. They go to the hospital and the white doctor treats them and they are well again. You might not believe it, there are some instruments I have seen with the white doctor there, which can detect the sickness in your body and then you're given the exact treatment that is required. At the hospital, they don't just give medicines. You won't believe it, they can ask you to urinate into a small container and they will use their instrument to examine your urine to find out the sickness in your body. With that, they will give you the right treatment. I think their method is more exact. Our herbs and roots are very good but I think ours still requires great improvement which modern education can make possible. I hear that the white man also makes his medicines from herbs and roots in their area like us and they have instruments of knowing the healing power of herbs and roots. Other instruments and machines are for the processing and grading of medicines into units of capacity. I think they have gone far ahead of us. But I believe we shall get there one day as our children begin to acquire knowledge about such things at school and apply them to our own herbs and roots. In that way, we will be helping one another to bring a better health condition to everybody round the world. The only advice I want to give our people, for now, is to tell their children who are in schools to help them read the instructions on the white man's medicine so that they know the use and how it is taken, and when such medicine will expire. Such information is usually found on the paper on the bottle or the packet of the medicine. They should have such information before they buy those medicines. Our people should not just rely on all that the medicine peddlers tell them. There is danger in relying solely on their information as they might only be interested in how much they can sell.'

The entry of four other chiefs into the house invigorated the liveliness among them, as they exchanged greetings and pleasantries. They were very influential chiefs in the community among them was the *Ugo*,[8] the official spokesman of Akpobaro. Their presence anywhere in the community was almost as good as the presence of the entire chiefs-in-Council of the community.

---

[8]The official spokesperson and the foremost leader of a village in some Urhobo communities.

Chief Akpovire looked at the bottle of roots and saw that it had gone down. He got up and picked the bottle on the floor by the central table - he wanted to send for more drink. Ochuko soon returned with another filled bottle of the local drink. He poured half of it into the bottle of roots and stood by, knowing very well that he would soon be told to serve the drink.

Before the four chiefs took their seats, two other chiefs came in and the excitement in the house began to brim over.

'Ah, where you people trailing us?' the *Ugo* said jokingly.

'No, we weren't trailing you,' said Ahwotu, one of the last two that had just come in, 'but when a good thing is about to happen in a place there is always a meeting of minds,' and they all began to laugh and shake hands.

When they had all sat down and the excitement had died down, Obire stood up to speak.

'*Ilorogun, Ugo,* and the entire house, I greet you all. At the time you entered,' referring to all those who had just come in, 'I'm sure you noticed what we were doing,' pointing at the bottle of drink on the table. 'Of course, in the house of a great *Olorogun* like Councillor, one should always expect a drink on the table.'

Everyone in the house nodded in agreement and laughed.

'So when we came he offered us that,' Obire pointed to the refilled *bottle of roots* on the table, 'we will not hide it from you. We offer you the same drink, also. My people, there is also kola-nut and two shillings in the saucer to *support* the drink.'

Chief Akpovire had added money to the offer as the occasion had assumed a semblance of formality.

'Please kindly accept them from us, I greet.'

Omonigho stood up after Obire had taken his seat to accept what were given. After which, Ochuko took the saucer of kola-nut to Akpojerho, the eldest man among the new entrants, who prayed with the kola-nut and the drink respectively to Chief Akpovire, followed by Omonigho, Obire was next, and the rest were served round according to age. When the kola-nut and drink had been passed round, they started enjoying their conviviality again.

'Great men seldom visit, they send messages,' began Chief Akpovire in an outburst of excitement. 'But when they do, it is to the honour of those they visit. That is why I feel greatly elated to have in my house, the *Ugo* and the rest of you, *Ilorogun,* who can decide the fate of the entire world. I salute you all.'

22

Though Chief Akpovire knew that the *Ugo* and the other four powerful *Ilorogun* were regular callers to his house, and he equally knew that his house was gradually becoming the place where very important decisions affecting Akpobaro were taken, as he had become one huge stature that radiated development and progress in the community, he still preferred to give credit to others with less social estimation rather than betrayed any consciousness of his greatness. Humans generally enjoy flattery though they pretend to the contrary. As soon as Chief Akpovire expressed his compliment, the *Ugo* and the three other chiefs who came with him began to brim with ecstasy. They were greatly elated to hear such encomium being lavished on them by the most respected man in the community. This was fully expressed in their smiling faces.

'We thank you for your good words, Councillor,' said the *Ugo* with a feeling of excitement, pretentiously couched in an unaffected mien. Everyone present was enthralled by the compliment which caused great laughter among them. After some other similar expressions of compliment and pleasantry had been shared in this way, amidst drinking and laughter, the *Ugo* related what actually prompted their coming.

'Councillor, while you were in Safa, some strangers from riverine area, fifteen men to be specific, came to request for some portion of land in the community to dwell in; they are interested in settling here and they pledge to abide by whatever terms we might give them. We told them to give us two weeks to think it over. We wanted to hear from you first before we know what to do,' the *Ugo* said. 'Unfortunately, you did not return from Safa when the two weeks ended and the *oguedion*[9] granted their stay. We feel we should still let you know now that you've returned,' the *Ugo* added.

****

Earlier, some strangers from that part of the region had come to dwell among them. Akpobaro community had granted some portion of land as settlement to the foreigners and they had settled and lived peacefully in the community – abiding by the rules and terms of the community - though living their own ways. Life was generally harmonious even though the settlers lived separately from the natives. Inspite of their differences, many of the settlers from the

---

[9] Townhall where traditional chiefs have regular meetings to deliberate and take decisions on matters affecting their community.

riverine area had made friends among Akpobaro people who helped them at the beginning to make the task of settling in a new place less difficult, by inviting them severally to their farms and after the day's work they would be given a head-load of foodstuff. In this way, the initial suspicion and distrust of Akpobaro people towards these riverine settlers in their midst gradually disappeared. One of the terms of their stay in Akpobaro, apart from respecting the community's customs, was to pay homage to the chiefs-in-Council yearly with a specific quantity of items derived from whatever occupations they engaged in, in addition to a jar of *ogogoro* and a saucer full of kola-nuts. The settlers were happy in Akpobaro, so they had no problem in meeting these terms. Infact, they did so with all gladness. Many of them had become more prosperous than the average natives.

All the villages of Omaurhie people, including Akpobaro, were particularly favoured by nature, as the entire land of Omaurhie to Safa was between the coastal region and the rain forest belt, so it had the features of both regions, and was well endowed. They had good land for farming, parts of which were several virgin forests from where timbers were produced. Some parts of their land were used also for growing rubber trees. The two factors made Omaurhie land one of the main fields to the growing industrialisation of Safa. But the people of Omaurhie were either mere field workers exploited by the major producers or small scale producers at the mercy of the major suppliers who dictated the prices, so they received mere crumbs of the thriving rubber and timber businesses at Safa. Many natural palm trees also grew on the land. Apart from the river which flowed across the length of Omaurhie to Safa, streams that flowed into the river were here and there. During the raining season, natural water-ways were well supplied with fishes. Around the river and the streams were swamp forests and raffia palm trees, so there were several natural occupations one could engage in for a living. However, only settlers could see beyond the traditional occupation of the people. The people of Akpobaro engaged in farming. Their men prepared the farm for their wives and children to cultivate and grow foodstuffs for the support of the household. After the planting season, the men would become less busy. Yam was regarded as the prize crop, and that was where the men belonged. They gave all their attention to its cultivation. But yam cultivation was not an all season occupation. After stemming its tendrils very little was left to do until harvest. This encouraged a little idleness among the men but they were quite complacent with it because that was what they grew up to know. Although with the coming of timber and rubber businesses, many of the young men had begun to engage in rubber tapping and timber activities - from felling to the haulage of logs into the river where they were floated to Safa for sale. But strangers who came to Akpobaro saw other potentials and resources that the indigenous inhabitants were blind to or did not want to engage in simply because they had never ventured into such activities before. So when strangers started engaging in such unfamiliar occupations as fishing, tapping and brewing of raffia palmwine into *ogogoro* and the cutting and harvesting of palm fruit which they used in producing palm oil and palm kernel, the people of Akpobaro saw no threat to their source of living. When a few other strangers from the eastern part of the country came with retail petty shops, they were hugged and welcomed in Akpobaro. Even if these settlers were to veer into Akpobaro's traditional occupation, there would not still be any problem; arable land was vast. This attitude of the people of Akpobaro had encouraged more people into their community. Chief Akpovire had particularly enjoined the people to welcome strangers into the village as he saw the presence of other peoples in their midst as a sign of development and progress. He knew it would generate socio-economic vibrancy and the spirit of enterprise in Akpobaro.

****

But as the *Ugo* gave him the information, he squinted with some alarm. He was just thinking into the future; he was considering the other side of the coin. Politics is a very sensitive matter. It touches the nerves of the people. Chief Akpovire was wary of the continuous incursion of strangers into Akpobaro which he thought might jeopardize its political stability in future. He knew that the settlers had been showing absolute loyalty to the community. There had never been any cause to suspect any disloyalty among them. But he felt that their children that would come after them who would have the privilege of being bred together with the children of Akpobaro might not entirely see themselves as settlers. And if they became greater in number and probably more prosperous than the natives, that might cause some restiveness in them, which could endanger the peaceful co-existence that was being enjoyed presently. *If there is a split in the ranks of the people, the tendency for each side to canvass the support of the settlers was there. God help the village in such an event,* thought he.

25

'Councillor, you're not talking! If the idea is not favourable, let us know. That is why we came,' said the *Ugo* with some concern after observing that the information was causing Chief Akpovire some anxiety.

Chief Akpovire shaking his head in the negative countered: 'I was only considering the number. Don't you think the number is rather too large at a time?'

'Just like you observe, I raised the issue of their number, but many *Ilorogun* argued that it does not matter as long as they can find work to do,' said the *Ugo*.

'In that case, we can leave the matter as they have agreed. But we must be very careful in admitting more,' cautioned Chief Akpovire.

'Councillor, sometimes you're too quick in accepting the ideas of the *Ilorogun*-in-Council. It was sad indeed that I was not at the *oguedion* during the last meeting. I would have protested strongly at the chiefs-in-Council for the admission of the fifteen men. You see, we the *Ilorogun* are becoming rather selfish. We're now more interested in the annual homage-paying of these strangers,' accused Mudiaga.

'I think it is time we stopped the influx of strangers into our land. We should not forget our children. They need the land and its resources, too,' Okpako chipped in.

'But you didn't say so at the *oguedion* last week. Is it because Councillor has expressed some reservation?' the *Ugo* challenged Okpako.

'You know I tried to but I was shouted down and I became annoyed,' Okpako argued.

'Why can't those strangers remain in their own land, after all?' another man said in protest. 'You think as you have many resources around you, so everybody? Imagine the people from the riverine area, they have no land for farming!' one other chief pointed out.

'But do you see them doing farming when they come here?' retorted the *Ugo*. 'Granted, they still carry out fishing but there's scarcity of foodstuffs in their land, hence they run here!' returned Okpako.

'Have you not heard that there are people living in desert, have they died?' Mudiaga chipped in.

'Some of you think that our people do not migrate to other lands because our land is abundantly blessed. Look very closely, you'll observe that some of us have equally sojourned among the riverine people. The world is like that.

26

It is not always because of what to eat that people move from their home place,' Obire stated.

'You are right Obire,' said Chief Akpovire calmly. 'The creator of the world is perfect in his work. That's why there is always a means of survival for every people of the world, no matter where they live. The Almighty Creator knew from beginning that the entire land would be inhabited, so he put what will sustain people in every land, no matter the conditions. In the desert there are means. In the waters there are means, and they are numerous. Some of these means are obvious, some are not so obvious. Some others require discovery. There are many that have not been discovered but they shall be discovered one day. So nobody is created to lack or to depend on others to survive. The truth is, some people are lazy or not creative and they prefer to be pests on others.'

The house became silent, an indication that Chief Akpovire had led them into the reality of existence.

Just then, Erhukaye, an elderly woman, walked in with a broad smile in her face, which covered all the sorrow and sadness she bore along. All attention immediately shifted to her as she greeted all.

'I am just from your house,' indicating the *Ugo*. 'Atake, my good sister,' referring to the *Ugo*'s most senior wife, 'told me you've just left to see Councillor, and I became happy. I never knew that OUR Councillor is back. I do ask after him among my good sisters that are looking after him. Only for me to be here to see that the entire village is here. God is with me!' she said with a dramatic heave of relief, as she placed her two palms on her chest to demonstrate it.

'Give her drink,' said Chief Akpovire, and the eldest man in the house prayed as he held the small glass of drink towards Erhukaye who was kneeling to receive the drink.

'*Avwebo*, our hearts leap with joy whenever we see you because you are an example of a good wife and how a mother should be. It is our prayer that the owner of heaven and earth will continue his favour upon your life. What does a woman pray for in marriage? Is it children? That he has granted you in abundance. We thank him. But there are still other things. What about long life with your husband? What about prosperity of your children? Certainly, they shall follow you because you are good and faithful in marriage. We always pray that our children will do better than we, ourselves. So shall it be

27

with you and *our brother*. We thank the mighty one above because he is always good to a good wife and mother. He'll favour and bless you always.'

'*I-s-e!* Erhukaye answered as she received the drink. '*Miguo*,' she greeted before gulping the drink, 'My respected fathers-in-marriage, I thank you all,' she said as she got up. 'I am very proud of you all. You have always been very good to me. Marriage is honey when you have very good and kind *fathers-in-marriage*[10] like you. I thank you all,' said she again.

'It is also true that a devoted wife and mother is a great strength to her husband, and that's what you are,' Chief Akpovire enthused.

'Yes,' all the men in the house acknowledged in unison.

'Thank you, my respected *fathers-in-marriage*,' laughed Erhukaye. 'It is like the story of the dogs as our people usually say it,' she went on. 'Where two dogs are playing, it is when each falls for the other in return that makes the play more interesting,' and they all began to laugh in full understanding.

'Actually, I came to initiate a case for the next *Ilorogun*-in-Council,' Erhukaye started in a mood of seriousness when the excitement had died down. 'But since our Councillor is around, I won't wait till then. I would like to present the case in his house here next market day,' untying the left edge of her wrapper to bring out money. 'I would like to initiate the case with one pound,' as she stretched out the money.

'Who are you contending against?' asked the *Ugo* as he received the money.

'Otuene, my son-in-law!' she said.

Every one of them broke down in laughter except Chief Akpovire. The story of Otuene and his wife was very well known in the village.

'It's a family matter,' declared Chief Akpovire calmly. '*Ugo*, please return her money. We shall settle the matter without making it a case,' he added.

'My respected *fathers-in-marriage*, do not take it as rudeness,' she knelt down. 'I want to make it a case and let the side that loses forfeit its money and buy elders drink for resolving the matter. That way, that stupid and ungrateful man will learn his lesson. Let him pay his one pound and lose it!' protested Erhukaye.

---

[10] Fathers-in-marriage: a respectful way a wife addresses the men of the family to which she is married. But Erhukaye used it in a general sense of respect to the men she addressed in the story by way of demonstrating her respectful manner.

28

'*Avwebo*, get up, we won't allow that,' insisted Chief Akpovire. 'Listen *Avwebo*, this evening, come with your daughter, I shall send for Otuene and his people and the matter shall be settled here.'

Erhukaye curtseyed in appreciation before leaving the house.

****

That evening Chief Akpovire convened the meeting of some very notable *Ilorogun*, to hear the matter in his house. The two parties were ably present with some of their relatives. Erhukaye presented her case when the house was complete with all the expected adjudicators. It was over a fight between Oke, Erhukaye's daughter and her husband, Otuene. Otuene was a cantankerous and irascible person. He used every slightest provocation to beat up his wife. Unfortunately, Oke was not also helping matters. She could hurt very much with her stinging tongue as Otuene lost his temper. As a result, they were always in constant bickering, which in most cases resulted in fight. Many people thought the marriage would have collapsed by now but had inexplicably survived, probably due to the tireless and unwavering efforts of Otuene's people who believed that the couple would soon overcome what they saw as 'the teething period of marriage'. But then, the constant brawl in the marriage had become so notorious that it became derisory amusement to the people of Akpobaro. In most cases, Oke would run back to her mother. She never returned until a deputation was sent from Otuene's family to appease her and her family with the promise that they would prevail on their son to mend his ways.

The last quarrel was over a supper. Otuene came home late that evening and was very hungry. He saw that Oke was just about to prepare the evening meal. His anger rose suddenly.

'Bad wife...just getting to cook when others have eaten and are enjoying their rest after the day's work?'

'Bad husband...never asks for explanation before barking.'

'Are you talking to me like that?' queried Otuene and gave Oke a blow on her head and *their show* started again. With the combination of hunger and anger in Otuene, he threw all caution to the wind and Oke was turned into a punching bag. Before neighbours came to separate them, great damage had been done...Oke's face was suddenly covered with bruises, and in one mad reaction, she almost chopped off her husband's lower lip with her teeth, while neighbours were prevailing on him and stormed out of the scene. Oke ran as fast as her legs could carry her until she reached her parents' home, knowing that if Otuene caught up with her on the way, perhaps only her corpse would get to her parents. Oke's father was furious when he saw his daughter badly battered and disfigured. He made up his mind immediately that Oke would never return to Otuene again.

Almost a year after, nothing was heard of Otuene and his people. In two instances, Oke was critically sick. Many people in the village came to comfort her. But Otuene and his people never did. After a while, Erhukaye became very concerned over her daughter's marriage and was thinking of what to do to save the marriage, but she dared not breathe a word of it to Emoyefe, her husband.

Later, that was one year and three months after Oke had run to her parents' home, Otuene's people came for settlement one day. As expected, Emoyefe turned them away. But Otuene's people were determined to take Oke back to her husband. They believed in the idea that if you cannot get to somebody directly you can get to him through those with whom he has deep and penetrating relation. And it worked. When they had succeeded in wooing over Erhukaye and Oke, they approached Omoyefe's closest friend, Erhuke and his closest brother Akpokona for help.

One day, Erhuke came to visit his friend, Emoyefe, over the matter. After they had spoken generally, Erhuke introduced the matter for the last time. 'You see, this life we are living is a very delicate one, and we have to be very careful the way we handle it. No matter how reasonable you can be, you must pray that whatever decision you take today is supported by circumstances of tomorrow so that you can be justified. It is the future that passes the judgement on the decisions and actions of today, whether we like it or not. What is sensible today may be seen as a mistake tomorrow and what appears foolish now may turn out well later. There are things beyond our understanding. But we should always take decisions based on our highest sense of judgement because it is that which is truly right that tomorrow is most likely to justify. In a situation where the person you are taking the decision for, does not support you, you should withdraw because if you insist, and tomorrow does not bless your decision, everybody will blame you for it, and that can torment you for the rest of your life. That is why we play the fool sometimes. To insist on your decision against all prevailing appeals is no wisdom. Your wife and your daughter, even your brothers are in favour of settlement of the marriage. Why don't you leave the matter for tomorrow to prove them wrong?'

When Erhuke had finished, Emoyefe thought for some time.

'Erhuke, your explanation has shed some light on an area I actually overlooked. Our people say, *You cannot munch a food and swallow it for a child;* he has to swallow it himself. I thank you very much for your advice,' Emoyefe said thoughtfully.

'Everybody knows you have done your best. You have given them your wise counsel. After all, your wife and your daughter are no children,' Erhuke explained further, having been encouraged by Emoyefe's favourable reaction. After that day, Emoyefe allowed the settlement.

But when Emoyefe became disposed to the settlement, surprisingly, Otuene's people did not come again, and Erhukaye felt betrayed and fooled. This annoyed her very much. She therefore decided to bring the matter before the highest adjudication of the village, which was the body of *Ilorogun,* the highest title holders of the community. When Erhukaye had narrated her side of the story at Chief Akpovire's house that evening, being the initiator of the matter, the *Ugo* asked the eldest man among Otuene's people if any of them would like to refute what Erhukaye had narrated or had any question to ask her in her presentation. He shook his head in the negative.

'That means everything she says is correct?' said the *Ugo.*

The man nodded his head in the affirmative. This implied that Otuene and his people had nothing else to say, by way of presenting their own side of the matter. The *Ugo* and the rest of the *Ilorogun* smiled to one another to indicate that the task at hand would be easy.

'Enotu,' the *Ugo* called the eldest man among Otuene's people again, 'do you have anything to say before we take our decision?'

And the eldest man stood up.

'My people, I greet you all. Actually, we are not here to argue with our beloved mother- in-law. We came here for settlement. Our desire is to see the young man and his wife back to their marriage. But if I end it with that, I may not be fair to my mind and to my family's in-laws. I'm quite sure you are all aware that since the last quarrel between Otuene and his wife, which is over a year now, our family has made a series of efforts to settle the matter. Our people say that when dogs fall for each other, their play becomes more exciting. The frequent quarrel between Otuene and his wife, Oke, is very well known in the village and I'm sure too that it is also well known that we, the husband's family, has always moved in swiftly to appease our daughter-in-law and her family, without wanting to know who was wrong. In fact, we always took the blame because we know who our son is and we always prefer to be grateful to our good mother- in-law for her understanding. We know that her sympathy towards her daughter's marriage has sometimes caused serious frictions in her matrimonial home.

But we are also aware that our daughter- in-law is not an angel; she has her own faults. But we don't want to look at that. What is actually surprising us is the complacency of our kind mother-in-law in welcoming our daughter-in-law each time she runs home. Our good mother- in-law has never one day, on her own, returned our daughter-in-law, after such escape, at least, to find out what actually happened and settled the matter. We do not like how she encourages our daughter-in-law to abandon her marriage and stay with her. It is not only in Otuene's marriage that quarrel occurs. It occurs in every young marriage at least, and with time, the couple grow up with experience _ they learn from their past mistakes and improve their relation. That cannot happen by running away to parents. We, parents, should not encourage such shirking. That's the little grudge we have against our mother-in-law. I greet the house,' he smiled and everybody laughed including Erhukaye.

'We thank Enotu because our people say a person who speaks out his grudge before his supposed offender and other persons wants settlement,' said the *Ugo*, and many in the house nodded their heads in the affirmative. 'You see, silence can be very dangerous where there is a dispute. It can complicate little problem. And reconciliation is very difficult when either of the side in a dispute refuses to open up. Such situation can render every good effort towards settlement useless. The one who expresses his feeling makes settlement easy. So, we thank you again, Enuto. *Avwebo*, you have heard Enuto, what do you have to say?' the *Ugo* turned to Erhukaye.

'My respected *fathers-in-marriage*, I thank you all,' she curtseyed. 'I also thank him,' referring to Enuto, 'in fact, he's been the sustainer of this mismatch.'

Everybody burst into laughter, knowing that she was referring to the marriage between her daughter, Oke and Otuene.

'And I pray his effort should not go unrewarded. My elders, what else will I say, other than to say I will mend my part,' *Avwebo* curtseyed again to signal that she had nothing else to say, and everyone in the room applauded.

32

'We thank both sides of the matter because when the two sides of a dispute are interested in peaceful settlement, a very difficult matter becomes easy to handle. So it is with this case. There is nothing to settle here; the matter has naturally resolved itself. Enuto, bring drink and let us share together and that settles it,' said Chief Akpovire in a matter-of-fact manner.

Chief Akpovire prayed with the drink and kola-nut. He held a shot before Otuene and Oke who were kneeling in his front, 'You are both settled. Oke, return to your husband...that is your home. Don't run away again. If Otuene fights you again or does anything that offends you and you cannot settle it with him, tell Enuto. I'm sure he will be able to put Otuene in his proper place. Is that not true, Enuto?'

'Yes, of course.'

And everybody laughed.

'But you must be patient with your husband,' he turned to Oke again. 'It is not every offence of a man to which his wife reacts. And when he is boiling, try to keep your cool. You can express your feeling later when he is calm and needs you. I guess you understand what I mean!'

Chief Akpovire beamed with smile and every other person in the house laughed knowingly while Oke and Otuene smiled shyly.

'You will discover surprisingly then that the lion is a lamb! When the man is flexing muscles, the woman knows where her power lies and if she applies it properly she will realise that she can tame the wildest lion in a man. So be wise my daughter. As for you,' Chief Akpovire turned his attention to Otuene disdainfully, 'it is not bravery to beat one's own wife. It is only a foolish man who turns his muscle against his wife. If you have strength, be like the horse and plough the farm and let people see it! A man's strength is meant to protect his wife and not to beat her.'

'She has a stinging tongue,' snapped Otuene.

'Keep quiet! Is there any woman who cannot hurt with her tongue?' returned Chief Akpovire. 'A man must be patient with the tongue of his wife. That's why you are a man.'

'Councillor, he's still young; he does not understand,' one of the men in the house said teasingly.

'He just has to understand as long as he keeps a woman at home,' reacted Chief Akpovire in a matter-of-fact manner. 'We believe after this settlement, you will never beat her again. But if you still persist, we shall order your age-group in the village to get you tied up for severe flogging. That day you will know what it means to defy elders.'

'He won't try it again!' said Enuto in an assuring tone, and everybody laughed as Otuene pledged so before the house.

After the settlement, they all began to drink and converse happily before dispersing that night.

The next day, Erhukaye came back to thank Chief Akpovire with a bunch of plantains for resolving what had been a great heartache for her for more than a year. She was very happy.

CHAPTER FOUR

Eight able-bodied young men were tramping the bush path in a file, each with a well-sharpened cutlass. One of them carried a container of water in addition. Another person among them held a file wrapped in cellophane with his cutlass in his right hand. It was early in the morning when the time was just unveiling Akpobaro for the day. Silent dew-drops from the trees fell upon them as they trod the bush-path from the main road of Akpobaro. The bush-path was like a dark tunnel, totally cut off from light, as darkness still enveloped it in the thick bushes: trees and undergrowth which grew massively together had added their own shadows to the grey dawn. This made the dawn looked like dead of night in the bush. But these early morning risers could feel their way through the bush-path in the thick darkness as they were already familiar with the path- way, and because their eyes had remained in the darkness for some time, somehow, they seemed to find some illumination on the way. Once in a while, they would come into an opening of the atmosphere, without shaded trees, where they could find the grey brightness of the dawn. These young men remained in their silence until they reached a big cherry tree and they picked all the fallen cherries of the night, being the first to be there, and they continued their walk until they came to the particular bush they were to clear. By this time, the day had wiped every form of darkness of the night from the entire horizon and the sky stood stainless in the stillness of the morning like a shining silver plate. The sun was just emerging in her characteristic glowing radiance in the dry season.

It was the beginning of the year, the time for planting. Each family had begun clearing their farmlands. Chief Akpovire had arranged with the eight young men the previous night to go and clear a portion of his ancestral farmland the following morning. Unlike the others in the village whose sole occupation was farming, Chief Akpovire only carried out farming for the fun of it and for the fact that farming was customary for rural dwellers, so he used his skeletal farming most particularly to engage his wives at Akpobaro, as it was totally unacceptable for women to be mere house keepers in a traditional setting like Akpobaro. Chief Akpovire used labourers to clear his farms. His wives only carried out planting and harvesting of crops on their farms.

That morning the eight men walked round the farmland for proper assessment. This was to know its length and breadth and where to start the clearing. They observed that it was a second grade forest which meant that the original forest had been cut down once for farming. But after nine years of fallowing, the farmland had almost replicated its original form.

'It does not look like second grade,' one of them said after a thorough examination. 'The land should be very fertile.'

'It's really a great labour,' another one of them added, while considering the densely folded clump of creepers in his front.

'Let us not complain yet. A man who has agreed to go to battle should not be afraid to fight,' said the one who would coordinate the clearing among them.

'I'm not complaining. I'm only saying what I observe,' defended Ovire.

'That's alright. We're not here to argue. Now, four of you,' the coordinator became business-like, 'spread yourselves on that end of the land,' he directed those on his left flank. 'The rest of us will start from the other end.'

This was the traditional way of starting the clearing of the undergrowth. The approach enabled each person to keep from one another to avoid being hurt by the flinging cutlass of the next person in the clearing. The second reason for the approach was for each person to have a chance of assessing the work of others on his side and keep pace with them if he was lagging behind. In some way, it allowed the spirit of competition. In this approach, each side worked towards the other until they became close. At that point, each side again would assess which side had gone farther. Most times, it generated controversy as the side that had not kept the pace would want to argue that their side was more able. All the same, the competition among those on the same side and those on the opposite side was always a healthy one, as nobody wanted to be derided or accused of lagging behind.

The greatest advantage in it was that it was self-regulatory. However, in the course of clearing, one must pray not to have the misfortune of having unevenly difficult part that could put one at great disadvantage, and not keeping the pace, which of course, might incur the derision of others.

Once the eight began chopping the creepers and all the other undergrowth on their parts with their cutlasses, the concentration became absolute. Only the uneven pattering of cutlasses from the two sides of the farmland was heard. But birds in small groups flew from one section to the other somewhat in panic over the ruffling of their tranquil habitation from time to time. The eight young men worked assiduously and were all covered

36

with sweat. But after a long period of uninterrupted clearing, one of them walked down to where the water was, and drew the container out from a thick foliage which shrouded it from direct sunlight and began to drink. The water was fresh in the coolness of where it was kept. As he sat down with a cup of water under a good shade of a tree, surveying the extent of work done in vague meditation, another one of them staggered down with exhaustion and threw himself down beside the first. Another followed, and the rest of them began to walk down one after the other to have a drink of water. They all began to drink. Drinking water was another way of resting. They had all been exhausted and were just waiting for one person among them to take the initiative. After drinking, they sat together for some time while assessing the area they had cleared. They observed that much was still remaining. They wished they had completed the work, as they were exhausted and hungry. They could feel the emptiness of their stomachs. But they still needed to continue the clearing before the arrival of Chief Akpovire's wives who would bring them food. Before they began clearing again, they sharpened their cutlasses with the file they came and carried on willy-nilly as it were, till their food would come.

Meanwhile, the three wives of Chief Akpovire had been preparing separate meals for the hired labourers back home. Customarily, the women in Akpobaro usually prepared plenty of food for men who were hired to clear their farmlands during the planting season. They fully appreciated the sapping nature of the work. They were also aware that the hired labourers always left home too early for the clearing, for them to eat in the morning, so the food they prepared to the farm on such occasion was always plentiful, more so when the new planting season usually followed the previous year's harvest period. Children were ever willing to follow their parents to farm on such days, even the most recalcitrant ones, as they knew there would be great feasting at the farm.

Efe was one child who did not know whether to bear food with his mother to the farm that day. It was Saturday when he enjoyed staying by the riverside to wave, with some other children in the village, to the band of whites who sped past Akpobaro in speedboats. There was one particular family among them that he always looked forward to seeing. In that family, one young boy about his age always returned his wave with equal affection, to the extent that a bond of friendship seemed to have been forged between them. After many repeated expressions of such mutual affection, Efe began to imagine the day the boy's parents would stop by, for both of them to meet and possibly take him home and show him their rich and beautiful house in Akpobaro. Then, he would proudly tell the white boy that his father was a great chief and had white people like his parents as friends in Safa. He also thought such an occasion would afford him the opportunity to have the boy's address in Safa with the hope of visiting him. He loved this thought very much and strongly believed it would come to pass one day. But when it would be was what he could not say. Being strongly rooted in this notion, he did not want to leave the riverside on Saturdays, lest they stopped by in his absence. So every Saturday, Efe would go to the riverside to swim or be involved in other forms of play with other young boys of his age. While he was doing that, his mind actually was on seeing the white little boy flew past with others. Once the sound of speedboats was heard from a distance, all the children at the riverside would begin to jump up repeatedly in great excitement and many others would run out from the village to the riverside, abandoning whatever they were doing, to join in the hand-waving and chorusing of, 'o-y-i-b-o! o-y-i-b-o! o-y-i-b-o!¹¹ Few of the whites would wave back in broad smile, gleaming with pleasure, as their boats flew past amidst splashes of water which waved the riverside for sometime. They seemed to enjoy this friendly acclamation very much, as they enjoyed their boat trip to the river source where they swam and splashed water all day. In their swimming, they would feel every aspect of the river source with relish. The river source was ever clean, pure and refreshing with sparkling sharp sand. They often plunged themselves into the deep, leaving their swimming tubes afloat to romance with the sharp sand at the bottom of the river like fish, only to reappear at the surface water and swim back to their tubes. Some other times, they would launch against the tide in their wildest excitement as if to grapple with it in its laughing run-away rush after they had allowed themselves to be carried away a bit by its current.

Here was the resort of the white colony at Safa on weekend. They always came with canned foods that would last them on the trip. Once they noticed to their displeasure that it was twilight, they would be seen tearing through the river in great splashes back to Safa.

One Saturday, Efe was at the river, looking forward to seeing his imagined friend. As it were, several speed-boats sped passed. As each successive one passed, Efe looked intently for his *friend,* to exchange their mutual hand-wavings in a most affectionate smile. But as all his peers and

---

¹¹ European or white person

38

others jumped up in excitement and chorused, 'oyibo!,' when the speed-boats were passing, Efe was only literally doing so until he saw *his friend*, which was usually the climax of his exciting moment. Unfortunately, that Saturday, the little boy and his parents did not turn up and Efe became very disappointed. 'They always come, they'll certainly come,' he said to himself. When their usual time of passing was over, Efe still believed they would come. He thought perhaps their boat had some fault and they were trying to have it fixed, to enable them join their colleagues later at the river source, so he kept waiting.

Meanwhile, his mother had been waiting in vain for Efe to return home with the bucket of water she sent him. She kept inquiring about Efe from everyone returning from the river. They would tell her that Efe was at the riverside. She sent word to him to return with his bucket of water. But Efe did not heed. He remained at the riverside until all the whites who had passed earlier were returning in the evening. It was just then, it struck him that *his friend* would not come and he went home dejected.

Otabunor, his mother, picked up a cane and struck him with it six times as Efe poured his water into a large basin, and he cried away as his mother spoke angrily to him, for spending the whole day at the river. He went to a quite corner and sat down alone, after wiping away his tears. He was wandering why *his friend* could not make it that day. He became more anxious, thinking that the little white boy and his family might stop coming altogether.

'Have they gone to their land?' he said to himself.

He dismissed the possibility from his mind.

'If they have gone, all those other whites who came would have gone, also. After all, they all came from their land together.'

He wondered why the colony of white people in Safa did not come to Akpobaro in the first place. *Is Akpobaro not a fine place? Many other people from other lands come here, why not the whites too?* He remembered hearing his father telling his friend, Mudiaga, one day that the white people neither farmed nor fished but were always writing on a table inside a building or supervising their black workers. *I wonder what kind of work they are doing by writing inside a house?* thought he. Efe remained there thinking about the world of the white man which remained buried in mystery in his mind until it became dark.

In the night, Efe could not eat his supper. Her mother thought he was still feeling hurt over the beating. On the contrary, he was filled with the thought of *his white friend.* That night he met the young white boy in Safa and they played together for a long time on a fine street lined with beautiful flowering trees. The boy later took him to their home and he saw a beautiful house with many beautiful things he had never seen before. In their conversation, he asked the boy why he did not go to the river source the previous Saturday and the boy told him that his parents had a visitor from their land that day. He promised Efe that they would not only come the following Saturday but he would entreat his parents to stop over at Akpobaro so that he could visit him. Just then, Efe woke up and painfully realised that it was only a dream. He wished it was really. For sometime, he thought deeply over the dream for what he could make out of it. He turned it over repeatedly in his mind. He eventually concluded that the dream was a pointer to his meeting with the boy at Safa very soon, and he became elated immediately that thought came to him.

The following morning, Efe walked to his father and told him, after greeting, that he would like to go with him to Safa in his next trip. Chief Akpovire looked at him for sometime and wondered what must have brought such thought to his mind that early morning. 'Why do you want to go to Safa?' he asked with some irritation. Efe could not say anything. He was only gazing at his father with all the entreaty of the world in his tender face. Chief Akpovire noticed that the boy's eyes were almost tearful and was quite nervous. He was very surprised. He kept wondering what had come over Efe. 'If you're so interested, I shall take you down in your next holiday,' he told his agitated son. Efe would have preferred that week to actualise his dream but who was he to trade words with his father? He greeted father and went away. His father felt that the boy must have had a strong reason for his request. He hoped to probe into it later when he found him in a more cheerful mood. Nevertheless, Efe was relieved by his father's promise, relishing in the belief that his dream would soon come through.

It was the following Saturday that Chief Akpovire sent labourers to his farmland for clearing. While the cooking was going on, Efe could see the plenty of fish and meat lavished in the soup. All the other children in the family were all excited about going with their parents to the farm that day including those who would not like to go ordinarily. Efe would like to be there, too. But that would make him miss *his friend* at the riverside. 'Will you go?' asked his mother, as she did not see any sign of such excitement in Efe. But Efe only looked away with an undecided mind. When the movement to the farm was to begin, Otabunor looked around for Efe but he had melted away beyond reach.

When Chief Akpovire and his band of food bearers reached the farmland, the labourers had done greater part of the clearing. As his three wives clustered by children noised into the farmland, the young men who had been waiting impatiently for them, pretended to be too engrossed in their work to notice them.

'*Vwadoh!*[12] Chief Akpovire greeted as he was carefully working towards them to survey the extent of the work done.

'*Miguo*,' the workmen greeted in return from their different positions including the other group behind who only heard his voice.

'Well-done,' said Chief Akpovire cheerfully, essentially to those who could not hear him clearly before. His wives and children took it up from there.

'*Vwadoh, vwadoh*,' they greeted the workmen. 'You have covered so much ground in such a short time?' Chief Akpovire added with satisfaction. 'You must have been so early.'

The boys answered in the affirmative.

'Well done,' he said again, you should stop for now. Come and have some food,' he urged. 'You must be very hungry.'

One by one the boys started coming to where Chief Akpovire and his wives were with all signs of exhaustion and hunger. The women and children greeted them again as they came gasping. The women cleared a spot under a shade of a big tree and set the food. When the workmen saw what was set before them, they could not hide their excitement and disbelief.

'All these for us!' exclaimed one of them.

'No, for the trees and bushes,' replied Chief Akpovire and they began to laugh.

While they settled down to the lavish dish, Chief Akpovire and his family were at a different spot to have theirs. The labourers agreed in their hushed tones that it was an honour to work for a great man who sincerely appreciated the good labour of the common folk. The oldest among them packed the meat and fish into one separate plate which formed a mountain on it. There were palm oil, *banga* and melon soups. When they saw the large quantity of food set before them vis-à-vis their empty stomachs, they thought there was going

---

[12] General greeting for more than one person.

to be some struggle among them to secure each person's portion. But before they could go half their respective portions, they were already filled. They looked at the left-over and regretted that they could not eat anymore.

'I wish there was a place for reserve in the belly,' said one of them and they all laughed. They could not even consume all the fish and the meat.

'Indeed, hunger is a lazy wrestler,' one of them said. 'That's what my father always says. A minute ago when I felt a crushing hunger in my belly, I thought I could crush anything. But here we are! We cannot even go half way.'

They called the children to take over the remains. The children were also filled. But as usual with them, they had insatiable appetite for fish and meat. So they rushed down and cleared the fish and the meat. They also licked up the soups. But yam, starch and plantains they did not touch.

Most probable, the animals would call for their own feast that night as the huge left-overs were thrown into a bush nearby.

While they were all relaxing after the heavy meal, they saw a group of monkeys jumping from tree to tree. The children became excited and were shouting at the monkeys. The monkeys seemed to be at a kind of game. They were in a single file, taking their leaps one after the other in exactly the same way. They were very smart and fast as if they were in a great athletic drill. The one in front seemed to be leading the rest. Chief Akpovire pointed the front one to his children who were completely possessed by the sight of the monkeys.

'That's their guide. It is the one that sees to it that there's no danger ahead,' he told them.

'If there's danger how does it make the others know since animals don't talk?' one of the children asked while they were still gazing at the monkeys. The monkeys were almost out of their sight then. Their movement seemed to be too fast for the children's desire. Chief Akpovire laughed at their ignorance.

'You think they don't talk? They do among themselves, just as we humans do. But only in whistles and signs, which were enough to pass all they require to say to one another. Probably, as they saw us watch them pass, they might have spoken about us.'

'Are they killed for meat?' another child asked.

'Why not? But it is not everybody that likes to eat them,' said Chief Akpovire.

'Probably because they look like humans!' another child chipped in while frowning at the monkeys as they were going out of sight.

'If we kill one now, won't you eat?' asked one of the labourers, smiling with some mischief, and all the children shrugged their shoulders with some awful expression in their faces.

'Ah, not me!'

'Not me...' they began to say, one after the other with patent disapproval, most probably because they saw the monkeys as living caricatures of humans.

'What will you do now since all the meat you all ate a few minutes ago was monkey?' the labourer advanced further in his mischief and all the grown-ups, including Chief Akpovire grinned, impatiently waiting to see how the children would react to the prank being played on them. At once, the children began to make attempt at vomiting and the adults began to laugh until one of the women shouted, 'S-t-o-p! It's not true,' and the laughter became louder as the children joined in it – laughing at the whole foolery.

When the labourers had fully relaxed, they sharpened their cutlasses once again for the last phase of the work. This time the sun had begun its downward journey home. After such a great meal and long rest, they set at the work with new vigour. When they began again, it was with steady effort as they felt they had enough time to complete the clearing before sunset. When they had cleared to some point, they encircled the remaining portion which was now small.

Meanwhile, an antelope had been trapped in that portion. The antelope had been stirred up from its resting place with the clattering of the cutlasses since the second phase began and it withdrew inward, waiting for a chance to run out of the danger. As the men waged on with the clearing, the antelope receded further inward to the thickest part of the remaining bush. When the labourers were unconsciously closing in on it, it became restless and desperate for an escape. It made a dodgy attempt, and it was a wrong move. The antelope's movement had rustled the dried leaves on the ground in the bush in its movement. Immediately, the workmen became aware of its presence and there was frenzy among them as they looked out for the game. One of the men cut a short thick stick and with a studied watch he threw it. The stick went violently through the bush in the direction of the antelope. Caught in a labyrinth of frightful confusion, the antelope ran out at once in an uncalculated flight. Quickly, one of the labourers dashed out his cutlass and the poor animal began to struggle, the third slashing with the cutlass snuffed life out of the antelope. Everybody around rushed forward with excitement to see the game. The children began to dance round the lifeless animal in jubilation.

After the brief excitement over the game, the workmen went back to work again. Their good fortune seemed to give them a new vigour. They were now very fast with the drive to finish up at once. In no time, they cleared the thickest part where the antelope hid and concentrated on some thick folded long grass. It was the remaining part of the clearing. It proved to be the toughest. But the workmen were not daunted. They tackled it with great vigour. In a short while, they cut it up to a dip that was covered with the same grass mixed with some creepers which they left for two men among them to finish.

While they were leaving, a porcupine sprang from the dip and began to struggle with the grass already cut. It tried to escape as it could but the grass was a great hindrance and with little effort it was killed. All the labourers dashed to the dip again to look closely. Behold, three others were lurking inside, looking for cover. Expectedly, none of them escaped the chilling slashing of the cutlass. 'What a fortune!' They all seemed to be saying as they gazed at the four games.

Later, the labourers brought the games to Chief Akpovire for sharing. He dismissed the idea outrightly.

"They are yours. I was not part of the killing.'

The workmen looked at Chief Akpovire with bewilderment. They were not convinced at all with his argument.

'If you had injured yourselves during the struggle to kill the animals would you have shared the injury with me?' smiled Chief Akpovire as he struggled to convince them.

'Our people say: *He, who finds a good fortune, has a smiling companion, also,*' the one who was co-ordinating the clearing among the workmen said,

'Yes, you're right. But that entirely depends on the fortunate person. He has not offended anyone if he chooses not to share his good fortune with anybody,' remarked Chief Akpovire.

'We don't want to be an example of such bad manners,' replied the workman.

'Well, that I leave to you – it's entirely your own affair.'

The workmen understood his point quite clearly and they argued no further. But they knew how to use their good sense of judgement. They

44

communed together and gave Chief Akpovire the antelope which was the choicest game.

'No, that's too much for me alone!' protested Chief Akpovire.

'Sir, it's entirely our own affair, remember?' and they all began to laugh. Truly, the offer was quite disagreeable to Chief Akpovire. He wished he had agreed to share the games in the first instance. All the same, he thanked them ad nauseam for being so generous to me.

CHAPTER FIVE

Chief Akpovire had been making every effort to realise his dream: the building of a college at Okuemo, a neighbouring village of Akpobaro. Okuemo had given him a good expanse of land for the college. The village was agog about the new status they would soon enjoy among the entire Omaurhie villages. The day Chief Akpovire went to see the elders of the village for the affirmation of the proposal, most Okuemo people did not go to their farms, as the wind of the significant event which was to be previewed to the village elders only, had swept across the entire village the previous night by hearsay, and the people did not want to say it from secondary source. Before noon that day, the compound of the *Okaorho*, the eldest man of the village, had been brimming over with people milling about with so much excitement and speculation. The noise in the compound and around it was deafening as almost all the people in the village gathered there – market noise was lesser. There was tension and anxiety, also; anxiety over the coming of Chief Akpovire who had been under intense pressure from all the villages of Omaurhie, on where to site the college, the pressure from his own village being the greatest. The people of Akpobaro wondered why Chief Akpovire would leave his birth place and give such a privilege and status to other people. They argued that, 'A man cannot go to someone else's farmland when his farmland is there, unused.'

****

One day, the elders of Akpobaro sent a deputation to Chief Akpovire over the matter. Mudiaga, his friend was included on purpose. After Chief Akpovire had offered them drink and kola-nuts, they presented the matter to him.

'Councillor, we thank you. We are always grateful to the Almighty Creator for raising a man like you in our community. He knew in advance our situation and gave you to us as a gift that will lift our village from darkness. It is our prayer that as you continue to look after our community, so the Almighty Creator and our ancestors will continue to look after you. No evil in the East, in the West, in the South, and in the North shall befall you,' said the *Ugo* prayerfully.

'*Ise*,' the entire house chorused.

'Councillor, our people say when a man sings praises of someone for too long in his presence, people will begin to think he is about to beg for something. So let me stop at that. Not to waste further time, we are sent here by the entire Council of Chiefs over a very important matter that borders on the development of our village,' he paused for a while. 'We hear that you are planning to build a college at Okuemo; something that has been a luxury to the entire Omaurhie people. We know that Okuemo and Akpobaro are kindred but we live in separate places and have our different interests. We would like the college therefore to be sited here, at Akpobaro, so that our children and those that are already in the modern secondary school are encouraged to attend. Unlike those of you who have the ideas of the white man, I may not have much to say about the beauty of a college but I do know that if not for such knowledge several good things we have had from government through you, would not have been possible. We need many *people like* you to bring development to the village and we believe the college will bring up such great people. We also believe that more of our children will attend the college if it is sited here in Akpobaro. If Okuemo desires great things they should pray for great men to come from their midst rather than have what naturally belongs to us, your immediate people. Do I speak the mind of our people?' asked the *Ugo*.

This was done to make it clear to Chief Akpovire that his word was the entire Akpobaro's stance on the matter.

'Yes, you have spoken well!' all the other chiefs answered. 'We greet you, Councillor,' and the *Ugo* ended his speech.

Chief Akpovire thanked them so much for their concern for the village.

'Sustainable progress and development can only come to a place when the interest of the children and upcoming generation preoccupies the minds of its leaders. This, you have demonstrated. You are indeed worthy leaders of the village and you deserve all esteem and reverence. Now, to answer you directly: when I came to settle among you after my two tenures at the Council, I had and have my plans and vision for the entire people of Omaurhie. I travelled round the country during my political days and I interacted with many great people including white men. I have also read several books to understand many issues about development of a society. From all of them, one thing remains clear: the entire world is changing. It is changing very fast. Our own country is even changing faster. And the changes are all in one direction: the direction of modern society. The world is moving towards a coalition of ideas that will transform it. So the world belongs to those who possess brilliant ideas for better society and you can only possess such ideas

47

through education. Without education, the world will leave you behind. It is in this regard, I am doing all that I can to bring education to our people. I know many of our children, through education, will move from here and become part of the great world. We must therefore encourage them to go to school. So that they move farther in the world and plough back the benefits to our community. This vision is not limited to Akpobaro alone but to the whole Omaurhie people. I have chosen Okuemo for the college because it happens to be the centre of Omaurhie. The college will therefore afford the great majority of the people the opportunity of attending a college, including those who will come from outside as accommodation and feeding shall be provided in the college. I know our people might not be able to afford the boarding. Our children can attend from here. They will not consider it too far if they know the benefits they stand to reap from it later. Please make it possible for your children to be there when it opens. I thank you all,' and Chief Akpovire ended somewhat with an air of finality.

There was silence for some minutes.

'Councillor, we thank you for your explanation,' the *Ugo* responded. 'We appreciate your explanation quite well but we cannot say anything now. We shall report what you have told us to the Council of Chiefs which sent us. Whatever they think, we shall let you know. We thank you.'

And the deputation went away. But they never came back again because they knew Chief Akpovire had made up his mind and his argument could not be faulted.

✳✳✳✳

While the people of Okuemo were anxiously waiting, they would ask one another, now and then, 'Will he come?' Many of them had their doubts because they were aware of the pressure piling on Chief Akpovire over where to site the college, especially the pressure from his village. Their fear was heightened as he had not shown up by noon. They feared that he might not keep the appointment, after all. They were more inclined to think that his own village might have pressurized him into changing his mind. But the *Okaorho*, the eldest man of Okuemo, repeatedly assured them that Chief Akpovire would come.

'Councillor is not a man to doubt. I know him. If he has changed his mind he would have let us know by now. You people don't know that man. He is a very considerate fellow; a rare breed among us. When people are saying he has changed his mind, I just laugh at their ignorance. Let me tell you; before that man takes any decision he must have weighed and considered every aspect of it, even things that we might never have thought of in the first place. And once he has made up his mind, let thunder rumble the sky, let lightning strike, and let the sea roar in its waves, he will not blink his eyes again. That man, his words are rock. The people of Akpobaro think Councillor belongs to them. They fail to realise that when a man shoots into prominence he becomes the sun that shines on everyone. I know that man does not think like the rest of us.'

Though, these words of assurance seemed to convince the people, but they still had their doubts lurking in a cloudy corner of their innermost minds until they saw Chief Akpovire.

At the outskirts of Okuemo, appeared three tiny figures on bicycles. The people of Okuemo became excitedly agitated when they spotted a flashing white bicycle among the three figures. It was very well known through out Omaurhie that only Chief Akpovire had the coveted white superb bicycle then. This further made him unique in the clan. Every time, the people of Akpobaro or any other village heard the sound of the white bicycle which sounded differently from the other bicycles, ticking, like the counting of a big clock, the people would look around for Chief Akpovire, knowing full well that he was the only one with such a bicycle. If he wanted to attract greater attention and amuse himself, which he loved to do sometimes, he would increase its speed in a manner of being in a hurry and relaxed the pedals. The bicycle would begin to ring loudly a rhythm which attracted greater attention with much admiration and it delighted him a great deal. Another way of knowing he was passing by with the bicycle was its bell. The white bicycle bell sounded exceedingly sharper than the black one. The people of Akpobaro in particular had come to associate the sounding of a white bicycle with Chief Akpovire.

****

But on a few occasions, he allowed his children to ride it for errands. The children always took advantage of such a rare opportunity by riding for pleasure. They would ride the bicycle round the village, showing off with it. Most cases, they would be so carried away with it that they kept their father waiting for a long time, which usually earned them some thrashing. Their friends, who often ran after them, soliciting earnestly for a short ride, were not also helping matters. The short ride was always much longer than they

49

promised. Not all their friends that ran after them usually had the privilege due to time constraint. Such Chief Akpovire's child on errand always hurried away with the promise of another day to his friends who could not ride that day, when he realised too late that he had over delayed. Those who had the privilege would jump up and down with pride, smiling effusively to the annoyance of the unlucky ones.

The last time Chief Akpovire allowed his children to use the white bicycle when they were sent on errand was when he sent Omovie a message with it. That was also the first time Omovie was riding the bicycle. And he became too excited with it. He was swaying from one side to the other, practising how to ride without holding the handle bars. A practice, children of his age often indulged in. Some of them had perfected the art and they claimed to be unbeatable while others looked for every opportunity to master it. But the children in the village only did so with the black bicycle which was common, having no special regard. But today, Omovie had the singular privilege of practising with the highly coveted white bicycle. At first, he only rode the bicycle until he reached a more auspicious place, where he began the art. Three of his school mates spotted him from a distance and they ran after him, shouting at him to stop for them. But Omovie did not heed. He knew they were coming to beg for a ride. He decided to raise the gear up to increase his speed. Unfortunately, the peddlers became totally loose and free from the gear at once, and he fell. Soon, the three boys caught up with him and lifted the bicycle off him. They began to assist him in fixing it, with the belief that Omovie would show gratitude later by allowing them to ride. They did all they could to fix the gear again. But all their efforts yielded no result. In their anxiety, they pressed the gear too forcefully and repeatedly and the gear became disconnected totally. Relentlessly, they kept trying, believing it could hook up any moment. Omovie's heart was pounding too hard now, fearing what his father might do to him. His eyes began to prickle with tears.

'What a devil? What will I say?' he lamented in his agony and tears began to stream down his cheeks.

Meanwhile, his father had been waiting. Chief Akpovire was with some persons in his living room, having some insipid conversation. Although his father was becoming uneasy over his delay, he did not betray it at first. He was just hoping that Omovie would be back soon. When their conversation had eventually trailed off, uncomfortable silence crept in. At that moment, Chief Akpovire stood up and walked out of the house to look for anybody he could

50

see to send word to Omovie to return immediately. But none of the children was around. He became veryy angry. He was just waiting for Omovie now to have him thoroughly beaten. He thought the boy must have been carried away in the indulgence of riding for pleasure. He was just waiting in the frontage of house, looking very angry and confused, not knowing what to do next in his agitation. Just then, two of his other sons rolled in the bicycle.

'He has spoiled it, heh?' Chief Akpovire asked curiously, as he saw them rolling the bicycle into the compound.

They nodded their heads in the affirmative.

'Where is he?'

The two boys made no response.

Chief Akpovire understood their silence. Omovie had gone into hiding, fearing the trouble awaiting him.

'Did you see Onovughe and Edafe?'

'They are on their way,' one of them answered.

Chief Akpovire's spirit became lifted.

'You have done well,' he told the two boys. 'Tell Omovie never to return home,' said Chief Akpovire in anger as he went inside.

Apart from severe beating Omovie received that day, Chief Akpovire never allowed his children to ride any bicycle again, not even their mothers' black bicycles whenever they were sent on errands…messages had to be carried out on foot, no matter the distance and the children grumbled within themselves when they were sent on errands and they never forgave Omovie for it.

****

The people of Okuemo peered intently with great excitement at the approaching figures at the outskirts.

'He's the one!' one of them shouted excitedly. Others looked more intensely, trying to be very sure.

'He's the one!' another voice announced.

'He is the one!' another followed.

At once every one of them burst into a loud shout of 'he's the one!' They began to dance and celebrate. Many of them could not hold their peace any longer. In their excitement, they ran towards the bearers of good tidings and welcomed them with songs of praise to the house of their *Okaorho*. Chief

Akpovire and his two companions were greatly elated by the way they were received.

Meanwhile, the *Okaorho,* the elders and chiefs of the village were seated in the *Okaorho's* sitting room, waiting the arrival of Chief Akpovire. When they heard the hysteria outside, they looked out with expectation and got the message, and they became very glad.

'I told you that he will come!' said the *Okaorho* excitedly.

'Yes, you said so,' many of them in the sitting room began to say.

When Chief Akpovire with his two companions eventually entered the sitting room, all the men who had been waiting, stood up to shake hands with him in warm greeting. Drinks and kola-nuts with some money were immediately presented to their august visitor, after they had all seated again. The supporting of the presentation with money by individuals was almost endless. Everybody wanted to support, a way of showing that they were all very happy with the coming of Chief Akpovire. The tray of money was becoming filled with coins. Immediately, another tray was brought in. At last, Mudiaga, one of the two that accompanied Chief Akpovire down, stood up with broad smile to accept the offers.

'If I had known, I would have brought a big sack,' and the people laughed. 'Well...I'm blaming myself because everyone knows in Omaurhie that our people from here are exceptional when it comes to hospitality.'

He then smiled broadly for something else.

'Besides your open generosity, we know you are highly favoured with beauties. Councillor,' turning to Chief Akpovire, 'don't you think our wives need assistance back home?'

Everybody burst into laughter.

'Yes, we have them, if Councillor and his men desire, why? We'll give them with all gladness, as many as they want,' an elderly woman said in jest.

And the laughter was renewed.

'Well, we thank you all for your generosity. We are indeed very grateful. We accept the drink, the kola-nut and the money,' Mudiaga said matter-of-factly, and he gave the two trays of money to the other co-companion of Chief Akpovire. 'And let the *Okaorho* bless the drink and kola-nut for our eating and drinking. I thank you all!'

And they began to drink while they talked about recent events in the clan.

When the drinks and kola-nuts had gone round, it became clear that Okuemo people were eager to hear Chief Akpovire. But Chief Akpovire was not in a hurry. He was still savouring the spirit of camaraderie in the gathering. He believed, after all, that such important news was not to be hurried over. But after a while their *Ugo* spoke again.

'People hardly see the elephant in the bush and if one happens to be seen, you know there must be great story to tell. Councillor, we know your coming might not be for nothing. If there is an important message for us we are ready to receive it with all gladness. We thank you and the ones that came with you.'

There was calmness after their *Ugo* had spoken. Everybody was excitedly waiting. Chief Akpovire thanked them for the enthusiastic welcome accorded him and his companions.

'I'm particularly pleased with your generosity. I know Okuemo to be very hospitable and kind. You all know that I have travelled a lot. I have met many kinds of people. I have also received many great kindnesses. But in all these, I had never received or seen the generous kindness you have shown to me today. Really, I was touched when I saw the poorest and the very aged among you enthusiastically offering what seemed to be their last to my reception. But what can words offer me to say? Sincerely, I cannot express the debt of my gratitude. True, there is poverty in language. Well, it is suffice to say that my companions and I are very grateful. We thank you so much.'

He paused for a while.

'I believe everyone knows why we came. But I know you want to hear it from me, directly. Now, let me make it clear and to the hearing of all the people of Okuemo that we have come to affirm that the college I am about to establish in Omaurhie shall be established here in Okuemo. There is no going back on this arrangement!'

And all the people yelled and leaped with joy and began to jubilate. Very many of them began to dance outside, and they eventually danced back to their various homes, celebrating the good news. While all the youths ran to the site the village had earmarked for the college with their sharpened cutlasses, and began to clear enthusiastically. It was a very large site.

****

Chief Akpovire had planned to make the college a model. He was prepared to put everything he had into it. He had been consulting with the principal of the Government College in Safa who was an experienced and tested educationist. The white man had been very willing to render every useful advice to Chief Akpovire in the establishment of the college. He was very happy and surprised

53

to see one of the natives showing such a great commitment to the building of a standard college in the area. Hitherto, he had recommended to Chief Akpovire the size of the land needed for the college. He had also brought in another white expert to design the school structures to the standard specifications obtainable in Great Britain.

Since that day when the site of the college was cleared, Chief Akpovire had been working assiduously to see the school take off. Fortunate enough, his timber business had been yielding good returns during the period; apart from using part of the timber proceeds to complete his bungalow at Safa, all other monies coming his way had been invested in the college. The small proceeds of the modern secondary school were not spared too for the development of the college. All the blocks of classrooms, dormitories and staff quarters had been completed within two years of development. Equipment, school facilities and materials still remained a huge challenge however.

Though, Chief Akpovire was happy that he had been able to secure government approval for the school after raising all the structures, there were still several things to be put in place. He was very eager to see the college start soon. He had been thinking of loan but he wanted that to be the last resort. In his determination, he had redoubled his effort in his timber business. He scarcely had time for community's matters nowadays. He would leave at cockcrow with his workmen to the forest for the felling of timbers while another group of workmen jerked the logs onto a makeshift rail-line that was meant to facilitate the rolling of the logs. The workmen used very strong stems afterwards to push the logs one after the other on the rail line to the river. From there, they would be floated to Safa for sale. The work was very hectic and laborious. It was usually from cockcrow to roost.

The risk of floating the logs to Safa which often took about two weeks was quite great. The line of logs could break apart in a strong tide and some of the logs might get lost in the process. There were also pirates in the night. The risks of one or both were high, and in such event, it was always like starting from scratch again, after experiencing such a huge loss. Until the logs reached Safa safely, the owner was always having sleepless nights of anxiety.

When the college was near completion three years later, after clearing the site, Chief Akpovire saw the need to sensitise his pupils and all other teenage children of Omaurhie. One day, he visited his modern secondary school; it was always unscheduled and rare. Chief Akpovire believed in seeing things as they are. From his political experience, he had observed the pretension in a scheduled official visit. Though the headmaster had adjusted to his approach, he still found himself discomfited sometimes on such occasions. In most cases, Chief Akpovire preferred to see the headmaster quietly and would leave briefly as he had come. This made his visit that day rather unique and special. It was early. The school bell had just been rung for assembly. The pupils filed themselves out according to their classes. The teachers were surprised to see their proprietor that morning because he had never come so early before. Though, it was the office of the teacher on duty for the week to conduct the assembly, the headmaster decided to take the responsibility that day. The presence of Chief Akpovire had put pressure on him and wanted to exhibit a high sense of responsibility. The teachers and the pupils understood and assisted by making themselves ever-willing follows. The pupils were orderly in their lines and conducted themselves properly without prompting. Class teachers left the veranda platform where they usually stood by the headmaster in front of the assembly ground to inspect and conduct their pupils more particularly.

When the headmaster had completed the routine of Morning Assembly, he looked towards the proprietor to draw the pupils and teachers attention to the all-important person in their midst.

'As you can see, we have an august visitor in our midst. The one who created the opportunity we are all enjoying here today. I don't really know how to introduce him formally to you. He is a man who has walked so many great paths that one does not know where to start. But you all know him. He really does not require any introduction. I only wanted to introduce him formally, even at that, I find it extremely tough. Herein lies his greatness,' he smiled. 'Well, I leave that headache to history. He is here to share some of his great ideas, should I say ideals, with us today. Sir,' he bowed his head in respect, 'we consider it a great honour to have you in our midst. You are most welcome.'

Chief Akpovire walked to the centre of the veranda platform and the pupils broke into a song of praise which was specially composed to welcome important visitors to the school. When the song ended, Chief Akpovire thanked the staff and pupils, particularly the headmaster, for the great achievements the school had recorded in a short time, most especially the last edition of the yearly football competition among modern secondary schools in the Council area, in which the school won the gold trophy. He enjoined them to maintain the high standard the school had set for itself in all aspects of education. After he had elaborated on the achievements, he went further to admonish them on the task of living a successful life.

'Like the coin, there are two sides to life: success and failure. How many of you want to be failures? Raise your hands.'

Expectedly, nobody raised his hand.

'Now, how many of you want to be a success?'

All hands were up including the ones of the headmaster and the teachers. And there was a general laughter.

'I just wanted to demonstrate the truth about life hence I asked the two questions which seem funny, and it was obvious that *everybody wants to be successful.* That is why we have this parlance: *failure is an orphan but success has many fathers, mothers, brothers, sisters. . . .* But much as everyone wants to be a success, in reality, there are many failures and few successes among individuals in a society. Is that not true?'

The pupils answered in the affirmative.

'The reason is simple: most of us want to be success without its ingredients, and that's not possible! There is this saying among the white people, *No pain, no gain,* which our people call, *Work before pleasure.* What that means is that you should be prepared to toil for success. Success is great will and perseverance. So many people cannot face its rigour and long trial, so they crash out. That's why many people are failures. There are others who are hard working but have no plan. They are like a ship without bearing. They could just be spinning round and round one spot. My good pupils, be wise! Don't be either. Plan and burn for your dream and you shall be great.

'Now, on a more particular matter, it is now common knowledge that the college at Okuemo will soon be open. I am working hard to see it open next year.'

The pupils and staff who had been listening with all attention applauded.

'I must confess that the great success of your school has really emboldened me to establish the college in the area.'

Another round of applause followed.

'And when I was conceiving it, my immediate concern is you,' he pointed at them. 'My vision for you is not for you to stop after the modern secondary school but to go further, to be that which will really make you glad to have education. What I mean is that, you must work very hard in your studies for you to have good grades in your final examination, which will qualify you for the college that is about to be opened in the area, because, you are going to compete with other intelligent pupils from other areas, especially the urban pupils.

'It is necessary to state emphatically that the college shall set a very high standard that will be difficult to beat. In that circumstance, we shall not compromise merit and excellence for any other considerations. It is my hope and desire to see as many of you as possible gain admission into the college. It is a great privilege and opportunity for you. Frankly speaking, it will be a great pain for me if many of you could not have access because you are the reason for the establishment of the college.

'I know many of you will not be able to afford the luxury of boarding hence I am establishing the school in our locality. It is my belief that the college will awaken educational consciousness in the area. One thing you must understand, education brings out the best in you. It can also make you get to very lofty positions you never dreamt of in the first instance. I know if you work hard and pursue your education further, many of you will become accomplished teachers, lawyers, doctors, writers, accountants, even statesmen and many more. This reminds me of what one of the Black Americans told us in a conference of Pan-Africanism held in Accra few years ago. He was addressing nationalists from all parts of Africa struggling for their countries' Independence. I was one of the delegates from our country here. He said, *Youcan be if you wanna be.* What he meant then was that, we could win Independence for our countries if we really fought hard for it. In the *same* token, let me tell you today, you can be one of the professionals I mentioned if you work hard for it. The ability is in you. All it takes is great effort. So you must take your studies very seriously. Dream big and work hard towards it and you will marvel at what God has deposited in you. How many of you will like to be in the college next year?'

Expectedly, every pupil raised his hand and there was a general laughter again.

'Good!' Chief Akpovire acknowledged. 'That becomes a challenge for each and every one of you. You have the key to open the door. And what is the key?' he asked, wanting to be very certain that the pupils understood him clearly.

'Hard work!' chorused the assembly.

'Fine, make sure you are there. One other thing: there will be scholarships to any Omaurhie pupils who have distinction in his final result and pass the entrance examination into the college.'

The assembly applauded excitedly.

'That's the second challenge for you. So you have no excuse for failing to take advantage of the college. I thank you all for having your audience.'

When Chief Akpovire had ended his speech, the headmaster thanked him and turned to his pupils, 'You are lucky to have this wonderful opportunity. I feel like living my life all over again. I wish I had this opportunity I would have gone far in education. You may not be able to appreciate this privilege you have now. I believe you will appreciate it better in your later life. All the same, be wise! Make good use of this great opportunity, like I always tell you, *Strike the iron when it is hot* if not...I leave the rest to you,' he smiled. 'Now let us give our proprietor three happy cheers for this great opportunity: 'Hip! Hip! Hip!' he shouted.

'Hurray!' chorused the assembly.

It was repeated accordingly and the atmosphere was charged with great joy.

Later, Chief Akpovire had another session with the staff of the school. First, he thanked them profusely for the good work they were doing. He told them theirs was not a job that could be paid for, adequately.

'It is only the Almighty Creator that can fully reward you. You are not only imparting knowledge, you are also moulding characters. Whatever the children turn out to be tomorrow is the work of your hands. I think your profession has placed you next to God.'

All the teachers, including the headmaster, clapped somewhat in amusement of having been highly flattered.

'This is not flattery, I mean it from the depth of my heart,' Chief Akpovire said with all seriousness. 'I appreciate all that you are doing here. You consider it a small work. But it is exceedingly greater than you think. The destinies of the children are in your hands. You can make or mar them. Whatever they become tomorrow to a very large extent depends on you! I believe you know that, for us to play this great role very well, we ourselves must be examples of what we teach. This is the greatest challenge of this venerable profession. Please, note that you are not accountable to me your employer. No, you cannot answer to me. It is to God. Yours requires a good and sensitive conscience, because one who builds up children builds up the next generation of a society. And no society can be better than those who constitute it.

Frankly speaking, I really appreciate your good work. And I will like to encourage you. Now that the college is about to commence, I will like some of you to advance your education so that you can be there in future. I will not hesitate to absorb you. I know money is a constraint but that shouldn't be if we can enter into a kind of agreement, by which, the college foots the cost of your further studies and you pay back by instalment later, when you have completed your studies and have been absorbed. It's a matter of solid arrangement. So, you too can further your studies without financial barrier. Remember, a teacher who earns his pupils' respect later, is the one who progresses as his pupils' progress.'

All the teachers were greatly excited and clapped repeatedly, by way of appreciating Chief Akpovire's benevolence and wise counsel, which brought into full consciousness, the practical reality of the profession. The headmaster once again thanked Chief Akpovire on behalf of the staff for his good words of encouragement and bounteous offer. He prayed that God should continue to prolong Chief Akpovire's life for his service to humanity.

CHAPTER SIX

'Chief, thank you very much. I've actually heard a lot about your kind assistance to the police in the area, but I didn't know it was really great like this. Thank you sir, you've saved me much trouble,' the police constable bowed in greeting.

'I quite appreciate the work of the police, it's so huge. Without the assistance of the general public, especially those of us at the grassroots, there's little they can do,' said Chief Akpovire.

'Chief, how many of us in the society truly appreciate this fact?'

'Quite few,' said Chief Akpovire.

'I wish there were many like you, our work would be much easier and interesting.'

'I think it depends on the relationship, officer. I believe the police can win the public support they really need, if they are seen as trustworthy public personnel and have a good rapport with the public generally. Perception counts a lot in building good relationship. I think we will get there some day,' said Chief Akpovire.

'Chief, I agree with you totally, and we're aware of this fact. But you see, things are messed up from the top; we at the bottom merely carry out orders. It's horrible sometimes, you know.'

'That's what I think too,' answered Chief Akpovire. The police constable shook hands with Chief Akpovire finally and bowed again in greeting before leaving.

****

Constable Akpan was from the police divisional headquarters in the area, to carry out an arrest or see a matter settled in Akpobaro. He was newly transferred to the Council area, so he was not familiar with Omaurhie villages. In fact, this was his first assignment to the area. Almost all the policemen in the division knew Chief Akpovire. He became close to the senior police officers when he was a councillor. Since then, he had had contacts with a good number of them. And being a foremost community leader in his area, the police always relied on him for assistance. The police superintendent officer in control of the Council area, once in a while, paid the local leaders in the area his respects. This was a legacy the former white police bosses in the area left

60

behind. The idea at the beginning was to build a good community relation with the police through local leaders. The police force then was understaffed and to have effective control of the localities, it was thought necessary, to maintain this kind of relationship for maximum cooperation from the local leaders. This was in line with the general policy of the colonial government in reducing administrative cost as much as possible in the territory. But when the country was decolonising, indigenous officers were promoted to head the various divisional units across the country and many more indigenes were recruited.

When Constable Akpan was to go for the Akpobaro assignment, his boss called him and he answered with a smart police salute.

'When you get to Akpobaro, ask for Chief Akpovire and report your mission. He's our man there. He knows what to do. Be very careful with him. He's a very learned and experienced person. If he decides to settle the matter for us, allow him, okay!'

'Yes sir!' Constable Akpan gave another swift salute.

'Sir, am I going alone?'

'There's no fear. Chief Akpovire can handle the situation, okay!'

'Yes sir,' another smart salute followed and Constable Akpan departed.

Ona had gone to the police station to seek the arrest of Omogevwe for breaking the head of his eldest son, Tobore, over a land dispute at their farmland. That day, Tobore and his two brothers had gone to the farmland to clear a new farm for their father. It was the beginning of the planting season. On getting to the farm, they observed that Omogevwe with a handful of labourers had cleared into their own portion of the land. Tobore drew his attention to the demarcating lines.

'What? you brat! Showing me the boundary of the farmland I have been tilling even before you were born? You children of nowadays have no respect; no manners!'

But Tobore was sure of the boundary. He was there seven years ago when his parents tilled the farm. He was just twelve then. He took food along with his mother to the men who cleared it. He also participated in the farming during the period and had been setting traps in it for rodents since then.

'This isn't a matter of respect! We're talking of facts, here. That's where the line passes,' Tobore pointing to his left side with much audacity.

This further infuriated Omogevwe. He was suddenly filled with scorn and haughty indignation. He considered Tobore too young to talk to him with such audacious defiance. He gazed at Tobore with stern warning in his eyes, as he was too angry to speak. But Tobore was too young to appreciate the flame of anger burning in the eyes of an irate man, so he was not intimidated. He was prepared to defy Omogevwe. He looked back into Omogevwe's eyes, '*What can you do?* he seemed to say. Omogevwe could not stand his affront any more. He drew very close. He was about to do something nasty.

'No,' he shook his head in restraint, 'you're too young! Let your father come and repeat exactly what you have said and you people shall get what you are asking for' said he.

The challenge to his father annoyed Tobore very much.

'What can you do?' retorted Tobore.

Omogevwe considered *this brat* for sometime as his anger rose to its limit. He was now panting nervously with fury.

Tobore braced himself for the challenge while his two younger brothers were waiting in support. Omogevwe's hired labourers who had been watching the situation from their working positions rushed forward as tension heightened. Omogevwe quickly looked around. His eyes flashed to one big stick nearby. At once, he grabbed at it and flung it on Tobore's head with all the strength of his anger. Least prepared for this, Tobore shouted in great pain and held his head. He felt the strike like a thunder. Omogevwe then rushed after the other two with the big stick in his hand. In a quick reflex, they took to their heels. Omogevwe pursued them. This quickened the pace of the workmen. They eventually got hold of Omogevwe with his stick and when they had returned with Omogevwe who was still spoiling for a fight, they were shocked to see the havoc he had caused. Tobore was lying on the ground, with his hand on his head, dripping with blood. On a particular spot in his head, blood was gushing out like the source of a river. Tobore's face was already covered with his blood when they got back to the scene of the incident. The blood was running down his body. Tobore was weeping ceaselessly as he kept wiping the stream of blood off his face with his fingers. But it was useless; the blood was flowing freely and endlessly.

When they saw the gory sight, they were overwhelmed with apprehension of a possible death in their hands and were all in panic. The horrific situation swallowed all the agitating hostility at once. Tobore's two brothers who were being pursued had returned. They were all darting about for a particular leaf whose sap could stop the haemorrhage. Tobore's two brothers were wailing now. Omogevwe was running mad for the leaf. A lump seized him in the throat. He tried hard not to shout in his terrifying agony. He could not imagine being a murderer. As he ran about, he found it extremely difficult to breathe. His entire body was vibrating with anxiety and his heart was pounding hard in his chest. The anxiety in him seemed like a bomb that was about to explode and shatter him to pieces, as he was groping about for the leaf. One of them ran down eventually with a bunch of the leaf. They all ran in that direction and brought more. They sprinkled little water on the leaves and began to crush them with their anxious hands for the sap, which they squeezed into the gushing spot. They squeezed more and more until the sap stopped the flow of Tobore's blood significantly. They splashed some water on him, as he appeared very weary and weak, in their effort to keep him alive, after they had washed his face and head slightly to remove the bloodstain. That done, they lifted him on their shoulders and were home bound.

They took Tobore to the dispensary before reporting the incident in Ona's compound. Tobore's parents and other people in their immediate neighbourhood who heard the bad news ran to the dispensary. When Ona saw the critical condition of his son, a combination of fear and exasperation shook him violently. The dried blood on Tobore's shirt and body was enough elaboration. He immediately went after Omogevwe in a flame of wild passion. But Omogevwe had sneaked away immediately they brought Tobore to the dispensary. He knew Tobore's condition could provoke uncontrollable anger in a dove. He went home to inform his people of what had happened. His wife and children were bewildered, anxious and upset. They prayed that nothing untoward happened toTobore. Omogevwe's elder brother told him to stay away while they, the family, tried to placate Ona and his people, as anger most times knew no caution. So when Ona with his kinsmen poured into Omogevwe's compound, they were disappointed at not meeting him at home. As he could not find Omogevwe, Ona went straight home, dressed up and set out to Ugbevwe where the police station in the area was. Before he left, he charged his wife to see to Tobore's treatment. Some of his people were suspicious and alarmed of his movement. They pleaded with him not to do anything rash but to see to his son's recovery first. But Ona did not listen to their entreaty. Some other persons, who suspected that he might be going to the police, persuaded him to see Chief Akpovire first. But Ona had already made up his mind. He headed straight to the police station at Ugbevwe. When Omogevwe and his family suspected that Ona might have gone to the police, they became worried. They thought it was something that should have been handled by the elders at Chief Akpovire's edifice since the elders-in-Council was still two market days ahead.

****

Police were highly dreaded by the people of Akpobaro. They saw the police as the force of government and law. So bringing the police to arrest somebody at Akpobaro was seen as bringing the entire government of the state to fight the person in the community. 'Who can fight government?' was always the question they asked whenever they heard of police arrest. And police arrest was considered the worst humiliation one could give to one's folk. Every man in Akpobaro would prefer to suffer any other indignity instead. It was an unbleachable stigma forever. The victim would ever be reminded of his open shame before the entire community, by anybody he had the misfortune of quarrelling with. This made the incidence of police arrest rare in Akpobaro. The few cases which the police had handled in the community were highly abused by them. They would put the suspect in handcuffs irrespective of the allegation and parade him through the village with kicking, pushing and whipping while the people watched with pity helplessly.

In one of such police arrests and brutalities something tragic occurred, the death of a prominent man in the village. The previous night, Ugbomah had a quarrel with Enughe over their children who fought during the day while they were away in the farm. When Enughe learnt of the fight in the evening, he started raining abuses on the family of Ugbomah. They were immediate neighbours, so Ugbomah and his family were hearing all that Enughe was saying. After a while, Ugbomah realised that Enughe's raving and cursing which he couched in proverbs were directed at him and his children. Enughe was always jealous of the growing prosperity of Ugbomah who suffered terribly when they were young. Ugbomah's father suffered a sudden fatal illness and died when Ugbomah was a little child. His mother went berserk in agony for weeks. Nobody could pacify her. A month later, she became mad and started roaming about in lamentation. One day, she walked into a bush fire and suffered severe burn. She died some days after. Ugbomah was her only child.

The unfortunate circumstance forced Ugbomah to stay with his aged grandmother. At this time, his grandmother was already stricken with age. She had been living on the support of her daughter, Ugbomah's mother, before misfortune wreaked its havoc, so she was most unsuitable to look after the poor little boy. But fate has a way of making such unthinkable and helpless circumstance bearable. At eight, Ugbomah had started to fend for his grandmother and himself with the help of a kind neighbour. Early in the morning, he would follow to the farm a kind woman in his neighbourhood who was always seeing to the needs of Ugbomah and his grandmother as possible as she could and had taken up the responsibility of fostering Ugbomah. She would organise men for the clearing of Ugbomah's grandmother's farmland and do the planting for them.

At that age, Ugbomah was already being taught how to plant cassava, cocoyam and yam in their moulds and he was learning very fast. He could weed and tend yam tendrils under the tutelage of his surrogate mother, Umi. At harvest, he would follow Umi to the farm. She taught him how to uproot the cassava, yam and cocoyam. Initially, it was really difficult. Ugbomah would cut the tubers in several places as he tried to uproot them. Some other times, he would not bring out all of them from the soil. Umi would be furious with him. But she would quickly realise that he was only a child. Oftentimes, she would begin to sob after charging at him, as she realised that his mates were enjoying the comfortable care of their parents and knew nothing about Ugbomah's world. One day, she almost cried herself out in one of such instances. She burst into tears and wailed profusely.

'Oh death, see your handiwork, see your handiwork,' she shook her head in agony instinctively repeatedly, as tears were flowing freely from her eyes. 'Death! Why do you do this to this poor innocent little boy? Why? Why...?' she began to wail profusely. She tried to suppress her emotion when she realised that the poor boy was gazing at her with a confused and worried look as he could not comprehend why she was just crying like a baby, and was at a loss what to do. Much as she tried, her tears were flowing unhindered; there was no restraining. She burst out again, 'O death, why? Why? I say why? Don't you have pity?' She broke down completely in tears and her tears kept flowing as she could not help herself.

But there was a silver lining in Ugbomah's dark cloud. When he was eighteen, he was already living like a man. He had several large farms which he tilled himself and his experience of life was exceedingly great. He was very matured and ahead of his peers in every respect. At twenty-two when his age mates were still living under their parents, he was already a man with a wife and two children. Parents readily pointed him out to their children for inspiration.

He eventually turned out to be one of the most prosperous men in the entire Omaurhie community. A community which believed that the defence of a man lay in the number of people around him would always encourage a lone star like Ugbomah to marry several wives and he did. As a result, his house was not lacking in numerous children. So when Ugbomah realised that he was the object of Enughe's vociferation, he became more attentive, not because of the anger such outburst could provoke in him, but as Akpobaro people often say, 'The words of your enemy, though bitter, can make you spot your bad side.'

Enughe always looked for the slightest opportunity to pick quarrel with him. He had never hidden his hatred for Ugbomah. In such acrimonious moments, he always loved to remind Ugbomah of all his bitter past, to plague his joy and crush his sense of accomplishment, as Enughe could not bring himself to the reality of that 'hopeless thing' of yesterday whose life had become the envy of the people.

That night, Ugbomah was able to deduce from the utterances of Enughe that there had been a fight between his children and Enughe's while they were away. He called one of his children who was always in the forefront of the feud. Oke narrated what transpired during the day. There was a fight between three of his children and Enughe's while they, the parents, were away. From her narration, the children of Enughe as always were on the offensive.

'But did I not tell you people to avoid those children, heh Oke?' Ugbomah charged at his daughter.

'They came to us,' answered Oke guiltily.

'And you fought after I had warned you!'

He quickly took his cane and whipped Oke thrice before she could run away, crying. Oke's mother ran down from their kitchen house on the other side of the compound when she heard her daughter's cry.

'What happened again?' she demanded from her daughter who narrated all that happened to her mother. Her mother, Titi, saw that her daughter and the other two of her half-sisters only fought back to defend themselves against the aggression of Enughe's children. She became angry with her husband who always beat his children each time they fought with Enughe's. She walked to her husband, pretending to be unaware of what actually happened.

'What did she do?'

'Have you not been hearing the raving of Enughe since?'

'Yes, I have been hearing him. Is it because of Enughe's children you beat Oke without finding out what happened?'

'Well, I was not interested in who were wrong or right. I beat her because she disobeyed me.'

'You don't know what you're doing, Papa Oke. You're only making your children timid and stupid, children who can never assert themselves among their peers. Enughe protects his own and we kill our own for them. Tell me why Enughe's children will not always want to fight them? It is not fair! And I will never support you in this!' Titi walked away angrily. Immediately, she came into the open on her way to her kitchen, she exploded.

'Only a foolish man will want to kill himself over little children's disagreement. When people talk of being a man, some foolish men think it is by having that *okra* between their thighs. It is behaviour! You cannot be a man when you are a child at heart!'

The Enughes heard Titi as she intentionally spoke very loud while facing their side for them to hear. Curiously, Enughe with his family had been looking out to see whether the bait of words he threw out would receive any catch. This, Ugbomah knew and had been trying to avoid playing into his hands hence he had been warning his family not to respond to their provocations. And the Enughes knew that Titi's insinuation was directed at Enughe, the head of their family.

Before Titi could finish her last word, Enughe, his two wives and all his children rushed out to her as they had been waiting for this moment.

'Are you insulting my husband eh?' Enughe's older wife shouted angrily when they came near, spoiling for a fight.

'You're the one labelling your husband. I never mentioned name!'

'To whom then were you referring? You cursed woman!' Enughe shouted in great anger.

'You're the one that is cursed, not I!'

'You're talking to my husband like that, eh?' The two wives of Enughe shouted together as they rushed at Titi. Titi replied with a resounding slap on the face of the older wife of Enughe and all the other members of Enughe's family joined in attacking Titi, including Enughe himself. Ugbomah dashed down at once. His other two wives followed, then his children. There was no asking of questions. The fight began. Ugbomah had three wives and more children. When he ran out to see the commotion, he was completely taken aback when he saw the entire Enughes fighting just one of his own. It was so

67

compelling that he did not really know when he struck Enughe a heavy blow and drew his attention for a one-to-one fight. The fight took a different shape. The entry of Ugbomah's household re-ordered it into one-to-one, as each of the Ugbomahs squared up to one of the Enughes' according to age. While the remaining ones watched for possible back-up. The Ugbomahs saw the fight as a very big challenge. They reasoned that for the Enughes to have the temerity to attack them in their own home was the most intrepid assault. This spirit emboldened them and they fought with all zeal and spirit – a fight to prove to the Enughes that their being on the defensive all along was not an act of cowardice – they were gaining the upper hand. They crushed the Enughes to their shame and disbelief before neighbours in the area came to their rescue.

The fight between Ugbomah and Enughe, the two heads of the disputing families, was the most dramatic. Ugbomah was greatly incensed when he saw the entire Enughes were fighting Titi as he rushed down, and with all the rage against his adversary's previous aggressions, he was mad. He fought like a wounded lion. It did not take him much time before he threw Enughe down and struck him many severe blows. He so overpowered Enughe that it did not look like a fight of equals. And when the people ran down to see what was happening, though, they were swift in separating them, they were quite happy over the outcome. The entire neighbourhood was aware of Enughe's aggressiveness towards Ugbomah and his family. While they calmed both sides down, they were gloating over the defeat of the Enughes.

No noisy braggart like Enughe would want to accept defeat. When he had been rescued from the crushing blows of Ugbomah, he became more aggressive. He was raving and cursing and spoiling for more fight, boasting that he was going to crush Ugbomah. He lied that some Ugbomah's children held his hands when the fight started. Though, he would not accept it, it was a way of alluding to the fact that Ugbomah defeated him in the fight. But the people knew that Enughe's affectation for more fight was to cover up his shame. At the end, they led him and his family to their own house and eventually calmed them down.

That night on his bed, Enughe went through the whole episode in his mind. He could not sleep. The shame and humiliation of the fight came to his full consciousness and he was very disturbed. He could feel the humiliation in his spine as he reflected on the fight again and he became very bitter. He could

68

feel sharply now the smouldering derision of the people who came to separate them from fighting and he thought it was just the beginning.

'It'll soon become the joke in the village,' he told himself.

His pride was further wounded when his mind flashed back to that *poor little devil* with heavy load from the farm while he and other children were at liberty of playing games in the afternoon, only to run home for their meals that had been waiting. He shook his head bitterly and became more spiteful. He thought of what to do. After a while, he smiled gleefully. He rolled over in his bed and went to where he kept his money. He wanted to be sure. He counted them carefully. They were correct. He kept them under his pillow anxiously waiting for dawn.

At second cockcrow he started. He took his bath and wore one of his outing clothes. Took his money and quietly locked his door. He tapped the door of his senior wife who opened her door immediately she recognised his voice.

'I'm leaving. Take care of the home. I shall be back in few hours.'

'Where are you going?' his senior wife said with apprehension when she noticed his outfit. She knew he was on a distant journey for something very important and urgent. She could smell it.

'Don't mind that,' Enughe returned as he was going away, not wanting to be disturbed on his avowal mission. He wanted to be out of the village before Akpobaro people rose from sleep and he was on time. His senior wife followed him with her eyes in his vague figure in the gray light of dawn until he disappeared. She was worried. She knew her husband's journey in such an unholy hour was not unconnected with the previous night incident. She just hoped Enughe would not do anything too rash.

Enughe was at the police station at Ugbevwe to complain. He told the police officer on duty that he and his family were maliciously attacked with clubs and cutlasses in their home by a family next to them, who were bent on doing them harm. He added that the same family had made several attempts at his life before.

'I had tried to be calm, believing that one day they would come to their senses. But the one of last night was too much for me to bear. At least, one of my family members would have been killed, if not for the kind people around that came in, immediately.'

The police officer looked at him after he had recorded his statement.

'Were any of you injured?'

Enughe wanted to nod his head in the affirmative but he quickly realised that he was before *the law.*

'No sir.'

The police officer knew that Enughe was not telling the truth.

'How could you and your family be attacked with dangerous weapons and none of you was injured?' the police officer said suspiciously.

Enughe was silent.

The police officer wrote on the paper again.

'Well, it's a matter for investigation,' he said.

When he had finished his writing, he called two police constables in the open registry. They came immediately and gave him a smart salute.

'Follow this man to Akpobaro and get one Ugbomah. Do that very quickly.'

'All correct, sir.' they saluted again before departing with Enughe.

Policemen at the lower level always abused their authority in their out-of-station assignments. They loved to display unlimited power as they understood the psyche of the rural folk. In such assignments, they always showed that they were the prosecutor, the judge and the executioner and the first person that came to them was their client in the matter. With this impression, any malicious person who wanted to humiliate and shame his foe would invite the police. As far as the people were concerned, this was the essence of police arrest. But the intrigue must be well perfected to trap the target at home. Otherwise 'the police's client' would have wasted his money.

'You mean the man came with a machete to attack you in your house?' one of the two constables asked Enughe on their way to Akpobaro.

'Yes, I cannot lie to you.'

'That man must be very wicked. We shall teach him a very bitter lesson,' the other police constable added.

'How much are you giving us? Remember, the way we will handle him ultimately depends on what you can offer,' the first one said.

'Officers, don't worry about that,' replied Enughe and to prove that he meant business, he dipped his hands into his bag and brought out two pounds. The two policemen looked at each other in pleasant surprise. In all their outside engagements, they had never received this much, which was higher than their monthly salary. They smiled to each other.

'That's good,' one of them said to Enughe. 'Don't worry, that man shall pay dearly for what he did,' added the senior police constable.

70

Enughe was happy that the two policemen were fully on his side. He was prepared to spend anything to make Ugbomah regret the day he touched *the tail of a tiger.*

It was still morning when they arrived at Akpobaro. The people were just preparing to go to farm. Enughe kept a distance ahead, from the two policemen so that they might not be linked to him, fearing that someone might decide to spoil their plan by alerting his perceived target, Ugbomah, for an escape. The two policemen moved into Ugbomah's compound from both ends and met him in his sitting room. He suddenly froze with fear where he sat. All his strength and courage left him at once.

'We're for you,' one of the two policemen said sternly. Ugbomah stared at Enughe who swelled with pride and pomposity, savouring the effect the arrest had produced in Ugbomah, as he seemed to be saying, 'Yes, that serves you right!' in his victorious eyes which oscillated between ecstasy and cruelty. Ugbomah's wives and children came to Ugbomah's sitting room one by one like panic-stricken chicks in search of their lost mother. They were all there in their cold helpless anxiety, fearing what would happen to their father and husband, though maintaining their distance from the menacing presence of *the law.*

The people's curiosity was aroused when they saw the two policemen in the village. They became anxious. From distance, they trailed the two policemen until they entered Ugbomah's compound and the people stood by, fearing for Ugbomah. They suspected Enughe had brought the police for what transpired the previous night. As they gathered in front of Ugbomah's compound, they murmured to one another in great anxiety.

'Was it over the quarrel of yesterday?' a woman who just came whispered.

'What else!' another one answered reluctantly.

'Enughe is wicked,' the first woman said soberly.

'Is it today you know?' the second woman returned in the same subdued manner. The others around merely stared at the inquirer. They were all too anxious to talk aloud.

At once, the crowd that gathered in front of Ugbomah's compound rushed forward when they heard a sudden screaming inside the house. It was Ugbomah's voice. The two policemen had started beating him with their batons. They were hitting him all over: on his head, back, sides, everywhere while they were also kicking and pushing him outside. At the centre of his compound, they tore his trousers and shirt before the eyes of every body

around. Ugbomah was almost naked to his pants. His head had started
dripping blood. His wives and children were wailing uncontrollably as they
watched helplessly the gory sight. Other sympathisers, particularly the woman
were screaming with horror as they closed their eyes or ears instinctively while
they watched. But the two policemen were not done yet. They were
determined to humiliate Ugbomah to the extent of hating himself. His face
was already covered with bruises. One of the two policemen saw some thick
hard wires fastened together like a rope by the side of some plantain trees in
the compound. He picked the wire-rope and began to whip Ugbomah with it.
It inflicted wounds on his body and Ugbomah began to wreathe on the
ground in great pain. His screaming was breaking every heart that heard him
and was almost tearing down heavens; it was the cry of a man watching his
own dying moment. Everybody at the scene was in excruciating pain of
anguish. Most of the women and children could no longer stand the sight.
They turned their eyes away in tears.

Later, the two policemen gave Ugbomah a marching order in handcuffs
for their onward journey to Ugbevwe. The entire village folk were annoyed to
see this unpleasant incident happening to one of their most respected men.
They felt Ugbamah's pain in their own hearts. The people realised that
Ugbomah was stronger than they thought, as he was able to survive the killing
maltreatment of the two policemen. As the two policemen led their captive
away in handcuffs after he had been thoroughly subdued and humiliated, it
brought back the painful memory of the slave trade when their kinsmen and
women were led away in chains before their eyes and sold away as slaves after
they had been thoroughly beaten.

Midway into their journey to Ugbevwe, Ugbomah told his captors that he
would like to pass waste matter. The two policemen looked at each other and
allowed him. At this time, they had removed the handcuffs from his hands, as
they wanted him to move faster with them, because the journey on foot from
Akpobaro to Ugbevwe was a long one, believing that they had beaten him to
the point that he would be too afraid or weak to run away. This feeling not
withstanding, they made Ugbomah to walk between them so that he could not
easily escaped if he dared. As Ugbomah entered the bush, his captors took him
for granted that he would not do anything unexpected because of the brutal
treatment he had received. Immediately he entered the bush, Ugbomah began
to weep silently. The degrading and humiliating treatment he had received in
the hands of the two policemen overwhelmed him afresh and he felt so

72

worthless. When he had walked out of the sight of the two policemen, he quickly pulled out his torn trousers and threw them round a branch of tree. Meanwhile, the two policemen and Enughe were waiting by the road. Enughe wanted Ugbomah to be thoroughly humiliated. But he felt now that the two policemen had over done it. Guilt and compunction began to well up inside him. He knew he was going to be the common hate back home. Enughe and the two policemen became uncomfortable when Ugbomah did not return from the bush after a while.

'We wouldn't have allowed him go alone,' one of the two policemen said anxiously. In their agitation, they thrust into the bush, and in a few metres from the road, they saw a figure hanging in a tree. They rushed forward and untied the poor figure. But it was useless. Ugbomah dropped down lifeless. The three men were perplexed and speechless, not knowing what to do. At once, Enughe broke down in tears, having stared at the corpse for sometime.

When the news came to Akpobaro, the whole village was thrown into wailing and mourning. The whole Akpobaro was pouring into Ugbomah's compound. The compound was sorrow-filled. The youths of Akpobaro were shocked to hear the death of Ugbomah in the hands of the police. They went wild in great anger and were running towards Enughe's compound - there was commotion and hysteria - and they brought down Enughe's house for bringing such a calamity to their community and in few minutes the house was put to ruin.

Later, the youths went to bring down the corpse. Ugbomah would be buried in a near-by bush immediately, without any ceremony, as their tradition frowned against suicide in the society. It was sad indeed that a man of his social standing should die the way he did. When his corpse was arriving, the entire village was again thrown into another wild flame of passion. The people became riotous to catch a glimpse of it as they wailed uncontrollable. Through out that week Akpobaro was like a cemetery. People remained in doors after farm. The social life of the village came to zero. It took about two weeks before life began to pick up again.

The police were not happy with the way their men handled the unfortunate affair. They felt there was need to mend fences with Akpobaro community. Chief Akpovire was the councillor of the area, then. And it was agreed that no policeman should make any arrest in Akpobaro community again without passing through their leaders. And since that arrangement,

Chief Akpovire had been doing the mending in matters involving the police in Akpobaro.

Omogevwe with two elders of his family went to see Chief Akpovire over the impending arrest, and to await his arrest at Chief Akpovire's. Chief Akpovire expressed surprise over Ona's action.

'But he should have come here, first,' said he.

While they were still waiting, they heard some excitement outside. They thought it was Ona and the police. But they were not. It was one of the immigrants from the riverine area who had just returned from his native place. He had brought two large sacks of dried fish to Chief Akpovire. Edema had gone to his birthplace to participate in their annual fish harvest. When Chief Akpovire, Omogevwe and his relatives looked through the windows, they saw the children dancing round the two sacks at the veranda. Just then, two children of Chief Akpovire ran into the house in great competition, 'Papa, Itsekiri man brought fish for you,' they both announced almost at the same time.

'Plenty, plenty fish!' one of them added in great excitement.

Chief Akpovire and the others in the house came out to see.

'You brought them for me to buy?' said Chief Akpovire.

'No, I brought six sacks from my place and I decided to bring two for you, Councillor,' Edema smiled.

'Six sacks and two for me!' Chief Akpovire screamed in disbelief. 'Thank you so much, Edema, for your generosity. But how did you come about these plenty fish?'

Edema smiled over Chief Akpovire's ignorance.

'I went to my place. You know, in my place fishing is our farm and it's harvest time.'

'And you can have so many as these?'

'Yes, so many. My place is surrounded by water and there are plenty, plenty fish during the raining season,' Edema smiled with unassuming pride.

'Ah, in the riverine area, fish is their blessing. Do you consider what we have here as fish? Go to the riverine area and see! You won't believe it,' one of the two elders of Omogevwe said.

'Eh-eh, is that so!' said Chief Akpovire, still wondering in surprise. 'There was one time when we were tracing one of my maternal cousins who sojourned to that area. For years we were not hearing from him. So we decided to look for him. And we eventually traced him to one riverine village.

When we got there, we saw fish, plenty, plenty fish in the village! We ate fish and became sick and tired of it. We couldn't take as many as we desired because there were no sacks when we were returning. We never envisaged it. Per adventure I go again, hm!'

And everybody burst into laughter.

When Edema had left with his two children who brought the sacks, Chief Akpovire called one of his children to take one sack into one of his rooms and turned to his visitors, 'Our people say if one comes across good fortune, his companion does, also. So the other sack is for the rest of your.'

'*Shuo!* the two elders looked at each other, then Chief Akpovire in disbelief. 'No, Councillor, we're not companions in this case. We're here to burden and inconvenience you with our own trouble,' one of them said.

'But does that deny the fact that you were with me when Edema presented his gift?' said Chief Akpovire.

'No, but ....'

'That answers the question, there's no *but* in it.'

'But in good conscience we cannot share equally with you.'

'I'm not sharing equally with you because you're three. Let's not argue over this any more,' Chief Akpovire ended matter-of-factly.

The two elders with Omogevwe knew Chief Akpovire did not want the argument stressed further, and they concurred. So, they accepted the offer which they felt they never deserved in the first instance and thanked Chief Akpovire for his over generosity.

****

Later, Ona arrived with Constable Akpan. He was unhappy to see Omogevwe and his two elder relatives already there, because he knew that, at the end of the day, Chief Akpovire would prevail and broker settlement and his purpose would be defeated.

When the policeman and Ona were seated with the rest who had been awaiting their arrival, Chief Akpovire put some palm wine and kola-nuts on the centre table for the entire house. But every other person knew that the presentation was meant specifically for the policeman – the guest in their midst – that they were only enjoying the drink and the kola-nuts for his sake. When they had eaten the kola-nut and washed it down their throats with the wine, Constable Akpan thanked Chief Akpovire for his generous reception and explained his mission and how his police boss instructed him to reach the ex-councillor for the matter.

'Who sent you to me? Is it Alfred or Alex?' asked Chief Akpovire with great interest, a way of showing to the constable that he knew everybody there.

'Alex,' answered Constable Akpan.

Chief Akpovire nodded his head in great delight, and the rest of them in the house except Ona nodded their heads too, expressing delight of amicable settlement at the end.

'Thank you for your coming. The accused person is here already,' Chief Akpovire pointed at Omogevwe who suddenly became nervous a bit. 'But the matter is easy. We shall settle it here. Your boss, Alex, understands how we handle matters here. Once, we can settle it, we do. If not, you people will take over, and I have handled many cases here – it's an understanding we reached with your station sometime ago. You're new, ask your boss, he'll tell you,' explained Chief Akpovire.

'I'm aware sir,' answered Constable Akpan.

'Oh, that's good,' replied Chief Akpovire. He immediately sent for *Ugo* and four other notable *Ilorogun*. When they had come, Chief Akpovire called on Ona to present his case. Ona said he knew very little of the matter, so he called Tobore and his other two sons who went to the farm where the incident occurred, to present the case. Tobore who had managed to come after his treated stated his case. Omogevwe was asked to confirm or refute Tobore's statement. He accused Tobore of not telling the truth in three instances and stated his own case in those areas. Then, Tobore's two brothers and Omogevwe's hired labourers to the farm were asked to testify. Though, their testimonies were not exactly the same, the elders and chiefs who were handling the matter knew where the truth lay from all they had said. After they had asked both sides some questions to clarify some grey areas, they went aside to further examine the facts and cross-examine them again among themselves before reaching judgement. They included the policeman and one elder from each side in the process of reaching decision. While they were out of earshot, they considered the weaknesses and the strengths of both sides, to the conviction of all those involved in reaching the judgement. Once they had agreed on a judgement, that judgement became final and binding. The role of the representative of each side to the matter in reaching judgement was to see that there was thorough fairness in the process of reaching judgment. That nothing was overlooked in the process, and also for the representative of the guilty party to plead for mitigation against harsh judgement. As they went back to the house, one could sometimes guess the judgement from the countenances of both representatives.

When they were all back to their seats, everybody became calm and anxious to hear the judgement. The *Ugo* cleared his throat, 'Well, we have considered the two sides of the matter. This is what we arrived at:

'Omogevwe, we found you guilty of wrong doing: That you stooped so low to fight with this boy,' pointing to Tobore,' a peer of your own son, is shameful. The proper thing to do was to ignore him and bring the matter up before his father in the first instance. And if Ona insisted on what his son has said, you know where to go the elders-in-Council who know the people that can identify and testify to the boundaries. I mean the other people that share boundaries with both of you in the disputed land and probably some other persons who should know. But you resorted to disgraceful act. For acting wrongly, you shall buy a drink and kola-nuts for the house to settle the matter. You shall also pay a fine of two pounds and five shillings, part of which shall settle the cost of bringing in the police. Thirdly, you shall bear the full cost of the treatment of Tobore.

'As for Tobore with his two brothers, we observed that his impudence provoked Omogevwe to act the way he did. Younger ones must respect their older ones. That is the propriety in every society. Next time he is found wanting in good behaviour, he shall be fined and punished. He is hereby warned!

'As for the land in dispute, we shall send people to go and identify the true boundaries. I thank you all,' ended the *Ugo*.

And everyone in the house nodded their heads with satisfaction for the sound judgement of the case.

After the pronouncement, the older of the two Omogevwe's siblings thanked the elders for their judgement but pleaded for the reduction of the fine. Omogevwe and all those in sympathy with him, apart from his two elders, knelt down and pleaded along. After much pleading, the *Ugo* reduced the fine to one pound five shillings. In reality, the *Ugo* knew that there would be plea on the part of the guilty party, so at first he announced a fine higher than the one agreed upon by those who handled the case. So, even when he was moved by emotion, he would not sway from the collective judgement. But there were times when the spokesman might be allowed to use his discretion in such circumstances, by the use of eye contact among those that participated in reaching a judgement.

After the judgement, Omogevwe and his people presented the drink, kola-nuts and money on the centre table. The drink and the kola-nuts were taken and everybody shared in them. This indicated that the dispute had been resolved.The people had a belief among themselves that once the two sides in a dispute had agreed to drink together after settlement, the capacity to continue the dispute would no longer exist. That was why they always drank together after the settlement of a dispute.

CHAPTER SEVEN

The Independence of the country from British colonial rule eventually came and the entire country was thrown into wild celebration. Jubilation was everywhere. The remotest part of the country was not left out in the celebration. The nationalists had long been singing of a land of abundance and splendour for everybody, in an atmosphere of freedom and this had encouraged the people to fight with zeal behind their nationalist leaders for independence, as they dreamt of the day and looked forward to it, day by day.

On the eve of Independence, Chief Akpovire sat together with some chiefs and friends in his house. They were drinking and talking merrily about the Independence.

'That we're no longer under the whites is enough to celebrate. It has been a great injury to our pride and dignity to be ruled by foreigners in our own land,' said Mudiaga.

'What is more insulting is that we have been one huge business venture whose great profit travelled into the purse of Britain, as they kept churning us for more. But now, all that is going to stop. We shall now use our resources and energies for ourselves. And you'll see how our country will change very soon,' Chief Akpovire said in ecstasy.

'Soon, the government will bring to all the nooks and crannies of the country good road network and electricity,' the headmaster of his school added.

'I hear that we shall not be using cutlass and hoe. Government will bring motor-machines for planting, weeding and harvesting our farms. Even the machine for making garri will be provided,' Karie said excitedly.

'Then, what shall we be doing?' said Agbamu.

'Just to see the machines do the work,' Karie replied.

'Ha-ha-ha,' Agbamu and others in the house laughed excitedly.

'Then, Jehovah's Kingdom, which the *Jehovah church* talks about, is here! Can it be real?' Agbamu asked in disbelief.

'They say it is so in the white man's land. It's just that the whites wouldn't want us to enjoy such things here, ask Councillor,' pursued Karie, and they all turned to Chief Akpovire whom they all thought knew everything of the world.

'Well, it is possible. I have heard it too that in the white man's land, that's how farming is done. So, now that Independence has come, why not?' Chief Akpovire answered.

They all began to dance. In their excitement, they brought out money individually and called for more drink. That evening they drank and talked so much about the Independence for a long time into the far night before they went separately to their individual homes.

On the day of Independence, there was celebration throughout the entire country; it never wanted to end. From the beginning of the day, the men had gathered in circles, drinking and shouting in celebration, congratulating each other with, 'Happy Independence!' While the women were busy cooking rice and frying chicken, as the children clustered around them, sniffing the aroma of this very special and privileged delicacy. 'Happy Independence!' was the greeting everywhere, both old and young, even little children were all saying it to one another in the spirit of congratulation.

The excitement was overwhelming in Akpobaro. When it was about noon, everybody in the village went to the only government presence besides the dispensary – the 'Local Authority Primary School'* as it was known through out the region, to be entertained with different cultural dances. Everybody came out in his Independence clothes which was the cloth for the celebration across the country. In the evening, there was a football match between the youths of Akpobaro and Okuemu. It was very exciting. At the end of the match which climaxed the activities for the celebration in Akpobaro, everyone retired to the remaining feast of rice and chicken which they started eating earlier in the day.

Before the Great Day, elaborate preparations had been made across the country to mark the historic event, starting from the 'Divisions' to the 'Provinces,' and the grandest one was at the country's capital. Chief Akpovire being one of the prominent leaders in his 'Division' was specially invited by the Council for the celebration. He was obviously enthusiastic. Not only because he participated in the series of political campaigns that culminated in the country's Independence, he did travel with prominent politicians across the country in the campaigns and rallies. Besides being a delegate to the first summit of Pan Africanism ever organised on the continent of Africa in Accra,

---

*Used to be Native Authority, now Local Authority as "native" had perjorative, racist connotation.

80

Ghana, he had also proved himself a successful grassroots political champion. Though, he was no longer in active politics, he felt highly elated to see to what he fully contributed coming through in the end.

The celebration was organised in the field of the public pavilion at Ugbevwe, the headquarters of his divisional Council. Many cultural dance bands had been invited. The dressing all through was the special independence cloth which generously displayed the map of the country with the robust portraits of the first indigenous Governor-General and the First Prime Minister who would kick-start the 'new country'. The cloth was sold throughout the country and almost everybody bought it including the poorest. It was the true manifest way of identifying with this 'new country', their hope of a good life.

On full display at the public pavilion was the symbol of the Independence, the new flag, green-white-green in colours and design. It had been replicated in a small size in large quantity with a handle to be displayed and waved by individuals. At the entrance to the large field of the public pavilion, the hawkers were making quick and easy sale of a booklet which contained the new national anthem, coat of arms, brief geography and history of the country, and the outlines of the biographies of the new 'Governor – General' and the Prime Minister. People that came for the celebration were all rushing to collect a copy. The numerous illiterates among them were also buying. They looked at the smiling faces of the two *messiahs* and smiled back at them – a perfect mutual smile of a great future awaiting them. They also turned to the coat of arms and the map showing the country's landscape and regions. They could not make much out of them but they loved them for their beauties. At any rate, it was serving its purpose – just to be prided.

The carnival procession at the public pavilion was huge and colourful. People in their thousands were streaming in and out for no specific purposes. Though, there were makeshift booths and benches for representatives of every invited community in the Council area, but the massive turn-out rendered such arrangement useless. It was a great carnival. People streamed about for sight-seeing while they also stopped to entertain themselves, as street hawkers brought in all manner of fast foods and drinks.

Later in the day, the occasion became organised. Several prominent persons in the Council area made important speeches on the Independence and paid glowing tributes to the famous nationalists who fought assiduously for it. There was always a huge applause for each name mentioned. The people were further reminded that the Independence would usher in great prosperity which would transform the life of every citizen, every community and the entire country.

'Above all, Independence sets you free from any forms of subjugation, deprivation and oppression which were the hallmarks of colonialism,' stated the chairman of the Council. 'It releases your creative energies for great accomplishment,' he added.

To set the stage for the celebration, those of them at the *high table* poured themselves drinks and toasted to the success and greatness of the *new country*. As glasses clinked each other, there was a huge shout of joy and every other person bought a drink and congratulated one another in celebration.

Other activities that spiced up the day were match-past and cultural dances, by contingents of all the districts in the Council area. The schools in the Council area were not left out in the march-past and cultural dances. Apart from their banners of identification which were held out in front, during the march-past, all participants in each contingent marched pointedly with their individuals' small independence flags which were distributed to schools freely for this purpose. The marching of school pupils was singularly unique. The pupils bursthilariously into joyous songs as they marched past the Council's chairman. The overflowing joy in their faces was most palpable as the overwhelming excitement of the Independence flowed into the march-past. And the whole marching exercise became one huge gaiety. Every one could feel the depth of the celebration of the Independence. After the pupils, came the women from each district. The women were more dramatic. Their march-past was turned into dancing. They danced past, singing and jubilating. By the time the actual dances were to feature, the atmosphere had been overcharged. Everybody entered into the field and beat all protocols; it was a celebration galore. They danced and danced and danced through out the day.

A week to the Independence Day, there had been a flurry of activities at the country's capital to mark the Independence. Seminars, conferences and cultural fiestas were held in a series. The seminars and conferences were organised for the newly elected political leaders who would assumed their offices following the Independence elections. The 'parliamentary system' had been in place but the departing colonial regime wanted to be certain that they were leaving behind a leadership that could sustain the British Westminster tradition. The seminars and conferences covered the following topics: *Law–Making and Government Business, Collective Responsibility of the Cabinet,*

Sustainability of the Parliamentary System in a New Democracy, and lastly, *Opposition and Shadow Cabinet in Parliamentary Democracy.* Experts from Great Britain were invited to lead the discussions including some very powerful voices in the House of Commons in Britain. These discussions were very lively as they engendered a lot of debate from leading nationalists who would form the new government in the country. At the end, all the aspects of the Westminster tradition were clearly expounded and the prospective leaders looked forward to the Independence Day when they would begin to play the various roles fully.

The cultural fiestas were organised to show the country's rich cultural diversity and pageantry with all its entertainments. The purpose was to show that: *Though in tongue and culture we differ, we are one,* and it was also to add to the general air of celebration. Varied folk dances and acrobatic displays were selected from the three regions of the country. One exciting and unique aspect of these dances was that, they were not just dances but dances which told memorable stories about their peoples – they were dance drama. In the dances, how some historical events were carried out would be demonstrated to amuse and remind the people of such events. Sometimes, they mimed the historical events, at other times, the stories would be told in the songs that accompanied the dances, so these folk dances were themselves histories. The cultural fiestas were well organised and the people were happy to realise that they had very rich cultures. The political leaders were more particularly happy, as the dazzling performances and cultural shows stung the world to realise the great future the Independence could bring. As one performance to another thrilled the delighted international audience, the nationalist leaders were happy with themselves that they could put up such a satisfactory performances and this, in their minds, became the first toast of the country's independence.

On the eve of the Independence, one special gala night was organised in the banquet hall at government house in the capital, in honour of the departing colonial 'Governor-General'. The occasion also doubled as the valedictory session for him. The young *National Arts Commission* of the country was able to put together a good number of troupes which performed spectacularly at the event. It was a night to be remembered as the leading lights of both political divides watched the troupes with great delight while they poured themselves choice drinks. It was an occasion to be remembered: A night that put away all the bitter acrimonies between the colonial administrators and the nationalists. True, after the rumbling in the sky, comes the rain that brings down the brittle air, for a refreshing beginning: A night that made mutual enemies to see themselves as partners that wrought together a potentially great country. It was a great joy to see the whole political struggle ending in this manner – no foes but friends and partners. Indeed, success is that enigma that can reconcile sworn enemies when they are brought together by its joy. It was not surprising therefore when the yesterday's *anarchists* and *seditionists* were dancing together and clinking glasses with their yesterday's *exploiters* and *fascists* in an atmosphere of conviviality. It was quite pleasing to hear one nationalist after another pouring endless encomium on the out-going 'Governor-General' for his great achievements. In rounding it off, the foremost nationalist leader described the achievements of the out-going 'Governor-General' whom he was to take over from as, 'dazzling starlights that will never dim.'

'With all sincerity, Your Excellency, they will never blink for a moment after you have gone, rather, they will ever remain to constantly remind us of the great strides in the past. Your Excellency, you have given us a great challenge and inspiration.'

And there was a resounding echoing of huge applause round the hall.

When it was the turn of the out-going 'Governor-General' to speak, standing ovation rent the hall for sometime. Obviously, he was the man of the moment. His face sparked with an overwhelming delight. He was an excellent man of imperial trim. Quite confident and calm, he held his audience in a firm position of undivided attention. It was time to engrave words on marble, as he delivered his speech with felicity and elegance. He was very thankful to the people, especially the political class and Her Royal Majesty, the Queen of Great Britain, for making his rule a memorable one. He was glad that his regime eventually brought to an end the British colonial rule in the country. He also thanked his fellow British nationals at the top level of his administration for their support and cooperation whom he credited with the success of his administration. After all the thanks, he had some words for the *new country* and its leadership to reflect on when he had left.

'Today, I feel so fulfilled. I have a strong sense of accomplishment because I am leaving behind men of honour and distinction who can continue effectively from where we stop. They are persons whose high leadership quality has been tested.'

There was a round of applause.

'I have no single doubt in their abilities.'

The audience repeated the applause.

'I have spent some years with you here – I understand how your pulse runs,' smiling. 'You are a people with so much energy, vibrancy and resilience: A people with so much social dynamism. I envy you sometimes.'

The audience applauded again.

'But these great plusses must be well managed. You must not squander them – they are delicate!' he alerted. 'You are made up of many peoples, cultures and several religions. Your country is a microcosm of Africa. So the greatest challenge you're going to face is how to use this rich diversity as a source of strength instead of division. Well, it depends on what you want to make out of it. But I am quite certain that your achievement will largely depend on your ability to manage the diversity and use it as an asset for development. It's a great challenge because if it is not properly handled, it might stand in the way of national cohesion, and there will be trouble, and you will never get anywhere.

'You must take practical steps to consolidate and strengthen the bond of unity independence has brought. You must strive to integrate all the ethnic groups into one solid indivisible nation. Once you can achieve that, the country will grow very fast, and it will be the envy of many nations. For you to succeed, you must first shed your ethnic and religious toga and turban yourself with statehood and be the father of all. Give every citizen a sense of belonging and perform every bit of your office for national interest. If you can do this, you will be able to carry every citizen along your vision and aspirations, and certainly, you shall achieve great results. Mahatma Gandhi did it so well in a more complex situation and translated himself into an icon of nationalism. Till death and after, he remains the father of India. If Gandhi made it, then, what stops you? I hope you shall be successful. I wish you all the strength and wisdom. I shall miss you very much. Certainly, I shall miss you vibrancy; your dynamism. I thank you all.'

And the audience clapped repeatedly for sometime – they never wanted to stop. It was a clear indication of their deep appreciation of the home-truth in the speech. At the end of the valedictory remark; souvenirs were presented to the out-going 'Governor-General' and the other top colonial officers with him.

By noon, the next day, the race-course at the country's capital was brimming over with people. Top political leaders from the few independent African countries had taken their seats. Great Britain's Queen, represented by a high-profile Royal Princess, was present with all her grace and majesty by proxy to officially declare the Independence of Namia. Her majesty's royal forces in their magnificent regalia were in array as the guard of honour. The well-decorated royal horses were also there for the parade. Also there, were all the first class traditional rulers in the country with some of their adoring chiefs. Many dignitaries within and outside the country could not be introduced. They all came to witness History. Different cultural dance bands were on their beats, entertaining. It was a huge glorious accasion.

After all the order of precedence had been observed, the Great Queen's representative, Princess Alexandra of Kent, with all her grace and elegance, went ahead to declare the Independence. In her brief remark, she congratulated the people of Namia for their Independence and spoke of the great expectation the world had of them, as they began the journey of nationhood.

'The world is watching and you have no reason to fail because you have all it takes to make a great nation, Great Britain shall give you all the necessary assistance that you might need as an infant country, which British prime minister shall unfold very soo...'

A great applause greeted the remark.

'Being an Independent Country we are now into a new relationship – we are now EQUAL partners.'

There was a general laughter.

'We join other nations in welcoming you to the comity of sovereign nations, congratulations! And I thank you all.'

Immediately, the whole gathering was to witness the high point of the Independence ceremony – the lowering of the *Union Jack* and the hoisting of the new green-white-green flag which everyone watched with breath-taking excitement, and suddenly, a great cheer went up. This was followed by many repeated fireworks thrust into the air as the new flag swung in the air in its poise position. Next, was the singing of the new independent national anthem. The people could not believe their eyes neither could they contain themselves as these historic events were happening in quick succession.

Next, was the swearing-in of the new 'Governor-General' who delievered one of the most gripping and boisterous speeches in recent times, in his flamboyant characteristic style. His language was grand and full of coinages of 'isms'. He had a great flair for rhetoric and the occasion offered him the proudest moment. He was down-to-earth grand, a style which he had used effectively to endear himself to the people and mobolised the country in his early days of nationalistic activism. The great majority of the people caught the fever of his wake-up campaign against colonialism then, and he was held with great awe. But today the story was almost different. Atavistic interests and sentiments had whittled down his high regard considerably. But one can still recognise a huge tree by its stump. He seemed to have bounced back to his full reckoning when he addressed the world today, as the first indigenous 'Governor-General' of the most pupolous Black Country in the world. He began his speech with a honeycomb of thanks: To the Queen, to Great Britain, to the out-going 'Governor-General,' to all Pan-African activists, to his co-travellers in nationalistic struggle, to traditional rulers, to the people of the country, to his own family and above all, to God Almighty. He stated emphatically in his speech that he appreciated the enormous responsibilities of his high office and avowed that he would not disappoint the people or the world. He promised to reel out very soon, a comprehensive plan of actions for the development of the country. He assured everyone that the Constituton would be the temple of the new government and the principles of the 'rule of law' would be his abiding faith.

'History has long proved that the only government that can guarantee freedom, liberty, equality and justice in any society is the one based on the "Rule of Law" and for the "Rule of Law" to guarantee these tenets it must be anchored on international principles of democratic government and the collective will of the citizens which our constitution today is a living testament.'

Unfortunately for the first indigenous 'Governor-General' with all his political sophistry, his power was not more than a mere seal in the office of the new prime minister, unlike his colonial predecessors that wielded so much power.

Somehow, the Governor-General's remark was alluding to the recent agitation of some minorities in the delta region of the country which greeted the advent of Independence. It was termed, 'The Fear of the Minorities in the South.' The region had enjoyed some relative development and sophistication in the country, arising from their long association with the whites since their first entry into the country. This had encouraged a great deal of commerce and entrepreneurship which had brought prosperity and modernity to the area. And Safa and other towns in the area were municipalities since colonial administration of the country, so all the series of decolonisation from bottom to top never affected them much. This had protected them from the influence of the major ethnic groups who had been acquiring political dominance since the Macpherson Constitution. And the minorities in the delta belt knew that their cocoon would be burgled the day the major ethnic groups took over the entire political machines of state, most particularly because of their thriving economy and their sea ports. So when these minorities screamed and sought a special sanctuary in the new 'Independence Constitution,' the out-going colonial government though acknowledged their fear, assuring them that the 'Independence Constitution' with comprehensive provisions of citizens' rights would be their bulwark and buffer against majority tyranny.

CHAPTER EIGHT

In the wake of the Independence, there was some ruffle of uncertainty among the white community in Safa. Most of them were in the various establishment of government: the police, the customs, the judiciary, the seaport, the municipality, etc. They were always at the top echelon of administration. But with the advent of independence, the fear of losing their positions with lots of privileges became real. Two weeks to the Independence Day, a directive was passed by the 'Colonial Office' in London, to all those on colonial posting in Namia, to report back for possible redeployment in the event of displacement. But many of the colonial officials knew that they had been enjoying positions and privileges they would never dreamt of back home: the chauffeur-driven official car, the official residence with well-kept lawn, official domestic aides etc would be a mere wishful thinking in Britain. Also, many of them had acclamatised to the locality and preferred the alluring comfortable residential 'European Quarter' in Safa with low cost of living to the expensive metropolitan life in UK.

Their initial reaction was one of excitement, going back home to fall into the warm embrace of relatives and friends, nice time to reminisce on old good times and amazing experiences in Africa, and reintegrate into one's glorious society. But counting the things they would miss, they became sad. Certainly, they would miss their prestige in the locality, the luxurant surrounding by the river and above all, the exciting sail and splashing savoury swim at weekend, which had become an unending craving among the white colony in Safa.

While they were chewing the cud on whether to stay or not, many of them appeared to see massive opportunities in Safa. They saw Safa as a great centre of commerce and industry under its municipality in a new independent country. They thought the business opportunity in Safa would continue to exist and expand. As a result, many of them decided to stay behind. They started by venturing into the lucrative businesses of timber and natural rubber in the area. Interestingly, the last colonial administration of Safa municipality decided to sell off the official residential houses in the 'European Quarter' in the wake of the Independence. These white government officials turned businessmen readily bought their coveted low-priced official residential houses from the government and began the business of shipping processed timber and natural rubber to Britain, using the business trips to see their relatives and friends back home in the United Kingdom.

But one of the few that responded positively to the directive of the 'Colonial Office' in London was Moore. Moore was the most senior doctor in the 'General Hospital' in Safa. He was invariably the director of the *General Hospital,* established by the municipality. Long before the coming of Independence, his wife, Susan, had been entreating him to leave for Britain, as she was not particularly pleased by what she considered as 'shut-out-of-civilization life' in Safa. Safa was rather too dull for her. She grew up in the heart of London and was accustomed to metropolitan life: the parks, the theatres, huge shopping complexes and all the frills at the city centre. She was a nurse in the *General Hospital.* After work, she found nothing particularly engaging during the week. She always locked herself up in her bedroom with novel-reading while Dr Moore would visit the golf-course in the evening with Skip, their only child. Her husband had tried to prod her interest in the evening gathering at the golf-course which was the common pastime of the whites in Safa. But the few occasions she went there with her husband, she found the place uninteresting. Some of the whites 'messed up' the guest-house with smoking and indecent gossips about their exploits with native girls. She was not interested in playing golf, either. The only occasion that fascinated her in Safa was the boat-sailing through the river at weekends. She enjoyed that and looked forward to it every week. As far as she was concerned, it was unique and magical. She enjoyed it so much that she often forgot, it would be dark in the evening. So when the opportunity for redeployment came with the Independence of Namia, the Moores readily embraced it.

But one person that would particularly miss them was Efe, who always exchanged heart-felt waving greetings with their son, Skip, at Akpobaro whenever they flew their boat past. This had registered a bond of affection between them.

The entry of many Britons who were previously in government service into timber and natural rubber businesses made competition keener. Hitherto, the few Europeans in the business only had to wait at Safa for their suppliers who brought the logs and the rubber lumps or sheets from the interior. They had their ready clienteles, so they only did a desk job. For the new entrants to gain access into the trade they had to look beyond Safa. They went into the hinterland to get their supplies directly from the source.

****

One early morning, Chief Akpovire was enjoying the warmth of the rising sun in his special deckchair in the frontage of his house when a car drove in and pulled up at a convenient place. Two smartly dressed white men with brief cases alighted and walked towards him. Chief Akpovire looked with vague expectation as they were walking towards him. He adjusted his sitting to give himself a poise posture, wondering what on earth must have made the two white men to come to their remote village that early morning. It was unimaginable to see a white man in Akpobaro. *What are they looking for?* Chief Akpovire kept thinking himself as they approached him. The last time he received white visitors at Akpobaro was seven years ago when some white missionary medical officials came from the Baptist Missionary Hospital, Ekroda. They wanted to vaccinate the people against small pox, at a time when the idea of inoculation was still very strange at Akpobaro. Chief Akpovire directed the town crier through the elders' Council, to pass the information round the village. But the people could not understand why somebody should be given treatment when he was not sick. Chief Akpovire assured them that the treatment was good for them. Nevertheless, the people remained sceptical. They could not trust strange white people with their lives; people they had heard so many weird stories about.

However, on the first day of the inoculation, some of the people came for the exercise at the primary school. Those were the curious ones. But when the first person was to be injected, they all ran away to tell the story that the white people wanted to pierce them with needle, which was very strange to them at that time. After that, nobody came forward to the missionary team anymore, for the vaccination. Those that remained within the school premises that day were just looking at the small number of whites and their instruments with curious and suspicious eyes, while maintaining their distance. They were amused by the conduct of the white missionaries and were waiting to see their next line of action. The missionary white doctor and nurses beckoned to them but they just smiled – a smile that revealed, 'We know your trick.' When those who stayed back home received the news later that day, they chuckled with satisfaction for knowing better. Urged by the white missionaries, Chief Akpovire instructed the town-crier to announce to the people again. But when the town-crier went round Akpobaro that night, the children and women came out to laugh at him. The news became a common joke in the village. The town crier came back that night to Chief Akpovire to relate the people's reaction.

'Thank you, very much. I knew they would not go, especially when it has to do with needle-piercing. I think the white people should have devised a more enticing method. But we have played our part by passing the information,' he said to the town-crier.

The following morning, Chief Akpovire informed the bewildered medical team that the people would not turn up. The missionaries who had prepared for a whole week exercise packed their bag and baggage that day and left Akpobaro.

'I thank you people   for your good work,' said Chief Akpovire to them when they were about to go. 'The people need time and awareness to fully appreciate your humanitarian concern.'

'Chief, I think it will take the example of people like you to convince them,' said the white doctor ruefully.

He was indirectly expressing his disappointment that Chief Akpovire too did not submit himself for the inoculation. As the foremost leader of the community, the doctor thought Chief Akpovire's participation would have made the difference. But Chief Akpovire who knew how the people revered him, could not have imagined himself being used as a sample for something the people had treated with disdain.

'Well, that might be next time,' Chief Akpovire offered.

So as the two white men approached him, he thought that the Baptist missionary health workers were back again with their vaccination. When the two white men came close to him, they smiled. Chief Akpovire smiled back with some curiosity. They shook hands with him.

'I 'm Mr. Jones,' the one speaking then pointed to his partner, 'Mr. Dentist,' he introduced with some vague smile on his face. 'I guess you're Chief Akpovire.'

'Yes, I am. Can I be of help?' Chief Akpovire beamed with a smile of positive disposition towards them.

And the two strange faces looked at each other and grinned also, not knowing whether to start business straight away. Chief Akpovire guessed from their smile that they had come for something more particular.

'Let's go in,' he said as he quickly got up from his chair and led them into his house. When they had taken their seats, the two white men took a quick look at the sitting room that had some peculiar attraction. Good furniture: a set of chairs with cushion – the high fashion for the rich in Safa – one large huge cupboard with a honeycomb of compartments which stored the many personal valuables of Chief Akpovire: each unit had one or two particular items like wrappers, beads, hats, shoes and sanders, golden cutlery and expensive breakable plates, tea cups and jugs, bedsheets and pillow cases, foreign gins and wines, etc. Most of the items were very expensive and were reserved for special use. The front of the cupboard was engraved with varied and numerous sculptural designs, which on first consideration gave the huge cupboard the look of aesthetic presentation. A large wall clock was in the living room. It sounded like piano with several pleasant notes. Also in the large sitting room were two giant mirrors opposite each other in the house. The gramophone stood on a portable table by a corner. Under it were old newspapers notably 'Daily Times'. Up on the wall were several portraits. History stood behind each one _ one could study the history of Namia with the portraits – they were all arranged in order of time: from Lord Federick Lugard, the first colonial 'Governor-General,' to the last colonial 'Governor-General,' James Robertson, were arranged on one side. On the opposite, were the great nationalists, Sir Herbert Macauley, the father of all of them, stood bold with his *wire* moustache which had become a symbol of his tough resistance against colonialism. He led the line. On the other two sides of the wall were Chief Akpovire personal portraits which recorded his glorious moments in his political days – his different poses with known nationalists or other notable political figures across the country. A first step into the sitting room would strike any visitor, no matter his social status, to realise that he was in a home of a man of note in the society.

The two white men almost felt intimidated by what they saw. They had thought that they were only going to see a timber dealer in the interior of Safa. But the house had given them greater picture of the man. They were now thinking of how to approach him. Chief Akpovire felt he had very important guests. He went into his bedroom and returned with a bunch of keys. He opened one unit of the large cupboard in the living room and brought out a brandy and one wine. Opened another unit and rolled out glasses and a saucer. He shouted for Efe, one of his sons, through the window and Efe raced down. He remembered kola-nut. He went into his bedroom again and came with a kola-nut which he put on the saucer beside the drinks on the centre table. He added some money to the kolanut, and eventually took his seat in his dignified manner and smiled.

'I don't know if you have ever visited an indigene of our area?'

The two strange curious white men shook their heads in the negative.

'Well, we've a custom of receiving a visitor. But for your sake, I'll not go into further ceremony. What you are seeing on the table, is my small way of receiving you. Kindly accept them from me.'

The two white men had heard that African people had ceremony for almost everything, but they knew nothing about them, so were somewhat confused over what were presented. They looked at the kola-nut and the money on the saucer and wondered what they would do with them. *But we did not come here to beg for money*, one of them thought. Even in their confusion, they could not help but appreciate the courtesy and hospitality which was contrary to the many crude and horrid stories they had heard about the natives in the hinterland, though, still at a loss over how to accept the offer.

'You can take the money. I know you won't eat the kola-nut. My son shall open either of the drinks or both if you choose,' said Chief Akpovire trying to help them out.

'Chief, we will take only the brandy,' one of them replied.

Efe who had been waiting on them opened the brandy and wanted to serve them but Mr. Jones and Mr. Dentist preferred to serve themselves, so Chief Akpovire gulped down the one already served by Efe and allowed the two white men to do as they pleased with the brandy.

While they were drinking, the two white men felt they might have offended Chief Akpovire, by not accepting the money, which might not favour the business for which they came. Though, they would not want to throw away their chance, they thought it was necessary to maintain their dignity and prestige by not accepting the money. As for the kola-nut, they could not imagine themselves chewing that 'rubbish'.

Chief Akpovire on his part was regretting throwing his people's cherished act of reception at strangers who could not appreciate the symbolic value. He acknowledged the fact that he and the two white men were of different stocks but he did not quite like the manner by which they quietly turned down some of his offer; he sat askance where he was, just waiting for what they would say.

At that moment, Scorchearth and Comrade, the two inseparable hunters who played buffoonery in the village came in. They had a way of making every situation amusing. They were almost taken for professional jesters in Akpobaro, and nobody felt offended when bantered by the two wags; such a person just laughed it away with others around. Scorchearth and Comrade always amused people wherever they went, particularly children who were fond of them. The children always called them their nicknames for which they were well-known whenever they saw them, to curry some jokes. Apart from like-mindedness, one other thing strung the two jesters together: During the Second World War, Scorchearth who was Johnson Oyono was conscripted into the 'Allied Forces'[13] by the British colonial government in Namia, when he was eighteen and was sent to Burma in India, against the Japan's forces. There, he met so many different nationals and because of his comic personality, he soon endeared himself to many and became popular in his camp. He also performed very well in all his trainings and combat-ready exercises, and so was well liked by his captain who became fond of him, too. His captain used to train his combatants about warfares and military tactics regularly. He was always very excited to relate encouraging news of military exploits by the army of the 'Allied Forces' in other battlefields. In such circumstances, he would demonstrate and swagger with military posturing to make it more dramatic. So when the news of how the gallant Russian army crushed the Germans reached him, he was wild with excitement. In one of his training sessions, he began to expatiate with great vigour on the tactics of 'scorchearth' in military strategy, which the Russians used against the Germans. And as he demonstrated with his hands, Johnson listened with an express rapture on his face. He was greatly inspired by the story, as related by his captain. From that day, the word 'scorchearth' never left his mouth. Not long later, his camp-mates started calling him 'Scorchearth' and he was happy about it. That was how he got the nickname.

At the end of the World War, Scorchearth was discharged and brought back home with thousands of other Namians. He later joined the security department of 'National Railway Corporation' where he met Okpemu *alias* 'Comrade'. While there, some of the ex-servicemen who knew him in Burma picked up his old nickname and very soon his real name was abandoned at the railway corporation.

---

[13]Armies of Britain, USA, France and Free Euope pitted against the military coalition forces of the countries against them, the Axis Forces (Hitler's German,Mussolini's Italian and Emperor Hito's Japanese forces) during World War II (1939-1945)

Scorchearth joined the corporation at a time when government workers became the fuelling fire of the struggle for the country's independence and the railway workers were most active, as the president of the workers' union nationwide was from there. Moreover, many ex-servicemen who joined government agencies were angry with the colonial government for demobilising them without any benefits. They rallied round the nationalists for the struggle against colonialism, by using the labour platform to organise strikes across the country. Okpemu was very intrepid in the struggle, which earned him the nickname 'Comrade.' Scorchearth was active too, and because they both came from Akpobaro, it did not take long before they took to each other at the railway corporation. They were later sacked along with many others after one major strike in the corporation, which paralysed it for three weeks, and the British management decided to sack all the activists in one fell swoop. Comrade and Scorchearth decided to return to Akpobaro, their native place, after the sack. With their last money, they bought two locally made guns. Scorchearth taught Comrade how to shoot for some days before they began hunting as their occupation in the village. Since then, they had been happy. They often came home every night with good games. Hunting together finally cast them into one pair of a seed. Since they began, they had formed the habit of bringing a game to Chief Akpovire once in a while. Akpobaro people loved to show gratitude individually and collectively to Chief Akpovire whenever occasions warranted it. Interestingly, Scorchearth and Comrade had demonstated the deepest appreciation of his good efforts in the community. During their work at the railway corporation at the country's capital, they saw great opportunities which colonialism had brought and they had watched helplessly how these great opportunities were taken by nondescript individuals because of their education. And such chances continued to exist as the country progressed into independence.

So when they returned home to witness the amazing effort of Chief Akpovire to transform their rustic community through establishment of schools, they could not help adoring him. Apart from coming with a game at regular intervals, they also helped him in his farm. This had endeared the duo to Chief Akpovire who saw them as truly enlightened individuals and loved to engage them in the community's affairs, which had also raised their reputation among the people, their frivolous nature notwithstanding.

Scorchearth and Comrade came into Chief Akpovire's house through the second door in the back of the compound, so the children did not see them when they entered. As soon as they entered, they began their usual dramatic military salute to Chief Akpovire. Scorchearth would start a mock parade and a military chant. As he chanted the military parade song they both marched to and fro with accurate military steps. At once, they stood still and gave a military salute to their over amused 'General' who was already overwhelmed with laughter. Immediately, the children inside the compound heard their song, they raced down to the main door. The children in their wild excitement would have been shouting their nicknames but for the presence of the two white men.

The two white men were equally enthralled by the duo's demonstration. They were taken aback to see an authoritative military demonstration and they watched with awe. When Scorchearth and Comrade noticed the deep interest of the two white men, their demonstration was intensified and made longer than usual. More children and women came to watch. They were at the doors and windows – the presence of the two buffoons usually attracted them as sugar attracts ants. The two white men were so captivated that one of them gave them a pound. Chief Akpovire was so excited. He offered them the unaccepted kola-nut, the money on the saucer and the brandy which the two white men had been taking, and they ate and drank with gratitude.

With so much ardour, the chidren ran after Scorchearth and Comrade as soon as they stepped out of the house and began to shout at the top of their voices repeatedly, 'Scorchearth! Scorchearth!' 'Destroy everything!' Scorchearth would say in return. At the same time, some of the children were shouting 'Comrade!' in like manner, all of them in a wild excitement, 'Always vigilant,' replied Comrade, which was the slogan of his former trade union. The children continued to follow them. They turned back when Scorcthearth and Comrade had disappeared from the quarter. They were always carried away whenever they saw Comrade and Scorchearth.

The duo had just brought a fox, after their hunting in the previous night. Chief Akpovire was so grateful. He instructed two of his children to dress it for cooking, which he shared among his wives later.

The coming of the two hunters created the right atmosphere for Chief Akpovire and the two white businessmen.

'I guess they're ex-soldiers,' said one of the two white men.

'One of them,' returned Chief Akpovire heartily.

'They're really amazing,' the second white man complimented.

Chief Akpovire smiled.

'You've not seen anything. You can never have a dull moment in the presence of those two,' laughed he.

The two white men took advantage of the warm situation to discuss their mission. They had come to discuss with Chief Akpovire to be their main supplier of timber, as their finding had shown that he was one of the major suppliers of timber to Safa. When they had made plain their mission, the rest of the discussion became business-like. Chief Akpovire saw their coming as an opportunity of having an edge in the business while the two white men were only interested in making in-roads. They hoped to explore possible business advantage later, when they had secured a place and had understood all the intricacies involved in the business. But they were careful not to trade off cheaply, as that might jeopardise their chances of staying on the business. Initially, Chief Akpovire pretended not to be keen.

'Well, I already have a customer. We've been carrying on for sometime and he has been good,' he said.

'We know that. But we're in business. If you have extra money over what you have been getting, will you turn it down?' replied Mr. Dentist who seemed to have more business acumen than Mr. Jones.

'Of course, I won't.'

'That's exactly what we mean!'

And a business smile spread across their faces.

'So how much can you offer?' said Chief Akpovire.

'Chief, let's know first, the price of a timber in the market currently.'

'Well, that depends on the wood.'

'We know but there's a pricelist for the different woods from time to time'

'That's true,' Chief Akpovire looked upwards and reflected for some seconds. But he was not absolutely sure. 'Just a minute,' said Chief Akpovire.

He stood up and went into his office chamber inside his house where he kept all his business documents. He returned with a note book where he wrote the current prices. He wore his glasses and read them out. Not to be doubted, he passed the note book with the right page to them. Mr. Dentist and Mr. Jones studied it for sometime and became more business-like.

'We shall add 5% to each species,' said Mr. Dentist.

'That's not good,' Chief Akpovire shook his head in the negative. 'Dont forget, doing business with you will cost me my good business relation with Mr. Smith. We have been doing business together for four good years now. Besides, you're new in the business, you're not stable yet. You may decide to quit tomorrow if business goes bad for you and where will you leave me? In the hands of Mr. Smith and his clique again? You know that'll be suicidal! So the only thing that'll make me try business with you is good money, nothing else. If you mean business add something reasonable.'

'Chief, leave your relation with Mr. Smith out of it: we're in business. If Mr. Smith gets a cheaper offer somewhere else today, will he not abandon you? That's business! But we do appreciate your fear of reliability as we are very new in the business. What about giving you some capital with the five per cent?' said Mr. Dentist.

Chief Akpovire thought for sometime.

'It's our assurance of staying with you,' Mr. Dentist chipped in, as he saw that Chief Akpovire was still finding it difficult to make up his mind.

Additional five per cent and more money to expand? That'll mean lots of money for the college, thought Chief Akpovire. He became excited.

'How much can you offer?'

'Much as you might need.'

And a smile reeled out from Chief Akpovire's mouth.

Mr. Jones and Mr.Dentist knew that the more capital they threw in, the more the supply and if the personality the entire house of Chief Akpovire presented to them was any measure, they thought their money was in a safe hand. So the negotiation was satisfactory to both sides. Mr.Jones and Mr Densist poured themselves more brandy in quiet celebration as their first attempt into the business was successful. Both parties could not hide their joy as they shook hands cheerfully and thanked each other when they had finished their negotiation.

Chief Akpovire saw them to their car. The car had attracted many of the village chidren who had been playing around it with all fervour. They touched it, felt it and peeped at the side mirrors to admire themselves while Mr. Dentist and Mr. Jones were with Chief Akpovire inside. Car was a privileged sight in their world. When the car was driven to Chief Akpovire's house, it attracted the children immediately. As soon as the white men stepped out of Chief Akpovire's house, the chidren ran from it. But immediately the car started moving, they came back and ran after it and began to shout 'Oyibo!

Oyibo! Oyibo!' They had only been seeing white people splashing through their river at weekends. But seeing them now so close in their village was unbelievable. Two smart, daring ones among them clung to the back of the car as soon as it started moving. They savoured the rare privilege of the ride and laughed hilariously. The rest of them pursued with greater vigour as they were so full of excitement, in their attempts to cling to it also. They were very determined as they saw the two lucky ones smiling, satisfactorily. 'O-y-i-b-o! O-y-i-b-o!' the children continued in their pursuit. Other children who heard their voices ran out and joined them.

Mr. Jones and Mr.Dentist did not know exactly what to do when they noticed what was happening. They thought moving very fast suddenly could be dangerous for the two already on the car, and to slow down would make the children to overcrowd the car and that could cause accident. They could see the wild excitement of the children. They continued to go on their not-too-fast pace, believing that as they drove out of the village, the children would go back. They were right. As they got out of the village, their number began to reduce. Many were already discouraged when they could not get near the car. Others became exhausted. But a few continued to pursue till the car got to the outskirts before they finally withdrew. At that point, the two that clung to the back jumped down and waved goodbye with satisfaction and gratitude.

That day the news of the two whitemen's visit to Chief Akpovire spread through out the village and across the entire Omaurhie. Hitherto, the people saw Chief Akpovire as a great man among them. They also believed he was also influential among important people across the entire country. And when they heard now that two whitemen came to visit him in his house, they realised that Chief Akpovire was greater than they had ever imagined. That day his reputation soared to the sky and it remained the talk of the village for sometime.

CHAPTER NINE

Every privilege goes with a price, so it was with the family of Chief Akpovire. As Chief Akpovire's image in Akpobaro was assuming a king-figure, its long shadow of greatness was also cast upon his wives and children. This conferred automatic respect on every one of them. An honour which also had its own inherent high standard regulation which every one of them was expected to abide by, and it was not easy, especially for his children who naturally would want to indulge in some playful distractions like other children in the village. But Chief Akpovire's children found themselves restricted from all such indulgences. Not that anybody told them not to indulge in such things. They just found it difficult to do such ordinary things with others. Akpobaro people saw them as very special individuals in the community and did not expect them to be doing ordinary things commonfolk in the village were doing. But Efe preferred to live a life of his own regardless of his family background.

After he had overcome his misfortune of Skip's disappearance from the boat sailing across Akpobaro, he found a new life with the river, he developed a great interest in fishing. It all began when he often stayed at the riverside on Saturday, waiting for the speed-boats of the white colony at Safa to pass Akpobaro. In the course of waiting, he became involved in the swimming game of 'first-to-reach-there' or 'catch me.' Most of the boys he played these two games with, were children whose parents came from the riverine area to settle in Akpobaro. They stayed by the river and mainly engaged in fishing. These children knew alot about fishing like their parents. Though, not matured enough to join their parents in the fishing occupation, they had small nets and several fish-hooks which they set in the shallow side of the river among the reeds while their parents went far in the river in their fishing. At intervals of their swimming games, the children would run through the mangrove swamps on the other side of the river to check their nets and hooks and if they caught any fish, they would roast them in the fire and eat them in a frolic-some manner. Efe began to accompany them and usually had a share. After sometime, Efe became more interested in fishing than the swimming games with the boys. There was little difficulty in getting him some hooks and a net. The boys were very happy and enthusiastic to have a boy from the most famous family in the community to be among them in their playful activities.

They provided him with all the necessary materials and he became fully involved.

Efe was always in the company of the riverine boys in running through the several footpaths in the mangrove swamps on the other side of the river to fish, when he had got his own hooks and net. He was learning very fast. Towards the afternoon after some swimming, they would dig up earth worms in the loamy soil under the shade of bamboo trees by the main riverside and put them in a coconut shell. They would cut each earth worm into small pieces which they fixed to the hooks which they set separately with their nets among the flora on the other side of the river, to which people hardly went. From experience, they knew fish explored its inhabitat in an undisturbed environment. After this, they would run back to the main side of the river, where people fetched water and had their bathings, besides washing activities. Immediately they got to there they would pull off their clothes and jump into the river, splash water here and there, and plunge into the deep, burst out their heads and began to gasp and leap backwards to the shallows again. After a casual wash there, they would launch back to the deep, splash water at each other, and their play would begin. When they became tired or began to catch cold, they would remember their hooks and nets they had set and rush out of the water, get into their clothes and began to run up the slope and pass through the mangroves to the other side of the river. Tread the slippery ageless tree trunks lying in the shallows of the river and began to check the hooks and nets. Get the fish out with exciting smile which spread over their entire faces, and reset their hooks and nets again. With all the fish in their hands, they would run to the fireside and have them roasted with some salt and pepper before eating. They enjoyed it this way and Efe saw it as a nice delicacy. After eating the fish, they would go to the main riverside for another round of swimming. As the sun was going down in the evening, they would begin their last round: dug up earthworms again, fixed them to the hooks after removing their fresh catches. Those that did not catch any fish and their baits were consumed would be supplied with fresh worm and might be properly reposition while those still hanging with their worm were left intact; all for over night catch. And the roasting of the evening catches would follow. This would be done in a hurry, as they were already expecting their parents to return home, and the home chores assigned to them had not been done. Lastly, they would take their individuals' nets to the main riverside which they set and shielded among the corals under water, in the area sloping towards the deep where they thought some fishes usually aboded, thinking that such fishes would come out at night, exploring all the edges of the reeds and florals in the shallows.

After all these, they would go about their assigned domestic chores with speed and anxiety, praying to get everything done before their parents would return. Sometimes, they might be lucky. But in most cases, they received beating for not doing their assigned home chores.

That was Saturday. But within the week when they attended school, only afternoon after school and early morning before school was all they had, which was based on their individuals' efforts, as each took home whatever their individuals' hooks and nets caught. And it was this, their parents knew about.

Everybody in Chief Akpovire's home knew that Efe loved going to the river. They also knew he had passion for seeing the white people speed past the riverside in their engine boats. They also noticed that he had added another dimension to it lately. So when he started coming home with some fish in the morning, nobody was surprised. Initially, his mother was very happy about it. She felt that Efe's somewhat wayward nature had its positive side, after all. She prayed that he should continue in this way. In fact, she was very proud that her child could bring fish to the house every morning. She sometimes served Chief Akpovire some of the fish in his meal and was always excited to tell him the source.

'You mean Efe can fish? Who taught him?' asked Chief Akpovire the first time he was served Efe's fish.

Otabunor smiled.

'He's been seeing people fishing.'

'Just like that?' retorted Chief Akpovire.

'I think he's simply demonstrating the ingenious stuff in him,' replied she.

'Well, that's good,' remarked her husband with some reservation.

Otabunor saw it as a sign of improvement in her son's conduct. She had heard several times from her mother when she was young that, 'children are like the weather; they change from time to time. *Efe might well be a bleak weather that is just brightening up?* Everybody knew that Efe was very obstinate and enigmatic; not even beating could sway him easily from doing what he wanted.

In the school, his performance had started dwindling. Fishing and swimming always occupied his mind. Either he was thinking of his hooks that might have caught fish or his swimming. His class teacher had observed his distraction and his declining performance, which made him keep his eyes on Efe most times when he was teaching. He had warned him several times without result. The next step he took was to ask him questions often. This had helped a little. One day the teacher was teaching multiplication sum. One method he favoured most in teaching a topic, he had previously introduced in Arithematic, was question-and-answer method, which engaged the class most actively. He always asked questions in moving the sum to the next stage and he expected the class to supply the answers. Sometimes, he threw the questions at individuals.

'Seven times six?' asked Mr. Okoh, and the pupils started figuring out.

'Forty-two!' chorused two pupils at once.

'Good, carry?'

'Carry four,' answered the pupils.

'Correct, eight times nine?'

The pupils began to think again. He looked up and saw Efe gazing at the window absent-mindedly. He suspected that Efe had something else on his mind, as he had not heard his voice since the lesson began.

'Yes, Efe?'

Efe looked towards the teacher unexpectedly. He had not been listening. He felt sharply the embarassment of his unpreparedness to answer the question. The teacher now knew he had not been attentive.

'Efe, we are waiting for you,' said he.

Some pupils had figured out the answer and had started shouting, 'I, sir,' 'I, sir,'.... with their right hands raised up. But Mr. Okoh fixed his accusing eyes on Efe who was becoming more embarrassed and ashame.

'What do you always think about? I will flog you next time if you don't pay attention.'

Having warned Efe, he allowed another pupil to supply the answer, and went on. Very soon Efe's mind wandered off again. He saw that six of his fifteen hooks had caught fish. He began to dance on one of the old trunks at the river. He displayed the hooks with the fish to his friends who were looking with envy. One of the fish was very big. It was still struggling in the hook. It could have dragged the hook away were it not for the end of the stick of the hook that was hooked into some reeds. This was the biggest fish he had ever caught. As soon as he collected them together, he ran home. There was a great cheering when he entered their compound. Everybody came out to look. Efe dropped down the other five fish and was displaying the big one with the hook to the admiration of every one. 'Efe, what is the total number?' said the teacher.

'Six fish!' Efe shouted unconsciously and the whole class was thrown into a convulsion of laughter.

Mr Okoh was scandalised as he gazed at the poor boy who was dripping with embarrassment now. The question hit Efe like a dynamite. It was just then, he realised that he had been day-dreaming and was full of regret and shame.

****

That evening Mr. Okoh went to see Chief Akpovire. Immediately, Efe sighted him in their compound he withdrew. Mr. Okoh had come to intimate Efe's father of Efe's dwindling performance and his lack of concentration in the class. At the beginning, Mr. Okoh thought he would be able to handle the situation. But he had reached his wit's end and was now compelled to table Efe's problem before his father who, by Mr. Okoh's estimation, should have brilliant and well-behaved children. He had wandered on his way what had become of the boy who was above average before.

Chief Akpovire welcomed Mr. Okoh heartily to his house. He brought out the left-over of an imported gin and placed it on the centre table. He put a kola-nut and two shillings in a saucer by it.

'Mr. Okoh, there's a drink on the table.'

Efe's teacher was pleasantly surprised. He did not expect Chief Akpovire to treat him like a dignitary in his house.

'Sir, a whisky from Europe? Kola-nut and money for me?' said he in a surprise tone.

'Mr. Okoh, you're deflating yourself. You're as important as every important person under the sun. The lives of children, indeed generation, are in your hands. Mr. Okoh, you're important!'

'Thank you, sir. I feel highly honoured,' Mr. Okoh smiled and became mirthful.

They began to drink and chew kola-nut.

'How was the school today?'

'Fine, sir.'

'How was your HM? It's long I heard from him.'

'He was fine.'

'Have you seen your boy, Efe?'

'No sir, and I'm here on his behalf.'

'On his behalf? Hope nothing is wrong.'

'Not quite sir, only that his studies and performance in class is no longer encouraging.'

'What's wrong?' asked Chief Akpovire with some concern.

'He's always distracted in class these days and this has affected his performance adversely. I'm afraid if he continues like that he might repeat the class and that's not good for him, especially as your son.'

Chief Akpovire became pensive. He pondered over the remark for sometime and sent for Efe. But Efe could not be found around.

'Imagine the other day,' Mr. Okoh began to narrate, 'we were working a sum, after we had finished all the multiplications, I simply asked him to add up, and he suddenly shouted "six fish". When, in fact, we were talking in thousands.'

'Six what?' said Chief Akpovire.

'Six fish,' returned the teacher and Chief Akpovire nodded his head knowingly. What he heard now had confirmed his fear.

'Thank you for your concern, Mr. Okoh. I shall look into the matter. I am indeed very grateful,' said Chief Akpovire with the air of knowing exactly what to do.

'Thanking me is unnecessary, sir, I 'm only performing my duty,' Mr. Okoh said as he was taking his leave.

Efe must be disengaged from his fishing activity at once, thought Chief Akpovire when the teacher had left.

That night Chief Akpovire waited for a long time to see Efe return from where ever he went. When it was getting late, everybody in the family became anxious. Though, Efe often visited his maternal grandmother in the other quarter of the village, he never stayed late except when he had committed an offence back home. But everyone in the family thought that Efe was not in the compound when his teacher came, so they all felt that he could not have known that his wrong-doing at school was reported. By this thinking, nobody expected that he would stay away from home. Chief Akpovire's children went round the neighbourhood that night but they could not find him.

To everyone's surprise, Efe was at his grandmother's. He was already sleeping after a good meal. His grandmother returned him after she had completed all her house chores. That was what she used to do each time Efe ran there to escape from punishment at home. And whenever she returned Efe, everyone in the family was certain that Efe would be free from any forms of punishment. Apart from lavish food and other special treats which always attracted Efe to his maternal grandmother, her place had also become his sanctuary against punishment and beating each time he did something wrong at home. So when his grandmother returned him that night, Chief Akpovire grudgingly put away his whip in deference to his mother-in-law.

'*Oniaye*',[14] Chief Akpovire called his mother-in-law with all tenderness, struggling not to betray his exasperation, as he thought his mother-in-law would soon spoil Efe. 'I'll not touch him since you have pleaded for him. But there's one thing....'

'What's it?' cut in his mother-in-law with curiosity.

'He must stay away from the riverine boys. Because he fishes with them, that's why he no longer pays attention at school, fishing has possessed him and nothing else matters to him anymore. His teacher was here this evening with the report.'

'Efe shall not mingle with them again,' the old woman declared. She drew closer to Efe, 'You have heard your father. Consider those boys lepers from today – no mixing. If you go to them again I will never come here to plead for you,' she warned.

Efe nodded his head calmly with some sense of relief in his mind. But this kind of warning by Efe's maternal grandmother to Efe had occurred repeatedly, each time she returned him home, after he had committed an offence in the home, that it has almost lost its meaning. That night, Efe's grandmother did not leave until Efe had gone to sleep. She always told one story or the other to delay her stay. This nattering was done to neutralise and bury any lingering intention of beating Efe after she had left.

She treated Efe among her grandchildren with singular tenderness. She would not allow anything to hurt him. She was always prepared to stave off anything that would make him sad. And Efe was taking advantage of his grandmother's affection for him, by always running to her whenever he did some wrong at home. This oftentimes upset Chief Akpovire who believed that

---

[14]Mother-in-law. Or Wife's Mother.

the old woman was spoiling Efe but was constrained by custom to restrain himself from anything that would strain his good relation with his mother-in-law. It was a customary duty for him to always show gratitude and respect to his in-laws, especially his parents-in-law, who had borne the burden of raising their daughters for him to marry. That was why it was a common saying among the people that *the payment of bride-price can never be completed.* This was in appreciation of the enormous responsibility of raising a girl-child to that stage where she would become attractive to a man and be given away in marriage. And to the people, in what other way could a husband pay back other than to demonstate forever his indebtedness to his wife's family. That was why the people always returned a small amount of the bride-price to the suitor of their daughter immediately after it was paid and said, 'Bride-price is never completed,' as a demonstrative symbol of this belief among them. It was only in the deepest sense of this belief one could appreciate why Chief Akpovire with all his towering social stature and king-figure in Akpobaro could allow his mother-in-law have her way in Efe against his personal inclination.

For sometime there was no problem. Efe kept to his father's warning. He knew how severe his father could be when he was disobeyed. But one shining Saturday afternoon, however, Efe went to the river to fetch water. He met some children playing 'First-to-reach-there,' which involved swimming from one end to the other in a competition in the river. Many of the children in Akpobaro enjoyed the game a lot. As a result, whenever they came to the river they often spent a lot of time playing this game. Efe joined them in the game. After sometime,they changed to 'Catch me'which they called '*opiri*' in their local language. In this game, one person would chase the rest in the river and any one of them he was able to touch before reaching the shallow side would take it up in the next round. If he failed to touch any of them, he would continue in each succeeding round until he touched one of them in the deep.

Ejaife was a township boy. He came to spend holidays with his grandparents at Akpobaro. He could swim but not with the experience of the village boys. In this game which he had come to love, the other boys always derided him for his inability to catch someone. He would stretch after one of them in pursuit. But once the person plunged into the deep, Ejaife would no longer be able to pursue. The person might emerge eventually at the shallower ends, only to be laughing at Ejaife who was still waiting for him in the deep parts of the river. However, he had learnt one trick. Since he could not plunge down in the deep, he would pursue faster in the surface, leaving no gap, so anyone who could not plunge down fast and early enough might be chased very far in the river until he was touched. He had tried three times to catch one of them without success. He became more determined as every one of them laughed at him.

'*Opiri o*,' he started at the shallows again.

'Eh!' replied the rest in the deep.

'I am coming now.'

'Come!'

And Ejaife leapt forward towards Efe. He pursued very fast. Efe could almost feel his hand behind. He swerved in the current and leaped forward with all his strength. He was swimming very fast too. Ejaife pressed hard behind. He was encouraged by getting so close. He kept pursuing Efe and Efe could feel him so close. The current was at its highest. After a while of intense pursuit, Ejaife looked back and noticed that they had crossed their usual swimming arena and were getting out of the general waterside view. He quickly turned backwards. But Efe was still stroking forward as fast as he could, thinking that Ejaife was still pressing after him. By the time he turned, he was shocked to discover that he had gone too far. He was already out of view, the river current had aided his effort. He could not believe his eyes. He began to make desperate effort to swim backwards. It was then, he realised the difficulty of swimming against the tide. He never moved an inch forward rather the current was pushing him backwards. He had heard many times among grown-ups that, 'It is easy and interesting to go with the tide but very difficult to go against.' He was realising the meaning first-hand. He became very apprehensive and desparate and was in a survival frenzy. But after sometime, he painfully realised that he would soon go under – he was now very tired and weak. He attempted to shout for help. Instead, he was gulping water, as he was already going down. He gulped more and more while struggling to push upwards with his hands in desperation.

Ejaife managed to get back to the shallow area and was panting ceaselessly. When he had rested for a few seconds, he turned to see if Efe was coming but Efe was not in view. All the rest of them became alarmed. They feared that the current might have carried him away. They all panicked for a canoe. The only one at the shallows was padlocked and there was no grown-up around. They screamed in great panic repeatedly and immediately raised greater alarm to the village. Three young men raced down the slope to the river at once and a mass of people soon flooded the waterside.

The three young men dived into the river as soon as they were told what was happening. A huge crowd of people were anxiously waiting at the bank of the river while more and more young men were diving in as they came, and the search began hysterically. There was panic and frenzy as they had not been able to see him. At once, the crowd heard a yell from a distance in the river. And the huge anxious crowd shouted back with much curiosity mixed with apprehension.

Behind the huge crowd was Otabunor. She was distraught and was wailing uncontrollably. Some women held her down as she was writhing on the ground in distress. So also was Efe's maternal grandmother, Arierie. She was completely devastated where she was. She had run down from her home on the other end of Akpobaro like many others who heard the distressing commotion, only to discover it was about Efe, her beloved. Two canoes had been mobilised from the next waterside while the search was going on.

Efe's body was finally found and lifted into one, which caused the yell in further up the the river. He was completely unconscious. As soon as the hysterical waiting crowd sighted his 'lifeless body', many of them began to wail. One of the men immediately lifted the body on his right shoulder on getting to the shallow end, placing Efe's swollen belly directly on his shoulder and began to run with it up the slope into the village as fast as he could. The other men ran after him. Water started gushing out of Efe's mouth and a streak of it from his nose. The particles of the last food he ate were also dropping. When the man became tired he handed over to another man and that one raced faster than before. More water with particles of food kept on flowing and dropping. The crowd of people ran after the man, anxiously looking with for a sign of revival, as their minds oscillated between fear and hope.

When it was thought that all the water he gulped had gone out of him, Efe was lowered onto the ground. The crowd surrounded him searching for a possible stirring but there was none. Two of the men took him up again and shook him violently. After some while, Efe's eyes opened, turned his face and the people thundered 'ewewu!'[15] The shout was like an explosion which

---

[15] An Urhobo exclamation of relief over someone having overcome death or survived very dangerous situation against overshelming odds.

resonated round the village. And everybody became happy, thanking God for his mercy.

The men led Efe into his father's compound when he had fully recovered. Chief Akpovire had been standing by with some chiefs observing the scene with great perturbation. He watched Efe carefully as he was being led into his compound. His eyes followed Efe until he entered his mother's apartment of two rooms in his wives' abode.

Chief Akpovire sent for all the young men in the rescue effort and they all came to his living room. He put drinks, kola-nuts and a handsome amount of money on the table in appreciation. Many other persons also came in for a drink, by way of celebrating. Throughout that week, many more people, including chiefs and other notables, came to express their joy to Chief Akpovire's family. The women were visiting Otabunor while the men visited Chief Akpovire. All the people that came thanked the Almighty Creator for his great mercy he had shown on Efe and Chief Akpovire's family. They were thanking the Almighty Creator because they believed that Efe did not drown by an odd quirk of fate. Those who came later after the revival would examine Efe repeatedly to express their unbelief and the mystery of his survival. And they would tell Efe, 'Your god and your ancestors are never asleep.' Some of them who knew Efe intimately would go further to warn him against his fondness with the river. Mudiaga observed him for sometime, after thanking the mighty creator and the ancestors of the land for saving him, when he came, and said to Efe, 'It is the fly which has lost caution that follows the corpse into the grave. You're too fond of the river. The river you think to be ordinary water, deep inside are mysteries and terrible things. You must be careful of the river. All the same, we thank the mighty one up there,' he pointed to the sky.

But Chief Akpovire and Otabunor never said a word to their son concerning the incident. They did not even bother to ask him how it all happened. The entire Chief Akpovire's household were too terrified to mention the hair-raising incident. Throughout that week the compound remained cold and calm, the coming of outsiders to express their concerns and joy, notwithstanding.

****

After three weeks, the shock of the ugly incident faded away in the family and nobody thought of it again. Efe too had put the unfortunate incident behind him and his normal life began again. He had improved upon his performance at school and his teacher was quite pleased with him. These days, he was seen more in the compound and had begun to assist his mother more readily in the domestic chores. But his mother thought it was too early to comment on his improved behaviour. 'Efe is eccentric, just when you think he has become good that's when he confounds you with the strangest thing,' Otabunor said to herself. The river to Efe was no longer something to fondle, rather it had become a source of fear and danger; of something to be wary.

But one day Efe was going to the river to fetch water and he saw the riverine boys running down from the mangrove side of the river. They had some fish with them.

'Hey Efe!' one of them called. 'We don't see you again? We've been catching many. You know it's rainy season, very many now in the river.'

'I won't join you again,' answered Efe uninterestedly.

'Why? The other day your hook caught a big one. But we didn't see you so we crunched it.'

The boy began to laugh as he demonstrated with his mouth. Efe looked at him with some jealousy.

'Efe, don't mind this fool,' the oldest one among them consoled him as he noticed that Efe was deeply upset and might want to cry. He offered Efe one of the fish. Efe quietly slipped it into his pocket.

'Don't worry, you can still join us. Tomorrow, we shall be out there,' he pointed to the direction of the mangrove swamp, where they set their fish hooks. 'Join us after school.'

Efe did not reply. But it set him thinking when the young anglers had gone. His father had warned him against moving with the riverine boys and he had obeyed that, he said to himself. His getting almost drowned had nothing to do with fishing, he continued his introspection. It was his carelessness, he told himself. *And if not for that incident that almost took my life...*he was close to tears now as he relived the experience. He roasted the fish on the fire when he got home and withdrew to a quiet place where he ate it. He enjoyed it very much, a delicacy he had been enjoying regularly before and became sad that he was missing it. That night he was weighing everything in his mind again.

The following afternoon, after Efe returned from school, he was sitting at a corner of the veranda of his father's house. He watched for sometime the goings and comings in their compound. His father was sleeping. The women had gone to farm. But there were children in the compound. He sneaked away when he noticed they were not mindful of his presence. As he went, he looked back from time to time to see if anyone was watching him. Close to the slope of the waterside, he diverted into the other side of the river and finally disappeared into the mangrove swamps. He was going far inside beyond where the riverine boys usually fished. He wanted to go it alone quietly this time. He had carefully taken his fish hooks from the former fishing spot that morning and hid them somewhere among some twigs. He took them out and also took his can of worms and kept going inside the swamps. He was moving farther and farther, going beyond human activities, and it was getting thicker and darker. He reached a point where it was difficult to tell the day from the night. But beyond this spot, was some opening into the river. It piqued his curiosity. He could see shafts of sunlight in front of him. And he was determined to get there. He slashed his way through the dark thick mangrove swamps with great care. The place had some mysterious air around it which seemed to ward off all human activities from it. The cold calmness of the place was terrifying. A sudden air of overwhelming fear whirled round Efe as he went. He began to tremble. His head was swelling with fear. A solemn voice inside him told him to run back. But he could feel another mysterious urging which he could not resist as he was hearing the pounding of his heart now. He continued moving forward, without really knowing what was propelling him, even though his entire being was dissolving in fears. At a point, he was completely seized by a spasm of trembling – and he could not move again. He was about to scream when he heard a loud and tumultous splashing into the river in his front, and he saw a large tail of fish with feminine human appearance surging into the deep. He leaped backwards unconsciously, abandoning everything and raced through the swamps, falling and rising. He could not feel the hindering creepers of the entire thick swamps. It seemed the encumbrance nature of the mangrove swamps never existed. He ran as quickly as he could and he never looked back. He kept running until he reached his father's veranda in the back and began to pant ceaselessly. The few persons, who saw him as he ran out of the swamps, thought that something dangerous was after his life. They looked back but could not see anything pursuing him. They began to wonder if the boy had gone insane as his running did not have any semblance of play: they saw real fright behind it.

When the tension in Efe had come down, he began to feel sharp pains in his body. He noticed for the first time that there were some injuries on his body which hurt him severely. He wanted to cry when he saw that he was badly bruised too but he quickly restrained himself for fear of attracting attention. He was thinking of how to hide the injuries from the inquisitive eyes of his mother to save him from explanations which might put him in trouble. He was happy that nobody in the compound saw him when he ran in. He peeped into the compound and saw his mother, Otabunor, and two other women conversing in front of her apartment. Though, he was not seeing his father, he could hear his voice from the other side of the veranda where he usually sat in his special deck-chair. He was still looking at the injuries and bruises on his body when he overheard his mother complaining that she had not seen Efe since she returned from farm, wondering where he must have gone. He became more attentive at that point.

'Mamma, I saw Efe jumping into the veranda in the back of the house, not long ago,' said Onojome, the youngest child in the family who was playing with other children at the centre of the compound.

'See, if he's still there,' Otabunor told the little boy.

Immediately Efe heard that, he ran away from the veranda. He would not have them see the wounds. After he had squeezed the sap of some leaves believed to heal wounds on the affected parts of his body, he began to catch some butterflies among a group of flowers around one uncompleted building that was a bit isolated from the rest houses in the quarter. And when he saw people passing he would duck among the tall grass in the building.

As soon as night began, the terror of what he saw inside the swamps came back to him. He ran out of the place and came to the back of his father's house again. He remained there watching people passed to and from the river until night enveloped him there.

When he eventually came home that night his mother asked him a few questions. Efe preferred to remain quiet. In her annoyance, his mother flung the broom upon him several times and Efe ran to a corner and began to cry. But he was happy that his mother did not notice anything

As he lay on his mat that night, the terror at the river that day returned to him .Whenever he closed his eyes as he tried to sleep, the frightful scene would flash across. He could hear the terrifying splashing all over again. His head began to swell again with fear where he lay and he was unable to sleep. In his anxious anticipation of dawn the tormenting night became endless.

CHAPTER TEN

Good as the 'Macpherson Constitution' was, for setting the stage for mass participation in the affairs of the country, it however foreshadowed tribal policking. All the nationalistic passion that was inspired by famous nationalists across the country, earlier, was neutralised by emerging educated local leaders whom the Constitution threw up and their tribal leaning was richly fertilized by the permutation of the country into three regions by the previous 'Richard Constitution'. These emerging political leaders were more interested in empire-building by making their particular ethnic groups the bases of their political parties, which were more of personality cults. And this dwarfed the nationalistic tendency of the people and nationalistic sentiment began to take the back seat in the affairs of the country. Since then, ethnicism or tribalism became the lens through which every political action was viewed. After Independence, tribalism grew rapidly into exceedingly huge ogre which terrorized the entire socio-political environment of the country. Tribalism later bore another political monster, politics of intolerance with some religious blend. And the two formed an unholy alliance against nation building in their ferocious attacks. All this crystalised in fierce election violence and rigging, especially *operation wetie*[16] in the western part of the country, and the country was heading towards precipice.

The military, almost by default, ostensibly emerged from their obscure barracks to remedy the situation. But they were also felled in one swoop by the same combined forces of tribalism and socio-political intolerance and in no time they plunged the country into a three-year long bloody civil war.

More than tribalism and political intolerance, the military governments which came in succession eventually sank down to corruption, plundering the country became their main interest. Encouraged by the discovery of vast petroleum deposits in the Niger Delta and its staggering wealth, many of their officers became overnight millionaires. They were not alone; the bureaucrats and top civil servants were happy that the young military rulers relied on them

---

[16] Official name for measures adopted by security and military forces to counteract the widespread arson and mayhem that followed the regional election of 1964 in Western Nigeria, which witnessed massive rigging in favour of a party supported by the federal government.

for guidance and ideas. And they celebrated like a jackpot winner who woke up one morning to find that he was stupendously rich. They began to compete with their military masters in amassing huge wealth for themselves. Not long after retirement, they began to parade themselves as 'captains of industries,' 'director of this...director of that...' and yet the people's lives remained almost the same. Huge amounts of money from oil proceeds were stashed away, breathing safely and quietly in foreign banks to enrich other lands. Practically every one of them who found himself in the corridors of power only thought of how much he could make by his office. Budget implementation, contract negotiation, project execution, and more, were ready avenues for amassing wealth for oneself. And all these government activities became rivers of money that flowed into individuals' bank accounts. This new tendency went down the ladder and soon turned into a national philosophy. Rather than increasing the national assets and productivity, the political class began to plunder the existing ones and spent their loots recklessly. And the country became an insatiable consumer of all manner of foreign goods. But not to worry, the oil wealth was always there.

The military regimes became so crimson in corruption that it made the politicians of old, saints in the eye of the world. Besides tribalism and intolerance, the politicians of old worked hard to develope their regions and their peoples. Whereas this army of occupation and their bureaucrats were in the main, concerned with lining their pockets, every sector of the country began to experience neglect and rot as the country experienced one military coup after another. The brief civilian interregnum that came much later did not do anything to stem the tide rather they believed it was their turn to enrich themselves, too.

The people watched helplessly with resignation. They struggled daily against all odds to survive the locust economic policies of the military elite. Life became unbearable for the ordinary people. Life began to lose meaning. It became too vulnerable and miserable and the people were desperate for survival. They could not vent their frustration against their predators because they knew that the bullet would trigger off in such event. But frustration must find a way of expression, and upon themselves they vented their frustration – they became selfish and exploited one another in their desperate bid to survive _ their God-given heart of love and kindness lost its natural impulse to react to pitiable circumstances among themselves. The only thing they could see in every circumstance was how to turn every situation to their personal gain. What crystalised out of all this, in the society, was insatiable naked greed and avarice and it was enacted in every facet of life including religion. And these new national ethos found expression in all forms of fraud and deceit among the citizens.

CHAPTER ELEVEN

When the news of the first military take-over of the reins of government in the country, came to Chief Akpovire in Akpobaro, he expressed very little surprise. Since he left government, he had been watching the political situation of the country with disgust, as politics was degenerating from issues and debates to fierce raw battle among politicians, and elections became a war theatre. He thought that the soldiers had come to restore sanity and order to the political scene. But when the young military officers started playing ethnic card with their coups, he began to lose confidence in them. He was also getting worried about their approach to governance. Without feeling the pulse of the people, they issued orders and commands and expected the people to comply with 'immediate effect' like robots. As he watched successive military governments sinking deeper into the mire of maladministration, he became very disenchanted with state affairs. At a point, he became anxious that the country might be heading towards the rock. But much as he feared the outcome, he never thought by any stretch of imagination that he would be a direct casualty of their misrule.

One hush Monday morning, just like another coup, the current military junta announced the cancellationof all 'modern secondary schools' from the education system and the take-over of all private schools in the country by government like a cross of the pen over a document. As usual with such military pronouncement, they made it clear that the concellation and the take-over were with immediate effect. The announcement came to Chief Akpovire like a bombblast. His face wrinkled with shock at once. 'No, it can't be,' he shouted unconsciously. He thought there was a mistake in his hearing. Chief Akpovire was more worried about the college in which he had invested so much. In his confusion, he became too agitated to have a clear mind. He desired to hear the news again - it was too quick a flash in his thought. He tried to convince himself that that was not exactly what he heard. He listened to the radio again but it was broadcasting other news. He turned it off and hissed in frustration. He stood up and walked to his dining room aimlessly. Came back, turned the radio on again and turned it off almost at the same time, and remained where he sat. Still, he could not contain himself. His breathing was now heavy and laboured. 'All modern secondary schools are cancelled forthwith. All other private schools across the country are hereby

118

taken-over by the government with immediate effect. Any act of disobedience against this order shall be ruthlessly dealth with.' The words re-echoed in his memory as Chief Akpovire reflected. In a reflex, he shook his head, probably in an attempt to shake the bad news off him but that could only be a wishful thinking. 'I think that was not what I heard,' he said to himself again. Unfortunately, he was alone in his living room. He needed somebody else to confirm it. Chief Akpovire went to sit in his deck-chair and began to think. He placed his hand on one side of his cheeks and allowed his thought to wander freely for sometime. *If this is true how am I going to do it? I have spent my last cash on that college and now....* the remaining words choked up in his throat as he became more consumed with the frightful uncertainty of the future. 'How can somebody be destroyed in this reckless manner,' he said to himself and suddenly became pale with anxiety where he sat. He heaved a sigh of vague relief when he heard in his mind again, *You might not have heard it, right. Why don't you confirm the news from others?* He thought that was the best thing to do and became a bit composed. He was just thinking of going over to his headmaster when he heard a flurry of knocks on his door. It was the headmaster and two senior teachers of the modern secondary school. Immediately Chief Akpovire saw their long faces and their ruffled composure, his face dropped in distress at once.

Later, the State Ministry of Education took over all the primary schools and the colleges that were privately owned including the *missions' schools* while the 'modern secondary school' was completely erased from the school system as earlier announced. The government argued that education was too important to be left in the hands of private individuals or groups.

Chief Akpovire's case was worse. Apart from the outright cancellation of his modern secondary school, his college had not started, so it was not taken over by government. As a result, he could not get the paltry hands-out government gave to those whose schools were taken as compensation for their property. The college was to have started the following academic session. All the preparations towards it were almost ready. The necessary blocks of class rooms and offices were ready including the expensive science laboratory. The principal and the teachers had been recruited and had just started the process of admission when the unexpected happened. All these were hitherto necessary for the registration of the college with the Ministry of Education, and to get all these requisites ready for the commencement of the college in the approaching session, the entire life of Chief Akpovire was sunk into it. Then the devastating news came, shattering the whole dream to pieces.

The tragedy was not only for Chief Akpovire. The entire Omaurhie people felt it and mourned it. It was the most ambitious project that was to come to them. In the last one month of entrance examination and interview into the college, Omaurhie community witnessed the influx of township men with their children, coming for admission into the college. For the first time, public transports had a route to Omaurhie. Few personal cars were also seen driving to Okuemo on regular basis, and the people knew they were all in connection with the college. They saw such happenings as a sign of great things to come, and were all looking forward to the opening day of the college. Like a mirror, many boys and a handful of girls in Omaurhie villages often trekked several miles to have a look at the college, dreaming of the day they would gain entrance into this great institution of learning. They admired the barbed wire fence, the array of splendid flowering trees on the main lane leading into the college, which had been planted since the time of conception, the main field, the lawn tennis, handball, volley ball and basket ball courts. Some of the newly recruited teachers had started enjoying the lawn tennis court. These boys and girls simply could not contain themselves in their admiration when they came to see the college. The people of Okuemo were most particularly happy. They had been watching all the developments of the college with keen interest, anxiously waiting for the college opening day, like a farmer patiently waiting to harvest his farm. So when the news of the concellation and take-over of private schools exploded in the village, the people of Okuemo were too confounded to believe it. At first, they dismissed it as the wild rumour of their jealous neighbours. And when it became clear, the embarrassing shock that befell them remained palpable for long. They could not imagine their dream of urban life coming to their village, Okuemo, disappearing into the air in a flash.

Chief Akpovire remained upset and crestfallen for days. Everyday, he sat in his house with a forlorn disposition, brooding over his misfortune. He hardly ate and when he did, it was to please his wives who were becoming alarmed over his wretched state. One day Otabunor, his most senior wife, came to him in his living room. 'The food is on the table,' she knelt down. 'Thank you,' answered Chief Akpovire absent-mindedly and Otabunor left. She would have waited to see her husband walk to the table, but these days Chief Akpovire preferred to be left alone. He had not said so but his attitude

120

said it all. Reluctantly, his wives kept away from him a little, to avoid any trouble, but their eyes never left him. One hour later, Otabunor came back. The food was still there untouched. 'Masa, you've not eaten your food?' 'I shall eat it,' said Chief Akpovire with some reluctance. Thirty minutes later, Otabunor came again to see. 'You still haven't eaten your meal? 'Don't worry yourself my dear, I shall eat it. 'You've been saying that, yet you don't move. Masa,' she sat by his side, 'you can't continue like this. Put it behind you and think of other means. Life must go on. It shouldn't depend on one thing. After all, you have lived by several other things. Your timber business is still there. Are you not the one that often say "Life is improbable"?' 'Yes, I often say that my dear wife. But this is different! Everything, all that I have, is in that college. The concellation has ruined my life. How will I start life again? With what?' lamented Chief Akpovire almost tears. Otabunor became short of words as she had never seen her husband betraying strong emotion in this manner. She was deeply touched by his reaction. She felt like crying for him. 'Well, Masa, time, the ultimate healer will heal this painful wound,' she said. Otabunor eventually succeeded in moving Chief Akpovire to the dining room. He tried to eat, at least to satisfy her. He took some morsels and some fish and pushed the food aside – he had no appetite.

Some days later, some eminent chiefs from the various Omaurhie villages came to see Chief Akpovire. They had come to commiserate with him. At the last central chiefs-in-Council at Ugbevwe, they agreed to send a delegation to him. The over all *Ugo* of the entire Omaurhie people led the deputation. When they came, Chief Akpovire was reading the previous day newspaper. As usual, he offered them drinks and kola-nuts. At the beginning, they talked about general news that inspired laughter among them and the situation became warm. Chief Akpovire participated and laughed with them. He *was* very happy to see many people around him. Their conversation gradually took a turn and gravitated towards the banning of private schools across the country.

'When these boys came to take over government, many people began to celebrate and say, "It's good for the country",' said Chief Okposio. 'I looked at them and laughed. I told them that they were celebrating too early. You see, you do not presume that a new wife is good simply because the previous one was bad. It is when a man has married another wife before he can truly tell whether the previous one was actually bad. What are we seeing now? Is this not madness?' he waved his hand with disdain and hissed.

'Okposio, you're right. Why should a big country like ours allow boys with hot blood to rule them? We have just started shouting. But I believe a time is coming when we cannot even shout but dumb-struck by their actions. When it gets to that point, only the Almighty Creator can deliver us from their hands,' said another Chief.

'Almighty Creator?' Mudiaga retorted. 'Will he come down from his abode beyond the sky? We have made our mistakes. Let me tell you, what we have just done by allowing those boys to rule is not different from giving a little boy a loaded gun to play with. You can imagine what he's going to do with it.'

And every one of them began to laugh.

'We can still laugh now,' Mudiaga went on, 'but those laughters shall soon cease.'

And they laughed even more.

'If they misbehave too much they shall be thrown out,' one of them said in a lighter mood.

'Throw who out?' said Mudiaga cynically. 'Who will throw them out? Those boys are not different from any young man you can scold and insult and nothing happens. But the same kind of boys will come to your house at night, brandishing guns and other dangerous weapons and you begin to convulse like a baby and obey their orders without questions while they loot you silly.'

All of them started laughing again.

'It's true, that's the situation we have in our hands now,' Chief Akpovire added with all air of seriousness and a silence of grave pessimism fell in.

The overall *Ugo* had been waiting for this opportunity. He was conscious of the fact that people could be carried away by the accessories of an important matter, if they formed an interesting conversation.

'Councillor,' the *Ugo* started, 'our people say that, *what humans do not experience in this wide world does not exist.* What they mean by that is that we will continue to experience strange things in this our world. That's why we should not be surprise when the unexpected happens to us.'

And all of them nodded their heads attentively in total agreement.

'We cannot avoid them. But the way we handle them determines whether we can overcome them or not, and they are equally a test of our maturity.'

122

The *Ugo* was not in a hurry, he was picking his words carefully and slowly so that they could have the desire effect, and he was happy to observe that Chief Akpovire and every other person in the house was nodding their heads with much appreciation as the words came upon them as pestle comes upon mortar. He could feel the grave mood which his words had turned the house.

'When the government strange news concerning the college and the modern secondary school came, it knocked down everybody in the entire Omaurhie. Councillor, you're not alone in this. We all are affected. We know what the two schools meant to us – the loss is everybody's in Omaurhie – as our people would say, *when a great tree falls, some other smaller ones beside it collapse with it.* But we also know that when a misfortune affects many people, there's a varying degree – there are the most affected – that's why we, the elders of our community thought that, even with the load of the grief in our hearts, we should still come to you and say, *doh.*[17] Because it is by so doing, we can share the grief together and reduce its weight, as we all know, when we allow one person or each of us in our own individual ways to bear it, we might crumble in it. Councillor, we must accept life as it is. I know you are a man of great strength of character and you must take this with such courage. I thank you.'

Chief Akpovire went over the *Ugo*'s words in his mind for sometime before responding.

'My people, I thank you all. I am quite happy to see you all around me at a time like this.'

He paused for a second.

'You see, when a great misfortune happens to a man and nobody comes to him, the thought of that alone may cause him greater pain than his misfortune. That is why we always go to a kinsman or woman in misfortune. It is a great healing. Let me tell you that, your coming has brought me much relief and I thank you all for it. Some of us might not appreciate the importance of this kind of visitation until they find themselves in a pit of misfortune; we should not wait for that to happen. One thing this experience has taught me is that, nobody is actually in charge of his own living. We're in a precarious world. Please, convey my gratitude to the entire elders-in-Council when you get back. I thank you all again.'

17

The deputation took a round of drink before their parting greeting.

When they had left, Chief Akpovire returned to his gloom. He was a man of great courage as the *Ugo* had said; a man of great resilience. That the situation could shatter him to the level it did showed the gravity of the devastation in his life. There was one question that kept rolling up in his mind: 'How am I going to start again?' He could feel the emptiness of a brave man who had been drained of his strength completely, and whenever he remembered the dream and vision and the tiresome effort he put into the college, he would feel like shattering into pieces.

But he did not betray his emotion to his visitors. Chief Akpovire was a man who conducted himself with great dignity before others. Once someone came in, he would cover his bruised ego in a dignified smile and comportment, so nobody really knew the depth of his sorrow except his wives who kept watching over him as a worried mother would over her dying sick baby

CHAPTER TWELVE

Chief Akpovire eventually pulled himself together after sometime. But not until his wives and some of his friends like Mudiaga had continuously comforted and consoled him for sometime. He soon resumed his timber business. It was not an easy beginning as he had spent all that he had on the college, especially when he had an obligation to supply his white customers – Mr. Jones and Mr. Dentist – certain quantity of logs for a quarter, and a good part of their credit had been urgently spent to complete the college with the firm belief that the money would be recouped after the admission of students. Arising from this financial constraint, he decided to raise capital from several sources including an overdraft from his bank at Safa, for his timber business to go on. And as he concentrated on his timber business his life began to improve again. His wives were very happy to see him radiating warmth again and his past dignity soon returned. Led by Otabunor, his three wives went round to thank Chief Akpovire's friends who joined them in making their husband overcome his grief.

Chief Akpovire was also very appreciative. One evening, he called his three wives in Akpobaro, to his living room after dinner. That was one of the days he returned from Safa after the sales of his timbers. They were somewhat agitated as it had never been his habit, to call his three wives at the same time. The circumstance was thought-provoking for his wives. They stood before him, not knowing what to expect. 'Have your seats, please,' said Chief Akpovire calmly as they entered. He got up from his deck-chair and went into his bedroom. Chief Akpovire soon returned with his cupboard keys. He opened the unit of drink and brought out one of the most expensive wine. He put it on the centre table. That done, he went for glasses. His youngest wife, Omatie, ran after him to take over whatever he required to do, as it was not customary for a husband to do such domestic chores before his wife. But Chief Akpovire shoved her. 'Leave everything for me,' said he, in a manner that suggested, 'It's my entire affair, keep off.' He brought out four glasses and a saucer and put them beside the wine. Very quickly, two big kola-nuts and a guinea stood in the saucer. With some kind of felicity and amusement, his wives watched their much respected husband dart here and there, domesticating like a house-wife. It was like an interesting life drama being enacted before them.

'Yes, my beloved wives,' began Chief Akpovire when the table was set, as he balanced in his couch with dignified carriage. 'Even our own cup we wash it,' Chief Akpovire said with a smile, 'so say our people. I just realise that a good and faithful wife is an integral and indispensable part of a man's greatness. No wonder, the ever wise Creator whose mighty hand is on everything that affects us, saw the need to create a woman for a man. I never appreciated this fact until very recently. My good and faithful wives, I can never express the depth of my appreciation. But I will never forget your mighty hands of resue when I was drowning in a ruthless action of government. I thank you very much.

'My Lord,' said Ogevwe the second wife, 'but we are your wives. We are here to support and comfort you.'

'You're right, my honourable wife and you have always been doing that. But I had never realised that that role is so deep and profound. I think I may have been taken it for granted. That I am alive and kicking today is because of you. You were solid clutches to accident lame victim, without which he wouldn't have been able to walk again. You can never appreciate what you did to pull me through that morass that would have swallowed me. I thank the Almighty One today that it is over. My good and faithful wives, words can never be enough but I must say this, you have made me realise that, of all that I have, you are the greatest and the most valuable of them all. I am sure the Almighty One that sees everything and rewards adequately will fully recompense you. However, I have a little, at least, to show to night, that I appreciate all that you did. Please accept it with all the love in your hearts. They are little, but they represent something in my heart which I cannot fully express.'

To each of them he gave the best valued wrapper money could buy at the time.

His three wives did not know what to say; they were too amused: they kept smiling and laughing interchangeably – too full of elation and surprise. As they received their choice wrappers, they went down on their knees, 'Masa *miguo*,' greeted each.

'*Shuu*! this is very fine,' one of them exclaimed as she kept admiring her own.

'Very fine!' the other two added almost together.

'*Migwo*, Masa,' they repeated their greetings almost unconsciously, as they still could not believe their eyes.

126

'Masa, you surprise us! Who knew I was going to have such an expensive wrapper?' said Otabunor excitedly.

'Even me,' Ogevwe added.

'How could we have known?' the youngest wife, Omatie, said amusingly.

Chief Akpovire was beaming with smile, too. He was very pleased to see his three wives reacting this way.

'But you deserve it,' he grinned.

'Yes, of course. Why shouldn't the wives of Chief Akpovire, the foremost chief in the entire Omaurhie, not tie a wrapper like this?' quipped the youngest wife in an outburst of joy. She tied the wrapper round her waist and began to swing her buttocks in apparent show-off. The other two joined her. They began to say and demonstrate to each other in a dance:

> Who is your husband?
> Chief Akpovire is my husband
> The foremost chief in the entire Omaurhie is my husband!
> Why then will I not show off in expensive clothes?
> Surely, I will!

They sang to each other as they shook their buttocks to the admiration of Chief Akpovire.

'Our great husband you have treated us with an uncommon honour and generosity,' said Otabunor while accepting the drink and the kola-nut and the money later. 'And we feel highly flattered by this singular treatment. Certainly, we accept our most amiable husband's drink, kola-nuts and money with all humility and gratitude. Our good and great husband, we thank you. As you have honoured us, your wives today, so shall the Almighty Creator honour you, bless you with good health, long life and more prosperity.'

'Amen!' chorused the other two.

'And I shall see many more beautiful ones in my bed,' Chief Akpovire chipped in teasingly and his three wives fell back at once with laughter where they sat as the tickle threw them backward like a bomb. And from then onward, it was all excitement, laughter and celebration. It lasted close to midnight – they never remembered sleep. It was a night that cast the three women who strove among themselves to have a better attention of one man into one mould of love, which knew no line; a night they wished could last forever – blissful, savouring and breath-taking.

CHAPTER THIRTEEN

Few years later, the modern secondary school and the college fell into ruin. Lizards and a few rodents had found a home in them and their surroundings. They ran about, enjoying themselves in their beautiful habitations, as creepers and bushes had taken over the two schools after abandonment. The people had also forgotten the existence of the schools. Even Chief Akpovire hardly thought of them now, his timber business was thriving and had been engaging him. His pre-eminent position as the foremost chief in the entire Omaurhie villages remained established. He still remained the liaison between the police and Akpobaro people. The people complacently carried on with their traditional farming and the land remained good and fertile. Fishing and cutting of palm fruit in the surrounding bushes remained attractive to settlers in the community. The chiefs-in-Council were ever satisfied with the royalties they received from them from time to time. The local distillers had no reason to complain. Their *ogogoro* travelled far places and the hunters returned home every morning with games. Scorchearth and Comrade continued in their buffoonery and the children remained excited always in their presence. The moonlight still summoned the children in Akpobaro to play and story-telling.

But one day, the people of Akpobaro woke up to find some strangers on their farmlands. They wore helmets, boots and overalls and they seemed to be doing some photographing and measurement of the land. The head of the group was a white man. Parked near-by, on the farm road, was their truck. They were marking trees, including rubber trees.

The Akpobaro people were stupefied by the sudden appearance of the strange workers on their farmlands. They observed them for sometime with some measure of discomfort, distrust and insecurity without really knowing what to do. That evening the story of the strangers on their farmlands went round the Akpobaro. Many of the people who did not go to that side of their farms the first day, went the following day to confirm the story. They saw the strangers with some apparatus as it was told. Most obvious of which was the one like the tripod of a camera. The sight of the white man among them heightened their curiosity. The third day, the strangers were still there. They came in their truck every morning. They did their survey for about three weeks. After a week or so the people became less mindful of them as they observed that the band of workers was never distracted by their presence. They were so concentrated on their work and had not done any damage to their farms, yet. They just marked and cleared the line but left the farms untouched on their survey.

Shockingly, when they had finished their markings, they started cutting down everything they had marked previously, including the rubber trees. They also cleared the farm crops and every other thing on their surveyed line. The people came to the chiefs to complain and emergency meeting of the chiefs-in-Council was summoned the following day. Unfortunately, Chief Akpovire was in Safa. At the end of the chiefs' meeting, the village resolved to wait for Chief Akpovire. They had always relied on him in external matters like this. While they were waiting, a message was passed round, through the town crier, advising the people to refrain from any action against the foreign workers on their land and the people heeded.

It was raining season, their farm road was gradually being damaged as the truck of the stranger workers conveyed them through the uneven farm road daily and after three weeks the road started having gullies of water. The women and men who plied the road everyday with their carrier-bicycles were now finding it increasingly difficult to ride the road with their farm loads. Most times, they found themselves rolling and pushing their heavily loaded bicycles through the gullies on the road rather than riding. The large majority of the villagers who tramped the road daily were not better off. They had to use one hand to fold their clothes up beyond their knees to pass the deepening gullies, while the other hand clung tenaciously to the farm loads on their heads. For the-not-so-strong - the old, the deformed and the children - the ordeal was ghastly. At each of the flooded gullies on the farm road, they had to be smart and clever in contriving their escape. Some of them had fallen in with their farm loads and got wet. When it became unbearable, Akpobaro's youths made a detour round each of the deep gullies which brought some relief. But often bicycles collided as they went the narrow winding paths which sometimes resulted in serious accidents.

On Chief Akpovire's return, the stranger workers had left. But investigation later revealed that they were workers of Bacco Company – a geological servicing company which came to prospect for oil in the area for Starling Oil Company. Akpobaro decided to write to Bacco, requesting them to rehabilitate their farm road which had been damaged by their truck and was now in a state of disrepair. They also wanted compensation for their damaged crops and economic trees.

Chief Akpovire had assured the people that their requests would be granted, as he believed that the two multinationals had standards of operations and were highly responsible. His confidence was rooted in the belief that their requests were genuine. He was elated about their prospecting into Akpobaro. Chief Akpovire told the people that if oil was found in the land, they should count themselves lucky, as it would bring great development and wealth to the community.

'We must tell our people that they should not unnecessarily be disturbed over the damage and disruption. I am sure all that will be settled later. But we must be patient. Multinational companies have standard procedures. We should give them time. I think what should be of greater concern to us is the discovery of oil in the bowels of our land. Their coming suggests that there's a prospect. If that happens, we shall find ourselves in another planet; a new world of splendour. You can never believe it! I have heard about lands where crude oil is found in other countries. The people on such lands have money like water,' and the chiefs almost burst into laughter. They knew Chief Akpovire was not a man to be doubted but they felt he was becoming too excited about the prospect of oil discovery in the community. Ordinarily, they would have exploded in real laughter but their 'Councillor' was never to be treated lightly.

'You cannot believe me, I know,' added Chief Akpovire. 'How can you? After all, we have never found oil in this country, except one very little one at Oloibiri in the riverine area. Just pray, and you will see what I am talking about.'

When Bacco Company received the letter of Akpobaro, they forwarded it to Starling. Starling wrote back, explaining that their requests were being looked into. Akpobaro community received Starling reply with joy and they began to trust all that Chief Akpovire had told them. They now looked forward to the upgrading of their farm road and a handsome compensation for their destroyed crops and economic trees.

For some months, they did not hear from Starling. But their confidence did not dimmed as Chief Akpovire had earlier admonished them about the standard procedures of the company.

Gradually, everything about the oil company and its prospecting in the area began to fade out of their memories. The surveyed line was fast being covered with growing bushes. Many of the painted pegs on the surveyed lane had fallen too. The few standing ones were no longer noticeable. The farm road too had levelled up in the following dry season. By the second year, every trace of the activities of oil prospecting in the area had disappeared and the idea of compensation was now remote in their memories, as the harvests of the affected farms were over. The new planting season had begun. The people were preoccupied with the cultivation of new farms. Some had planted their first farms which began with the end of the harmattan. In their first farms, they planted cassava and water-yam. The planting of the normal yam was reserved for their main farms which began around March, as it could not survive the period from the dried harmattan to the entry of the rainy season. The planting season was the busiest. Once they finished their first farms, farming would begin in earnest. They would rise very early in the morning to their farms and come back in the twilight. The proper farming was very demanding and challenging. It separated the big farmers from the lazy and the small ones. During the period, only children and the invalid were seen in the village in the day.

In spite of the attention giving to planting during the period, the foodstuffs they brought to the market on market day did not diminish. The period called for extra effort. The people had to double their effort to get their farm produce ready for market day. Their market was the biggest among the Omaurhie villages. Akpobaro was geographically strategic. It was a border town. The people of Uloh were their eastern neighbour and they always came to the market with their farm produce. Many communities on the other side of the river ferried to the market by large commercial engine boats built like a house. They were mainly traders. They would bring finished products to sell while some others came to buy foodstuffs which they took to bigger markets elsewhere. People also came by lorries from Safa. The market often engulfed the entire village by midday – that was its peak. For a first comer, it was always difficult to locate the market place at this time. Many petty traders hawked their wares round the village including the medicine sellers. The Hausa traders from the up north also came with their locally made perfume. All these hawkers roved everywhere for buyers. One often heard now and then, 'fried rice', 'cooked eggs', 'buy medicine', 'fried groundnuts', 'sweet buns', 'buy pomade...' all in discordant voices like the sounds of a great number of frogs in a large pool of stagnant water. Their voices were often rendered in musical catchy tunes, quite distinct from their natural voices, with strong patronising appeal which often had great effect on the people.

The Akpobaro people were a tiny fraction among those who bought these wares. Many of the villagers far and near poured into Akpobaro on their market day to sell and buy things, especially people from the neighbouring villages who brought their foodstuffs for sale. Young boys and girls assisted their mothers in bringing down loads of foodstuffs on foot. To encourage them, some of the food items which they considered special were bought for them. It was also a day of shopping for the women, as most of the articles were only available on market days so both the women of Akpobaro and those of other villages bought all they needed before the next market day, which were mainly food ingredients that they were not producing on their farms.

****

On one market day, as usual, the whole Akpobaro was brimming over with buying and selling when a repeated sound of explosion shook the entire village and beyond for sometime. The very foundation of the earth seemed to be crumbling in the tremor. It caused a great panic. People ran here and there in great confusion, seeking for place to hide. Those outside dashed into any coverings they could find. Those in their houses ran under beds, tables or dashed into the inner rooms for safety. The hawkers did not know when they threw their wares away and ran for safety. The entire Akpobaro was panic-stricken. People thought of all sorts of things; it was an earthquake or the *Armageddon*. Fear gripped the entire village and the entire people were dead with fear where each of them hid. Akpobaro was suddenly turned into a ghost village, all the bustling market activities disappeared in a second. There was complete nervous calmness for sometime.

When the explosion had stopped, some of the men of Akpobaro came out. Others were still cautious. Many more came out after some minutes and the rest followed. The tension and anxiety started coming down. Although they were a bit relieved, it was with great caution they began to make inquiry about the incident. Very soon the news came that they were blasts carried out by some people believed to be those that came to damage their crops and farm road two years ago.

'Those people again!' shouted a woman.

'That's what the men who went to find out are saying,' answered another woman.

More of the seismic blasts were later heard from another location in the river.

****

A good quantity of crude oil had been found in the locality and Bacco Company had begun their seismic operation and it went on for days. The company encamped in one area in the farmland. Heavy duty trucks had moved in caravans, heavy machines and big pipes. To facilitate their operations, a narrow rough tarring of the farm road to their base, their central oil location, was effected in no time. The road was no longer the route of farmers. It had become very busy as different trucks drove past now and then. White men in over-alls decked with different kinds of helmets had become a regular sight on the road. At the beginning they always heard 'oyibo! oyibo!' when they drove past the local folk, particularly from the children. But the excitement of seeing them soon trailed off as they became too familiar after sometime.

Not only Bacco trucks plied the road now. Many business men and women from town also drove to their base regularly. They were contractors and suppliers of Bacco and Starling. They brought foodstuffs, drinks, tools and all the needed stocks to the camp. Some of these firms also handled some specific minor engineering services for Bacco. They had their own workers too and their camp became a beehive of activities. Accommodation became very scarce in Akpobaro. Many of the workers and a good number of Bacco workers who could not get accommodation in the camp at their central location had to find a place to stay in Akpobaro and the entire village became overwhelmed with strangers during this time. Many of the workers who could not secure accommodation in Akpobaro were forced to stay in the neighbouring villages. Some Akpobaro's youths were lucky to find menial jobs at the various sites of construction activities.

But the camp which was the central oil location was also the centre of all the operations. A huge derrick was being raised at the camp. The camp was to be the flow-station to all the various oil-wells being constructed on the sprawling farmland and beyond. Several engineering activities were taking place, day and night. Many people from the other Omaurhie villages often came to see for themselves as they could not believe the story about the camp at the central location when they were told. They saw a crane lifting things and workmen on the rig; and the risk in their operations. They saw a heavy machine being driven underground. They also saw a helicopter flying in and out with workers almost on daily basis.

At the camp, there was a residential side, made up of caravans arranged in rows. The first rate and highly skilled workers, mainly the whites occupied the choicest rows, followed by the second rate workers who were the senior staff of both companies, and the last rows were for the technicians, artisans and the sundry support staff in the site. The entire site was adorned with flood lights, both the operational and the residential areas of the camp were highly illuminated at night. All the necessary facilities that would make the camp a real home were well provided in the residential area. For maximum security, a very high barbed wire fence was erected round the site besides the heavy presence of policemen and well-trained security men with giant dogs.

As many oil-wells were being constructed in several places in Akpobaro's farmland, pipelines connecting these oil-wells to the flow-station began to criss-cross Akpobaro's land and beyond. The laying of pipelines also brought more jobs to Akpobaro's youths, as they were being taken as 'helpers' to the welders doing the main jobs. New social lifestyle also came with the 'oil activities.' Bacco's junior workers and their contractors' workers resident in Akpobaro had so much money. The oil industry was very lucrative and had a lot of fringe benefits for their workers and allied staff. These workers paid any amounts for food items they wanted at first asking; they never bargained. Food suppliers to their camp also began to source food items from the area too. They realised that the prices of foodstuffs were much cheaper than the ones they were previously getting from middlemen in town, besides the cost of transporting them down to the site. So they were encouraged to make their purchases at Akpobaro. All of which raised the prices of foodstuffs in Akpobaro.

The people of Akpobaro were very happy when the prices of their food items began to go up. With many job offers to their youths in the oil operations, they soon began to earn huge sums of money they never dreamt of in their lives.

Expectedly, house rents became suddenly very high and quickly formed a good source of income for Akpobaro community. As a result of the high demand for accommodation, kitchen houses and other accommodation attachments in a compound that were used for some special purposes other than accommodation were modified for rents. Hitherto, rented accommodations were remote in Akpobaro, apart from riverine settlers who had their own settlement in the community, all other residents were natives who lived in their traditional houses, so one could easily separate the natives from the settlers. But with the oil activities, the old order gave way. The high rent was so irresistible that there was hardly any house without oil worker tenants. The vacant partitioned rooms in their traditional women's abode which their young men used to stay before they built their own houses when they began family life were all let out. Others went beyond that to make an outlet into one or two rooms in their main houses and blocked the inner doors leading to the living room and let them out. Yet, some went further to erect makeshift accommodations for rent in their compounds and very soon the whole Akpobaro was overcrowded with these makeshift structures, as rents became a great source of income to this rural community that was once contented with very small amounts of income from their farm produce.

And life in Akpobaro witnessed a dramatic change. Hitherto, the people relished their cultural dances and music at festivals. Besides the festivals, music bands also entertained people at funerals, marriages and such other occasions that brought the people together, especially the youths who used such social gatherings to entertain themselves very well, especially in dance.

But the coming of many oil workers with township lifestyle following the oil activities in Akpobaro set a new standard of social behaviour among the youths. Just as sugar attracts ants so also money attracts easy life. Not long after, mobile film shows were staged twice in a week at Akpobaro in the evening by cinema centres at Safa, through local agents, and there was always a huge turn-out for them. Because of the high profit, more cinema centres in Safa entered the business and film shows became a daily night feature at Akpobaro and it was always a huge turn-out, to the extent that some of the middle-age men began to join the youths at the show. As time went by, disco was introduced.

Thick fence of palm fronds which was firmly secured with strong sticks was built round a large space in the village where the disco was organised. On the first day, a huge exciting crowd of youths took their turn to pay for tickets at the entrance. Makeshift bars soon appeared in its front for easy access to drinks, cigarettes, and the likes. At night, especially weekends, crowd of youths were regularly seen around the disco rendezvous. And as they partied through the night with intermittent sittings at the various makeshift bars to buy cigarettes and have some drinks. Sometimes, goat meat pepper soup was also provided in these bars and life became full for the youths. Many youths from the neighbouring villages also came in groups to have a full feel of the high life at Akpobaro at night.

For the native youths of Akpobaro the social change was most welcome. They saw it as a great release from what they now considered the conservative life they had hitherto been living, so they were happy.

With the regular visits of glamorous township girls to their boyfriends working in the oil companies at Akpobaro, it did not take long before the village girls began to follow their footsteps by engaging in sexual relationships with the oil workers, albeit secretly for fear of their parents and older relatives. This was only at the beginning. Gradually, they started going to the disco rendezvous and were seen drinking and freely romancing with the oil workers like their township counterparts to the displeasure of the village older members, and many cherished village values of decency began to give way as the youths now considered them primitive. All manner of fashions from the city were embraced by the local youths and Akpobaro began to wear some vague semblance of a town. Girls no longer remained in the cocoons of their family homes at night. They no longer ran away from the boys. But they now walked up to them when they whispered.

The elders and the chiefs in Akpobaro became very disturbed over the situation. They decided to use the village town-crier to warn against obscene behaviours in the village. But Akpobaro had gone beyond their grip. There were now too many strangers in the village. The youths now saw their elders and chiefs as people who could not understand the rhythm of the modern life and were no longer interested in what they now considered as 'the primitive life their elders lived in the past,' so the shows went on unhindered.

CHAPTER FOURTEEN

New developments continued to unfold. At the national level, military coups were staged in succession by army officers to topple one another, in their desperate bids to take a chance at government. But there was nothing new except fresh faces nay old faces, taking over more prominent positions. Their coup announcements had become so rehashed that they had lost their excitement. The people had long realised that military coup was not the solution rather it had become one dominant part of the country's political problem. What concerned the people each time they heard, 'Fellow Niamians ...' on radio at dawn, was to know if any of their ethnic persons was among the military officers that formed the new military junta. They looked forward to this for no other reason than to console themselves that the new junta had one of their indigenes benefiting from the government. This became the basis for supporting a government. If a citizen studied the list of names that formed the new military regime and could not find any trace of his ethnic people, he foreclosed any chance of benefits coming to his area. He quickly turned his back on the government and focused his full attention and hope on his personal struggle. In his ignorance, he thought that he could make his life meaningful without government, after all. Yet as he buzzed through the day and even the night, he still could hardly make ends meet. He had to brave all the many odds in the country to survive with his family yet he found it difficult to cope. Then, disillusionment would set in and he would become frustrated, bearing all the strains of his struggle on his face, yet he remained determined, believing that he would certainly make it someday, so his spirit remained unbreakable.

Like a bolt from the blue, came the news one early morning that one native of Akpobaro was among the prominent names in the latest military coup after several others, and he was appointed the Minister of Science and Technology. He was Brigadier-General Shevre Orode. There was a great celebration when the news reached Akpobaro. They thought that the sun of government was rising at Akpobaro and its sunshine would definitely illuminate everywhere in their land. It was more delightful to Chief Akpovire to know that the Brig-General Orode was a product of his erstwhile modern secondary school. Many products of the old school had also dispersed into several professions after climbing up the education ladder. Whenever they came home to the village they always paid their respects to Chief Akpovire like a chief paying his annual homage to his king who had installed him a prominent person in the society. The people of Akpobaro expected their Brigadier-General to come home and celebrate with them. But he never did. The army officers in government always considered such action derogatory, 'the attitude of bloody civilians.'

Like their predecessors, when they came to power, they talked tough with military arrogance about some drastic changes they planned to carry out to correct all the prevailing wrongs in the society. But the people knew that it was only a bluff. They had heard it several times before. They knew that their plans would soon crystallise into the continuum of ineptitude and corruption of other previous military rules with some cosmetic differences here and there. And one of such cosmetics was the appointment of a community-based leader as the sole administrator of every Council in the country. The previous military government appointed top civil servants to head the councils. There was no need to find out whether the previous mode was good or not, but let the people know that a new government had come. And the person appointed for Ugbevwe, the Council headquarters of Omaurhie was one Vremudia. He was not a member of the chiefs-in-Council at Akpobaro where he came from. He was ordinary, not everyone knew him in Akpobaro, but he happened to be the immediate elder brother of Brig-General Shevre Orode. Everybody in Omaurhie villages believed that he was not qualified for the position. However, they were not surprised because they obviously knew from where the appointment was coming. Nevertheless, there was some grumbling over the appointment across the various villages in Omaurhie. Vremudia was soon given an official car with a chauffeur. Not long, he started attaching 'Honourable' to his name, which in his estimation was a more elevating title than chief. A month later, government appointed him 'Justice of Peace'.

Power tickles the less prudent, and in most cases, it goes into his head. For the shallow mind, power is voluptuous: it makes him obsessed with possession and self-glorification, so it was with Vremudia. He knew he was not even popular in Akpobaro let alone in all the Omaurhie villages and for him to gain the popularity which his position commanded, he thought he needed to cut down the mighty tree which had all the sunshine of attention and would definitely shade him away from all public focus, for which he desperately craved. And his target was Chief Akpovire. He began by enticing some of the ordinary men, mostly the youths to himself. Of course, he stood no chance with the notables in Akpobaro. He always invited them to his house immediately he returned from Ugbevwe in his car, and offered them foreign gin instead of the locally brewed *ogogoro*. His invitees were also treated to a lavish dish of goat meat and yam spiced with some vegetable after their drink in his house. The news of such feasting soon spread round Akpobaro and many more people flocked to him. After sometime, he was no longer sending for people. They always came to him and very soon his house was always brimming over with people whenever he was around. They had become very loyal to him. Some of them were always there in his house and eventually became his domestic attendants. They no longer called him by his name. They simply called him 'Honourable'. And very quietly, a rumour was beginning to spread round that 'Honourable' had become the foremost leader in Akpobaro, so all such matters that were brought before Chief Akpovire must now go to him. When the rumour reached the chiefs-in-Council, they laughed.

'This man does not seem to know where he belongs. He is a government man. They appointed him. His dealings begin and end at Ugbevwe, the Council headquarters. He has nothing to do with us, here,' said the *Ugo*.

'*Ugo*, I think he should be properly told his limit so that he does not puff himself unnecessarily,' Chief Erayoma added.

They began to argue whether to invite him to their *oguedion* and caution him.

'I think that's not necessary yet,' said the *Ugo*. 'It's only a rumour. He'll surely deny it, so let us still leave it at that level. We shouldn't be seen to be over-reacting. I know Vremudia has been behaving like an evil-spirit possessed masquerade who refused to return home after the festival and live a normal life since his appointment. But we must act on good grounds lest we're accused of jealousy.'

Majority of them agreed with the *Ugo*. But one person that was very furious about the rumour was Chief Mudiaga.

'Who is Vremudia to say he has taken over from Councillor? If he's not careful, I'll smash him down in that his match-box house!' he said angrily.

'Ignore him. He's nobody. How can he compare himself with Councillor who is well-known all over the world – a man who has established a great reputation for himself over the years? Does Vremudia think Councillor's position is a government award or something to be picked up from the street

139

by sheer luck? If he thinks so, he's fooling himself. Reputable leadership like that of Councillor is not a title or an appointment. It is something one builds and earns over time by hard work and committed selfless service to the people,' posited the *Ugo*. It was with this statement they ended their meeting.

When the *amplified* version of the discussion at the *oguedion* concerning Vremudia reached him, he did not say anything. He merely laughed, a laugh that smacked of some sinister intent.

Chief Akpovire, on the other hand, did not blink at such rumour. He was rather indifferent. He could not contemplate the prospect of struggling over the leadership of Akpobaro with a person like Vremudia.

'Let him have all the posts of the world, he cannot be my equal,' he said to himself as he ruminated upon the rumour in his deck-chair in front of his house one evening. After sometime, the rumour died as it had come and there seemed not to be any leadership tussle, in Akpobaro and life generally went on as before. The people still looked up to Chief Akpovire as their foremost leader in the entire Omaurhie and they came to him as before to settle disputes and cases. The chiefs-in-Council remained steadfast in their loyalty to him.

While Vremudia continued to make merry among his loyalists. He had even begun to court the youths in the settlers' quarter who were not natives of Akpobaro. Not long, he erected a magnificent edifice for himself; one that took all the shine from Chief Akpovire's. It was an ultra modern house. It had glass louvres in its windows rather that the old-fashioned glass shutters of Chief Akpovire's. He furnished the living room with modern, elegant seats including a large glass shelf which showcased some of his exotic personal effects that he bought recently – all in a bid to outclass Chief Akpovire. With these fabulous possessions, Vremudia began to flourish as an important figure in Akpobaro. But all these could not put him in the same standing with Chief Akpovire in general estimation.

One day, a man in his thirties from Okuemo came to Chief Akpovire. He wanted to resettle with his wife, Veronica, after two years of separation. Veronica had run away from her marriage after a serious fight with her husband. Aforke, her husband, had a concubine in his village, and he often stole away from his matrimonial home at night, leaving Veronica lonely. This had caused several quarrels and fights between them. Aforke's people had always intervened in such instances. But their young man never yielded to their advice after each settlement. It had come to a point where they did not know what to do over the affair. They came to the conclusion that Aforke must have been bewitched with a love potion. One morning, Veronica's mother in-law came to plead with her to be patient with her son.

'Men are the same,' she told her. 'The more you fight and kick against their amorous indulgence the more they get involved. They don't like being pushed. Just keep calm and endure it. Believe me, it won't last. He'll certainly come back to his senses and be fully committed to you again on his own accord. That's how they are,' she persuaded.

Veronica would have heeded her mother-in-law's advice but there was a night she could no longer bear it, a night every woman would like to wrap herself with her husband's arms and enjoyed the warmth of his body. It was a very cold night and it rained all through that night. But Aforke stole out that night to sleep with his concubine, a divorcee. Veronica waited for a long time, eagerly expecting to hear her husband's knock on their door that night. When she became tired of waiting, she sat down and began to think of her life. She saw herself as a fire set to give warmth in a home during the harmattan but had been despised and abandoned, having nobody to appreciate its radiating warmth. She began to cry.

'Why did he come to me in the first place? He should have married her,' she said in her cry. She allowed her bitterness to well up until it saturated her soul and she wept profusely, soaking her pillow with tears. She felt thoroughly humiliated and was heart-broken. When the day was about to break, she put all her important clothes in a bag and kept it by the bed where she could easily fling it away at any moment.

Aforke returned home that morning when the people of Okuemo were just getting out of bed. He was looking spent in his weary eyes. It was very obvious that he did not sleep that night. Anger and jealousy rose quickly in Veronica as soon as her husband came in. She was like a bomb waiting to explode in the next second. Her face was as red as beetroot.

'Where are you coming from?' she asked.

Aforke pretended not to hear her.

'Why do you come back? It's she you prefer, go back to her!' continued Veronica.

Aforke ignored her and went straight to the bedroom to change his clothes. This further infuriated Veronica. She walked up to him and seized him by the collar.

'Why are you here? Go back to her!' she exploded.

'Please get your hand off me. It's too early in the day to quarrel,' answered Aforke angrily as he tried to resist her.

'No, you must go back to her, go back!'

Veronica began to push him with all her strength. They began to struggle against each other. In the struggle Veronica tore her husband's shirt. At that point Aforke could no longer tolerate her affront and he slapped her in the face. This was exactly what Veronica had been asking for.

'You slapped me! You'll kill me today!' She rushed at Aforke at once and they began to fight. Aforke was not really interested in the fight, he was only trying to resist her. But Veronica kept charging at him and was tearing his shirt in her rage. When she was satisfied with that, she immediately raised a loud cry. Before the immediate neighbours could rush down, Veronica had taken her bag and was leaving. As she was going, she began to wail, 'I 'm tired! I'm tired! Is this marriage?' she cried. Nobody could console her or made her return. She ignored all entreaties and kept going, raving and cursing.

At Akpobaro, her parents expected to hear from Aforke. But he did not come. They believed he would come one day, sooner or later. Meanwhile, Veronica was gradually readjusting to her old life before marriage. She still had the look of a maiden. She had no child yet and some of her peers were still around unmarried, so it was easy to readjust. As she reconnected herself to her friends, her old ways began to return. She soon began to look more attractive than before. She was regularly seen at the disco and other social arenas in company of her friends. At first, she attended as an onlooker. But as time went by, she became more enthusiastic and would like to participate in the dance like her unmarried friends. But no boy came to her for a dance as her marriage label was like a masquerade that scared away the boys.

One night, at the disco, the boys were taking the girls by the hand into the dance. Veronica had gone with her friends to the disco too. But one by one, they had all been taken into the dance. She was left alone where she was, making her look like abandoned fruit on a tree, very ripe, but nobody could touch it because the owner had placed on it a charm which put a curse on whoever plucked it. She liked to be 'harassed' and danced with like other girls. She had watched such affair at social arenas with embarrassing disgust and self-pity, cursing under her breath, the condition Aforke had kept her. Several times, she had resolved not to attend the disco. Still, she found herself strolling

142

to the disco at night. She could not stay back when all her mates of both sexes crowded themselves together, having all the fun in their time.

While she was contemplating whether to go home or continue in the torment of being left alone in the disco rapture, a hand slipped into her arm. She looked back and saw a smiling dashing young man beside her. Instinctively, she smiled back and almost found herself in the boy's arms readily. The boy took her hand and led her into the dancing, and they danced together through out the night, and were very excited being together, and Veronica was quite happy with the boy.

'You're a stranger here, I guess,' said the boy after the dance. 'I'd never seen you around.'

'You're the stranger, I believe,' Veronica smiled, unable to hold back her relish, as the boy led her home in the middle of the night. They came to an uncompleted house and hung there.

'You're right in a way. I 'm not a native. I came here with my parents two years ago. Nevertheless, I can identify almost every girl and boy in the village. Anyhow, we do meet. I think I have met virtually all of them. But you're new! You can't tell me, you've been staying in this village for the past one year.'

'Well, I've not been around for sometime. But I 'm a native,' returned Veronica.

The boy thought for sometime.

'Are you going back very soon?'

'Eh ... I don't know. I can't tell,' she shook her head in laughter.

'All the same, it's good to meet. I'm Thomas. I stay in the settlers' quarter.'

'You're really a stranger,' smiled Veronica.

'That was before. I 'm so close to the people now that I no longer see myself as a stranger. In fact, I've made many friends among the boys and I get involved in many things they do,' he paused for a while. 'Am I a stranger? No, not really. Well, let's put that aside, may I know your name?'

'Veronica.'

'That's nice. When can we see again?'

'When can we see, again?' Veronica repeated reflectively. 'Well, that's up to you.'

'I understand,' smiled Thomas. 'Then, may I know your place.'

'You want to visit me?'

'Yes, of course.'

'You'd better not.'

'Oh, afraid of parents or what?' said Thomas in a manner of teasing.

'Well, I've told you.'

'How do I see you then?'

'How did you see me today?'

'Okay, that's alright,' concluded Thomas with some air of understanding.

He saw Veronica close to her father's compound and bade her good bye. Since then, their relationship began to grow from strength to strength as Vero thought she needed some sparkle of romance in her life after her marital neglect. But she thought extreme caution must be maintained in doing it.

For a long time, Aforke did not come as Veronica's parents expected and Veronica's thought hardly went to him. She was enjoying her secret romance with Thomas. She loved Thomas who had shown so much affection for her and her love life began to blossom again. But love like the beacon burns where ever it is, it cannot be hidden, so it did not take long before the story of their love affair began to spread quietly across Akpobaro, and soon it became a common gossip. As the people of Akpobaro often said, "If one hears a gossip about oneself, the gossip must have been rotten with maggots by then." So when someone made a face at the other persons around and they laughed when Veronica or either of her parents passed them, she or her parents never knew that they were the object of the people's derision.

Thomas was one of Vremudia's loyalists. He spent most of his time at Vremudia's house. He and some other riverine boys hung around Vremudia as dogs follow their owners, for all manner of services, to the extent that they had gradually taken over all his domestic chores in his house. In return, they got lavish dishes and drinks and some pocket-money which was relatively handsome. Expectedly, Vremudia felt gratified with the servility of his hangers-on.

Aforke eventually came with his people to Chief Akpovire for reconciliation with Veronica after three years of separation. When Veronica's people received the cheering news, they were very happy, especially her parents who had been afraid that their daughter's long stay from her marriage might expose her to temptation that could smear their family's image in the community. But Vero was cold towards the reunion and she kept her distance from all the talk about it in the family. Unfortunately, she could not express her disapproval to her parents whom she knew very well would not listen to her. On the day of the settlement she followed her parents to Chief Akpovire's house willy nilly. After some conversation and drink, by way of settling down, Chief Akpovire explained the purpose of the meeting to the gathering and asked the spokesman of Aforke's family to initiate their presentation, as the meeting was at their instance.

'*Ilorogun, Ugo* and the entire house, I greet you all. We believe a person who recognises his wrong-doing and makes amend on his own, is wiser than the one who waited for someone else to point it out to him. We have decided on our own to come here to tell our in-laws and our beloved wife, Veronica, that we have wronged them. We are not here for any case: we are guilty and we plead for forgiveness.'

He and all his people including Aforke knelt down before their in-laws,

'Our in-laws we are sorry,' they pleaded.

'Stand up! Stand up! Our in-laws, it shouldn't be kneeling yet,' Veronica's father and his relatives said and their in-laws stood up reluctantly.

'In what other way can we express our gratitude and apology? We cannot be too old to kneel down before the one who gives his daughter to us in marriage. It is the greatest offer,' said Aforke's family's spokesman as they stood up. 'If we think of the lots of corn that have been used to feed a fowl, nobody can afford it in the market,' continued the spokesman humorously. 'That's why the receiving in-laws cannot stop kneeling in gratitude for their benevolent in-laws.'

'It is so,' the house responded and there was a general laughter and the atmosphere became warm. It was exactly this, the spokesman of Aforke's family wanted to achievement with his felicity.

'As I was saying,' Aforke's family's spokesman started again while standing before the full house, 'we are not here to argue with our respected in-laws. If I may borrow the language of oyibo court, "We are guilty as charged",' he stated in English, and they all started laughing again. 'We are therefore promising that, that silly misdemeanour of our son, Aforke, shall never occur again. I am giving you our word. We had to ensure that his bad habit had been thoroughly checked before we came for the settlement. That was why we delayed a bit, if not, we will be fooling ourselves. We shall therefore be very grateful if our most respected Councillor, the *Ugo* and other eminent chiefs here will reunite us with our in-laws so that our wife can return to us again –

our son Aforke is missing his wife greatly. We thank you all,' and the spokesman sat down.

'It is well spoken,' said the *Ugo* as he turned to Veronica's family on the other side of the house. 'My people, you have heard your in-laws, our in-laws. Can we now know your mind over what they have said?

The spokesman of Veronica's family quickly communed with Veronica's father and two other elderly men in their family before responding.

'Our respected Councillor, the *Ugo, Ilorogun*, my people, we thank you all for arranging the settlement. Our in-laws, we also thank you for initiating the reconciliation. Let me begin by saying that your good and conciliatory words have melted away all the anger in our hearts. You have also assured us that the cause of the friction and quarrel in their marriage has been dealt with. We heard that from you,' referring to Aforke's spokesman. 'But our people say that you cannot swallow food for your child, or someone else.'

Everybody nodded in agreement.

'Before we say anything therefore, we will like to hear directly from our son in-law, Aforke.'

And all attention shifted to Aforke. He stood up with some embarrassment before the house, 'I swear, I'll not look side ways again.'

And everybody laughed amusingly.

'Our people say that when dogs fall for each other their play becomes more interesting,' said the spokesman of Veronica's family. 'You have initiated the settlement. You have apologised for your wrong. You have also assured us that the cause of the wrong has been uprooted. What else do we desire? Unless we want to tell you that we are no longer interested in the marriage.'

Everyone nodded.

'Our in-laws,' continued Veronica's family's spokesman, 'we are still very much interested in the union. You befit us don't we befit you too?' laughing.

'Why not? you befit us,' Aforke's people said in return and there was a general laughter. 'So let our daughter be reunited with her husband, that is what my people say. In fact, we want to see a baby in the marriage very soon. We are becoming anxious.'

They all laughed again in concordance.

'We are glad,' said the *Ugo* after Veronica's family's spokesman had sat down. 'Two conditions spoil settlement,' the *Ugo* went on. 'Where the one at fault refuses to admit his guilt and apologise. But if he admits, settlement can still be elusive if the one to whom apology is offered, refuses to accept it and forgives. In these two thorny aspects of settlement, you have not been found wanting. We thank both sides for their willingness to embrace reconciliation. In doing so, you have made our task easy, we thank you. The last person who will respond to the settlement is our lovely daughter,' continued the *Ugo*. 'I know as a good daughter, she will not dishonour her family by toeing a different line. However, we still need to know her mind; she has the final say in the matter. 'My lovely daughter, can we hear you?' persuaded the *Ugo*.

But Veronica remained moody and motionless where she sat.

'I know women are shy when it comes to matter of open acceptance of their love relations in the open. Our in-laws what are you waiting for? Are you telling us that our daughter is not beautiful enough to be spoilt a little with petting?'

On the *Ugo*'s prompting, Aforke and his people came forward and pelted Veronica with some coins. But rather than the expected smile of acceptance, Veronica protested vehemently against their appeasement. She started sobbing. The in-laws pelted her with more money. But it became obvious that she meant her rejection of the settlement. Everyone in the house became disappointed. Her immediate people crowded her in impassioned plea but she would not yield. The entire house became suddenly calm and quiet by the surprises her refusal produced.

'What's the matter with you Vero?' her father charged.

'No, no, I won't. Aforke has suffered me enough,' she cried.

'My daughter, he won't hurt you again, take my word! All that is buried,' pleaded Aforke's father.

'No, no, he can't change, I know him,' she answered and kept crying.

'My daughter, why not try him again and see,' said her father.

'No, no, I'm not ready for that nightmare again,' she began to wail.

They all became confused, not knowing exactly what to do.

'Vero, you must be ready to go back to your husband,' charged her father in alarmed, decisive and firm voice. 'As far as I am concerned the matter is settled. You must go! You cannot disgrace me in this village,' her father said angrily. He had had a quick thought over the matter and the possible reason why his daughter was so bent in her refusal against all expectation and pleading, and his mind suddenly flashed to Veronica's closeness to Thomas. Hitherto, he had been very uncomfortable with it. But he wanted to give his daughter the benefit of the doubt and he saw the reconciliation as a welcome

147

relief. With Veronica's rejection of reunion, his fear of her daughter having a conjugal relationship with Thomas became very strong.

'Veronica! I have married you out! You cannot stay in my house after today,' he threatened with all fury.

'Then, I'll die,' replied Veronica in her cry.

'You must die then!' returned her father as he rushed at her with several slaps and Veronica ran out of the house while the people held back her father. And Aforke and his people went back to Okuemo utterly disappointed.

For two days, Veronica could not be found. Thomas too was not seen in Akpobaro. On the third day a police jeep entered Akpobaro. It drove straight to Chief Akpovire's compound. The four policemen looked tough and stern. They brandished their guns against any 'nonsense'. Chief Akpovire recognised them. He had had several contacts with them before. He thought they had come to notify him of another arrest or the possible settlement of such a dispute in his house as before. The only thing that set him thinking was their aggressive and menacing conduct and their brandishing guns; they had never come in that manner. 'This must be a serious matter,' Chief Akpovire said to himself as they stepped into his house.

'Chief, we want to see the following persons immediately, *Ugo*, Chief Obiebie, Chief Mudiaga, Chief Idogho and Emuobasa, the father of one Veronica.'

The most senior of the policemen read the names from a piece of paper with most unfamiliar attitude. The names were the prominent persons involved in the marriage settlement between Veronica and Aforke in his house three days ago. The names which included Veronica's father immediately sent alarm signals to Chief Akpovire. He knew the matter did not warrant police arrest. *Was the girl found dead?'* he thought and became a bit agitated.

'Officer, I shall send for them directly but may I know what the matter is?' 'You shall know when the time comes,' said the most senior policeman disaffectionately. Not long, all of them came except Chief Obiebie who was said to be away from home.

'His wife must go with us, in that case!' the sergeant insisted. 'Now put them in handcuffs!' he ordered the rest policemen, and a shocking alarm whirled over all the four of them, as they looked at each other in dreaming surprise.

148

'Officer, but you have not told me the matter! said Chief Akpovire angrily. The sergeant considered Chief Akpovire for some seconds, 'Chief, you too are under arrest!'

'Me!'

'Yes, you!'

It was like a dream to Chief Akpovire.

'Over what?'

'Well, you shall get that when we get to the station but for your position and the deep respect the police have for you, you shall not be handcuffed.'

'Where is your warrant? If you do not show me, I leave no where: That's the law!'

The sergeant smiled over what he considered as Chief Akpovire's bluff.

'Chief, do you want to resist arrest? Now, march them into the jeep!' the sergeant shouted to his subordinates in a decisive manner. And all of them in handcuffs immediately dashed forward and moved out of the house quickly and walked straight into the back of the jeep before any harm. Chief Akpovire remained in his couch completely crossed and embarrassed but comported himself in a most dignified manner, to impress the irate police sergeant that he was too important, to be treated shabbily. He could feel the embarrassment in his marrow. He was now the focus of all attention. The constables were agitatedly impatient for order. The atmosphere was charged and tense. Many of the local people hung around in disbelief.

'Chief, respect yourself or you shall be thoroughly sorry for this.'

'I've not seen your warrant yet! Besides, I deserve to know why I 'm being arrested. I'm not a criminal!'

'Chief, are you teaching me my work? Now, constables!' Before the constables could swing into action, many Akpobaro people who had been watching with great sympathy from the windows and the main door immediately surged forward and formed a phalanx between the policemen and Chief Akpovire. They begged Chief Akpovire to follow them to avoid any humiliation. His wives were on their knees, pleading to him with tears. Reluctantly, Chief Akpovire dressed up and went into the jeep, and in a swagger the policemen jumped in. Before the jeep sped off, the sergeant announced, 'whoever knows Chief Obiebie should tell him to report at the station if not, his wife shall never be released.'

That day Akpobaro's sun was cast down and a cold intimidating darkness fell upon it. There was confusion in the minds of Akpobaro people after the arrest. In their wildest dream, they never thought Chief Akpovire could be subjected to such commoners' indignity. A man they thought was a living legend among them. Someone they saw as their bulwark, whose life and leadership was the shining light of their collective existence as a people. The entire Akpobaro saw their own insecurity and helplessness in his arrest. The news of Chief Akpovire's arrest spread across the entire Omaurhie villages rapidly and they were all sad and shocked. Nobody could decipher the cause of the arres,. though many people in Akpobaro believed that it had to do with Veronica's marriage settlement. But the *Okaorho*[18] dismissed the insinuation that Veronica's husband's people at Okuemo were behind it.

'I don't think so. I know the people in that family. The people behind the arrest must be very powerful and influential. My people, it must be a great government man. Don't forget, my people, that Councillor and the entire police at Ugbevwe have been very close,' he told the people who came to him over the matter.

He paused for a while.

'Ah, for Councilor to be treated like that!' he shook his head.

'Those behind this thing must be very great.'

'What could be their reason?' one of the chiefs said.

'I don't know. Nobody knows either,' replied the *Okaorho* meditatively. 'That remains a puzzle.'

'Which one is not a puzzle? Is the whole arrest not a puzzle?' reacted another chief angrily. 'Only God can tell,' one chief added helplessly, and for sometime they remained silent and confused, and were completely at a loss over what to think.

The entire village slept late that day. They gathered in circles and talked about the incident in whispers. They were all shocked with fear. Nobody knew what was happening. But the whole story hung on their minds with great perturbation. That night, the *Okaorho* and the chiefs had decided to send three chiefs to Ugbevwe the following day to find out more about the arrest.

---

[18] The eldest man and the spiritual leader of a village

When Chief Akpovire and the others arrested with him got to the police station at Ugbevwe, they were all thrown behind bars except Chief Akpovire who sat at their reception office throughout the night. They remained there till the following day when the three delegates from Akpobaro came. And when the Divisional Police Officer, DPO, learnt of the delegates, he summoned them to his office and ordered that those of them arrested from Akpobaro be brought before him, and they were led in by two constables.

'Please have your seats,' the DPO said without looking up. He looked at a note before he wrote down some words.

'I am quite happy that your village people have sent down representatives to the station. This is what we expected before going further on the matter, and their quick response might save you from further detention. You have been charged with conspiracy and attempt to murder. You have equally been found flouting government order, though many of you might be ignorant of this. But ignorance is no excuse in law. Two days ago, a case was reported here of how you were forcing one Veronica to marry a man she never wanted to marry. In your insistence, you all began to beat her and she narrowly escaped death in your hands, and as at yesterday we were told the said Veronica had not been found. Whether you have succeeded in killing her we don't know yet. Police have begun their investigation, and your arrest is part of that investigation. So we're going to take your statements right away. Constable, get them some papers and biros.

'The other charge borders on your rude violation of government order. If the rest of you claim ignorant, Chief Akpovire cannot. He knows that it is an appointed "Justice of Peace" that is expected to settle cases among community folks, and that is why government has appointed JPs all over the place for the peace and harmony of the country. You have one in your community in the person of Most Honourable Vremudia Orode. Yet, you do not give him due recognition. He was given that title by the state government in recognition of his eminent role in settling disputes among your people in the past. So you must recognise him and give him his due respect. Let me make it clear to all of you, Chief Akpovire is not a JP, so he has no right to handle disputes in the area. All such cases must be referred to Most Honourable Vremudia Orode. If not, you shall soon incur the wrath of government. A word, they say, is enough for the wise!' concluded the divisional police officer.

After they had made their statements, they were led back to the police cell while Chief Akpovire went to the Reception. The DPO later told the dejected delegates that the families of the arrested persons must pay ₦20,000 each, before those arrested would be released on bail. On hearing this, the delegates were devastated, as the money was too much for simple villagers like they were.

When the news of the DPO's charges and condition for bail was broken at Akpobaro, the people were wild with anger. They began to curse whoever that was fomenting the trouble. The suspicion was upon Vremudia. But the major challenge now was how to raise the huge sums to bail Chief Akpovire and the other chiefs arrested with him.

It took a fortnight before they were eventually set free. By then, they were completely overwhelmed with lassitude and vexation. When they reached Akpobaro in the evening of that day, the people poured out in large number to receive them, and as they separated to their individuals' homes, the people followed each of them to their homes. Those that followed Chief Akpovire were more. This was understandable. His towering image attracted much greater sympathy. Unlike the others who narrated all the ordeals they went through, at the police station, before their bewildered audience, who wanted to hear everything first-hand, Chief Akpovire got home and slumped into his couch, looking completely displeased with everything around him and did not say a word. He was just listening to the people with equanimity. Many people who heard of his return later, flooded his house. The ordinary people, mostly the women and the young men, limited themselves to the windows. They curiously wanted to see how their great chief looked, after the untoward experience at the police station. There were furious discussions inside his house that day. Many of the people were expressing their shock and anger over the arrest and detention. They were cursing whoever that might have wrought the evil. All this was probably done to elicit the reaction of their great chief. But Chief Akpovire was too confounded to talk. When the people had congregated in this way for sometime without any response from him, they began to disperse in small numbers one after the other, having expressed their final sympathy to Chief Akpovire who only nodded his head in response. In that way they all left. Those who came much later in the evening did the same thing. Like before, Chief Akpovire only responded to their greetings quietly.

The two weeks of absence of the notable leaders of Akpobaro was an opportune time for Vremudia to plot his way to prominence. He hurriedly organised the opening ceremony of his new edifice. Apart from using it to draw all attention to himself, he wanted to put the consciousness in the minds of the people that he was now a man of means. Vremudia used the occasion to make a loud statement. In the ceremony which attracted many people, foods and drinks were in lavished supply. A music band was hired for life performance to entertain invitees. Many government dignitaries came with Brig-Gen Orode to grace the occasion. It was the biggest occasion ever staged by a single individual in the entire Omaurhie clan. Before the ceremony, Vremudia personally went round to invite the remaining chiefs in the village to the ceremony, and some of them that went were treated with great ceremony of recognition. He personally visited each of them the following day after the occasion to thank them for their attendance. Then onwards, he either visited them or sent for them.

CHAPTER FIFTEEN

The oil activities at Akpobaro suddenly wound up just as they had come. The construction of the flow-station and all the oil-wells had been completed. Construction of oil-pipelines from the various oil-wells to the flow-station had also been completed, and Starling's servicing companies and their suppliers packed their equipment and facilities, and left the place with their workers. Those who were hired in the period of the operation were disengaged. Only skeletal routine maintenance work at the flow-station by Starling workers remained, and the curtain was drawn on the economic and social boom the oil activities brought upon Akpobaro.

This affected the people of Akpobaro severely. Life went back almost to the level prior to the oil discovery. The main problem that resulted from this was the vacuum the oil activities left behind. Those who were fortunate to have enjoyed the juicy fridge benefits of the oil industry found it difficult to go back to their traditional farming. Working in the oil industry became an eye-opener to the fact that farming was a hard and miserable occupation, so it was no longer attractive to many youths. Also, those who were encouraged by the oil boom to set up small businesses and became petty traders, bar owners and others in the emerging leisure or entertainment industry suddenly realised that they had lost their businesses. The ordinary individuals in the community were not better off. The makeshift rented accommodations in all the places became a waste and a great discomfort to good surrounding. The high profit from foodstuffs also disappeared and all the high life in Akpobaro suddenly melted away.

After a long time of the geological survey in Akpobaro, some staff of Starling came to Akpobaro to hand out paltry sums to individuals whose farms were affected by their survey. The people were happy because they did not believe they could still get compensation for their damaged crops after three years, when they had forgotten everything about their damaged crops. So the money seemed a bonanza to them, which otherwise would have been rejected by a more informed people who should have insisted on the use of a competent independent valuer to ascertain the true cost of the damage before payment. More over, the people of Akpobaro knew very little about good money before the coming of Starling to the area. Even when Starling Company underpaid the people in compensation, the company's 'damage clerk' who paid them the money further exploited their ignorance by cutting some fraction from every compensation for himself.

When the payment had been effected, though belatedly, Starling's 'Public Affairs Department,' otherwise known as PAD, decided to hold a meeting with the chiefs and elders of Akpobaro at the village *oguedion*. It was to brief the people of the company's plan to carry out oil exploitation in the area and what the people of Akpobaro should expect. From the outset, the officials made it clear to them that there was a new statute of government which entrusted all the minerals in the land to government, so all negotiations over exploitation of minerals by their company had to be with the government.

'Whatever compensaton we have paid and might pay later to you or any other communities shall be for their economic trees and crops. But for good relation with our oil-bearing communities, our company sometimes goes beyond business interest. We have a policy of assisting our oil-bearing communities in building some social infrastructure or facilities for their better living, in order to establish a good relation with them, for this reason, Starling has decided to tar your road to the main road that leads to Safa. This, in our belief will open up your area to the rest of the country.'

And the people started jubilating.

'More shall come. In return, we expect your community to be supportive of our operations and protect our installations in the area.'

The following day, the news went round the entire Omaurhie villages and there was much greater jubilation which thrust the entire people into their streets, dancing in celebration. Two days later, major national newspapers in the country carried the news in screaming headlines. One particular newspaper captioned the news in extra bold print on its front page: STARLING TO LINK OBSCURE COMMUNITIES TO SAFA WITH A MULTI-BILLION NAIRA ROAD CONSTRUCTION. But what eventually came out of this, was a rough tarring of their road which terminated at the newly constructed Starling oil flow-station at Akpobaro, and by the end of all the oil installation in the area, the road had been riddled with many pot-holes.

After a careful assessment of the oil activities in Akpobaro for sometime, Chief Akpovire felt there was need for Akpobaro to enter into a memorandum of understanding, MOU, with Starling Company. He had seen the shoddy construction of the road. He had also observed the constant emissions of the gas flames out of the derricks of oil-wells in their farmlands. It had become a common sight nowadays to see strange rain water in Akpobaro. Though, Chief Akpovire did not exactly know what it meant, he knew it would surely have some damage on their land and vegetation. Following these observations, Chief Akpovire decided to convene a meeting of chiefs and elders of Akpobaro at the *oguedion* to ventilate his concern before them. They were very delighted.

And after a good deliberation, they all agreed that a letter expressing their observations and concern over the negative impact of the oil operations in their land and the need for a memorandum of understanding with Starling be dispatched to the company. When the head of 'Public Affairs Department' of Starling Company, Mr. Olaniyi, went through the letter, he was surprised. He took the matter immediately to his area general manager.

'What? They want MOU over what?' the area general manager queried.

'I don't know, but I guess it has to do with the complaints in their letter,' answered the PAD's manager.

'What do they know about MOU? Poor wretched villagers!' hissed the area general manager and dismissed the letter. 'You know that we have no contractual commitment with village dwellers,' the white man pointed out to the PAD manager. 'We talk with government and government alone, okay?'

'Yes sir,' concurred the PAD manager with total submission.

'At any rate, you know what to do. That's your office and they are your people,' stated the white manager pointedly to the PAD manager who always accepted his boss's views without much dissent.

Mr. Olaniyi mulled over the matter for a few days before writing back to Akpobaro's community, proposing a meeting with them.

On the day of the meeting, Chief Akpovire and several other chiefs were all well dressed in their traditional chieftaincy regalia. As early as nine in the morning, they were already waiting the arrival of Starling Company's officials. For the past three days, Chief Akpovire had been thinking over what they would present to the oil company as conditions of relationship. He was to be the spokesman of Akpobaro. The chiefs-in-Council had anticipated that the official representatives of Starling Company coming to the meeting would be highly educated officials and they too needed a well-informed person to handle their own side, during the horse trading. And they were really very proud to have a person of Chief Akpovire in the community for a matter like this. While they were busy discussing their next Council meeting, Mr. Olaniyi and his two assistant managers in the 'Public Affairs Department' of Starling drove in. They walked into the *oguedion* with some air of importance. They thought they had come to discuss with simple villagers who should feel honoured by their presence. For these Starling's staff members, it was a matter of dispatch; they had come to hand out to Akpobaro community, their company's policy of no relationship with the communities in their areas of operations and no more. So they did not waste any further time, after the ceremony of presenting drinks and kolanuts.

'You have a great tradition of reception and hospitality here,' smiled Mr. Olaniyi. 'I thank you all for making us beneficiaries. Well, coming to the business of today, I would like to inform you that Starling is a transnational company. It is operating almost everywhere across the globe and it has a standard policy of relation with its areas of operation, based on the legal framework of each local environment. In Namia, there is a law which entrusts all the minerals in the land to government. So we as a company owe all our obligations to the government as the sole owner of the oil in your area. As a result, we have already, an existing MOU with the government as partner. It is our belief therefore, that government will use some of the huge profit she realises from the joint venture to make the necessary provisions to the people in our areas of operation; it is government duty. We wish to advise you therefore to channel all your needs to government. It is simple. Our obligation is to government and government in turn has obligation to you. So the idea of having MOU with you is completely ruled out. Be that as it may, we might get out of our business way to assist you from time to time. Remember, it is not an obligation. We are sorry we have to say this again. We thank you,' Mr. Olaniyi stated very clearly.

'We thank you for making the condition of your business environment in Namia very clear to us. But one important fact that must be made clear to Starling is that, no matter the arbitrary law that has been drawn up by government, Starling cannot ignore the people in its areas of operation. Starling's oil exploration and exploitation in the area is taking heavy toll on our environment. Much of our land has been taken over by your activities and the remaining land is being despoiled by your operation. For the first time, we are now experiencing acidic rain water. The huge flames constantly being emitted from Starling rigs into our environment are a great pollution and you should know its effect on our health and on our crops and on the entire environment. Please, don't talk about government to us. Government is a stranger we do not know. Look at our community. Do you perceive any smell of government?' Chief Akpovire waved his hand sideways as if to show Mr. Olaniyi the entire Akpobaro. 'The only people and things we see and affect us here are you and your activities. Starling must draw up a plan of action to make up for the damage and think of how to control the devasting effects of its activities in its areas of operation. It must tell government so and get the money out of their so called mutual deal. If not, I see great problem in future. This is the idea we have for calling for MOU. Right now, our people are becoming disenchanted. That's why we, the leaders of our community are bringing the matter to your table. We think it is wise for you to consider the issue before it poses a great danger to our relationship,' Chief Akpovire told them.

Swayed by a superior argument, Mr. Olaniyi reluctantly promised to take their idea to the company's management for consideration at the end of the meeting. He also promised to inform them of its outcome. He however added that the people of Akpobaro should not be very hopeful as their demand is in conflict with his company's policies.

On their way back to Starling Company, Mr. Olaniyi and his two assistants could not help but be impressed by the views of Chief Akpovire. They saw the claims made by Akpobaro community as quite legitimate and germane. How wrong they were to have thought they were going to face some villagers who knew next to nothing. But the way Chief Akpovire articulated the community points and how he was able to link the huge flames from the oil derricks to the polluted rain water in the area stunned them. Hitherto, they in the oil industry knew that oil exploitation had its negative consequences on lives and environment. But since none of the inhabitants of such areas had complained and such negative effects of exploitation had not actually caused obvious damage in any of the areas, they had not given them the least consideration. But here was a man who could perceive very deeply and discern what many could not see. Mr. Olaniyi was really encouraged by Chief Akpovire's argument and he hoped to pursue the cause to the highest management level where the company's policies were articulated and formulated. In fact, Chief Akpovire had opened his eyes to the realisation of possible outbreak of protests and hostilities in the oil-bearing communities in future if nothing urgent was done now to ameliorate the negative impact, especially of gas-burning at the rigs. He had read that the gas being burnt away in realising crude oil could be converted to another source of income.

He remembered reading something on the process of converting the gas to liquefied gas which was very useful in the industrial sector. He therefore hoped to raise the possibility in his report to the area general manager and possibly to the top management at their head office. There was one other thing he had learnt from the meeting, the need to have a consultative forum with community leaders in their areas of operation. He believed there was a lot to learn from such mutual interactions, in order to promote a harmonious relationship. These and other ideas he hoped to articulate to top management of Starling. As he went over these ideas in his mind, he remembered 'we-know-better' attitude of the management when in actual fact, they knew very little about what was happening at operational level, he thought. *'They're not on ground_ they see nothing – yet they feel they know it all,'* Mr. Olaniyi said in his mind. *'Communication is a two-way traffic: top to bottom and bottom to top.'* He became angry at that point. But this was one case he hoped to pursue vigorously. As far as he was concerned he was prepared to take the matter to the highest level of the company's management.

CHAPTER SIXTEEN

The return of Chief Akpovire and others from the police detention caused some quiet stir against Vremudia at Akpobaro because the whole story emanating from the arrest pointed to his direction. Rumour had it that Veronica and Thomas were seen together at Safa. After the release of Chief Akpovire and the other chiefs, the police did not pursue the case further. The people were already accustomed to Chief Akpovire in handling their matters. They still went to him to settle their cases despite the police warning, though, Vremudia had succeeded in winning some of the chiefs over by financial inducements to fight the majority in the chiefs-in-Council. This had made decision-making very difficult in the *oguedion*, as opinions were now formed along this divisive line. To give more muscle to his group in the tussle, Vremudia gave the chiefs supporting him several petty contracts at the Council at Ugbevwe, which had further strengthened their loyalty to him. As time went by, the village too was dragged into the tussle.

Chief Akpovire was not really interested in the imbroglio. He feared it might tear the village to pieces. He had carefully weighed the situation and he knew that the odds were against him, and he was prepared to remove his hands off the community affairs.

'If someone is eager to take the people's aches off me, why should I worry? I am willing to give it up. It's been at a great personal cost,' he said to himself one evening as his mind wandered in that direction while he was relaxing in his deck-chair in the frontage of his house. But he knew that the matter was not just the assumption of the community's leadership; it had gone beyond such a simple decision. It had become a great challenge; a war as it seemed. At least, that was the way Vremudia and the entire chiefs were seeing it, and he knew that his loyalists and supporters who were in the majority in the village were not prepared to see Vremudia winning the battle against him. They were prepared to do battle with Vremudia and his hirelings. In fact, the *Ugo*, Chief Mudiaga, and the other chiefs arrested with him were already preparing for a real show-down on the matter. It would be a great betrayal to them if he gave up the fight. Therein lay his dilemma.

He had turned the matter over repeatedly in his mind. As he sat in his deck-chair in front of his house that evening, he was seriously weighing the matter in his mind again. *If it is a matter of handling Vremudia, that's easy. He's not a problem, but the government. All the weapons of government are available to him. Fighting him means fighting the entire state, a state at the whims of some individuals for that matter!*

He shook his head.

'No, it'll be foolish,' he said to himself. 'Standing in his way is standing in front of a bull-dozer. But how can I make the people understand?' he said to himself.

This was the crux of the matter. They still saw Vremudia just the way he was before his brother became minister, a nobody in the village who now wanted to assault his betters with his new position. They felt he should be made to know his place in the community, his recent fortune notwithstanding.

****

Vremudia was quite happy over the way events were unfolding. He was sure of his way. And recent developments had not given him any cause to doubt that. The successful arrest of Chief Akpovire by the police was a great delight to him. He thought that alone had demystified Chief Akpovire's larger-than-life image in Akpobaro. With his new edifice, which was second to none in the whole of Omaurhie, his increasing tribe of youths and the few chiefs that were loyal to him had become very loud and confident in promoting him vigorously at the *oguedion*. And now, he was beginning to gain reckoning in Akpobaro. Many people began to see him as Chief Akpovire's rival. He felt he was getting close to the mark, that of axing down Chief Akpovire to assume the community's absolute rulership, a prize he thought he must win at all cost. He knew it was a matter of time.

He was absolutely fixated on that awesome place of Chief Akpovire, having all the people coming to him with deference. He thought once Chief Akpovire had been successfully uprooted, his great position of leadership would naturally come to him. But what he did not know was that Chief Akpovire did not attain his glory by being a councillor or by dominating others. It was a reward that came naturally with his selfless leadership. In his avowed determination, Vremudia knew that the people's attachment to Chief Akpovire was strong and deep-rooted, and it would take more than his personal effort to uproot him. He felt he needed the assistance of his big brother, Brig. Gen. Orode, the Federal Minister of Science and Technology.

One day, he travelled to the Minister and told him that Chief Akpovire had become very jealous of him. Indeed, inventing vicious stories to bring the Brigadier-General against Chief Akpovire became his latest scheme.

'I don't know why some persons feel it should always be them and no one else! Is the community created for that fossil alone?' Brig. Gen. Orode exploded one day in his annoyance after Vremudia had told him another hateful lie against Chief Akpovire. 'I was a little boy when he started leading the whole Omaurhie,' he added in his smouldering rage.

'Ah, that man, he doesn't want any other person to come up. I tell you since you helped me with that appointment, he has declared me his number one enemy. It has been one allegation or the other against me. And he has his ready soldiers in the *Ugo* and those other chiefs around him.'

'But why did they decide to ostracise you now? Why? What is your offence?'

'Offence? What offence? They say I am not the one who should be JP. Chief Akpovire told them that the position is his, that you used your political influence to rob him. Shevre, you don't know those people. They're terrible! They'll stop at nothing to frustrate me out of the position! I think I'm going to resign my office as Council chairman, so that I can have my peace at Akpobaro. I'm tired, tired of their trouble!'

'No, you mustn't do that!'

'My brother, I must do, I don't want to die yet. I just came to tell you so 'cos it'll not be nice to resign without letting you know.'

'You mean it has come to that! I thought Chief Akpovire was very liberal, reasonable and enlightened.'

'It's been all pretence, I've come to know better,' Vremudia replied, trying to make sure Shevre had no iota of respect for him any more.

'You shall not resign! I'm coming home. If it means using all my powers to keep you in the office I'll do. I'll tell that old rascal that he's only a local champion if it comes to that.'

Vremudia returned home that weekend satisfied. When the handful of chiefs who were loyal to him came to see him after that visit to his brother, he bragged to them, 'Very soon, Chief Akpovire and his loyalists shall be crippled. Just wait and see,' he told his enthusiastic listeners. 'The *Ugo* and that foul-mouthed Mudiaga shall come here to beg me. You shall see it with

162

your own eyes. They shall soon realise that their master is nobody,' he added with a smug smile spreading over his face.

Meanwhile, Vremudia had been thinking of stirring some disturbances in the village to compel Chief Akpovire's loyalists to fight him. He needed it as a clear proof of his many allegations that he had been telling his brother, Brigadier-General Orode, against Chief Akpovire, when he eventually comes.

One day, he returned from Ugbevwe pretending to be in great anger. He immediately summoned his lackey supporter chiefs in the chiefs-in-Council to his house.

'When I told you that Chief Akpovire is a wolf in a sheep, you didn't believe me. I've just uncovered, from the vantage point of my office, that he has been collecting huge sums regularly from Starling for the maintenance of our road all these years. You know our community wrote Starling on the road matter at the beginning of its operation, remember?'

The chiefs nodded their heads with revealing interest.

'Yes, you're right,' one of them answered.

'And nothing actually came out of that effort.'

'So that man has been deceiving us,' said one of the chiefs.

'Yes, he's been deceiving us, yet he claims to be working selflessly for the community!' said Vremudia in a mock anger. 'Now listen, this is a matter I want you to raise in the *oguedion*. I have all the proofs! And I'm prepared to deal with that old fox. Enough of his tricks!'

That day the bad news swept across Akpobaro like a wildfire. Chief Akpovire was very angry when Mudiaga came to inform him about the news that was spreading round the village.

'Councillor, are you hearing the story?'

'What story?'

'The rotten rumour that you have been embezzling the funds, the oil company sends down for the maintenance of our road. They say Starling gives you money yearly to maintain the bad state of the road.'

'Who are those spreading such wicked rumour?' Chief Akpovire asked with great uneasiness. 'Who are those spreading it?'

'It's all over the village like rainfall,' replied Mudiaga.

Chief Akpovire fell back on his couch at once and was quiet; not knowing what to say.

Since the police arrest, he had almost become very placid. The shock of the police's *volte-face* against him was still raw in his mind. It hurt him like a fresh wound. The betrayal had almost erased his faith in human being. Considering his closeness and his selfless service to the police over many years, he never had the least presentiment that they could be an instrument of humiliating him. He still could hardly believe it any time he thought of it. He thought that human being could no longer hear his conscience, or was it that his conscience was now dead? These and other similar issues concerning conscience overwhelmingly dominated his thoughts.

Since the arrest, he found it hard to relate warmly with people like before. *Now, the same person who used the police to assault and humiliate me is again vilifying my reputation built over the years.* As he ruminated upon the damaging and unfounded rumour, anger and vengeance began to well up in him.

'Can you guess who is behind this?' asked Mudiaga knowingly.

'Guess? Who else other than that wicked Vremudia,' replied Chief Akpovire angrily.

'Councillor, that idiot needs to be taught some very hard lessons. I think you're rather too soft with him,' replied Mudiaga.

Chief Akpovire gave him a hard look, a look that was saying, *the problem is more than what you think* and Mudiaga became affected with Chief Akpovire's overwhelming sense of equanimity and he recoiled in silence as well.

The people of Akpobaro were confused over the story. These days nobody knew what to believe. Several wild allegations had been levelled against Chief Akpovire in the village by Vremudia and his supporters. The people just talked about them without any definite opinions dominating their minds. They expected Chief Akpovire to come out and clear himself or crush the perpetrators of such damaging rumours. But they were not seeing either of such actions from him. This attitude of Chief Akpovire tended to make them less inclined to disbelieve the several wild allegations. They waited to see *their king* rise up to the challenge but they had been disappointed by his silence. This smack of weakness was becoming more irritating to them than the false allegations.

While Vremudia continued his affront on Chief Akpovire, Mudiaga, *Ugo* and some other notable chiefs were provoked one day in the chiefs-in-Council when it was reported that Efe was beaten up by two settler boys on the prompting of Vremudia while Chief Akpovire was away in Safa. They all decided to march to Vremudia and warn him against using strangers to cause trouble in the village. They met Vremudia and his boys in their usual gaiety, drinking, when they got there. The stormy appearance of Mudiaga, *Ugo* and the other chiefs drew away all the cheering at Vremudia's. At once, an atmosphere of nervous confrontation set in when they noticed that the intruders were from the *opposition camp*. Vremudia watched them with anger and disdain as they came close.

'What do you want here?'

'To warn you over the trouble you're using strangers to cause in the village,' returned the *Ugo* calmly.

'To warn me?' retorted Vremudia with a sneer on his face. 'Over which strangers?'

'These boys you use to cause problem in the village,' Mudiaga pointed to the boys with him.

'Nobody should call us strangers in this village,' answered one of the boys angrily.

'We're no strangers,' chorused the rest of the boys in defiance.'

'Are your parents natives of this place?' shouted Mudiaga.

'They're no strangers! And if that's the reason why you have come, you had better leave. I won't entertain such silly argument in my house,' exploded Vremudia.

'Well, we have warned you. It won't be pleasant next time,' returned the *Ugo* as they turned to go.

'What do you mean?' Vremudia stood up in rage.

'We have told you!' Mudiaga used his walking stick to emphasize the warning as they walked away.

'Nonsense, what right have you to come here and challenge me in my own house?'

Vremudia ran towards them, spoiling for a fight.

The *Ugo* turned to answer but Mudiaga held his hand in a sneering smile, 'Do you mind the rant of an adulterous child?'

On hearing these words, Vremudia quickened his pace in an uncontrollable rage.

'What did you say?' he thundered.

Vremudia was rumoured to have had a controversial circumstance of birth. The story went round long ago, during the time of his birth that his mother was having a secret extra-marital affair with a herbalist who was massaging and giving her potions for child-bearing before the pregnancy of Vremudia, so his true parentage generated some quiet suspicion in Akpobaro. Rumour had it that his father disowned Vremudia when he was born, and it took a long time after repeated appeals from some close relatives before his father reluctantly showed some acceptance. It was said also that till his death, his father never openly called him his son, neither did he show any visible interest in him. So it was one aspect of Vremudia's life to which he was most sensitive.

'Repeat what you just said to the *Ugo*!' he closed up on Mudiaga like a pointing cannon about to explode.

Mudiaga did not answer and was walking away with the rest. Vremudia seized him by the shoulders and forced him to face him.

'I say repeat what you said!'

'Get your filthy hands off me or you shall receive what you're asking for!'

Mudiaga also became furious. All Vremudia's boys in his house came forward with intending support for their master. The *Ugo* and the other chiefs tried to free Mudiaga from the grip of Vremudia. They were all shocked when a loud slap descended on *Ugo's* face. His face twitched with unexpected signs of great shock. The *Ugo* touched the affected cheek dreamingly as if to be sure whether the slap was real. Being the spokesman of the community, the *Ugo* was highly respected among the people.

'You slapped me?'

'You slapped the *Ugo*!' the *Ugo* and the other chiefs shouted almost together in disbelief.

'Yes, I slapped the *Ugo*! What can you people do?' Vremudia charged towards the other chiefs.

'Nonsense!' he spat with fury and was very despiteful.

The chiefs beheld him in his *madness* for a moment and took away the *Ugo* who was still grievously agitated.

'Let's go. There're better ways to handle the ferocity of a madman,' Mudiaga said as he and the other chiefs urged the *Ugo* away.

Meanwhile Vremudia was still raving and cursing.

'None of you can do me anything. Dogs! that's what you all are!' he shouted in an overwhelming rage. 'I'll crush any of you who cross my way, even your master,' he boasted.

When the people of Akpobaro heard about the incident, they were very unhappy. They agreed that Vremudia was becoming a loose, angry cow that was attacking everything on its way. It needed to be tied up! That night the village youth held a quiet meeting. The following morning, in agreement with the elders, they attacked Vremudia and his tribe of youths. It was a fierce clash. The village youths were much more in numbers, so they had the upper hand. They destroyed Vremudia's two cars and smashed his doors and windows open. Vremudia managed to escape with some wounds. Many of his boys had severe injuries too.

The people of Akpobaro could not hide their joy. They were happy that Vremudia with his nuisance boys had been subdued, as he was carrying on as if the world belonged to him. They heaved sighs of relief and chuckled in satisfaction as they talked about the incidence.

The following day the noisy Vremudia and his tribe of youths seemed to be non-existent. The village youths in their savouring air of a victorious army, for that was how they saw themselves, gathered together at the main entrance of the village, fully armed with clubs and machetes, believing that Vremudia and his tribe of boys would want to fight back. But in the following two days nobody heard anything about them. But on the third day something unusual happened in Akpobaro. About 5.00 in the morning when it was thought that nobody had come out of his house, four army trucks filled with soldiers, stopped at the outskirts of Akpobaro and all the soldiers jumped out of the truck, and began moving in circumference of the village in order to lay siege to it. They were so furtive in their circulation that a fly could hardly notice their movement, and they were fully armed. When it was some minutes to six, the last six soldiers began to walk directly into the village. As soon as the six were at the edge of Akpobaro, they released rapid gunshots into the air for about a minute. The youth immediately fled their positions and scattered in different directions in escape. When, the six soldiers ceased firing, those other soldiers laying seige began their shooting into the air. It seemed the sky was being shot down upon Akpobaro. Panic seized the entire village. Several people who were already out that early morning raced back into their houses. Everybody shut himself in, in great fear; afraid of what would happen next. Even the goats, sheep, fowls, and other domestic animals took cover in any hiding place in the village. Akpobaro was literally dead after the rapid shootings. Five minutes later, the soldiers emerged from all directions, and were break into houses. The villagers had fragile locks so it was easy. They smashed every door open in search of the village youths. Everyone was trembling. The women and children of every house were wailing in horror as the soldiers smashed doors and windows open and dragged out with kicks and whipping, every young man they found. They eventually gathered all the young men together and marched them to the village square. Chief Mudiaga, *Ugo* and the other chiefs who had a row with Vremudia earlier were also marched to the village square, where they were thoroughly beaten and tortured by the soldiers. There, the youths were given additional beating and were made to frog jump about for hours.

Later, around ten that morning, Bridadier-General Shevre Orode rode in a grand jeep into the village and headed straight with some soldiers to Chief Akpovire's compound. He was so disappointed to learn that Chief Akpovire had travelled to Safa two days earlier. He ordered the soldiers that came with him to smash all his doors and windows down. Chief Akpovire's wives and children were severely beaten with military whips. The Brigadier-General threatened to kill all of them. After calling Chief Akpovire all manner of names, he left and headed to the village square where the youths had already been treated to severe punitive military torture meant for erring soldiers in the barracks and had been crying.

'You old fools!' barked Brig. Gen. Shevre, when he swaggered into the village square with all air of military might.

He was referring to the *Ugo* and the other chiefs who had been thoroughly humiliated and were completely shame-faced.

'You used the youths to unleash violence upon my brother. By the time I finish with you, you shall know that soldiers are different breeds,' he said to them. He began to strike each of them with his military staff.

After the youths had been tortured severely with military whips at the village square, Brigadier-General Shevre summoned all the chiefs in Akpobaro together.

'Now, listen to me! Oviri is no longer the *Ugo*. Onokero is the new *Ugo*. Did you hear that?' he said peremptorily.'

All the chiefs who were overwhelmingly afrighted nodded their heads submissively. Onokero was one of the few chiefs loyal to Vremudia.

168

'If you disobey him, I'll throw all of you into police cell and you know what that means. Chief Akpovire is lucky. Next time, no absence, no mistake about him. I swear!'

That day the whole Akpobaro was beset with the tremor of the military brutality. The people were too frightened to talk about it. At most, they whispered it, while looking here and there – as if the walls of their houses were standing soldiers on guard. They had never experienced such brutality and humiliation before. For the first time, some of them began to realise why Chief Akpovire had been quiet over the unrestrained provocations of Vremudia. They knew Chief Akpovire had lost out, though they still had their sympathy for him. But what was the use of their sympathy in the present circumstance? They painfully had to surrender their loyalty to Vremudia and Onokero, the new *Ugo*, if they did not want a repeat of the horrible military invasion and torturing, and they thought such a repeat would be on a higher magnitude.

Ordinarily, the appointment of Onokero as the *Ugo* would have been unthinkable. Besides his unimpressive and feckless personality, Onokero did not also come from the quarter to which the coveted title would have rotated in the community. In fact, Akpobaro people seethed especially those from the entitled quarter when they heard about the arbitrary appointment. But they all knew they had no choice in the matter. And this realisation had also silenced all the resistance against Vremudia, and the coast became very clear for him and his cronies to assert themselves fully in Akpobaro.

When Chief Akpovire returned from Safa, he was shocked to see his house in such a deplorable condition. He felt completely humiliated. He examined the damage quietly and thought of what to do. He was absolutely absorbed in how to redeem his personal dignity and pride. Hitherto, he had been very careful because he never wanted the situation to get to this embarrassing level but now that it had reached it, he felt there was no dignity and honour to protect any more. To him, it had come to the point where an adversary had thrown dust in one's eyes and dared one to do his worst. This time, he was not expecting any support from the people who had been dislodged from the struggle. Also, the police and other security agencies were also out of the question. *What's my weapon of resistance?* pondered he. He must be seen to have some muscle to earn some respect in the community.

'Chief, your case is an example of brazen military abuse of political authority and I shall prosecute it with all the abilities in me, at least, to prove a point that these *military boys* should be made to realise their limits. They can't just be behaving as if there was no law in the country, simply because they're in power. After all, if every citizen disregards the law as they do, can they rule?'

'But Barrister, are you sure the justice system is still effective under these military dispensations?'

'Yes, we in the legal profession will not allow them to temper with the legal process. We, lawyers, fight with all our strength to resist military dictatorship. Chief, you know that the court is the bastion of law and order in the society. If the judicial system fails, anarchy and lawlessness becomes the order. That's why no government toys with its justice system. It is the last pillar of any organised society. No matter the pollution outside, it cannot be allowed to infiltrate the justice system. Every government is careful about that because they know if they allow the justice system to be corrupted, they're indirectly subverting their own government – no government no matter how powerful, survives anarchy.'

'Barrister-at-law! Even in a very corrupt and irresponsible military junta called government?'

'Chief, don't worry, have no fear. I'll have wanted to go into legal niceties and history to prove my point. But it's not necessary. The justice system remains the last hope of the oppressed in seeking redress.'

'That's alright Barrister, you can then initiate the legal action.'

'Chief, I thought you were well-informed about this thing. Not me – the police –it's a criminal case. I believe you have reported the matter to them for proper investigation.'

'Report what matter to whom?'

'Report the matter to the police, of course.'

Immediately, Chief Akpovire face became wrinkled with frustration and helplessness.

I can't go to the police!'

'Why, chief? It's their duty to carry out investigation and initiate the matter in court, because it's a criminal matter. In fact, we need their proper investigation to prosecute the case in court.'

'I know but I thought we could do without them.'

'No, we need their report in court.'

'I see,' said Chief Akpovire as he lowered his face with complete resignation and thought for sometime. 'Lawyer, let's forget everthing altogether,' said Chief Akpovire as he turned to go.

'Chief, you can't leave this case. I know in your heart of heart you want to go to court to seek redress. What other option do you have against oppressive military might other than the law? Consider your personal dignity and self-esteem that has suffered terribly. No, chief, you can't let go!'

'Lawyer, you don't understand,' Chief Akpovire shook his head repeatedly. 'No, no, I don't want to get involved with them.'

'You mean with the police?'

Chief Akpovire nodded in the affirmative.

And the attorney, Mr. Okeme, observed that Chief Akpovire would not want to be persuaded further on the police matter.

'That's alright, I'm your attorney and solicitor, I can do that for you.'

'You can do that without my involvement?'

'Yes, of course.'

'Then, I'll forever be grateful.'

Mr. Okeme, Chief Akpovire's attorney, had a rough time getting the police to initiate the case in court. But he handled the case with much spirit and passion. He was not looking at what Chief Akpovire would offer him, rather he wanted to use the case to prove to the overbearing military government and the entire citizenry that military officers were not above the law and they needed to operate within the law, even while holding political offices.

From day one the police at Ugbevwe were completely uninterested in the matter. They wanted to frustrate Mr. Okeme's efforts by repeatedly telling him to come some other appointed time. They pretended to be too occupied to look into the case. And after many repeated and failed promises with this excuse they realised that it was no longer tenable. So they began to tell Mr. Okeme that they needed clearance from *above* as the matter was involving a highly placed military figure in the country. The divisional police officer at Ugbevwe assured Mr. Okeme that as soon as they got clearance, they would give the matter all the attention it deserved. Mr. Okeme was a very patient person and had also realised that the police were not willing to investigate the matter but he knew deceit would not last long where patience persisted. The attorney actually wanted to allow the police to come to their own folly. He was conscious of all his argument to Chief Akpovire on the efficacy of the justice system even in a corrupt military dictatorship and he was prepared to prove it to Chief Akpovire with the case. In this light, Mr. Okeme saw the case as a great challenge to him and he approached it in that spirit. The last time Chief Akpovire came to his chamber to know the extent he had gone with the police. The vivacious attorney had very little to say. He merely quoted this popular saying in the legal profession to Chief Akpovire, *though the wheels of justice may run slowly, it must surely get to its destination.*

When it was obvious that the police had no more tenable excuse in their chicanery as already predicted by Mr. Okeme, the divisional police officer, DPO, started avoiding him completely.

'Constable, tell the lawyer that I can't see him today,' said the DPO to the constable who had just brought Mr. Okeme visitor's form to his office.

'That was what he also told me the last time I was here. I won't take all this nonsense any more,' exploded Mr. Okeme, and stormed into the office of the DPO.

'DPO, it's very obvious to me now that you're not ready to prosecute the case. But if you don't investigate the matter and bring it to court within the next two weeks, I'll petition you to the Inspector General of Police, the Attorney-General of the Federation and initiate a case against you and the police in court on this your deliberate refusal to prosecute a criminal matter, which by law, you're duty bound to do. And be sure, the Press shall hear of it. Good day!' Mr. Okeme left the police station in fury and refused to heed the call of the DPO who was urging him to come back to his office.

The threat worked. The police investigated the matter at Akpobaro and initiated it in court. However, they refused to invite Brigadier-General Shevre Orode, the Minister of Science and Technology and the soldiers he used in torturing Chief Akpovire's wives and children, for questioning. But as expected, Mr. Okeme was not to worry. He was relying on the massive evidence of destruction at Akpobaro and the people's testimonies, which he considered were enough to see the case through successfully.

When the case had been initiated in court, Mr. Okeme worked very hard to see it through. He studied day and night with all zest as he saw his own fate sealed with the case. Besides the fact that it was a high profile case that would

172

drag in both the government and the entire army, he also knew that the case might put the current military government on the spotlight locally and internationally. And in such event, he reckoned that he too would be in the limelight. So he was putting in all his brilliance and expertise. At the beginning of the proceeding in court, there seemed to be nothing special with the case; it started like every other case, and it seemed to be going through the due process of judicial proceeding. But on the fourth hearing of the case in court Mr. Okeme realised that he had a huge road block on his way. The presiding judge began to treat the case with withering contempt. Though, the army sent a legal representation after being put on notice, he was only coming with excuses to put off the case each time the case came up, which the judge always willing to grant without looking at its merit.

When Chief Akpovire noticed the furtive scheme to frustrate the case in this manner, he was not surprised. From the start, he felt his effort might come to naught, inspite of his attorney's assurance. But the human nature does not allow the freedom of inaction in the face of extreme provocation. This was what prompted him to go to court.

After about two years of court feet-dragging on the case in the court, Chief Akpovire decided to withdraw from the matter, especially when the case could not make any impression on the people of Akpobaro. By that time, the spirit and determination of his attorney had also been dampened, following several military harassments and threats to his life. All the same, Chief Akpovire appreciated his bold and courageous effort and actually acknowledged it in a letter he wrote to him to signify his withdrawal.

'Thank you, my dear Mr. Okeme for all your effort, it has been exceedingly great. But depressingly, the much raving of the mother-hen will not make the hawk to return its chick.'

CHAPTER SEVENTEEN

The drumbeats, the songs and the dances were varied and resounding in the endless procession towards the river at Oteheri, the ancestral home-town of all Omaurhie people. Each of the villages that made up Omaurhie came with its own dance. The dances and all the accompanying exciting crowds were all moving toward the *Okunovu shrine*. Besides its dancing group, each village or quarter in Oteheri and some individuals who felt blessed that year by *Okunovu* came with their loads of offerings, which were the best of their harvests: large tubers of yams, big bunches of plantains, prize he-goats, rams, etc. Came also were potters with some of their finest well-designed pots. The hunters were there with dressed smoked dried choice animals. Those whose occupation was palm oil making also came with large containers of palm oil. These offerings were deposited at the shrine of *okunovu*. And after these presentations, the dancing and celebration continued round the town until evening when everyone and every group would depart to his village or quarter. This was usually the climax of the *Ughokun* festival which lasted for nine days in the entire Omaurhie villages. It was celebrated annually in the worship of their god, *Okunovu*.

The *Ughokun* festival was very important in the life of Omaurhie people. Apart from *Iyeri* and *Ore* festivals which were periods for worshipping and serving the ancestors of every family at the family ancestral shrine, in the custody of the eldest man of each extended family, the *Ughokun* festival was the biggest festival in Omaurhie. It was devoted to the worship of *Okunovu,* the god of the entire people of the land which they worshipped under its priest, the *Orhere*. The *Orhere* was highly respected among them. He was second only to the *Ovie*, their traditional ruler, as he was the oracle of the people; through him the people heard from their god. The priest had no other engagement other than his total devotion to the people's god. On this all-important occasion, he sacrificed a specially-bred cow, which they reared for use at sacred ceremonies, at the shrine of *Okunovu* and offered prayers for the peace and progress of the entire Omaurhie land.

The life of the *Orhere* was a sacred and privileged one: one that was revered to the sky. Apart from having all the people's offerings for *Okunovu* at this great festival, he had anything he wanted free, and without question in all the villages in the clan. For instance, every year, in one of the nine days of *Ughokun* festival, girls who were entering puberty across the entire villages had to go to the *Okunovu* shrine together, stark naked, to have the blessings of marriage from *Okunovu,* just before their circumcisions. And if there be anyone that attracted the *Orhere* at the shrine, during the performances of their marriage blessings, he could put his priesthood beads on her neck, which authomatically conferred priestly wife upon the young girl, and the girl would be his wife. Nobody questioned the *Orhere* decision. But the *Orhere* also knew that the people expected him to excercise his privileges and authority with the highest sense of responsibility and discipline, so he always acted with decorum and self-restraint. On ordinary day, there were many among the people who felt obliged to send one food item or the other to the *Orhere* in appreciation of his devotedness in the service of the entire people. The people saw him as one who looked after the entire society while the rest individuals were looking after themselves. So the individual people always felt obliged to send the *Orhere* the most valuable food items on their farms. It was only the year of the locusts the *Orhere* had his supplies greatly reduced. But he was still much better off than individuals as the entire people believed and ensured that their god could never go hungry. That was long ago.

The Omaurhie people always celebrated the *Ughokun* festival with joy of gratitude, as they had always had bumper yields on their farms. The hunters too had never ceased to come home with good games. The fishes in their river were always there for catch, even though, the people saw fishing as a casual and pastime activity, which explained why those engaged in it, were either children who only saw it, as an indulgence or the riverine settlers who were traditionally fishermen and women. The palm trees grew on their land without planting, so they belonged to the entire community, and those who cared to make palm fruit cutting their real occupation were merely required to send a handful of palm fruit to the chiefs-in-Council, every quarter of the year, by way of showing gratitude to the community. But those who only cut palm fruit for their domestic use did not need to do that. There were others who engaged in making palm fruit into palm oil and kernels which they sold to others for domestic use or for export. They too used to present some of their productions to chiefs-in-Council quarterly. And because of this beneficence of providence in the land, the people always celebrated the *Ughokun* festival as if that was their last day on earth here. The next day after the ceremony, heaps of foods; the reminants of what were left-over after the great feast would be found at their dumpsides.

Nine good days were usually declared for the observance of the *Ughokun* festival in Omaurhie. During this period absolute peace was expected to prevail. No dispute, no quarrel, no fighting and no protest. This was to ensure that nothing was done in the land that could offend *okunovu*, the general god of Omaurhie people, so that he would accept the people's thanksgiving and offerings and blessed the entire land. In consequence, any acts or actions that had the potency to break the peace were overlooked and the perpetrators carried on with impunity during the period. This often tempted some young people who had been looking for opportunity to indulge themselves in some forms of immorality to exploit the period, knowing that they would not be disciplined if they were caught. Rumours had it that some amorous men lured women including the married ones that they had been eyeing secretly to bed at this time. Though, cases of this had never come to the open.

Akpobaro people were already preparing toward the year's *Ughokun* festival, as it was only three weeks to its festivity. Just like the year before it, they had started putting aside the food items they would take down to Oteheri. All the people were expected to go to Oteheri except the children and the aged for the celebration. Apart from those who went to represent the village and some individuals who went to present their best harvests in thanksgiving, many others went for the fun and the excitement. Nobody would want to miss the great fun; no one wanted to be told of how the different dances, the huge procession, all the enormous presentations and the entire celebration went at Oteheri. Everybody from all the villages of Omaurhie wanted to be part of the great festival. Besides the show, many people from other villages always saw the festival as an opportunity to be with their kith and kin at Oteheri, the genealogical root of the entire Omaurhie people – eating and drinking together. So the festival always brought together members of the same extended family who had been separated. It was a time family members who had sojourned to different places would like to come home with their immediate families. This had helped to know all the extended family members in a lineage. The whole of Oteheri was always boisterous at this time. There was always so much frolicking everywhere in the town during the festival.

176

Efe was one person, perhaps, the only one who did not look forward to this year's *Ughokun* festival. This was not because of fear of being beaten by his father, as he had grown up into full boyhood, and was already in college at Safa. He had a secret romance with Oyovo, one of the young belles in Akpobaro. When he was on holidays, Efe always monitored her movement and cornered her whenever she was on an errand, because such a secret affair was always kept secret, as romance among minors was considered a serious offence and was much disapproved by the community. So no boy or girl would want to experience the scandal and shame it bore. That was why Efe and Oyovo only met secretly. And such chances hardly come readily. Apart from market day when there was free movement, they seldom had the chance except for the occasional errands Oyovo usually ran for her parents.

As the parents of Oyovo were making adequate preparations for her circumcision that year, the news filtered out to Efe, and it was causing him great distress. Efe's friends believed that the *Orhere,* the priest of *Okunovu,* might take Oyovo for his wife at the *Okunovu* shrine as she was believed to be the most beautiful upcoming girl in the entire Omaurhie kngdom. Efe became very worried and apprehensive as soon as this notion was dropped into him. He had been thinking of how to reach Oyovo to confirm the story and plan a possible way of preventing her from going to *Okunovu* shrine that year. He knew that there was little he could do to prevent her from going but he wanted to convince her to postpone her circumcision to the following year. He wished an unforeseen circumstance could occur to stop the girls going to *Okunovu* shrine for marriage blessing that year. Efe was desperate to see Oyovo. Everyday, he would go near her place and hung by, hoping that she might be sent out on an errand. After some days, Gueke, a shopkeeper by Oyovo's father's compound had noticed that Efe was constantly lottering around there. As he saw him again, he said, 'What's Councillor's son doing around here everyday? He's always there alone most times.' The man he was talking with looked at Efe for sometime and smiled. He understood. He had seen Efe and Oyovo together before at a remote bend, near the bush path in one evening, holding hands and laughing. He knew there was some secret affair between them. But he had never expressed his feeling to anybody. He thought that if they were indulging in secret romance, one day it would come to the open.

'Leave the poor boy alone. His presence there won't rob you anything, will it?' the man told the shopkeeper.

'Of course not, I'm only being curious like every other human being.'

'But don't be curious to the extent where you put your mouth in a place where it's not wanted.'

And they both laughed.

Just then, Oyovo came out of her compound and was going the opposite direction. She had noticed Efe and became very nervous. She did not want him to come near her, as she had seen the two men at the shop looking her direction with curiousity when she came out of her compound. She quickened her steps and pretended that she did not see Efe. When Efe saw her going, his heart started leaping with anxiety. He did not know what to do now that he had seen Oyovo whom he had been craving to see. Instinct almost made him to follow her immediately. But he tried to be careful and act properly, else Oyovo would be offended and that would damage everything. So he hesitated a while. But he realised he had a rare chance at hand and must use it. He began to move discreetly in her direction, after glancing at the shop and around to see if some persons were looking. The two men at the shop seemed to be absorbed in themselves now, as he walked behind Oyovo. Very soon, he walked up to her and the tension in both of them rose. Oyovo looked the other side pretendingly as Efe whispered to her.

'I heard you're going to Okunovu.'

'My parents say I should go.'

'Why are your parents in a hurry? You can make it next year.'

'They're not in a hurry, all my age mates are going.'

Oyovo who was becoming very uncomfortable, thinking some persons might be observing, quickened her steps, to separate herself from Efe.

Efe understood her shyness and fear. For sometime, he was not sure of what to say and was silent while struggling to keep pace with her.

'What if Orhere puts his beads on your neck?' said Efe accusingly.

Oyovo suddenly understood Efe's fear.

'He won't do so,' she answered softly.

'What if he does?' Efe retorted.

Oyovo was rather uncomfortable with the notion.

'I don't expect it.'

'It's not a matter of expectation. That he-goat can do anything nasty and thinks he's beyond question. It's all nonsense!'

178

'Why would you speak of Orhere like that? Are you not afraid? You know Orhere is a spirit man, he hears things and can decide to do you harm,' cautioned Oyovo.

'Spirit man my foot! He should go and eat shit!' exploded Efe.

Oyovo opened her eyes wide with shock and covered her opened mouth with her hand at such blaspheming. She was full of fear and pity for Efe. The approaching of three women from the opposite direction eventually disrupted their conversation and Efe went away.

That night Efe could not sleep. He was reflecting very deeply on the authority of the *Orhere* to have any woman of his desire. He was doing so with much disgust. He had several painful questions on his mind against the *Orhere* and was wondering why one man should have the right and privilege to take any young woman as wife, even when such a girl might not like it. He was even more furious at the people who instituted the practice and those who continued to accept it as a tradition. *What a stupid religious practice and a coward society!* he protested within himself. *The Orhere can't harm shit. He has no power. The powers of the Orhere are all lies. They only exist in the minds of Omaurhie people. He's no such god anywhere.* He saw the Omaurhie people as people who needed to be liberated from the entire concept of *Okunovu* and its priest. He thought when he grew into a full man he would mobilise brave men like him, march to the *Okunovu* shrine and smash everything there. He wished he was a full man now. He thought of talking to his friends about dismantling the *Okunovu* shrine should the *Orhere* put his beads on Oyovo. But he soon realised that they certainly would not go with him. *Everybody is afraid of the Orhere and Okunovu. But I'm not! I'll smash the shrine on my own if those old dirty fingers touch Oyovo.*

CHAPTER EIGHTEEN

Mr. Olaniyi did a lot of study of the oil exploitation activities in the oil-bearing communities and found out that Chief Akpovire's alarm was correct. After his study, he prepared a report that gave a detailed analysis of the situation which he packaged as a proposal for Starling Company. He had worked on the report for months with his two immediate assistants. He alluded to some of the negative impacts of oil exploitation on the vegetation and its inhabitants in their areas of operation and suggested ways to avert the likely furore that might ensue. He also recommended the conversion of gas into liquefied gas as a way of stopping gas-emission into the atmosphere in the process of drilling crude oil from oil-well. 'This is what obtains in other oil-producing countries,' he stated. At the end of the laborious job, he and his two assistants congratulated themselves and thought that the management would commend them for such a well-articulated report, and they also believed the proposal would have a foot-hold on the company's public relation policy. They submitted the report to the Starling management at the headquarters through their area general manager and copied each unit of management at the operational level. Management annual general meeting soon drew near.

During the annual general meeting, the top management of Starling Company adopted the proposals in the report in principle, after an extensive deliberation, except the conversion of gas into liquefied gas which they thought might still take sometime because of the huge capital involved. They presented the proposal to government, their sole-partner, before fully adopting them as their policies. The main thrust of Starling's proposals to government was that, 5% of their mutual profit be set aside for the rehabilitation, preservation and development of the oil-bearing communities and their environments, so that the negative impact of exploration and exploitation could be minimised in those areas.

But contrary to their expectation, the government officials expressed surprise and disappointment at the proposals. They wandered when Starling Company became the advocate of the people in the oil-bearing communities. They considered the proposals as an indictment on government. In their argument, they reminded Starling Company that they were in the country for business and they should mind just that. They went further to say that government is fully aware of its responsibility to guarantee a peaceful atmosphere for Starling Company's business operation. They further stated that it was only when they could not meet that obligation before Starling Company would have the cause to complain. The government representatives also admonished Starling Company and all other multinational oil companies to always alert government any time the peace of their areas of operation was threatened. Finally, they warned the oil companies to avoid being dragged into local politics as that might be counter-productive. 'Government is aware of her citizens' needs and she is always willing to meet them within her financial limits. They need no one to remind her about them!' the spokesperson admonished.

When Starling management received the government response, they immediately realised that they were a bit meddlesome and regretted their action which they communicated back to government, saying that they were misinformed.

The covert reactions that followed almost cost Mr. Olaniyi his job. Queries were fired at him severally for no plausible cause. For more than three months he was under intense pressure of having to explain one thing or the other at both his local office and at Starling headquarters. It seemed the management was looking for every means to get rid of him. But he was particularly fortunate for maintaining a clean record and for having a godfather at the top. When the storm was over, he vowed never to think of community's interest again in Starling's operations in his assignment.

Meanwhile, oil discovery had become widespread in the delta belt of the country. Oil had also been found in several villages in Omaurhie that their entire land was fast becoming a vast oil-field. At Akpobaro more oil-wells had been constructed which had taken much of the land. Exploratory and exploitive oil activities were still ongoing in the area. Three more flow-stations had been added to the existing one. The workers who carried out the various oil operational activities in the area were mainly professionals and highly skilled technicians. But it was unlike before when many of the workers were staying in the community. A large, high-brow housing estate had been built for the workers and all their daily needs, including foodstuffs, were supplied through their registered contractors. And most of their foods were canned and processed foreign items. Their workers were mainly recruited from Starling headquarters and sent to the various operational offices where they were deployed to oil locations for work after some training. The artisans and the clerical workers who assisted the professionals on the job were recruited from the operational office at Ukoti which was not near, either. Apart from some irregular casual work that required local hands, the natives of Akpobaro were not employed in the oil-rich business. Although, some inhabitants of Akpobaro and other Omaurhie villages were now boasted professionals who graduated from various tertiary educational institutions, they had not been able to secure a job in the oil and gas industry which they dreamed of everyday. But the recruitment policy of Starling Company did not favour them, as the recruitment was always done at their headquarters at the capital, so they stood no chance. And many more people from the area were struggling everyday to go to higher schools. When they saw the great comfort the professional oil workers were enjoying in their land, they could not wish for anything less.

The estate which 'oil workers', as they were now called, stayed at Akpobaro was well provided with all the modern comforts of life, including air-conditioners, outdoor recreational facilities as swimming pool and lawn-tennis courts. Floodlights all through the night made it possible for these games to be played at night. The moon never showed its face here. Their catering, bar and laundry unit which they called 'service unit' was better than what very good hotels in the cities could offer. The estate was well-lawned with greenery. Also in the estate was a well-equipped clinic with expatriate doctors that rendered on-the-spot service, twenty four hours. The medical personnel ran two-week shift schedule here, which was supervised by their main clinic at Ukoti, their operational office in the region. The only black doctors employed in Starling were those who had their training in the advanced world. Well-treated pipe borne water was in constant supply. All the lanes linking each other in the estate were tarred. Their security personnel with fierce-looking giant dogs could detect any intruders thirty metres away. It was from the estate the main workers filed out to the various oil locations in Omaurhie each morning in a series of trucks like ants. They criss-crossed the entire land with their pipe-lines.

Understandingly, the ordinary people of Akpobaro never thought of getting near their amenities in the estate, apart from the excitement and curiosity that greeted the oil activities and the presence of white men at the

182

beginning. Their own circumstances made it impossible for them to contemplate getting close. They had always been living simple agrarian traditional life devoid of modern amenities, so they never saw the need for a good medical centre as they relied mostly on indigenous and traditional medicine or herbs for treatment. They saw the high and sophisticated living of the oil workers in their estate as luxury far beyond their reach and they thought they never deserved such grand comfort. They believed such a standard of living was only meant for the whites and the highly educated black people. So the people of Akpobaro never grudged the oil workers of their good fortune. They only wished that some day their own educated people would be in the company's employ and enjoyed these high modern living like other educated oil workers.

The only thing that was giving them cause for concern was the way the oil activities had been eating up their land, especially their farmland and the disruption of their traditional living. They felt being invaded sometimes and wished the oil company would pack up some day and leave them alone. Meanwhile, the road to Akpobaro had become so bad that the earlier condition of the road before Starling gave it a rough tarring was much better. Starling trucks plied the road regularly to the various locations, yet they did not see the need to maintain it. There has been a smouldering wind of disaffection over the ruination of the farmland and bushes by the oil activities. The youths in Akpobaro engaged in hunting and rubber-tapping, which had been their main occupations, but now the land had been decimated by Starling operations and games taken flight. The oil exploration and exploitation had drastically reduced rubber-tapping in the area also. Timber business, which also engaged the youths, was being reduced by oil activities in the area, too.

Chief Akpovire and the elders of Akpobaro had waited for the reply Mr. Olaniyi promised them but to no avail. They wrote several letters of reminder, but there was no response. Later, two very ugly incidents erupted in quick succession in a manner of conspiracy. One day, the people of Akpobaro woke up to see crude oil floating on the surface of their river which they depended on for all their domestic use and recreation. At first, they did not know what was wrong. They began to trace the source of the seepage, only to find that crude oil was gushing out from the oil pipeline near the river. Part of it was also going into the bushes nearby. The Starling workers at the station radioed their operational office and very soon, a helicopter flew some white men down to inspect the eruption. Many fishes were seen the following day belly-up in the river, floating. The oil workers warned that those fishes should not be eaten, and it was sounded round the village and other places. The people resorted to a far away stream for water. For two weeks normal life was disrupted until the emergency effort of Starling to clean up the affected area was carried out and a major repair was effected on one of the pipes linking an oil-well to the flow-station in the area.

Three months later, Starling engineers in their routine inspection discovered that one of the oil-wells in the farmland had a major crack and was emitting gas into the atmosphere. It caused a great trepidation among the workers that morning. They wondered why it had not incinerated the farmland. They were happy that the crack was discovered in time. They did not alert the villagers, to avoid any panic and agitation. But the company quickly passed an express order to them to keep out naked light or flame within three kilometres radius until further notice, an embarrassing arduous task for Mr. Olaniyi who had been keeping away from Akpobaro all this while. He told them a lie that the company's management was considering entering into an MOU with them as they earlier requested and assured them of approval, when the incident compelled him to meet with Akpobaro chiefs again.

Starling knew the danger the gas leakage posed if adequate precautions were not taken. They immediately dispatched policemen numbering over fifty attached to the company to the entire farmland to monitor the farmers. Bold billboards were placed in strategic locations on the farmland with the inscription: DANGER: NO NAKED FIRE! They immediately commissioned one of their contractor firms to construct a pipeline to the river, as a source of water supply to their fire-fighting facilities at their estate, in readiness against any fire out-break which they thought could be devastating, considering their extensive oil installations in the area. The distance of the fire-fighting equipment to the river was about ten kilometres. All these red alert measures remained in place until another oil well was constructed to replace the cracked one. Fortunately, Starling averted the latent disaster.

But the two unfortunate occurrences were trying times for Akpobaro people. The clean-up exercise was not thorough. The crude oil hung on their river for weeks after the clean-up. For about a month the people were always going to the far-away stream to fetch water which was not easy.

184

The path to the stream was almost covered with growing grass, as the people hardly went to the stream now. The few bicycle owners could not enjoy the privilege of riding to the stream. The path was narrow, rough and undulating. Many children fell with their water on their way from the stream and sometimes had their plastic containers torn or perforated, and cried back home in frustration. The women were more careful. But it was a tough time for them because they bore this extra burden in addition to their other routine activities.

The smell of crude oil hung upon the village for a long time and the portion of land affected had begun to give up all its natural features. The trees, particularly the rubbers began to wither. Their leaves began to turn yellow and fell off after sometime. At first, it looked like the season when trees shed their leaves but new replacement never followed. Next, the bodies of the trees began to decay. It was so gradual that the people could not notice it until after sometime. For the undergrowth, they never woke up again after the oil spill. They perished and decayed with the remnant of the crude oil after the clean-up, and for many years the area could not bring forth normal vegetation. The few that sprouted out came with miserable yellow colour and after sometime they withered away, and the area remained a permanent scar that kept reminding the people of the unpleasant incident.

The riverine settlers who had been enjoying undisturbed boom in fishing turned out the worst hit. After about a month, the river became skyly clean again but all the fishes had disappeared. The fishermen toiled all day, cast their nets everywhere in the river with anxious expectation. But when they drew the net together, to their dismay, not even one fish would be in it. The drought of fish in the river was very disturbing to them as days entered weeks and weeks entered months. When they returned home in the evening without a catch, each night became a night of deep thought; overwhelming thought of survival. In their dire straits, some took to farming which was like a man learning to walk again; fishing had always been the occupation they knew from childhood. Those who could not adjust to farming left Akpobaro in search of another settlement.

But the hardship of the oil spillage paled into insignificance when compared with the one of gas leakage. Akpobaro people had always worked with fire on their farmlands. They burnt the cleared, dried debris after two weeks of farm preparation ahead of planting. Unfortunately, the planting season coincided with the gas linkage. This meant that they had to suspend all the planting activities of that year. By the time the construction of the new oil-well was completed, they were already on the threshold of the rainy season, so very little was cultivated that year as they spent very little time in farming during the period, unlike before when they took enough food along with them to their farms which they warmed with fire before eating later in the day. They were also used to preparing some local fast food at the farm. But the banning of naked fire put a stop to all of that, which resulted in poor harvest and hardship that year.

Strangely, the people of Akpobaro began to experience some awful and unusual developments in their land. Though, a good portion of their land had been taken over by the oil activities, they noticed to their chagrin that the remaining land was no longer turning out normal yields. The cassava stems and leaves looked quite juicy as before but their tubers were rack and ruin with very bad smell when harvested. Very little could be got out of them. Though, the yams were not rotten, their yield was so poor that it was not worth the labour any more, and yam was the men's crop. The corn had only few ears on the cobs, so were many other minor crops. The fruits were not spared. Many plants bore deficient fruits while some other could not bear fruits any more.

The people began to realise as they bemoaned their lot, that they were gradually being estranged from their own land and felt highly constrained by the oil activities in the area. As each day passed, they bore their frustration quietly, longing for the day the oil activities would come to an end. Everyday, this uncertainty of life tormented them like excruciating pain in the body.

Their fish harvest festival which occurred towards the end of the year was not celebrated the following year after the oil spill. Their natural water-way was filled to the brim that year as usual with the coming of the rainy season. The water flowed from the river to the source of the natural water-way one night in a heavy rain. Through out the night, the rain was just pouring down. The following day water was running down the natural water-way that criss-crossed Akpobaro and flooded everywhere around its source, where most families had ponds. The ponds were all covered with water. The people went out the following morning to see the extent of the water coverage amidst random croaking of numerous frogs in the flood. They were quite happy to observe that the water covered all the ponds. The children were excited too, as they usually swam and fished in the running natural-water-way. The coming of the running water from the river at the peak of the rainy season each year was always greeted with great excitement as it reminded the people of the great fish harvest ahead.

When the dry season set in, and the flood began to recede, every family would cut palm fronds to cover their own ponds for fear that the heat of the sun might kill the fishes except for those ponds in the thick bushes, totally shaded by trees. A month later, when the flood around the source had completely dried and the natural-water way was getting empty, the town-crier went round the village one evening, announcing the day for the fish harvest as fixed by the chiefs-in-Council. The people as usual were looking forward to a bumper fish harvest that year. On the appointed day, every family turned out very early in the morning with their variety of hand-made baskets of cane and palm tree straw which they used to sieve fishes from the ponds. Also taken along were buckets to bale the water from the ponds. That morning the pond field was swarmed with people full of excitement and expectation.

By noon, the men began to climb out of their ponds totally appalled and alarmed. There were no fishes in the ponds! The first family to discover the uncanny situation was struck dumb. The men came out of their ponds fretful and crestfallen, with mounting frustration. They could not believe it. It had never happened. Immediately, they wanted to find out if they were alone in this mind-boggling inexplicable misfortune and they went to see other ponds. By 2.00 in the afternoon, it became clear to the entire Akpobaro that the expected fish feast was doomed. Not one fish was found in any of the ponds. Gloom of disappointment enveloped the entire village that day, as they all returned home from the ponds with long faces. They believed that the marine goddess, a section of them worshipped at the river, was angry with them.

The following morning, a procession of *Igbe* members[19] led by its priestess, were dancing towards the riverside. They were believed to possess the marine spirit and were worshippers of the marine goddess. As usual, they dressed in white apparel and their faces and bodies were extensively designed with native white chalk. Many on-lookers, especially children, trailed behind, maintaining some distance. A white cock was held by a woman in front, a goat was being led along by one of them. Some tubers of yams, a bunch of plantains, three bottles of mineral waters and some native chalks were in a big basin carried by a maiden. The ethereal spiritual songs, which tended to

---

[19] A religious sect or group devoted to the worship of marine goddess

influence the conduct of the priestess who was at the centre of the small procession, were poignant and esoteric. The priestess was never steady. She was always staggering about in a seeming drunken manner and unable control herself, yet never falling. Sometimes, she would be in frenzy. And in a rare moment in the height of her frenzy, she would race forward as if she was pursuing something, only to run back again. In each of these dramatic moves, the singers and the drummers also responded by a change in pitch. When they reached the riverside, the dancing became more vigorous. Everyone of them became more dramatic in the singing and dancing, making some eerie and weird sounds, which were believed to be the language of the marine spirit and the priestess swayed uncontrollable as if she was about to be blown down by a strong wind. In a moment, she raced forward in absolute frenzy, ran back and ran past the group forward and backward , left and right, snatched the white cock, turned it round her head seven times and round the group once before casting it into the river. A loud shout of approval followed, as the cock struggled on the river several times before going down. And the dancing resumed again. After sometime, the priestess marched forward again and muttered some incoherent incantation which only the world of marine spirit understood, before breaking into the following eulogy:

The owner of the marine world
We greet you and your host
The queen of the coast
We greet you and your host
The goddess of favour
We greet you and your host
Our great provider
We your host greet you and

We have come again
To give thanks
We thank you and your host
We offer you these ones:

She started throwing the rest of the items one after the other into the river.

188

The ruler of the marine world
Bless our land
Bless our ponds
Bless our waters
Bless our fish harvest
It glorifies you
It celebrates you

Bless your people

And the goat, the last and prize offer, was thrown into the river which was followed by a loud cheer. And the singing and dancing resumed homeward on the slope into the village.

As they returned, one of the women shouted at once, 'She's calling! She's calling me!' She was moving back towards the river. The rest of the group members held her but they could not. Her body had become too slippery and was breaking loose. They called for help. Many people ran to them and helped. But she could not be held. She had broken into hysteria and was moving down. Many more people came, men and women, and formed a huge phalanx on her way but she managed to sway through! She had possessed extraordinary strength and became too slippery to hold. The people shouted and became frantic.

'No, I must go! She's c-a-l-l-i-n-g!' she kept repeating, struggled and was going closer to the river.

The crowd surged here and there to prevent her. They believed that if she could get to the river she might disappear. And after about five minutes of intense struggle, she became completely calm, weak and numb. They carried her home in her unconscious state. She became normal again when she woke up the following morning.

It sometimes happens to some of the members who catch the marine spirit. Any non-initiate who is possessed by the marine spirit would be taken to her shrine for full initiation and participation in all her rites and worship and if she refuses to be initiated, the belief is that she would die. In any case, none of such persons believed to have been possessed with the marine spirit has ever refused.

Regrettably, the following year and other subsequent years fishes never came   with the running water from the river, during the rainy season, so the ponds remained without fish and the fish harvest and its feast were lost to history.

CHAPTER NINETEEN

After the military invasion of Akpobaro, every opposition gave way for Vremudia to be in full control. Buoyed by the military terror his brother visited on the village, Vremudia saw himself bestriding Akpobaro like a cowboy on his horse and thought he could ride the village as he pleased. He took decisions for the entire people. The new *Ugo*, Chief Onokero, and the faction of chiefs who were loyal to him simply reported at his house, to take instructions, which they related to the rest chiefs at the chiefs-in-Council.

At first, many chiefs were not pleased with the new development but they were afraid to oppose it. To keep their pride and reputation, some of the notable ones were no longer attending the chiefs-in-Council meetings. They thought that was the best way to avoid trouble with Vremudia and his cronies. But Vremudia with his men saw their action as a refusal to acknowledge his leadership. Soon, rumour started going round Akpobaro that the names of the chiefs who were distancing themselves from *oguedion* meeting were being compiled in Vremudia's house for sanction.

Expectedly, the next *oguedion* meeting witnessed the coming of all the chiefs except Mudiaga, even the deposed *Ugo* who since the military torture had never entered the *oguedion,* also attended. After that day, every chief pretended to be a friend of Vremudia. Those of them who had vowed earlier never to associate with him began to visit him regularly and often eulogised him for his *good leadership* as they sat with him. And this pleased Vremudia very much. After sometime, the chiefs saw their regular visits to him as a duty and were doing it religiously.

Now that he had taken over everything and his house had become where every decision of the village was taken, one would have thought that Vremudia would be satisfied. You know that the wicked are always afraid and are in constant sense of insecurity, irrespective of the physical protection around them. In the mould of somebody who attained his position unfairly, Vremudia began to anticipate evils towards himself, without really knowing how such harms would be plotted by those he displaced and offended. So he began to think of the best way to survive and consolidate his position against his phantom enemies. This further drove him to plot more evil.

Vremudia particularly believed that as long as Chief Akpovire still lived with some honour, he would not enjoy the full loyalty of the entire Akpobaro. He felt Chief Akpovire's gracious presence in the village still cast doubt on his authority and leadership and this worried him a lot. Anytime his thoughts went to Chief Akpovire, he was always uncomfortable. And the more he thought about it, the more his worry increased. For sometime, he kept his anxiety to himself. He had been thinking of the next action to take.

One day, he summoned his core loyal boys to one of his inner chambers one mid-night. He told them that he had uncovered a plot by Chief Akpovire and Mudiaga to eliminate him. He did not elaborate. These days, he never thought it necessary to explain or make his point clear to others. He considered such a thing quite demeaning to his position. Vremudia was happy to see his boys becoming furious and vexed at the drop of his allegation.

'When he was the leader, everyone of us gave him support and respect. I never sought his downfall. But now that I'm the leader he no longer sleeps. I hear of his plot against me everyday. If not for God and the good people of the village, what'll have become of me?' lamented he. 'How long shall I live in his constant threat?'

'Leader, we'll handle him. He can't pose any danger to you when we're here,' said the leader of his boys.

'He shall surely regret it,' one of the boys added, the rest of the boys nodding their heads in agreement.

'Now, listen boys! This is one issue we shouldn't brag about,' Vremudia told them confidentially, having been satisfied with their reactions. 'We must be clever! Let no one else hear of our plan.'

At that point, he pulled out a charm-object from the back of the door.

'Now each of us must swear,' Vremudia became fiercely business like. 'Now swear!' he ordered as he placed the charm-object in front of the leader of his goons to swear the oath of secrecy and loyalty to whatever plot they were to carry out against Chief Akpovire. He swore and passed the charm-object to the next person and all the boys swore sheepishly with the charm-object, not knowing exactly what to expect.

For a while, Vremudia stared at the boys with some evil intent, while his eyes were rolling over some sinister thoughts. He was thinking of how to divulge his evil intent to the boys as he flashed his eyes from one boy to the other. The boys were now filled with fear of what Vremudia was about to assign them.

192

'Now listen, all of you! Next Sunday, you shall go to Akpovire in the night and waste him! Disguise yourselves! Rob and kill! Understand?'

The boys were silent.

'Clear?' roared he.

'Yes, leader,' they answered, trembling.

'I shall give you arms. You must act with tact, squeak-free; no trace! Right?' he bellowed.

'Yes leader.'

'Good, no fear. I'll give you protection. We can't fold our arms to see Akpovire destroy us. We must act fast before he does us harm, understand?'

'Yes leader,' they answered reluctantly.

The boys went to sleep later with great unease. They could not imagine themselves shedding innocent blood, let alone of one who was so good and honourable in the village. They were really worried about having a hand in Chief Akpovire's death. But they could not now show any act of disloyalty or ingratitude to their master who had been so kind to them. Besides, they had sworn to a charm or fetish which they believed would have a curse placed upon them if they failed to abide by what they had sworn to.

Samuel was most disturbed among them. When he got home that night, he was restless. He was one of those settler boys with whom Efe was fishing when he was very young and since then they had remained friends. Samuel becoming one of Vremudia's boys was totally unplanned. Samuel never imagined that one day he would ever come near Vremudia. He had always disliked Vremudia from his closeness to Efe and because he had heard many stories of his malevolence towards Chief Akpovire, and had even wondered why the man was so heartless. But one day, he went with his fellow riverine boys to play football at the primary school field. The village boys usually played football there most evenings. Sometimes, he was lucky to be chosen to take part. But when he was not, he would be watching from the sideline like many other boys, as many boys often turned out for the game in the evening. Those selected were chosen on the strength of their previous performances. Sentiments were always put aside; each side would want to have the day in order to deride their opponents. After the football game that evening, his fellow riverine boys whom he came with were strolling into the village. They persuaded him to follow them. They told him they wanted to see someone before heading home. And he did without knowing the exact person. He was already in the house of Vremudia before he knew Vremudia was the object of their visit and it was too late for him to turn back. Vremudia welcomed them heartily and gave them drink. In his chat with the boys, he became particularly interested in Samuel whom he had never met before, and he was often looking at him for expected response in his conversation. Vremudia seemed to have taken to him. When the boys were leaving later and were about five metres away, he called Samuel back, and slipped a note in his hand, 'I'll like to see you again,' he whispered to him. The money produced a feeling of involuntary repulsion in Samuel as he looked at Vremudia who seemed to betray some vague insincerity in his smile. Samuel thanked him and ran back to meet his friends. He was surprised at Vremudia's sudden interest in him, and was at a loss what to make out of it. But somehow his feet kept taking him to Vremudia's with the rest of the riverine boys willy nilly, and as time went by, the tie grew, especially when Vremudia continued to encourage him with generous gifts. After sometime, he did not see anything wrong with Vremudia again, and he started going there so regularly that he eventually became one of his most reliable and devoted boys. While he was gravitating to Vremudia, his relationship with Efe was gradually being eroded as Efe went to college at Safa. They seldom met after that and when they did, they would interact briefly as old friends and went their separate ways. Visit to each other as before no longer existed between them. And as Efe continued staying out of Akpobaro for his college education, his chances of interacting with Samuel became very slim and had almost thinned out. But in the deepest recesses of their minds they still considered each other a friend.

Since the night they agreed to eliminate Chief Akpovire, Samuel had not been himself. He found it extremely hard to get his mind round on the matter. Everyday, the idea lay on his conscience like an excruciating injury. He could not sleep at night. Not only did he not want to have a hand, he was also thinking of how to save Chief Akpovire's life without betraying Vremudia and the other boys. It was a complex issue that had no easy way out. But four days to the execution of the plot, Samuel went to see Efe in the evening. He led him to a corner from his friends.

'What I want to tell you is at the risk of my personal life. But I can't help it – so my life is at your mercy,' said Samuel soberly. 'Your father must not sleep his house Thursday night.'

'Why?' said Efe with fear.

'I've told you. Please, be wise.'

There were several questions Efe wanted to ask him but Samuel would not say any more under any circumstances. He could perceive that the little Samuel had divulged was done at great pain.

'Thanks,' said Efe with much inclination to know more about the matter, which he expressed clearly in his anxious look.

'What I've told you is enough, just act on it,' instructed Samuel as he was walking away, not wanting to say more.

When he had left, Efe was very worried. He knew Samuel was Vremudia's boy and he suspected Vremudia had some evil plan against his father the coming Thursday night. He was full of appreciation for Samuel's great courage and expression of true friendship. But his greatest challenge now was how to get his father out of his house the Thursday night. He knew his father would not be persuaded to leave his house, for some where else at night under any circumstance.

That night, Efe could not sleep. He stayed up till one o'clock in the night, turning his mind over and over without any lead. The following early morning, he went to see Mudiaga. When he got there, Mudiaga was already up from bed. He was sitting in his living room, taking some shots from his bottle of *ogogoro* of several herbal roots – it was his way of 'warming' his stomach for the day, just like most men in Akpobaro.

'*Miguo*,' Efe greeted while bending down one of his kneels as he entered Mudiaga's house.

'*Vredo*,'[20] answered Mudiaga with some surprise on his face. 'Efe, you're here this early morning? Hope nothing is wrong?'

He was looking at Efe intently for possible signs of bad news, as Efe had never come to him at such time. His fear was further heightened when he reckoned that Efe was the most unlikely choice, Chief Akpovire would use among his children for normal errands. 'You say nothing is wrong?'

'Nothing is wrong,' answered Efe as he shook his head in the negative.

'Is everybody in the family well?'

'Yes,' Efe nodded his head positively.

'Is your father well?'

'Yes.'

'What about the women and the children?'

[20] Response to the greeting '*miguo*'. *Miguo* means "my knees are down" out of respect for the older person. While "vren" or "vre" means "get up" or "stand up", and "doh" thank you for the gesture of kneeling.

'They're all fine.'

'You say you're all well?'

'Yes.'

Mudiaga paused for a while, 'there's a drink,' he pointed at the table.

Efe shook his head in the negative and bowed his head in appreciation.

'Take a little, it's good for the stomach,' Mudiaga persuaded.

Efe shook his head again.

Though, most young men like Efe often refused to accept drink from the elderly as a mark of respect, even when they desired it very strongly, but Efe was not for such propriety – he was very worried inside. He was trying hard not to betray it. He did not want Mudiaga to anticipate what he wanted to tell him.

When there was nothing else to say, Efe told Mudiaga all that Samuel told him.

'You mean what you're saying?' reacted Mudiaga with some alarm.

Efe nodded his head in the affirmative calmly.

'Alright, my son, I have heard you. I'll see your father and discuss the matter with him,' said Mudiaga after some agitated reflection.

Efe stood up to leave. But something was hanging on his mind.

'Papa, please let no one hear it, it's a secret,' said Efe as he was stepping out.

'My son, you're not talking to a fool,' returned Mudiaga.

That evening Mudiaga strolled over to Chief Akpovire. Chief Akpovire had just finished his supper and was sitting in the frontage of his house. The breeze was gentle and refreshing. He always loved to nestle in his deck-chair like this in the mellowing evening. That was the time he allowed his thought to roam freely like the bird in the air. And some issues he might have overlooked would come to his consciousness again. It was also a time he usually analysed a nagging and thorny issue for resolution, and his mind would be working like the clock. That evening, he was just thinking about the present situation of Akpobaro: how Akpobaro was just drifting very badly. He realised that nobody cared any more for the community and he was very worried about it. He feared that the situation of the village might turn awry, as a result. He had already seen the signs; how the village had regressed sharply. Painfully, he saw himself being part of that regression: how events had made

196

him the pebbled shore being rocked and washed away by the tide. He shook his head with disgust. He became sad at that moment.

'Life is worthless if it has nothing to offer society,' he said to himself. Chief Akpovire believed that the most miserable person on earth was that person who had the privilege to give to society but unfortunately choosing to take from it, rather.

It was in this mood and reflection that Mudiaga met him that evening.

'*Otemunoruemu!*[21] *Okpirhevagho!*[22]...' Mudiaga started showering Chief Akpovire with nicknames associated with greatness as soon as he sighted him. He wanted to put Chief Akpovire in a robust liveliness because he knew what he wanted to discuss with him was alarming. It was also an attempt to get him off the life of sobriety that he had come to embrace these days, as Mudiaga was increasingly becoming bored with his companionship recently.

It worked. Chief Akpovire was all smiles to receive his most loyal friend. He stretched out his hand enthusiastically in warm greeting when Mudiaga became close, while one of his children ran inside the house to fetch a chair as usual. When Mudiaga had taken his seat, they continued their pleasantry which soon drifted to some general matters. Mudiaga became very critical of the rest of the chiefs, who out of fear, went against their good conscience to surrender to Vremudia. He was particularly angry with the deposed *Ugo* whom he criticized severely.

'Councillor, some people have no pride, no shame: cowards!' laughed he sarcastically. 'How could the *Ugo* of all persons cross over to that scoundrel after what his brother did to him? I can't imagine it. God forbid! I used to respect him. I never knew he was such a coward.'

'I think they have no choice,' observed Chief Akpovire.

'What choice?' exploded Mudiaga. 'Councillor, are you telling me I had a choice when I defied Vremudia the other time?'

'Well...' Chief Akpovire wanted to say something but he quickly swallowed it. He wanted to say that Mudiaga was too close to him to have gone to Vremudia but he quickly realised that would amount to ingratitude on his part.

'There's no "well" there. They all simply show that they're cowards, complete cowards!' ranted Mudiaga.

---

[21] One who is exceedingly able and exceedingly carries out great deeds.

[22] Mighty tree with well-established roots which can withstand any weather

'But who knows what would have happened if they'd not gone over? Probably, somebody would have been more desperate and that could mean more trouble for us all,' offered Chief Akpovire.

'Well,' conceded Mudiaga reluctantly as he immediately came to the consciousness of what Efe had revealed to him. 'All the same, I hate them all – they're the ones making that animal to feel that he's somebody we should all look up to. He's nothing but a beast, a mere beast, that's what he is. It won't last…Vremudia cannot handle the slightest problem in this our community. He sees leadership position as something to be acquired like a property. I mean some kind of expensive and beautiful clothes to be worn. He does not know that leadership is a huge responsibility and challenge and it takes a great mind and uncommon courage to handle it successfully,' asserted Mudiaga.

Chief Akpovire truly appreciated all that Mudiaga had said but did not comment, as he thought his comment might indirectly advertise himself, which he always tried to avoid.

When Mudiaga had said all that he wanted to say about the chiefs and Vremudia, they became silent for sometime, which ushered the dreadful news Mudiaga had brought. Chief Akpovire rather than frightened by it, reacted with some unaffected equanimity.

'Plotting to kill me? Let him come,' said Chief Akpovire calmly. 'The elephant thinks it's the biggest animal in the world but one day it shall encounter the hippopotamus!' sniffed he.

Mudiaga wanted to know what he planned to do to counter Vremudia.

'Mudiaga, I've no plan! Let him come. Is it not my life he wants? It's here waiting for him.'

'Just like that?' said Mudiaga in bewilderment.

'Mudiaga, what do you want me to do?'

'Travel to Safa,' said Mudiaga.

'Run away? I can't run away for that bastard! I won't be seen to be afraid of him! That's the last thing I'll surrender to him.'

'So you'll wait here and be butchered?'

'Let them come and do whatever they want to do. Is it not my life Vremudia wants? By all means, let him come and take it! If he takes it today, can he still come and take it again?'

Chief Akpovire paused for sometime.

'If Vremudia observes that I'm afraid of him. When will he leave me alone? And how long will I continue to run? Mudiaga, I'm tired of all this!

I'm really tired of it all. Listen, there's an extent to which a person is pursued that he can no longer run. And when he gets to that point, he either fight back or he surrenders completely. That's the point I am now, and If I have to fight, it's either to kill him or be killed by him, that's the only way to settle the matter with Vremudia, as it stands now, and I don't want to shed blood.'

'So you'll wait here and be butchered?' said Mudiaga again.

'Let him come. I'm tired.'

Mudiaga considered Chief Akpovire for sometime and was full of worry and concern for him since he could not persuade him to travel to Safa.

That night Mudiaga was thinking of what to do to save his friend. He lay blank in his bed with his eyes blinking repeatedly for an idea until sleep overcame him.

The next morning he sent for Efe. He was thinking of how to raise a counter-attack against Vremudia. Interestingly, Efe equally had such a plan in mind if his father refused to stay away. He pleaded with Mudiaga to leave everything to him, assuring him that he could handle Mudiaga's evil intent. Though with some doubts, Mudiaga reluctantly committed the plan to repulse Vremudia to Efe, as he had pleaded. However, he hoped to monitor it for proper guidance.

Contrary to Mudiaga's misgiving, Efe was quite circumspect and cautious about his plan. He was close to a number of boys among the natives and the settlers. He spoke to some that he could trust and they were ready to help in the repulsion. When he had got the required number, the next move Efe made was to get at least two locally-made guns which they would fire into the air at the approach of Vremudia's attack. Getting that done would not be easy. The hunters in Akpobaro were so organised that they entered the bush at night as a group and returned the same way, so getting a gun from one of them might raise questions that would betray the cause. This turned out to be the single major obstacle. Efe had thought over it repeatedly without solution.

One day, he decided to see Mudiaga. Mudiaga had been very keen to know how Efe was going about the plan and had always shown the readiness to assist and guide in any way he could. Initially, Efe preferred to keep his detailed plan to his chest, fearing that Mudiaga might not support some aspect of it. He so believed in himself that he did not want any other person to come into the full arrangement. As he plodded his way to see Mudiaga that evening, he was doing so with a divided mind. But his spirit was quite high on his return. Mudiaga directed him pointedly to call in Scorchearth and Comrade whom he thought would fit into the plan perfectly and would not hesitate to come in.

More than expected, the duo effectively took over the whole arrangement and evolved a new strategy. They divided Efe and his friends into four organised armed units, which Scorchearth termed 'Alert I,' 'Alert II,' 'Response' and 'Reinforcement'. Scorchearth drilled the boys on how to take position and what to do at their respective positions in the counter-attack. The boys were so thrilled and excited that they responded to Scorchearth's military drills with much gusto. Scorchearth was reliving his military days and he ensured that his instructions were carried out with all seriousness and responsibility in the strictest military sense. Efe was awestruck to observe Scorchearth's expertise and experience which reminded him that he was only a boy. His idea of firing two shots into the air at the approach of the enemy to scare them away was jettisoned by Scorchearth.

'Just firing at the approach of your enemy might not scare a serious enemy away. On the contrary, they might only pull back and take cover, waiting for further action from you, and if there's no further action they'll take a different route stealthily and launch their attack from where you never expected, catching you off guard. They will not abandon the fight!' explained Scorchearth. He had earlier told them to drop the idea of using machetes, knives and battle axes. He assured them that their two guns would suffice if they were effectively deployed.

In the night of the attack, Vremudia called his boys for the operation to one of his chambers.

'Tonight, we shall go on our mission. You all know that we need to be very sure and careful. It must be a mission accomplished! The fight we're about to embark on is not my fight alone. Chief Akpovire and his supporters have never hidden their hatred for settlers in this village, and you know it. I don't need to remind you what led to the first fight: they came here calling you strangers and trouble-makers and later they instigated the village youths against you. It was I, through my brother, the minister that came to your rescue. Imagine what would have happened to you. Through that singular rescue, you're still breathing your freedom here. Remember, they made your parents to part with some of their hard labour quarterly, to remind them that they're strangers here. And you, their children and down the lines, will forever remain strangers and in this village, not minding whether you were all born and grown up here like their children. But now, you have this chance to change all that; to save yourselves and your lines this humiliating bondage. It is my belief that the Creator of this earth who creates everyone, never creates anyone superior to another. We are all equal! But Chief Akpovire with his loyalists dislikes me very much for this my belief. Chief Akpovire hates me because I welcome and accept you freely into my house and treat you settlers as natives of Akpobaro. He has accused me of betraying my own people for supporting you settlers in this village. But I don't give a damn because I know I'm doing the right thing. They have plotted severally to eliminate me. But by sheer luck and divine protection, I've survived them. Yet they're never tired. They're so bent! You should know that the very day they succeed in eliminating me, you're in big trouble: They'll surely turn the sentiment of the whole village against you settlers. I have to tell you all this, so that you don't think I'm merely using you. We're fighting a common cause. I had been patient, believing that some day they would become tired. But I was wrong. Recently, I got a tip that Chief Akpovire is planning to use some dangerous armed bandits in Safa to attack me on my way to Ugbevwe under the guise of armed robbery. I'm now convinced that if we don't fight back, he'll certainly kill me soon. This is why we cannot afford to throw away this chance. Risk everything to accomplish the task. Don't fear anything! You've all the protection under heavens: The police, the army, even the court are our friends, so there's nothing to fear.'

The boys nodded their heads approvingly to every of his word.

When Vremudia had assured himself of the full co-operation of the boys, he went over to his wives and barked for the boys' meal which his three wives brought to his sitting room immediately. It was rich and lavish. The boys ate to their fill, relishing its tastefulness. After that, Vremudia rolled out drinks which the boys gulped down until all the bottles were empty, and he thought the drinks would embolden them in their dreadful mission. The boys were now tipsy. When it was midnight, Vremudia went into his reserved chamber and brought out guns which he handed out to each of them.

'Be mindful,' cautioned Vremudia, 'they're loaded already.'

After other vital instructions, he dispatched them into the stark cold dark night. This was about 12:30 a.m.

The last boy carried one heavy rod for break-in. They took the longer rough path that was ominously shady and calm, with few houses that were separated apart. As they slipped through the path, the sounds of their careful steps were all they could hear. The boys very much wished their steps were soundless, as they kept reminding them of the dangerous mission they were embarking on. As soon as the assailants stepped into Chief Akpovire's quarter, they were filled with a huge flood of tension and they became nervous.

It was past midnight and the entire Akpobaro had gone to sleep. Scorchearth, Comrade and their boys emerged. Scorchearth placed his 'Alert I', 'Alert II', 'Response' and 'Reinforcement' in four different positions in the quarter. 'Alert I' took cover at the mouth of the quarter in which Chief Akpovire lived. 'Alert II' were positioned at the end of the quarter. 'Response' and 'Reinforcement' were lined along the quarter between the two. They were in the flank to ensure that there was no escape for the attackers when 'Alert I, or 'Alert II' signalled their arrival. They would close in on them when they had been allowed fully into the quarter. The entire arrangement was like a web. They were all instructed to watch for any sign of movement in their take-cover positions in the quarter.

Samuel had told Efe that evening that their group had planned to enter the quarter by its main entrance. But as they were coming that night the Vremudia's boys changed their mind, for fear of attracting attention. They reasoned that the other unsmooth path which entered the quarter by its end was shaded with bushes and was less populated which they thought could shroud their mission. In his determination to save his father from the imminent attack, Efe had on several occasions reconnoitred over to his mole at night to get tips on Vremudia's side and he believed whatever Samuel had been telling him.

Samuel was full of anxiety that night when they, the Vremudia boys, decided to change their route, because he feared Efe would be misled by his earlier information, and there could be a mistake by Efe's side. He thought in such event, his well-intended useful information would be misconstrued. As they entered Chief Akpovire's quarter that night, Samuel's heart was almost leaping out of him in his anxiety.

Efe had earlier argued with Scorchearth and Comrade to accept it as a *fait accompli* that their foes would come through the broad side of the quarter, as he had been primed. But Scorchearth emphasized that in military operation, nothing was taken for granted and he favoured total defence in their formation, which eventually prevailed.

202

At the point of entrying the quarter, Vremudia's lackeys stopped at a bush patch to seal their final arrangement. Their leader took a survey of the sleeping quarter and noted that the mission was safe.

'Look, we must act without a mistake; Chief Akpovire is our target and nobody else. He must be struck and killed. We must be quick. Lastly, no shooting until we get close. We must hit him point blank. And once he's down everyone must disappear fast!'

While they were still there, the Scorchearth group noticed their presence and regrouped stealthily. They allowed them into the street. And as they started breaking Chief Akpovire's door, Scorchearth and Comrade disarmed their three men keeping watch around the house quietly and before they knew it, all of them were surrounded with overwhelming number of young men. And there was commotion. The people in the quarter started coming out to see. First, were the men, women and children followed later. At first, there was fear. But when they began to hear the discordant voices of farmiliar people, many who were initially hesitant began to open their doors.

Scorchearth and Comrade were panting in rage. Efe was not different. They had rounded up all their captives in one place, with their hands tied and were made to sit on the ground shame-faced. Their rifles were laid beside them after they were unloaded, as evidence of their evil.

'You don't want to talk?' shouted Scorchearth in great anger.

'Talk! talk! before we descend on you,' added the rest in the capture, with all the authority of victory in their voices. Scorchearth and Comrade waved their hands for silence and the entire crowd of people became silent.

'You're still silent! Probably, you need some beating, first,' Scorchearth swaggered through the crowd and returned swiftly with a long stick. 'Now, tell me, who sent you?'

'Oh, we beg. We are sorry,' the captives pleaded.'

'Beg what? Tell me, who sent you? Or else!' Scorchearth struck one of them very hard on his head with the stick and the rest of them who had been itching to have the Vremudia's assailants thoroughly beaten began to hit each of them repeatedly.

'Oh, we're sorry, don't beat us. We won't do it, again,' Vremudia's boys began to cry in pain.

'Talk, I say talk' and the beating continued amidst wailing. Sorchearth raised his hand to stop the beating. And there was silence again.

'Now, let us hear you,' charged Scorchearth.

203

'Please, forgive us. We are sorry,' Vremudia's emissaries of death continued, pretending to be unaware of the question repeatedly asked.

'Oh, I forgot that saying that, *Palm kernel does not yield oil unless it is heated severely,*' said Scorchearth in great fury, and he started striking them repeatedly and anyhow. Comrade and all the capturing boys followed. The on-lookers that came did not also spare the assailants – it was smashing of all sorts. The spasm of wailing that followed attracted more people into the scene. At first, all the on-lookers took the Vremudia's boys for thieves. Theft which was a rare occurrence at the time was carried out without dangerous weapons. The thief merely sneaked into a place and took away his targeted object. The objects of theft were usually domestic animals like goats, pigs and cocks. Many curious on-lookers were shocked to see guns with the *thieves,* not knowing what was really happening. Chief Akpovire requested Scorchearth and co to halt the beating.

'Please, take them to the Idugbu,[23] rather than making them objects of entertainment here,' he ordered.

Scorchearth and Comrade complied immediately. They marched Vremudia's boys down to the house of the chairman of *Idugbu.* Some of the on-lookers, especially youths who were excited with the beating followed them while the rest of the people returned to their sleep. The *Idugbu* was a group of energetic and responsible able-bodied men appointed by the Chiefs-in-Council to detect, check and investigate all criminal matters in Akpobaro. And after their full investigation of a matter, they would bring the matter before the chiefs-in-Council for judgement if there was enough substance of proof.

Incidentally, Scorchearth and Comrade were among the *Idugbu.* The *Idugbu* ministered further beating to Vremudia's boys to extract confessions from them. They knew how to handle such offenders. They believed that there was nobody, no matter how hardened he was, would always confess his crime when he could no longer bear the horrible beating, so beating was to the Idugbu's weapon of extracting confession from suspected criminals. After severe torturing, the boys confessed their mission to Chief Akpovire's house that night to the bewilderment of their audience who could not believe their ears. By then, the Vremudia's emissaries of death were almost gored to death as they dripped with blood from the injuries in their bodies.

---

[23] Traditional village police or investigator

The story went round the village the next morning. It struck the whole Akpobaro like a lethal arrow. By noon, notable chiefs from the entire Omaurhie villages had begun to visit Chief Akpovire to confirm what they had heard and to rejoice with him.

'You mean Vremudia could harbour such evil?' One of the chiefs from a neighbouring village said in his disbelief when he came.

'*Shuu!*[24] this is not what ears should hear. It is too evil; too strange for the ears,' he added.

'I'm too shocked to believe that such a plot could germinate in Omaurhie,' responded Chief Mudiaga, who was always around to give detailed account of the dastardly act.

'It was unthinkable! Akpobaro is no longer our village; it's a strange land!' added Chief Akpovire.

'*Shuu*! this world is full of strange things that will always shock us,' said the chief from the neighbouring village again.

Later that day, three elderly chiefs from another village came.

'When we heard it we were shocked. We could not believe it. Our *Ugo* decided to send us down to confirm the story.

'*Shuo*! so it is true,' one of them said after they had heard everything.

'Councillor, your god really does not sleep,' one of the three remarked.

'Of course, your god will never allow such evil to happen to you, Councillor,' the eldest man among them affirmed.

'*Isie o,*' the house chorused.

'Councillor, you're too good to die in such wicked act. You shall never die in the hands of your enemies,' stated the elderly man prayerfully.

'*Isie o,*' chorused the entire house again.

'We thank the Mighty Creator,' answered Chief Akpovire. He never said anything beyond that in his quietism.

'Councillor, don't be afraid. Your good works will always plead for you before the Almighty Creator. The world knows that you harbour no evil against anybody. So anyone who wants to do you harm shall surely have his evil upon himself,' continued the eldest man in a much stronger emotion.

'*Isie o,*' the house chorused in a congratulatory tone.

---

[24] Shuo or Shuu: exclamation of shock or surprise

'If you do no wrong, you do not die wrongly,' somebody in the house chipped in.

'It is true,' the house answered.

It was always this kind of expressions that the people often said to Chief Akpovire when they came. It was to build his confidence and remove any sense of insecurity and fear in his mind.

Stealthily, forces of evil lure and will every coward into misdeed, but like a trailor, abandons him in open shame when the truth thrusts up its conquering light, shattering even the most shameless and hardened criminal in self-pity. Vremudia could not wait till the following morning before he fled Akpobaro that night. He anxiously waited the return of his emissaries of death in his house that night. When it was about three in the early morning, he became anxious. He dashed to a vantage window in his living room and peeped through, for any signs of movement after a slight opening. He was there with his heart pumping with fear. He remained there for sometime, not knowing what to do. After some minutes, he tiptoed to the door, leading outside, unlocked it quietly and slipped out. He was walking stealthily towards the main path of the village. When he got to the point where his sight could project into Akpobaro clearly, he peered into the grey darkness of the night for the faintest possible signs of what might be happening, with all his imagination and power of hearing raised to their full consciousness. At that time, his minions were being grilled by the *Idugbu*, when all the noise and excitement about their capture had ended. Unable to get any cues, Vremudia returned to his house, sat down in his living room in great agitation. He was overwhelmed with sudden paleness. All his courage and audacity left him. He sat there for sometime, rolling his eyes for an idea in his confused state. Then a sudden fit of anxiety hit him. He darted into his bedroom at once, pulled into some presentable clothes he could find and dashed to his wives' section of the building and summoned his three wives to his living room.

'Please take care of the home, the children, everything... I'm going out of the village. It's very urgent!' he gasped.

'Is it not too early? Besides, you've not told us where you're going and when you'll return,' the senior wife said while they were all petrified by his manner of leaving.

'Don't worry. I'll be back. I'll be back soon,' Vremudia said as he opened the door to go.

After their confessions, the *Idugbu* took Vremudia's boys to the *oguedion,* the following day. Though the leadership of the chiefs-in-Council were tied to the apron strings of Vremudia, the facts and evidence resulting from Vremudia's boys' confessions and the numerous witnesses to their misdeed were too glaringly overwhelming for their manipulations. Besides, the incident had turned all sentiment against Vremudia, so much that his closest ally would be afraid to speak for him at that moment.

The youths of the village were enraged over Vremudia's plot to eliminate Chief Akpovire. They came to Chief Akpovire the following morning as a mark of solidarity with him. They was a large crowd. Chief Akpovire thanked them for their concern but pleaded that they should not take the law into their hands as the leaders of Akpobaro would handle the matter as it were. When the youths left Chief Akpovire, they danced round the town singing to the shame, cowardice and evil of Vremudia. They later marched to the *Idugbu*'s chairman and the *Ugo,* warning that they would impose their justice, if the matter was not properly handled.

'We know that some people are carrying on in this village as if nobody else mattered: They're the law and they do whatever they like, thinking nobody can dare them, simply because they have government behind them. They brought soldiers the other time to kick our buttocks, whip our backs and break our heads. We were all sore. But we'll not fear! This is our village, inherited from our fore-fathers. Nobody can enslave us in it. Nobody can kick us like a football in it. We won't submit to any cowardly intimidation and brutality. No matter how powerful they might be. Very soon, very soon, we shall smash and clear out all their recklessness and rescue the community from their hold,' the youths' spokesman boasted to the new *Ugo,* before they left his place.

The dancing of the youths round the village had galvanished the entire Akpobaro to support Chief Akpovire. The men and women were proud and happy to see the youths in their display of rare courage against the brazen oppression of Vremudia whose conduct in the village had left no one in doubt about his overbearing self-importance. They condemned the cowardly attitude of the chiefs and elders of Akpobaro for submitting so cheaply to Vremudia's dominance. They praised the boys as they danced past.

Later, the elders-in-Council found Vremudia's boys guilty of attempting to murder Chief Akpovire. Though, the assailant boys confessed Vremudia as the person that sent them, the chiefs did not mention him in their judgement.

The punishment meted out to Vremudia's boys was expectedly severe. They were to be flogged forty hard strokes of the cane, a fine of a he-goat, a bottle of *ogogoro* and four thousand naira each each. The money involved was by all accounts a huge amount at this time in the village. The other option was that they would be made to dance naked round the village with their hands tied together and a loose chain round their feet to restrain their movement, to the entertainment of the people. And as the *Idugbu* marched such capital offenders round the village, they would be jeered at, stoned and struck with whip by over-zealous youths. The second option was more dreadful, as the offender would be inflicted with great injuries and in most cases, injured beyond recognition, and might die at the end. If he managed to survive, the stigma of nakedness and humiliation before the entire village remained with the offender like a permanent scar for life. Because of the severity, shame and stigma, people hardly committed capital offences in the village.

Unfortunately, for the Vremudia's minions, they could not pay the fine. Their parents and relatives totally distanced themselves from them, to show that they had no hand in their ignoble act or to prove that they were equally offended by what they did or both. So on the second day, they were stripped naked and were made to dance round all the quarters, while the *Idugbu* thrashed them. It was a great amusement in the village. As they walked past each quarter, people came out to jeer at them. Some spat at them, some others threw stones at them which they struggled vainly to avoid. By evening, they had been beaten beyond recognition, and were left to suffer their bruises and injuries.

Three days later, Vremudia came back with policemen to arrest the *Idugbu* chairman and other persons that were actively involved in the arrest and the beating of his boys. Comrade was among those arrested. Luckily, for Scorchearth, he was away in the farm when the police came. The arrested persons were taken to the police station at Ugbevwe. They were accused of taking the law into their hands. The police also took the tortured Vremudia's boys purportedly to their station for interrogation. But they were instead taken to the general hospital in Safa for proper treatment and recuperation. Vremudia did not return to the village until two months later. Before then, he had sent some fierced-looking miscreants from Safa who were armed to the teeth to guard his house, as he learnt of the plan by Akpobaro youths to burn it down. Those arrested by the police were subsequently arraigned in a magistrate court after a month and were each sentenced to ten years imprisonment with hard labour.

****

Two months later, those Vremudia's boys who attempted the murder of Chief Akpovire appeared in the village, looking very healthy in fine attires. They came to take the place of the fierce-looking township boys on guards at Vremudia's. Since that time, they all began to stay with Vremudia. Vremudia wanted to prove to the people that he was the man of the moment, an authority of government in the village and whoever touched him or his representatives touched government and all its authorities. He was using the latest incident as a pointer to the fact that Chief Akpovire was a man of the past; spent and irrelevant. Many who came to give Chief Akpovire kudos and support immediately after the attempted murder went into recess, as many of them were now afraid of Vremudia after *Idugbu* chairman and other members involved in the handling of his assailant boys were jailed. Once again, the reputation of Chief Akpovire took a nosedive, and nobody talked about him any more in public matter.

And Vremudia and his close allies bounced back to full reckoning and remained in charge of Akpobaro. And life went on as if the attempted murder incident never took place in the first instance. However, Vremudia had become more careful in the village. This made him to act more cautiously in dealing with the people.

One person that suffered the severest blow in the fall-out of the incident was Scorchearth. He was shocked and baffled by the way the entire incident turned out. Most baffling was the imprisonment of his inseparable friend, Comrade. Scorchearth began to have a completely different view about life, more particularly about justice and its entire mechanism. He saw a deep contradiction in the justice system and was completely taking aback by what happened. He eventually retired into his shell, which gave him more time to reflect on life and the way it rippled and ruffled individuals and the society in endless waves of uncertainty. He could not understand the meaning of justice any more. He kept wondering who should be said to be guilty in the whole episode. *Is it those who stopped the murder of a prominent and innocent person and strictly ensured that the perpetrators of such evil intent were punished or those who conspired and wanted to murder?*

He also could not understand why a superimposed justice system that was totally alien to the people was merely being used to oppress the weak and serve the interest of only the mighty and powerful in the society. These and other similar posers engaged his mind few days after the news that Comrade and the others arrested were jailed. *Why were the law operatives totally blind to the murder attempt and saw only the so-called wrong-doing of those who took the law into their hands?* This mind-boggling question Scorchearth could not find answer. 'Justice, justice, what a depraved concept!' he shook his head as he wondered aloud in utter disappointment one night in his confounded and depressed state.

CHAPTER TWENTY

Akpobaro now had many educated youths without jobs. Some of them were university graduates. Their frustration grew every day when they saw their counterparts in Starling estate at Akpobaro living in great comfort. They had travelled to Starling head office to seek for jobs but they were never recruited. They had no people in government that could give them jobs either. Everybody in high position of authority only thought of giving the few available jobs to those who were close to him, as unemployment was biting everywhere. When companies and government advertised vacant positions, it was only done as a matter of procedure. Everybody knew that at the end, only those who were connected to the top would get the jobs. Unfortunately for Akpobaro, they never had the opportunity of early education because there were no schools in their area then. So now that they had educated people, there was nobody in top positions to assist them in getting jobs.

Their farmland could no longer yield well. Fishes were no longer in their rivers too. Their two significant festivals could no longer hold because the blessings of their land and water which inspired the two festivals no longer existed. Everything was oil and its activities, with its devastating toll on its operational environment. The atmosphere had become very hot: the hotness was becoming unbearable. Pregnant women always go to the river to cool themselves. Most men wore only shorts, sometimes trousers, leaving their bodies bare.

The people did not know exactly what had gone wrong. Some people believed that their fore-fathers and the gods of the land were angry and had decided to punish the community for their wrongs. But many others refused to accept this because many a time their ancestors and the gods had been appeased, but nothing came out of such sacrifices. The few Christians in Akpobaro - for there had been some converts after several Christian crusades by Safa churches lately - were saying that the inclemency was a sign of the apocalypse. They had the story in their Bible and they started worshipping more fervently, telling the people that they should turn to the church, for the Great Kingdom of Jesus Christ was at hand. Life was falling deeper in the abyss of frustration and hopelessness everyday. 'Jesus is the light of hope and salvation,' the Christians asserted. They were winning people and the church grew rapidly in Akpobaro.

The leadership of Akpobaro had also sunk down. The chiefs hardly attended meetings nowadays. On such days, few chiefs would only come to bemoan the circumstances that had befallen the village. While the many others flocked to Vremudia to have drinks and foods. Vremudia had gained full ascendancy. Many more people had joined his flock. He was the only rich man now in Akpobaro, and was very outstanding. Apart from his position in the Council which brought him a lot of money, he had also become the only man with whom Starling officials related in matters concerning their oil operations in the whole Omaurhie villages. And Starling Company had been giving him so much attention and goodwill. He had become one of their major contractors and suppliers. Nobody knew the extent of his involvement with the oil officials. But the whole Akpobaro knew that he was their only friend and a kind of liaison between the oil company and the entire Omaurhie. All the token compensations for damaged crops on their farmlands were usually paid through him. He had boasted several times that he would assist the unemployed graduates in Akpobaro to secure jobs in Starling Company. Because of this, a retinue of graduates flocked to him and started serving him in some of his domestic chores. Some parents brought foodstuffs to him repeatedly to remind him of his promise to assist their graduate children into Starling employ. He always assured them of fulfilling his promise. He would tell them that he had finalised with the white boss supervising all the company's operations in the area and he had promised to absorb his boys into the company. But in all his promises, he had not helped anybody. He had four cars now, the only ones in the village and had married four additional wives. There were stories that he had built some edifices in Safa. Vremudia was now very fat. His neck was gradually swallowing up his head and now grunted heavily whenever he talked.

Another oil spill occurred after a long interval. It was a hole in one of the pipes carrying crude oil from some oil-wells to the first flowstation. It started in the night. By early morning the next day, the crude oil had covered a large space. The stench hung badly upon the village. The people knew that oil spill had occurred again when they woke up the following morning for they had come to know the smell. That people trooped into the bush to locate the spill and saw a large pool of it in a section of the oil pipeline. The pipe was still gushing out crude oil in great quantity.

212

The chairman and some members of the *Idugbu* went to the estate to alert Starling Company's officials. But before they got there, they met some of its workers for routine maintenance on their way. Messages were immediately sent through their communication radio to their Area Office while the engineers on site had gone to detect the affected pipe and the oil-wells in order to stop the flow. Immediately, a team of experts were flown in by Starling helicopter that day for inspection, and within three days repair was effected and normal operation resumed. But the spill was not cleaned up; the large pool of crude oil still remained there. The people would not have bothered about it but for the smell. The smell was strong and seemed to be affecting them. Many people began to throw up their foods now and then, particularly the children. The people believed that it was the stench of the crude oil that was responsible. These days, nobody complained. But they expected Vremudia to speak to the top officials of Starling about it, as he was the only one who was close to them. But he never did. A month later, some strange patches of rashes began to spread in Akpobaro.

One day, a group of youths were playing draughts at one of the small shops in the village. Draughts-playing was one major way the youths used in relieving themselves of their frustration of joblessness. They sat to play and watch draughts in the sheds of the small retail shops in Akpobaro. On such occasions, they joked and laughed at one another. Most often, the loser of each round of the game was their butt. The teasing was usually vicious, often directed at what would most likely touch the loser most. One needed to develop real thick skin to absorb the *hard punches* if not one would certainly fight somebody. But they never fought: it was a question of 'If you hit me hard from the blue angle, I'll hit you hard from the red angle.' But like the game of boxing: 'Don't hit below the belt' - non-involvement of close ones.

The loser of the first round had thick patches of rashes on his body. '*krokro* skin, get up! That's how you lose your skin to Starling spill. See, see, it's growing on your body,' one of the boys pointed at the patches, as the loser was getting out of the game.

'Sure, it's g-r-o-w-i-n-g all over him,' many others chorused and began to laugh, pointing their fingers at the patches on his body.

'It's growing everywhere, not only on my body. See, see...' said the loser, pointing to other boys there that had it. 'There's no shame any more.'

And they all burst into laughter.

213

'What are we really laughing about? It's no longer a laughing matter,' one of the older boys exploded like a thunder. 'How can this useless company be doing this to us and we keep quiet! I pity those of you laughing now. Soon, I say very soon, it will catch up with you. Be laughing, idiots.'

They all became sober at once – everyone of them got the message very clearly.

'Are we cowards? Don't we have a voice to tell Starling to clean up their stink? We've got to or we perish by it,' another strong voice added.

'Yes, we've got to tell them; enough of the nonsense!' said another angry voice.

A strong feeling of indignation and fury was welling up in them now and the feeling to do something very urgent and probably nasty to prove a point was sweeping across them.

'We must go to them now and let them know!' one stoutly built boy with daring eyes said.

'Let's go! many voices concurred and they all began to head in the direction of the estate. They broke into a protesting song:

> We no go gree o*
> We no go gree!
> *Oya, oya*, we no go gree!

As they sang along, many people in Akpobaro were attracted to them, and by the time they were at the end of the village, nearly all the young men were already part of them. So it turned out to be a huge crowd. They sang with the highest spirit of solidarity and before they knew it, they had walked the three kilometres to the estate.

Before they reached the gate, the company was already alarmed by their clamorous chants which bombarded their usual serenity. Many of the workers in the estate were looking out to know what the unusual commotion was all about. The security personnel had firmly secured the huge iron-gate and were on red alert. When the mob of youths saw that the gate was locked, they increased the tempo of their song, and began to dance with much greater vigour, increasing commotion at the gate. This was to let the company realise that they came for them. When no counter-reaction came forth for a few

---

*"We won't accept" in Pidgin English

minutes, in their increasing infuriation the young men started banging on the gate.

There was no response still.

They kept banging the gate in their noisy clamour and after about thirty minutes, two helicopters flew into the estate. The boys saw them but did not give any thought to them, as it was usual to see helicopters flying in and out of the estate. It was the arrival of anti-riot police men. The site chief engineer overseeing all the oil operations in Omaurhie had related the disturbance at the estate to the area office. As the white man was relating the incident in the radio room, he looked out through a window upstairs, trying to describe the irate youths. One statement that signalled great danger to the estate and which called for a full combative response was when the chief engineer said, 'It may be over with us any moment. Now, they're breaking... Oh, my God!' shouted he as he heard the banging at the gate. The white man was so frightened by what he thought was a hair-raising mob riot against them. The area manager was panic-stricken at the other end.

When the police flew in, the boys were still banging on the gate in a most clamorous manner. The anti-riot police held their breath and marched straight to the gate and the estate security officials opened the gate at once. When the boys saw the purple-faced anti-riot policemen in helmets, holding out AK-47 rifles, they could not believe their eyes. They took to their heels, falling over one another as they ran. The policemen scowled at them for a while. They knew the boys did not prepare for a fight. But in their characteristic manner of demonstrating and satisfying their blood-thirsty braggadocio, they fired at the boys. That was the only way to report back that their mission was accomplished. No anti-riot squad that went on a mission without a story of killings; it was unheard of. They fired more and more and many of the boys began to fall down.

That day Akpobaro was immersed in deep sorrow. The village was frantic. There was crying everywhere. In all their life they had never experienced anything near this. It was too horrific and unimaginable. The village lost one-third of its young men in the shooting. For more than three weeks, the poignancy of the sorrow remained palpable in the village. Life seemed to have left Akpobaro. The elders and chiefs gathered daily at the *oguedion* in the first week and began to shake their heads in silence, every now and then. They could not speak. They shook their heads in deep sorrow as the tragedy continued to rock them inside. When the mind is too heavy with sorrow, words become difficult to utter. All-day long they remained in this mood. Every morning they went to the *oguedion* and mourned together. The woman could not go anywhere. They remained in their houses grieving. Everyone was affected, even those who did not lose anybody. It was not an individual tragedy. It was the whole Akpobaro.

One day, while the chiefs and elders remained in their solemn session at the *oguedion*, reflecting about their fate, three reporters came. They had earlier visited Starling area office at Ukoti where the company public affairs manager told them that Starling was not in any way responsible for the incident at Akpobaro.

'Well, it is unfortunate. But what could Starling have done in the circumstance? We were confronted by a mob disturbance right there at the estate. As law-abiding people, we invited the police – it is their job, you know – but we did not envisage, it would turn out nasty. It's really very unfortunate,' he shook his head regrettably.

The three reporters were in Akpobaro to confirm the police statement that the young men in the disturbance were armed with dangerous weapons.

'We'll not contradict what government has said. No, we cannot,' said the *Ugo* shaking his head solemnly.

The other chiefs and elders nodded their heads silently in approval.

'Nobody can disprove government,' repeated the *Ugo* reflectively. 'But now that you news people are here, there's one thing we will want you to tell government and the world: we're fed up with the oil operations on our land. We beg government to remove the oil company from of our land,' said the *Ugo* with great distress.

The other chiefs and elders nodded their heads again in agreement.

'Tell government that the fence which protected the homestead has been broken,' added one of the chiefs proverbially as he shook his head, looking downward.

Silence prevailed for some moments.

The three reporters were beginning to be affected by the overwhelming palpability of their sorrow.

'I know you people in the press are well respected in the society,' resumed the *Ugo* poignantly. 'Government listens to you. Please, we plead with all our heart, tell government that we're tired, tired of the oil thing!' shaking his head sorrowfully, as he was still overwhelmed with the whole pain of the police shooting.

The reporters nodded their heads in sympathy. They could perceive the pain, the frustration and the anguish of Akpobaro in the *Ugo*'s voice.

When the three reporters left the *oguedion,* they went to the spill site that was believed to be the cause of the tragic episode. While they were going with their guide, they were attracted by an old-fashioned modern edifice with some rustic elitist appeal. They wondered who might have built such a stately house in a lost village like Akpobaro years back. They became curious.

'He was the over all chief before and a very great one,' their guide told them.

The three reporters became more curious when they saw that the doors and the shutters of the house were open, and they went in. What they saw in the house made them agape and they became much more curious. At one end of the living room, they saw one old man in an armchair reading a book with his glasses. Deeply absorbed in his reading, Chief Akpovire had not noticed the strange faces at his door. But when he did at last, he felt rather disturbed by what seemed to be an intrusion into a world of absolute quiet to which he had resigned himself. He considered his unwanted visitors for some seconds, not knowing whether to invite them in or not.

'Who are you?' he asked with some hesitation which reinforced his uninviting attitude.

'Em...we 're sorry to disturb you, sir. We are reporters. '

'Reporters!' said Chief Akpovire. He quickly adjusted his body to give himself a poise. 'What are you doing here?' he added.

'Our paper is doing a feature on the killing and we're here for an insight,' one of the reporters said apologetically.

'I see. Well, you may wish to come in,' he said calmly while observing them intensely as they walked in. When they had taken their seats, Chief Akpovire shambled into his bedroom and came back with a wine. The wine had seen many years in his inner cupboard. He offered it to the reporters and they drank quietly.

'Sir, you look so different here,' one of the reporters prompted with the intent of unlocking the man's past which Chief Akpovire was most unwilling to go into.

'I don't think so. I'm like every other person in the village. No difference.'

217

'But your house and everything about you point you out as a man who has seen the world over.'

'But that's different from being entirely different from my people. I was born here, and for years now, I have been living together with them. We share all the woes together. We have a common lot.'

'Woes? What are the woes you've experienced here?' true to type, another reporter quickly chipped in. He considered it a good opening into the misfortune of the oil operations in the area.

For a while, Chief Akpovire was silent and thoughtful.

'But you're no strangers to all these things happening to us,' answered he.

'Like what?'

'You mean you have not been hearing of our good rain water turning rather grey and acidic? The rack crops, the scrub land, what is left? Look around and see for yourselves. Every time I look at the situation, the horror of one year when we experienced locusts that covered every part of our earth is what I see. That year, all the crops on our farms were destroyed; famine and hunger was all we knew. Many people died, especially children, and many also left the land. The experience was terrible, yet it was only our crops that were affected and for only one year. But today we are talking about everything of our existence and for how long? Where are they driving us to? I think only the Almighty Creator knows.' Chief Akpovire shook his head with total sense of despair.

'Our sympathy, sir. But you have not complained,' said the third reporter.

'Complain to who?' snapped Chief Akpovire grimly. 'Where are the youths that complained? Where are they?'

The trick of the reporters had started yielding fruit, Chief Akpovire was now forth-coming.

'As a whole community, you mean, nothing can be done about this naked injustice?' another reporter chipped in.

Chief Akpovire looked at the particular reporter and shook his head sadly.

'My son,' he said, 'there are many issues you do not understand here. And I plead we shouldn't go into all that – it's a very sad, lengthy and boring chapter,' he said. 'Our people often say, *it is the house that fell, the goat treads upon.* Let's close it at that,' pleaded he once again.

There was uncomfortable silence for sometime.

218

'Like we told you sir, we are covering the killing incident, is there anything you'd like to pass across. I mean how you people feel about the oil disruption in your land?'

'Well, I thank you for the opportunity. I consider it a special favour and privilege, though I have sworn not to meddle in the affairs of the community, I'll break that now, as a way of appreciating your genuine concern. You see, I've read in papers so many views canvassing for equity and justice, concerning the plight of the oil-bearing communities in the country. But let it be known to the world that those of us in the unfortunate situation don't even talk about equity. Equity will rather be unfair to the rest of our people out there. Equity in this instance emphasizes natural right and by that standard, the oil in our land naturally belongs to us, the oil-bearing communities, so its wealth. Generally speaking, that may not be fair to all concerned. By the same token, it is absolutely selfish and bad, for some people to legislate in the guise of government that all the land in the country and its mineral resources belong to the government. We have a common belief among our people here, that where someone is a companion in good fortune, in all conscience, he deserves a share in the good fortune. So let the one that has the fortune and his companions have their shares proportionately, while some measures are taken to preserve the vegetation and the environment, full stop.'

On their way to the spill site, the three reporters began to examine the view of Chief Akpovire. They were stung by his profound and magisterial insight in handling the thorny issue and they considered his idea quite excellent and magnanimous. They hoped to share his perspective in their writing.

'But why on earth, such a prodigy of wisdom and experience is rotting away in such a remote village?' observed one of them.

More surprising to them was that, he was not even part of the village leadership.

'Something is wrong in the village, I suppose,' said another regrettably.

'No, not the village but with all of us as a people. There are many of such men of experience, knowledge and stately disposition rotting away in this country while some empty-headed bluffers are calling the shots,' asserted the last one, and they all agreed. They had just realised that in putting their reports together, there was need to raise the issue of good leadership which they considered critical to genuine peace and development of the polity. They were already thinking of a new title for their assignment.

CHAPTER TWENTY-ONE

Safa began to sink continuously from every glory she had attained earlier, after Independence. At first, it was unnoticed. But after the Civil War, it became a free fall. The war did worst devastation to Safa in all its tolls. The war dispersed all the different peoples who had made Safa their home back to their original roots and all the booming activities suddenly came to a halt. Most of the whites could not stand the war, either. They abandoned their coveted European quarters and fled back the country.

Unfortunately, the end of the Civil War did not bring any improvement afterwards. Incidentally, oil was discovered in larger commercial quantity in the region, just when Safa was in this sinking condition. And the government and the people told their blessed souls, 'Now, eat and enjoy; No more sweat!' And Safa and all its enterprises were abandoned for the nearest oil town, Ukoti, where several oil companies had their operational bases, and the engine boat of productive enterprises began to sink down into the depth of inertia. People began to drift to Ukoti for business and employment. Over night, many people became contractors, business moguls in the petroleum industry and in government. Safa was not a place for either, so it was not long before the cosmopolitan Safa began to gather dust.

Oil was big money and big money was oil, and oil began to magnet all attention. Those in government and civil servants were in enjoyment stupor, as they became the main beneficiaries of the oil wealth. Money was like river that continued to flow everyday into the bank accounts of government officials without stopping. They embarked on vain capital projects in capital cities. Several administrative units, called states, were created and several more became the major achievement of successive military juntas that came for the oil money. Councils became too numerous to count. And many more were being agitated for, as the people had come to realise that the only way to share in the oil wealth was to have a unit of government in their locality. The sole purpose of replicating governance structures all over the place was to extend the supply line to other privileged few. The oil was there and would ever remain, so it was wasteful to think of other sources of income for government. And when such plan was conceived, it was never executed - nay turned out to be another supply line to other well-connected few. Voluptuary became the only thing man lived for and should live for.

But as government and governance was being replicated daily, the revenue allocation accruing to the political units became small and continued to decline. But that did not bother anybody; anyhow government would survive. Voluptuary would survive. At least, those in power would ensure theirs. While those cut off from the supply line would continue to be desperate. All this would continue to create a chaos that was ugly, shameful and dehumanizing.

But in all these kaleidoscopic replications of government, Safa was forgotten: bad and martial politics that gave only to those in the corridors of power, and perhaps to a few others who were near-by, made the situation terribly devastating. Unfortunately such calibre of people was not from Safa, so Safa became a living history, all her early great starts became relics of its past glory.

CHAPTER TWENTY-TWO

Chief Akpovire was sitting in the frontage of his house, and allowed his mind to wander gently like the evening breeze which he was enjoying at that moment. It was an ample time as he often did nowadays, to ruminate on several issues, as his thoughts wondered about. It had become one of the ways he engaged himself nowadays. He was reflecting on his glorious days in politics. He more often preferred to relive the past these days. His thought this time was on one of his speeches he considered brilliant then. He delivered it on the day he was sworn in as the presiding councillor for his Council, some years before independence. He had titled it, 'Roadmap to Indigenous Advancement'. He could still recall the week prior to that day when he buried himself in books and old newspapers to glean materials for his speech. He was so excited about it. He wanted to impress his audience, particularly the white colonial officials in their midst. Though he was disappointed to observe that the white officials were absent at the ceremony, he thought his speech would surely impress his fellow compatriots. But when he ended his speech, there was a confusing silence, as though he had been speaking to himself. The applause that followed was rather too hollow for any meaningful appreciation. His audience were bemused by his overuse of grandiloquent expressions which were more or less over-dramatized verbiage that merely assaulted their hearing and impaired the free flow of his ideas. The people were just wondering that the white man confused them by what they considered his nasal accent which made him rather too fast for their understanding. Now, they were more upset that one of their own was again confusing them with 'isms' of the English language. They wondered if all these were part of the trick in the white man's language.

After the speech, Chief Akpovire left the Council Office very disappointed, considering all the effort he had put into it. As he recalled the occasion, he began to beam, laughing at his own naivety and stupidity of trying to impress his own people with the language neither he nor his people understood very well.

'Would I have been able to impress the white men if they had been present?' he asked himself and chuckled.

He was greatly amused over his foolery then. He was almost becoming overwhelmed with laughter as he remembered the time when all of them who managed to acquire some level of English education, relished in the use of pompous words and expressions which they neither knew their functional meanings clearly nor how they could be effectively and skilfully deployed, but only used them because they wanted to sound lofty and important in their bid to show off their *high civilization.*

While he was still struggling to overcome the amusement his folly of old produced in him, he heard a cheerful acclamation in the compound. Night was already close, visibility was not very clear, but he could guess the fellow that was approaching. It was Edema, one of the reverine settlers who used to bring him a lot of dried fish on his return from his village fish harvest festival yearly. But for about eight years, he had left Akpobaro along with many other settlers and since that time he had not come back, hence his coming was generating a great interest in the compound.

'Edema, is it you, we are seeing or your ghost?' exclaimed Otabunor, Chief Akpovire's most senior wife. 'I can hardly believe my eyes! We never saw you again all this while?

You had been pretending to be our friend,' Ogevwe, Chief Akpovire's second wife added as they closely scrutinised Edema as if to ascertain whether he was really the person they used to know very well.

'Oh, my good women, I'm still Edema, your friend,' said Edema smiling shyly as he walked towards Chief Akpovire.

'How can you say so when you can keep away for so long,' Ogevwe replied.

'Ha ha ha,' laughed Edema. 'You see, life rolls and it can roll a full man like football. Sometimes, it can just roll you away to some place you never expected. Life is like that sometimes, so you can't blame me,' protested Edema. He robbed his face with his hand and laughed and did not know what to say again, while the two women were still gazing at him with disbelief. 'It is so,' he burst into another round of laughter, as he moved towards Chief Akpovire.

'No fish for us?' said Ogevwe disappointedly.

'Oh, fish, fish,' the word faltered in Edema's mouth as he replied and suddenly became pale and drawn with sadness. 'No fish in our area again,' he shook his head apologetically.

'What happened?' said the two women almost simultaneously.

Edema robbed his head with his hand again for explanation.

224

'My sisters, the thing surprise everybody o. Fish just disappear from our waters, nobody knows why. But some people are saying the oil companies cause it. Me, I don't know. Our fish harvest festival sef no dey again, 'cos no more fish to harvest.'

The two women looked at each other in bewilderment.

'Those oil people have gone there, too?' piped Ogevwe.

The two women without any further words went back to their apartments, leaving Edema with their husband.

Edema had come to Okuemo to visit an old friend and he felt he should use the opportunity to pay his respects to Chief Akpovire, a man he held in very high regard. While they were enjoying themselves in warm conversation, reminiscing on their past relationship, Efe and two of his friends strolled into the compound and after thirty minutes, they were on their way out. Their movement was so determinate, suggesting they were out for some very urgent and important engagement.

'Where are you going?' Chief Akpovire called Efe back, fearing that Efe might stay out that night, if what he could read of them was any guide. Chief Akpovire had become most particularly solicitous about Efe among his children nowadays.

The growing bond started long before Efe saved him from the death plot of Vremudia. Efe, who used to be the reprobate of the family, had turned out to be his father's favourite among his children, following his entry into college. He had been mounting the ladder of success in every step of his educational advancement ever since. Efe's stepping into college at Safa brought tremendous rapid improvement in him and all his waywardness gave way to a sublime character at his college.

But it was hard-won. When he checked into the school boarding house after his admission, he met a completely different world. At first, he found it extremely difficult to adjust to the hard and fast set of rules of the college. All students' activities in the boarding school were regimented and regularised and every student had to observe the rules. Mechanisms to ensure strict compliance were also put in place and had been very effective. More disturbing to Efe was the siesta after lunch. He found it extremely incomprehensible to force somebody to sleep. He could not also do without talking during prep. He was notorious for always having excuses to gallivant around during classes. He could not sit quietly in one place for hours so the

225

class was particularly distressful to him. He found the college environment totally disagreeable and was having very difficult times. He was like a caged bird.

One day, he was going around the school in his early days when he discovered a lot of fruit in the college orchard, and he took particular note of them. During one of the seistas, he stole into the orchard and began to pluck some fruit. While he was busy having his fun, the security men caught him and brought him to his House Master who made Efe to clear grass for one week. That was a great punishment for him; his palms were blistered for days.

There was another day when he rode the bicycle of one of his classmates, a day-student, into the town during long break, without permission from the student and his class master. In his excitement, he lost his way. Meanwhile, the boy who owned the bicycle had reported to their class master of his 'stolen' bicycle. That day the entire class and security men combed the entire school, including the dormitories, in search of the bicycle. Only for Efe to ride the bicycle back when the boarding students were already observing their seista after the close of school. His classmaster and housemaster were so angry that Efe was flogged all over his body and was made to uproot a stump of an old mango tree in the school. It took him one week without classes to carry out the punishment, and he felt thoroughly sorry.

He had also been made to 'touch his toes' for hours many times for noise-making and other minor offences during prep and seister which made him cry. In fact, the first year in the college was a real crucible for him. But it purged him of all his wild and passionate indulgences. By the end of the third term which terminated his first year in college, he had begun to mend his ways. In his second year, he had become a truly disciplined person and had thoroughly adjusted to the high procedural standards of the school. Since then, he had been making rapid progress in the college, so much that he went away with the coveted award for the overall best student, apart from several other awards in his final year, as the school system made him to channel his passionate, vibrant and dogged nature into positive engagements.

At the moment, Efe was already studying Geophysics at the Premier University, the oldest and most prestigious university in Namia. He hoped to work in one of the oil companies. He had a dream of making the oil companies to establish a good and harmonious relationship with their host communities.

Following the change, Chief Akpovire had become very fond of him. He saw Efe now as the off-shoot of his decaying life and this had made him very sensitive to everything about the boy. More particularly, he felt very anxious about Efe whenever he went out in Akpobaro and would be greatly disturbed. From all that had happened to him in the village, he could no longer feel safe, and he thought if his enemies could not get at him, they might want to get at his closest person. There lay his fear for Efe who was always swarmed by many boys in the village, as they saw him as their model, nay idol, and were very devoted to him. They always wanted to be around him.

These two opposing interests about Efe were causing some kind of uneasiness. His father preferred having him around, at home always to mixing freely with his numerous devoted friends in the village whenever he was on holidays. Chief Akpovire realised most times that Efe was becoming an adult and needed some freedom with his peers, so he should not spoil his happy companionship with them. But he often found himself struggling between his anxiety and Efe's right of adulthood. Most cases, he allowed the latter to prevail with great pain.

'There's a burial at Oteheri and we would like to be there,' Efe replied his father.

'But you just returned from school today. You haven't had time with your family. You've not even seen your mother who has been looking forward to your coming home. Don't you consider it necessary to acquaint yourselves with what has been going on in your home since you left, at least for a little while first? Your friends should know that you need a little rest after the long journey,' said Chief Akpovire, obliquely accusing Efe's two friends whom he thought were luring him into this night movement as his sharp angry voice was visible when he referred to them.

As they heard this, Efe's two friends began to walk away very fast.

'Papa, it's only this night. Surely, I'll have all my holidays here, so there'll be enough time for all that,' pleaded Efe.

Chief Akpovire was hesitant. In him was some vague fear against Efe's going to the burial that night. It was subtle yet strong. He was pensive for some time. He had a strong inclination to stop Efe, but he knew Efe would be unhappy if he did not allow him, so he allowed Efe have his way.

Efe hurried to meet his two friends who were waiting few metres away. They were glad that Efe's father eventually allowed him and they immediately set out to Oteheri. They were early. They knew the burial would start much later, but Efe wanted to have sometime with his girlfriend, Oyovo, whose parents had relocated to Oteheri before attending the ceremony. That was their real object of going. The burial was an ample opportunity to have some good time with her, because such freedom for the girls could only come on such occasions. Though, there was no prior notice, Efe knew it would be a heady excitement for Oyovo to see him unexpectedly.

As soon as they reached Oteheri, they sent an old friend to whisper Efe's presence to Oyovo while they were waiting her at a local joint. They hoped to leave for the burial from there.

Meanwhile, there was acute scarcity of petrol and other refined petroleum products across the country. The three refineries in the country had almost become moribund. Refinery workers were constantly agitating for improved conditions. Vehicles had been on queues on end at few petrol stations that had been pumping to customers by fits and starts. Soldiers and other security operatives were drafted in to enforce order out of the inadvertent and unavoidable chaos and ensure that the little refined products the refineries could churn out were made available to the public at normal prices. As it were, the security personnel assigned to the task saw great opportunity to line their pockets. Most of the little fuel that was available found their way into the black market with their prices beyond reach. Bursting the pipeline that carried refined petroleum products to the northern part of the country began to tempt those who had unbridled passion for lucre.

Vremudia and some of the oil workers at the field of Omaurhie had been making quiet, good money from the compensations due to individuals and communities whose crops and sacred grounds were damaged by oil exploration activities. They made sure that not less than half of the entire compensation money was in their pockets. The oil company was defrauded also by recording several fictitious but destroyed sacred lands, like shrines, which attracted larger amounts into the damage compensations for handsome receipts. It was always a secret deal which no one else knew about except those involved. But for sometime now, no new explorations had been carried out in the area. It seemed all the oil deposits had been found and the hope of new finds seemed dimmed. This made 'business' very bad for Vremudia and his collaborators. The boom in the black market was longer lasting, and because of its quick turnover, many unscrupulous businessmen and women turned their attention to it.

228

One day, an idea came to Vremudia as he drove past Oteheri where the pipelines that conveyed refined petroleum products to the north crossed Omaurhie. He quickly drove to the waterside where the pipelines stood out by the river. He gazed at the unburied pipelines for sometime, as his eyes rolled over by idea repeatedly in his thought. He noticed valves that connected the pipeline to another set of pipelines after the river. They were joints which could be unlocked. Only that it would require great expertise and finesse to undo it without damage. As Vremudia looked at the joints, he imagined the flow of refined oil inside. *This oil that has become gold now is here. Huge money! Yet...and yet...*he was in deep thought. He was completely engrossed with a possible idea of huge amount of money quickly coming his way like a strike on a huge gold deposit. That evening he drove to Starling estate at Akpobaro to see two of his allies among the oil workers.

There was a great gathering of people at a burial that night at Oteheri. The whole arena was swarmed. There were two sections. The traditional section attracted the older people. The older men and women and the elderly were shaking their heads and legs where they sat, humming delightfully along with the band, as they remembered their youthful days when they danced to the tunes. They realised how time had flown. Apart from the older people, there were also some well-arrayed young men and women watching the band, especially the steps of their dances with great pleasure. They all felt thrilled at the arena and seemed to have forgotten the dead person whose life the occasion was meant to celebrate. She was an aged woman of one hundred and five years. Many people in the village believed that her journey back to the spiritual world would be smooth as the woman was known to be very beneficent which reflected in her entire life of peace and grace. When she passed on, the people though were sad, were joyful that she led a good life and would be well received by the ancestral world. This also translated into the burial ceremony, for a departed one who had a glorious life on earth such burial was seen as a celebration rather than grieving. That was why the turn out for this aged woman's burial was gargantuan. Both the old and the young from different communities came to pay their last respects in celebration with her children and children's children. There were many ties that emptied the world into the burial: ties of in-laws, maternal and paternal blood relations across generations, each of whom came with other relations and friends and well-wishers. And this had a strong pull on others that were not directly or indirectly connected. That was why many people came from different communities to feast at least their eyes, as they would not want to miss such a great show that happened infrequently.

The second was a disco section organised by the grandchildren and great grandchildren of the deceased, many of whom were youths. They were more comfortable with the disco. Most of the youths took their place in this section. Mostly attracted to the section were college students who were on holidays from their various schools outside the locality. On such occasions, they always wanted to exhibit township and modern manner which they acquired from school, was quite distinct from their local way. They preferred speaking English to the local language. The girls would wear mini-skirts or trousers which were obscene in the eyes of older local folks. At parties and burials, these boys and girls held tight in their dances. They no longer liked the folk dance. They always wanted to get-together in their own way. Efe, his friends and Oyovo were in this section. They had been dancing and enjoying the occasion. It was a huge social gathering.

At the beginning, many college boys and girls and a few privileged undergraduates were engaged in some kind of badinage, as they mingled among themselves, getting to know one another in a genial social atmosphere, relating their different experiences at school amusingly.

Throughout the night, the ceremony remained peaceful and enjoyable. The deceased's children and grandchildren who were expensively dressed were very generous with drinks and foods. Take-away plastics and handkerchiefs bearing the portrait of the deceased with her age and the date of her burial on them were handed out as souvenirs during the ceremony.

While the people were having their last moment of the burial at dawn, the following day, news came that petrol was gushing out from one of the pipelines at the riverside. Many people ran down to see. Initially, it was just out of excitement, just to satisfy their curiosity, as it was strange and unbelievable to have petrol that had become a rare and very expensive commodity for sometime now across the country, just pouring out like ordinary water at their backyard. But some people stayed behind, dismissing it as one of those wild rumours. However, when evidence of the unbelievable began to come, they all ran down.

Petrol was gushing out from the joint at which two pipes where connected near the river. Beneath the spot was a dug pit. Some disconnection had taken place there the previous night, and the oil thieves could not fix back the valve between the two pipes and left in a hurry, probably when dawn crawled in. The gushing fuel had already filled the pit and was seeping into the surrounding bush. It had formed several lines. The smell had begun to spread too. Many people quickly ran back home to get buckets and all manner of containers and began to scoop the fuel.

The news spread with the speed of light and it did not take long before many people from neighbouring towns and villages swarmed the place. Cars and other vehicles soon filled every available space that was near, and many more were coming. The struggle to get the fuel became intense. There was jostling of people with scoops, pushing their way towards the gushing fuel. All the grass and bushes around the place had disappeared in a matter of minutes. It appeared they were never there before. People had covered everywhere. In the thick struggle, people could not get anywhere. Those who had earlier got to the pit soon found that they could not make their way out with their fuel and those who were coming to fill their containers could not get near the pit either. There was a huge gridlock of people. This caused anxiety.

But solution soon came. They began to form partnership; those going exchanged their empty containers with those coming with filled containers at the point of the jam, with the understanding that the one taking the fuel away to the buyers and motorists would return the container and the money as he would be collecting his filled container back at the point of exchange. The arrangement worked perfectly. Sometimes, one had to wait for the other at the agreed exchange point. And the process continued afresh again. Many returns were made in this way. There were many others who had their chance and struggled with all perseverance to get through the thick crowd and did not return, knowing full well that they would not have access again. The struggle, the buying and selling, continued in this manner as long as the fuel from the pipe was still gushing out. The news had gone far and wide so quickly, and more people with containers were now coming from distant places and there were endless lines of vehicular queues waiting to have fuel at a relatively cheap price. So much money and fuel were changing hands. The buyers were happy for having fuel at all and happier for having it at a much reduced price, and the sellers were happy also for all the cheap earnings.

At dawn, Efe and his two friends from Akpobaro led Oyovo home after the ceremony and took their weary and unsteady steps to one of their friends' places at Oteheri where they slumped into sleep. By two in the afternoon when they woke up, the whole Oteheri town had been swallowed by the fuel boom. The small town was brimming and bubbling with so many people from all places. Efe and his two friends caught the intriguing excitement immediately and they went for a sight-seeing, as the booming fuel activities had worn a carnival look, and many were there to catch the excitement.

At three, a helicopter flew in and hovered round the spot, warning the people to stay off the arena. They announced to the teeming crowd the great risk of being around the seepage. But the people were too numerous and too excited to listen. In fact, they saw the coming of the helicopter from the nearby refinery at Ukoti as the icing on the cake of the whole heady excitement and the warning was lost in the euphoria the helicopter brought. The people laughed hilariously and shouted with joy as soon as the helicopter appeared and they waved at it. Efe and his two friends took advantage of the further rollicking stirring the helicopter brought to get near the pipeline and they saw the pit and the gushing fuel.

But as the helicopter zoomed away, after repeated warnings, the unexpected happened. At once, a huge thick smoke covered the arena at once. The fire raced through the arena like lightning. The people were desperate. They could not see in the thick smoke and a deafening huge resonance of endless agonising wailings drowned the entire Oteheri and beyond. They were the cryings of dying people in a sprawling all-consuming fire. Crowd of people were running in all directions, many of them were burning with fire. The agonising cries of pain with all instincts for survival reverbrated round the area. The earth and the sky were rumbling! It was hell let loose. Commotion was everywhere. People darted here and there senselessly as if the end had come.

A great horror had befallen Omaurhie and in their wailings and mourning, there was no one to console the other, every family, everyone was bereaved!

Chief Akpovire was sitting alone in his deckchair at his frontage three days later. He remained pensive and peevish since the news of Efe's death. Tears were still tracing their lines once in a while on his face, converging at his chin. The drops on his chest had wet the shirt he had been wearing since the news, and was now spreading to his stomach. He remained deeply hurt as he poured out his soul freely once in a while. The pain was like a sharp small

232

blade cutting his heart endlessly. It was a blow his pride and equanimity could not withstand. Chief Akpovire was a man of great strength of character. But this one was too much for him. It had crushed the man in him and left behind the pain of endless grief. Nobody could console him. As he sat there lifelessly in tears, the sharp pain of losing Efe in the conflagration reverbrated and he began to weep more intensely than ever before.

Just then, the statement of Gen. Umah, the military head of state, on the fire disaster came to him again and his eyes dimmed with more pain which rampaged through all his entire being.

'How can he say the fire victims are national saboteurs and any one still alive should be arrested when the whole world are all rushing down with humanitarian assistance?' he said painfully to himself.

At that moment, he found himself in one of the solidarity rallies for the country's Independence.

'We must chase those colonial masters back to their own country, Britain. Compatriots, we must fight until we gain independence for our dear country,' urged the man on the podium. 'No amount of colonial harassment and brutality can stop us. We should be prepared to pay any price; no price is too great, even if it means surrendering our lives, for our dear country. Compatriots, fellow compatriots, listen, nothing on earth can hold us down in Egypt, not even the red sea! We must get to the promise land that flows with milk and honey. Compatriots! We must set ourselves free and have our independence where no person, no tribe, no citizen is oppressed: free society, free citizenship! No domination; no oppression – a happy people with common destiny. Fellow compatriots, let's fight and support each other even with our last drop of blood and overthrow this stark humiliating shame of colonialism…'

As Chief Akpovire relived the situation, he collapsed. His two wives who were sitting by him noticed that his breathing was ceasing and the man was dying. They raised alarm and in a minute Chief Akpovire's house was full of people. They all tried to revive him but it was too late. The old man had given up the ghost and everybody around began to cry while more people were still racing down.

Mudiaga who left him two hours ago was one of them. He looked at Chief Akpovire intensely for sometime and shook his head without a word. He touched him and shook him severally as he called him, expecting an answer. But there was no response. It was then it dawned on him that his best and only intimate friend and confidant was no more and he began to weep uncontrollably. Many chiefs and elders had come and were all sitting in the living room completely speechless. But their look was enough to tell what was going on in their minds: that the mighty tree under which Akpobaro people once took shelter from rain and hot sun was no more. At last, when Mudiaga became sober, he looked at the entire people wearing long faces in the house, cleaned up his tears on his eyes and said: 'Councillor would have lived longer and better for a happier people. But we are in a very wicked world, a world that celebrates evil and vices: a world that destroys good and virtues. The death of Councillor is an instance of how the world turns fine to ugly; goodness to rottenness. Councillor was good and honourable, great and gracious but the world is not for his kind. O Councillor, why did the Creator of the universe allow you here? You're too good, too decent for this sinful world. This malevolence called our world,' and he began to weep uncontrollable again and more weeping and wailings were heard in the house and everywhere in Akpobaro.